Flight for Fenella

By Roy Baldwin

Creative Gateway

Acknowledgement

Readers of previous books in this science-themed fantasy series may recall that a major source of inspiration came from my participating in the annual NaNoWriMo writing competition. Flight for Fenella, however, has gathered pace and come together differently, breaking momentum of that opportunity I undertook, for all writers new and experienced, to create a fifty-thousand-word novel within a disciplined timeframe of the thirty days of November. This time, I've taken a sabbatical from that worthy activity and in parallel with other science research, I decided to undertake a deep forage into my family history archives where intriguing mysteries and strange secrets have been residing, unsolved, for many decades and generations. As most people discover, I too have reached a stage of life when I feel an urgent desire to explore my ancestral roots, exacerbated by the knowledge that few people remain alive who can add personal recollections and tales of those unique eras past, never to be repeated. How much I wish I had asked more questions when that was possible. Now, the challenge of online archives and research detective work alongside forensic searches of old and interesting graveyards remains the only viable mode of attack. Suffice it to say, the rewards and revelations unearthed have been truly amazing. I discover that my heritage is intimately entwined with the former West Lancashire community of Leeds and Liverpool canal boat people, existing alongside a parallel group of pioneering maritime explorers, active throughout the nineteenth century. Ancestors made the first discovery of the Mary Rose shipwreck, a famous warship of King Henry VIII's navy, and engaged trials of the first commercial diving helmet in the 1830s. How it might have been for such seafaring families in those tough Victorian times has been captured in the story, providing some personal historical realism to the plot.

So, Flight for Fenella continues where Morag, book three of the Mauveine series, left off. An unexpected knock at the door of Orsbrick Hall heralds the arrival of a most peculiar visitor. Slowly but surely, this unexpected event triggers a series of frightening family ramifications for scientist Victoria McKenzie which nobody could have imagined was possible. Just when they finally thought the family turmoil was over at long last, they discover, too late, it isn't.

More people than I can thank from all around the world including relatives I never knew existed have provided me with valuable knowledge and inspiration. I would especially like to thank my immediate family and friends for the ongoing encouragement to keep thinking and researching out of the box and to persist against the odds, especially when the going gets tough and the writing hand becomes creatively immobile.

So, dear reader … enjoy.

Roy Baldwin
June 2017

About the Author

Roy Baldwin was born in West Lancashire and has lived and worked around the UK in various mathematical and scientific guises as an educationalist, civil servant and management consultant. Flight for Fenella is his ninth novel and the fourth book in the Mauveine Series, a collection of historic fantasy ghost stories based around the former aristocratic family of Victoria McKenzie, a modern-day scientist.

Other novels (2017) include Morag, Prism of Purpurine, Mauveine, Rhapsody of Moon, Rhapsody of Succession, Rhapsody of Fate, Rhapsody of Power, Rhapsody of Restraint. Roy Baldwin is a published author and book designer who regularly commentates on books and indie publishing.
In between writing and publishing, Roy tries to enjoy the fabulous beauty of the Norfolk countryside and seashore where he now lives. All Roy Baldwin's novels can be bought in eBook and print versions from online bookstores worldwide.

Further information can be obtained from the author's site. http://creativepubtalk.com

Chapter One

April 2026: London, St James's Square

A bucket of sweat poured from his skin and seeped uncomfortably through the back of his shirt. The media had warned this year would prove even hotter than the last which had been hotter than the year before, and so the story ran on forever, ad nauseam. A sequence of regular ranting that the end of the world was nigh flowed across the customer television screen, never failing to bleat continuously when the temperature hit over thirty degrees, a regular BBC news ritual since 2017 after America had unilaterally pulled out of the UN Paris climate change agreement. They even dug out coal again big time using a fracking technology which enabled old discarded mines to find sudden rejuvenation. Who would have thought eight years ago that exporting cheap coal to out of date power stations in Africa would provide the catalyst for America and the Soviet Union, suitably renamed in 2020, to engage in a bosom-buddy partnership? Going right down to the wire, the two crazy Presidents engaged in a friendly nuclear button standoff to see who would blink first, when a missile accidentally fired off. Unfortunately, someone got their coordinates muddled. Washington and Moscow ended up labelled Pyongyang, receiving an unexpected double-fire nuclear whammy, but China was finally happy. Boys will be boys and accidents do happen. The small number of refugees left alive in North Korea were easily accommodated, a beautiful wall was built to isolate the no-go area and already, a jointly administered US-Soviet-Sino enclave had reclaimed the remaining country and turned it into a thriving digital economy to rival South Korea. Unification was only ever going to be a pipe-dream. They said it during Afghanistan when America allowed India to absorb the country in 2021 after the Taliban were encouraged to invade Pakistan once the nukes had been forcibly removed by the new US-Soviet world taskforce ...

"You know, Harry, I wish you'd concentrate on your job instead of forever reminiscing about the good old days in the SAS."

Harry Aughton, head of office security, slowly put down his mug of tea and looked up nonchalantly at his boss, Eric. A graduate pen-pusher to the core, Eric never saw a day's action in his life. Harry still missed Afghanistan, even though he had to be retired off with a good pension after blowing his hand to smithereens on an IOD disguised as a child's teddy bear. He should have known better although the micro-chipped prosthesis worked a dream.

"You know, maybe there is something in this global warming stuff," Harry muttered with a growl. Since both the American and Soviet Union Presidents retired from the world stage via a glitzy joint announcement on the same day in 2024, a semblance of rapid realignment to normality from the last crazy decade was finally taking place, led by female administrations in both countries and starting with a world ban on coal mining in 2027. "Today, for some strange reason, it feels incredibly warm for April even for my highly tolerant self and I'm used to the heat."

"I think it's more because those idiots from maintenance are servicing the boiler downstairs and put the thermostats up, sod everyone else," Eric replied in a monotone. "Don't you read your office memos, Harry, I painstakingly prepare every week? I'm just going to readjust the master stat. It's absolutely roasting in here. I could do with a pint."

Harry smiled and resumed drinking his tea. No, he didn't look at any of that memo nonsense. Why bother reading anything that arsehole writes.

"Jesus Christ, who the fuck is that?" Eric shouted jerking his head towards the screens. The security cameras had caught a stunning, dark-haired woman in her mid-thirties, wearing a smart, orange flowery dress and dark red jacket, wandering slowly around a meeting room on the fourth floor. "I thought that room had been locked up all week. In fact, the whole area is still closed off. The new biotech company, Banjorama, haven't moved in yet have they? Can you focus the cameras in, Harry? She looks like she's off her skull on something."

They stared hard whilst Harry adjusted the monitor and both suddenly got a close up of the person, her hair bobbed in fashionable curls around an intense face, gazing in amazement at her surroundings. Harry was perplexed. A quick shot of the door showed the lock indicator was still on red. How the hell had she got inside and why?

"Maybe Jimmy has let her in for some reason," Eric murmured. "Where is he anyway? He should be down here with you."

"There," Harry replied, swinging the downstairs monitor around, irritated with his jobsworth overseer. "He's standing in at reception over lunch. Some leaving celebration in the Queen's Arms has overrun, I suspect. I'll go and fetch him and we'll grab hold of the intruder and find out what's going on. I agree, she definitely seems well out of it."

He leapt from his seat, checked his taser meticulously and headed off through the door to extricate colleague Jimmy from the reception desk. Eric continued to stare in fascination at the surprise visitor.

Inside the meeting room, the woman was gently feeling the smooth, white painted walls in awe and stared up in disbelief at the high suspended ceiling, filled with tiny LED lights which projected an unfamiliar illumination everywhere. She then sat in one of the meeting chairs, positioned around the oval twelve seater table and gazed nostalgically through the large triple-glazed windows, totally perplexed with the crowded London skyline and the myriad of people scurrying about their daily business below. All those self-propelled moving vehicles, not a horse anywhere and the streets looked amazingly clean. Suddenly she recognised the essence of the original surroundings she knew and loved so well and began to breathe purposely and heavily, desperately trying to avoid a panic attack as her heart raced relentlessly. Was she back in St James's Square? Returning her gaze to the room and the original, old Adam fireplace, it seemed incongruous amongst these other indescribable surroundings. She pondered over the expensive paintings, rare ornaments and coloured drapes which would have adorned the luscious furniture that once sat in this room. This stuff was so cold and clinical, featureless, but clearly utilitarian of purpose. The white ceiling although still high was much lower than she remembered and was covered in strange interlocking tiles with those peculiar lights embedded inside. How on earth did they work?

She walked again to the window and sat in a most unusual chair on wheels, all black leather and rotatable, catching a glimpse of St Paul's Cathedral. The old familiar dome still dominated the view. Some things had definitely not changed, and she smiled when suddenly the door rattled ominously and burst wide open. Six-foot-five-inch Harry had lunged inside, both hands firmly holding his new laser-taser gun to his prey, like a cop in an American crime movie, with colleague Jimmy a few steps behind. Both being ex-Special Forces veterans, old habits die hard even though the environment was as far removed from Kandahar as anyone could possibly imagine.

The woman looked up startled, at the burly but rather good-looking man who reminded her of someone else special in the distant past, if only she could get her brain into proper order.

"Stand up, slowly. Raise your hands madam, now, and move away from your handbag," Harry bawled, only too aware that there had been stranger incidents happen in London offices in the last ten years even through the UK terror alert was low.

She stared at the luxurious and unusual Hermes handbag on the table. She didn't know until then she had a handbag, and what a strange uniform this individual wore, certainly well cut and clean but unlike anything she had ever seen.

"On your feet please, now, I won't say it again. I'm sure you won't want to feel fifty thousand painful volts through your chest, will you."

Whatever fifty thousand volts felt like, she instantly assessed that it sounded an undesirable attribute to acquire and stood up quietly, holding her hands in the air. What a bizarre situation.

Jimmy had whipped out a high-frequency sonar scanner with a small LED screen from his back pocket and pointed it at her, a red dot appearing between her breasts which she realised felt remarkably supported by something under her dress. "No suicide vest, boss," he mumbled, rifling through the Hermes bag, "and nothing but the usual female paraphernalia here. No contents in her jacket. I think we can downgrade her."

Harry put down his taser and waved for her to lower her arms and take a seat again whilst he drew up a chair next to her. "I do apologise madam but after that attack three years ago in the Regus offices down the road, we never take chances. I'm sure you will appreciate the benefit of effective security protocol," he growled stiffly, never being comfortable with addressing women, especially attractive ones.

"I'm so sorry, what is a suicide vest and how does it work?" she replied, with an accent so pristine upper class it made both cockney Harry and scouse Jimmy look up sharply from writing notes on their tablets with digital pens. "And what are those things you're both writing on? I don't see any ink passing, really quite fascinating implements."

Harry and Jimmy looked at one another and smirked. What kind of bubble had this weird individual been living inside? Three North Korean suicide bombers had taken the side off the Regus technology building thinking they were inside the US Embassy, killing ten young business people with them, and fifty people in the street below. The worst terror attack in London since March 2017, but the whole world knew in an instant through social media and the internet.

Harry ignored her eager but strange questions. "Before we ask you what you are doing inside this building and why, perhaps you could show me some identification? Maybe you have a driving licence, passport or identity card inside your handbag?" he demanded forcefully. From that plum voice, she most likely was a rich and well-connected woman but God knows what medication she was on as he couldn't smell any drink on her breath.

She had no idea what he was talking about but opened the clasp of the bag, admiring its expensive calf brown leather. Although dubious of the style she stared at the contents that looked quite unfamiliar apart from a suede purse. A piece of a smooth and shiny flat material embossed with lettering lay at the bottom which she pulled out carefully.

"Ahh ... a credit card. May I, madam?" Harry said softly and for the first time he forced a smile but remained on his guard. Well-connected women were inevitably dangerous.

She handed him the card which he peered at intensely, noting the unique individuality and the three crowns hologram. His supposition of significant wealth was well-founded. This interview needed to conclude and he had to get her out of the place.

"Thank you, everything seems to be in order. So, may I ask how you managed to get in here and why?" he continued, handing her the card back.

The card material, definitely neither paper nor cardboard, certainly puzzled her but the lettering and the status she could relate to instantly. Miss Elizabeth Milbanke was stamped clearly onto a Coutts black bank card. She also spotted a blue silk handkerchief with a gold jewel encrusted compact mirror inside her bag. A wry grin passed over her face thinking of the delicious irony of it all ... her mother must be turning in her grave.

She watched the presumed policeman rub his glasses carefully on a tissue whilst he waited for her to answer when the connection suddenly flashed across her brain. She did remember after all and ... well ... another delicious thought to savour later. She was right all along but she had to think very carefully on her feet now. Very shortly she would need to leave this building and try and orientate herself into some semblance of normality ... at least money could be located. Banking with Coutts in the Strand was a definite act of supreme and pleasant familiarity. "May I ask? Sorry, I didn't catch your name or what number this building is in the Square?" she said softly.

"I'm Harry, Madam, chief security officer and this is my colleague, Jimmy. Twelve is the street number designation so to speak. These are the premises of Ruhrtechnical Holdings, specialist offices for technology startup companies."

She breathed in deeply. So much change, it was quite mind-blowing. "Of course, no wonder I became disoriented. I intended to head for the London Library next door but must have got in a muddle somehow. Difficult family problems were rather on my mind you see and I just walked up the stairs not, of course, thinking logically and wandered right in here wondering where the books had gone!" She giggled stupidly, hoping that the London Library still existed. Harry, she mused, what a quaint name. The man seemed quite unconvinced. Her brain ran on to explain further excuses which might have better credence.

Harry knew she was either lying or bonkers and would check the CCTV to confirm later, although how they had missed her walking past reception was anyone's guess. Jimmy was becoming careless, he would have to exchange words later. Harry had already concluded that bonkers, with more money than sense, was the most likely explanation. Perhaps she had mental problems and her medication had run out. Whatever, all he now wanted was to move this individual out of there fast, avoid Eric and saunter down to the Queen's Arms for his welcome pie and a pint lunch. He was starving.

"Fine, Miss Milbanke. Let me show you the exit so you can resume your way on to number fourteen. Jimmy, will you check the locks please on all the doors. This whole area is supposed to be secured for the week. You've been slipping up somewhere."

Jimmy walked out of the door in a huff. Rubbing his glasses again and making her smile, Harry led her out into the wide, carpeted corridor. She looked around at the unfamiliar glass windows, staring into other rooms; all appeared boringly the same, with bland white walls and matching ceilings. Some contained desks but the others were mainly empty and in the middle of decoration. She followed tentatively behind, intrigued when he pressed the lift button. The only object that caught her eye instantly was a large, antique chess set, placed like some ornamental decoration at the end of the corridor and looking remarkably familiar. The lift doors swished open, the lights subdued, and she gazed wide-eyed inside at the garish full-length mirrors lining the walls. But instantly, as she was always capable of doing, she gathered an immediate air of decorum and presence and strode in, watching eagerly as he pushed the down button. The lift descended quickly to the ground floor, a strange, whirring sensation and sound. There was, she concluded, an electric motor powering this moving box somewhere. So many things to get used to but already she was looking forward to exploring everything. The lift doors opened opposite a revolving glass door straight to the outside. She breathed an inner sigh of relief to see the old Square in all its green splendour, albeit surrounded by the most peculiar artefacts. Dazzling shops and busy happenings on the street bombarded her senses, with so many people rushing about and clad most peculiar.

"There you go, Miss Milbanke, just out to your left. Have a good day."

"Goodbye Harry and thank you for not shooting volts at me with that strange weapon," she replied coquettishly, turning and strutting eloquently towards the door, but she saw instantly her riposte was wasted. Harry was obviously an unsophisticated artisan of the time. Hopefully, she would soon be able to meet aristocratic society intellectuals. She needed to walk into her Square, sit down somewhere and reflect long and hard.

Chapter Two

Morning of April 20th, 2026 at Orsbrick Hall:

Quietness had spread like no other. A silence, pervasive as the greatest depth of outer space, filled the air with Victoria's sudden clipped announcement of 'welcome to the McKenzie family.' Abby, stunned and shaking from the discovery that before them was one Lady Fenella Kirkby, calculated the ancestry tally in complete disbelief. A tall, pretty twenty-four-year-old, Fenella's luscious mane of black curls were parted neatly in the middle and her long and billowing, yellow muslin skirt exhibited a picture of total incongruity as she stared upwards at the ceiling, mystified and frightened with what Victoria had announced. Such a thing was simply not conceivable. How could the date be so far ahead? But when Fenella looked around the room, especially at Madeleine and Belle who were smiling back in as friendly a manner as they could muster, understanding exactly what Fenella must be experiencing, all she could feel was abject panic. Her cheeks reddened alarmingly and her breath quickened. A jolt of adrenaline hit, causing beads of sweat to loom large across her forehead.

Abby topped up Fenella's brandy then swigged the rest of her own glass down in one gulp followed by another top up. But Fenella had gone inert as if her brain was dead and her limbs paralysed. Maddie sat next to Fenella and held her hand gently whilst they waited. They could plainly see her working through the immensity of what she had just been told, that today was not April 20th, 1865, like it was before she had gone dizzy waiting on the lawns of Orsbrick Hall for her grandfather to come out, but she had woken up on April 20th, 2026, one hundred and sixty-one years into the future. There was only one explanation. She had died from apoplexy like her aunt and this is what happened when you die, but these people had no wings. They didn't sound like angels and were dressed in the most peculiar apparel. She could only think of Archibald, a meaningful jolt back to familiarity and normality. She had to fight and muster up her full mental powers and retain his memory, he was so precious. Archibald the son of her mother's friend Lady Caitriona Endersby had been born the same year as her. They had been close friends since early childhood. Maybe she loved him but she didn't really know because she was discouraged from thinking of male suitors and especially meeting them. Her grandmother insisted she study hard and diligently, certainly, she never wanted for anything. Every comfort and need had been provided for unstintingly by her wealthy grandfather. But Archibald had become the new vicar of the parish church of Burscough and had renounced his aristocratic title to follow orders and embrace the church. He wanted to spend his life ministering to the poor and she would willingly have gone with him and support his every need if he had asked her, but he never asked. She had been so excited when she arrived at Orsbrick Hall to visit him having corresponded copiously the whole year before. Archibald, like her, had never known his father either. The resemblance to that man, Julian, Victoria's husband, was so uncanny. Perhaps they had set a trap to confuse her even more. She intended to see Archibald after the planned business of her grandfather and her with James McKenzie and his precocious sixteen-year-old step-daughter, Mauveine, but that never happened because in a flash she was here, still in Orsbrick Hall but in the far ahead year of 2026. Everything appeared so curiously strange around her, incomprehensible but instead perhaps she was in a dream. That must be it, of course, so if she pinched herself hard she would return to her grandfather.

She did.

Nothing happened.

Her Alice in Wonderland situation was complete but who was the Queen of Hearts? Was it Victoria? And was that outlandish individual, Sabrina, the Mad Hatter … or were they all insane? She realised that someone was speaking to her again and swigged down another large gulp of brandy.

Maddie, still holding her hand and observing sensibly, decided to intervene. "Fenella, we understand you've had a terrible shock but can I suggest something? Would you like instead to come up to my bedroom with my sister Belle and me, just for a chat? I can see you're already familiar with Orsbrick Hall. I bet you're intrigued what it may be like now aren't you?"

Fenella looked blankly at Maddie but somehow this was the one person who she felt instinctively she could trust and relate to and she appeared genuinely kind and sincere.

"Yes please, I'd like that."

Simultaneously in her head, Maddie was running through necessary practicalities, noting that Fenella was similar in height and build to both her and Belle. A change of clothes would be a good start.

Victoria, having complete confidence in her daughters nodded approvingly. She and Abby needed to discuss Mauveine and how on earth they could introduce Fenella to Julian, Lynton and the boys. From a glancing grin between Abby and Maddie, it was clear the suggestion received a double approval. A rattling of the back door immediately made everyone look around. Sabrina had successfully oiled her creaking metal hand and taken the opportunity to walk the dogs before they became fretful. The heavy door swung wide open and both family wolfhounds, Jeb and Kai, bounded in tails wagging. Barking gently, they ran straight over to Fenella and began to nuzzle her legs for their favourite ear strokes.

Victoria, instantly alarmed, rose to stop them. Those huge dogs would frighten the life out of anyone let alone poor Fenella in the state she was in. But a shaking head glance from Abby and the unexpected lack of fear from Fenella who was smiling warmly and rubbing their heads, in turn, made Victoria realise. Clearly, Fenella was used to these animals. A distinct relaxation had settled over her and Jeb and Kai sensed it. Maybe they even smelt the original scent.

"Oh how wonderful, Rufus and Sebastian my pet wolfhounds," Fenella cried, beaming for the first time. "Sorry Victoria, I realise they are not but I was missing them so badly whilst away from home with my grandfather. What are their names? They are so similar in both colour and temperament."

The dogs had slumped down at her feet, tired from their exercise along the canal. Everyone was thinking the same. Was this a potential breakthrough? Maybe they can actually manage this weird situation.

"Jeb and Kai," Victoria replied, smiling. "They are only three years old and brothers. Jeb is the slightly darker one. We bought them from a local farm. We've always had wolfhounds ever since I inherited Orsbrick Hall."

Fenella looked up at Victoria and took in her facial features. Her mind was clearing and whatever was happening to her she needed to go with the flow and she was feeling hungry.

"Come on, let's walk up to my room now," Maddie said softly, easing Fenella up out of the chair. "I think we can help to explain what you have just heard."

Victoria and Abby watched her swish out of the door in her long dress behind Maddie and Belle towards the famed wide marble staircase.

Abby turned to Victoria. "Fashions apart, can't you just see the resemblance now, especially to Maddie. She even walks with the same confident poise."

"I was thinking the same thing. There's another story we have to hear and understand yet. How she survived. Obviously, what we read about and surmised in those old newspapers didn't happen as reported. Amongst all that tragedy, Fenella really was born alive. But I wonder whether she knows who her father is and that Morag was her mother?"

Abby was pondering hard. That second glass of brandy had finally calmed her down, although why she had felt so agitated she didn't really understand, given how normally she was calm and composed in emergencies. Then a notion spread through her mind. "Actually, when she first came in, do you remember? She said, 'I can see this is Orsbrick Hall but not my Orsbrick Hall, or what should be mine.' I think Fenella knows or has some idea of her parentage and I suspect the business she had come for with James McKenzie and Mauveine before being whisked into the future was related to some perceived inheritance."

"I didn't hear her say that," Victoria replied. "My brain was going six to the dozen, but the logical sense of your argument is definitely persuasive. What did you whisper to Belle as they went out?"

"Don't mention Mauveine, given who or what we may be bumping into later."

15

"Actually that was good thinking, Abby. Fenella would have been James's half-sister, albeit illegitimate so Mauveine would have been her niece. Of course, at that time Mauveine was understood as his adopted daughter. How the true nature of Mauveine's parentage by James manifested to the outside world is still not clear, is it. And Fenella was illegitimate too. There were a lot of complications going on during that period in the mid-1860s but in order of priority of inheritance, Fenella would have come before Mauveine."

"Don't forget there was also Lydia, a legitimate sibling of James and his deceased wife Susannah. Where did she fit in? Also, we never did find out …"

"Find out what?"

"About why Mauveine was looking for Fenella on the Queen Lusitania. Was Lady Fenella Kirby the one she was looking for all along and for what purpose?"

"Oh my God, just when we thought everything would be settled and back to normal, it decidedly isn't. We'd better agree how to handle meeting my so-called sister, Alice Langton, down at St John the Baptist. For the time being, it doesn't sound like a good idea for either Fenella or Mauveine to be aware of each other's presence until we've worked out what to do and the reason Fenella is here."

"Agreed completely. And there's the small problem of explaining away Fenella, who knows nothing of the twenty-first century, to Julian, Lynton and the boys when we head for the pub, and I'm starving."

"So am I … fuck it all."

Suddenly, Sabrina marched in holding a tray of small cakes and a large pot of black coffee, a black suede glove covering her metal hand. "My rational sensors tell me that there is an intricate problem compiling with the arrival of this person

Fenella so I decided to bake quickly and provide you with suitable and required biological thinking energy before your visit to the George. I plugged into my ultra-capacitor for a jolt of electrical adrenaline too. I feel a deep mind session coming on."

Abby giggled stupidly and Sabrina immediately looked blank, uncomprehending of any illogicality to her words and actions. However, Victoria realised how hard Sabrina was trying to fit in and become part of the family, especially after they returned. It seemed that the fire in the barn incident, where Sabrina could easily have melted into a plastic blob, had triggered an internal reassessment of her concept of self and her role at Orsbrick Hall.

Victoria replied immediately. "Sabrina, thank you so much, that is really lovely and timely. Yes indeed, we do need to sit down and think through some rather difficult issues. Abby has had a few too many brandies for this time of the morning, so please excuse her mild levity today," ignoring a glare from Abby who was already tucking into the largest, pink-iced fairy cake. Sabrina poured out a large mug of coffee for both of them. "I shall call you if we need some input but I think at this stage Abby and I should be able to manage at least initially."

"Thank you, Victoria," Sabrina replied calmly. "In which case I shall return to designing and making the electronic control assembly for the new ground pump trial we dug out near the burial area, or should I more precisely articulate … Julian and Lynton undertook the digging with assistance from Ned and Zac."

"Really," Victoria cried, smiling. "I was told that Julian supervised and directed the project and that you provided all the cooking."

"Oh no, a false premise has been circulating. Unfortunately, Julian cannot function at a sufficient technological capability for that task. I had to take over complete supervision immediately and ensure they worked to exact parameters, or failure would have been inevitable. He was much better undertaking the digging and the George provided them with the necessary nightly nutrient sustenance."

Victoria laughed. "Yes, I'm sure. Well done again Sabrina."

They watched her fly determinedly out of the other door, this time wearing a pair of old baggy overalls, off towards the workshop with a laptop and large soldering iron from the kitchen tucked under her arm. Victoria turned to Abby and grabbed a cake. "Lynton will be disappointed."

"What with?" a puzzled Abby replied, pointedly.

"The sombre and utilitarian uniform change of course. Spicy mini-skirts definitely seem out. Oh come on Abby, don't look so glum. I was only joking. We've got some serious thinking to do and quickly. I hope Maddie and Belle are making headway up there with Fenella, whatever headway will turn out to be."

Curiously touching the smooth painted walls near the marble staircase, Fenella wondered where the beautiful ornate tapestry of the River Mersey had gone and pondered the unnamed picture of the white-coated female scientist busy in her Victorian laboratory. Who was that? Gazing down the first-floor corridor, all bright and airy with ceiling lights providing a warm welcome, Fenella's brain started orienting towards the reality of where she was ... and how she had managed to cross over a century's worth of time barrier. The whole Orsbrick environment was incontrovertibly changed and there was so much she had to understand.

Maddie and Belle had a large bedroom each with individual ensuite bathrooms next to each other, all exactingly done out to their indulgent tastes by their father. The moment they entered Maddie's room, the wall to ceiling bookcases filled with all manner of paperbacks and hardbacks on politics, art, literature, science and mathematics, grabbed Fenella's attention. She walked slowly up to the first packed shelf and pulled out a book on advanced calculus, peered inside quickly and put it back again with a wide smile, fingering the Cambridge exam papers on the oak desk, one of the original heirlooms which Maddie had lovingly restored and varnished up herself. Fenella stared, hesitated and then nervously touched the tablet screen which was displaying a rotating set of canal boat pictures. She jumped back startled when the pictures changed to photos of Janine on the Harvard campus recently sent by Maddie's best friend.

Maddie winked at Belle who whispered back. "Interesting reactions, we must find her some modern clothes and quickly."

"So, Fenella, what do you think of my room?" Maddie said warmly, indicating to Fenella to sit down on one of her comfortable chairs. Fenella gazed quietly at the decor, taking in the colour scheme the likes of which she had never seen in her life. The rear wall was papered in an expensive and dark rust-red fabric, against which Maddie's king-sized bed stood. A warm duvet with a rust and white spotted cover lay over it, replete with half a dozen fluffy matching pillows. A thick brown rug was stretched out in front. Matching velvet floor-to-ceiling curtains drawn back in front of the original windows provided an overall effect of luxury alongside the other wall, papered in a light-orange. Fitted wardrobes with matching oak doors, an expansive dressing table and a small coffee table finished off the room, all varnished to match the finish of the polished oak floors, which Julian had painstakingly sanded, smoothed, and oiled. A small chandelier hung from the white smooth ceiling, edged with tiny LED lights.

Fenella walked quietly to the window and stared out. Maddie had one of the best rooms in the house with a stunning view of the pond and the surrounding trees, the canal weaving through the fields in the distance. "Your room is very beautiful, Madeleine, unlike mine at home which is so dark and dull in comparison. I do recognise the view but I'm sure there were a lot more woods."

"Yes, there was," Belle replied. "Woodland in England has been heavily depleted over the last hundred years although much replanting is being done as part of rejuvenating the natural environment again."

"You know, there are lots of materials and objects here I don't recognise. What is this thing and what is it made of?" Fenella continued, picking up Maddie's black hairdryer and feeling the smoothness carefully.

"You use it to dry your hair and it runs, like most things, off electricity and it's made from an artificially manufactured substance called plastic which comes from oil," Maddie replied.

"Electricity? You mean the same thing that my grandfather and I went to see at the Liverpool Science Exhibition in 1861, where we saw a horseless carriage moving around the yard run by something called a battery and a motor. We also saw electric arc lights. They were very bright but so noisy and didn't run for long. I assume all those lights on the ceiling are the same idea? Tell me truthfully, am I really in 2026?"

"Yes, you are, Fenella. We know exactly how you feel and how much of a shock this is. We do have a lot to talk about," Belle replied whilst stroking her hand gently.

Maddie rummaged inside her walk-in wardrobe, emerging with a pair of skinny jeans, a floppy tee-shirt, and a new set of underwear, an unopened present from Janine of decorated blue boy shorts and matching bra. "Now, through that other door there's a water-closet and a shower with running hot water, not like you may have been used to, in fact probably sheer luxury in comparison. We're going to dress you up 2026 style and I bet you would love a hot shower experience. I'll show you in a second how to put this bra on, which I can assure you is much more comfortable than a chemise. I must admit those Victorian black ankle boots are very fashionable presently, you can wear these jeans over the top of them. Belle, have you got a spare pair of socks? I reckon you're about my size too, serendipity, don't you think?"

Fenella laughed for the first time. She felt so comfortable in Madeleine's company, and picked up the dark-blue skinny jeans, running her hand over the material. "Cotton?"

"Of course. Just as fashionable now as in 1865, especially in West Lancashire. This is a zipper, you pull it up like so."

"Gosh, Oh my Lord in heaven above, that is quite amazing."

"Just gosh from now on Fenella, no 1860s expletives, there's lots of new conversation to learn," Maddie replied as they both giggled. The Fenella ice wrap was melting. "In you go. I'll show you how to turn the tap on, use the shower gel in that plastic bottle and then we'll dry your hair when you come out. You'll be a 2020's girl in no time whatsoever."

Fenella wandered in tentatively, wide-eyed by the modernity and the thick, soft, fluffy towels but soon Maddie and Belle heard the shower running and a very pleasant singing of some kind of Irish ditty. Clearly, an influence of the Emerald Isle must have permeated her family roots, presumably on the Kirkby side. Emerging ten minutes later to a round of claps, Fenella, still in a daze but now genuinely smiling, liked the fit and comfort of everything, especially the so-called 'jeans' despite the unfamiliar material and style. They dried her natural, long and black, curly, wet hair and Madeleine put on a dollop of green eye shadow and red lipstick whilst Belle bundled up Fenella's Victorian dress carefully with the other clothes and put them inside a large bag in the wardrobe, well out of sight.

Fenella was gorgeous with distinctive Roma exotic looks and long, natural lashes which stood out remarkably with a little black mascara over them.

"Wow, Fenella, you look absolutely stunning," Belle spluttered, amazed at the transformation, as Fenella stood in front of Maddie's wardrobe mirror and gasped. She didn't recognise herself but rather liked the effect.

"Is absolutely stunning a kind of compliment?" she asked, fluffing her curls. "My grandfather often used to call me Nell but I never really liked it, I always associated the name with whores."

Maddie grinned. "Absolutely, I mean the compliment. To be honest, I like Fenella. It's a lovely name and suits you totally, very classy."

Belle nodded in agreement.

But where do they start? They needed to find some common language but what could it be?

Fenella eyed Maddie's desk again and casually picked up a set of Cambridge University scholarship papers in mathematics which Maddie had sat in March, agreed with Victoria as her backup if she didn't end up starting her dream artificial intelligence course at Harvard. Watched curiously by Maddie and Belle, Fenella silently read through all the questions, picked up a pencil and solved a complicated integration by parts question in seconds, one which Maddie had ticked and struggled over. Fascinated, Fenella's cheeks glowed with excitement. A sudden wave of confidence had swept over her. Mathematics, which she adored, looked the same in 2026 as in 1865 and she promptly burst into tears. Maddie and Belle realised that Fenella had unusually followed an educated science pathway like Morag her mother and was just as gifted … something at last in common amongst the three.

Maddie comforted Fenella as Belle cut up a jam sponge cake and poured out the teas. It was also obvious that Fenella was hungry and thirsty because she stopped crying immediately and tucked heartily into the cake. The time had come to talk. In detail, Maddie carefully explained who they were and the background to the McKenzie family, including the place of Abby and her relationship but decided to mention nothing of their 1841 return or about Mauveine. But Maddie did imply that the McKenzie females were psychic and being scientists and artists were sensitive to forces as yet unknown which enabled transfer through universes in space and time. Maddie crossed her fingers and took a gamble that Fenella would likely want to recall her own background rather than enquire whether she and Belle had moved across time too. That seemed to work. Maddie, as usual running her brain over realistic practicalities, had decided to propose a story to explain Fenella's sudden appearance to the rest of the world and especially to her father, Lynton, Ned and Zac. A couple of gentle knocks on the door made them turn. Victoria and Abby wanted to come in.

Marching in first, Abby gasped eyeing over the unexpected sight of Fenella looking now for the entire world like a student friend of the girls. "I must say, Fenella, your change of clothes is immensely transformational, you've become a different woman. Modern fashions definitely suit you. Are you pleased with the effect?"

Fenella smiled. "Yes most decidedly, thank you, Abby. May I ask? Will you be eating soon? I'm so used to having a good lunch and I'm starving despite the wonderful cake."

"Good to see you have a healthy appetite, something else you share with the McKenzie's," Maddie replied.

"And the Warren's," Abby chimed, relieved that whatever Maddie and Belle had been doing and saying, Fenella was beginning to look far less tense and stressed.

Maddie interrupted. "Okay. First, let me run this idea by all of you because once we walk out of the front door, we need to avert the obvious questions immediately. Fenella Kirkby and let's drop 'Lady' for now to make it easier, is a long-lost cousin of my friend Janine in the US, snatched as a baby from Boston and brought up in a closed and secretive convent in remote Cork in Ireland as an aristocratic nineteenth century orphan with a small group of other girls. One night she escaped, confused and dazed, never having been into the outside world before and was brought covertly by the CIA in Dublin to Orsbrick Hall because I had offered Janine and her parents, Fenella's closest relatives, to try and initially rehabilitate her here into the 21st century."

"My goodness, hell and damnation as Fenella would say, you couldn't make that up!" Belle cried.

Victoria stayed silent, her brain working logically through the pros and cons at speed. Abby was immediately sceptical. The story was so odd, although she agreed strange things had happened in the past regarding baby snatching and religious cults in Ireland but most importantly time was short and nobody could think of anything better.

Fenella, quiet and reflective, agreed. She knew her situation demanded something, however unusual, to explain why all she knew about was her life in 1865. If she had returned backwards to the eighteenth century she could have coped easier but she knew nothing of this future and would have to learn and adapt very quickly and felt confident if Maddie was alongside. She looked directly at Victoria. "I think I could help make that story work. I've always been good since being a little girl at story-telling. So much of my life has been closeted up with females anyway and I know a lot about convents. I've seen little of the outside world—my aunt was actually a nun."

Victoria smiled. She had nothing better to offer and they needed to move on to the George as expected. "I'm confident you can, Fenella. Now you are one of the family, it looks like we're going to have to put you up here for the time being, so we can all work out what to do next. At least you know Orsbrick Hall has space. Let me take you to the nicest guest room we have which is next door here to Maddie's. It's actually two rooms made into one, like a bedroom and a sitting room. I hope you like it. Then we'll take you to the George and we'll have some lunch and meet the rest of the family. And don't worry about cost and money, which is not a problem just as it wouldn't have been in 1865 either. We'll get you sorted out in no time."

Fenella visibly cheered. "Thank you so very much, Victoria, I don't know what to say but no longer feel so, well … err …"

"Alice in Wonderland?" Belle chipped in, to laughter all round.

Walking along the canal to the George, Fenella stared avidly at the changed scenery and the myriad of horseless pleasure boats sailing up and down the water, having traversed the tortuous system of original locks further back. Tourism and enjoyment of the canal heritage were important for the local community and the many people employed by it.

"But Victoria, where are the boat families and the horses that I knew so well? These barges propel themselves but I see no steam from an engine and no cargo."

"They are driven by engines, but not steam propulsion, they're called diesel engines and they run on oil. You have a lot to understand, one small step at a time, I suggest."

"You mean like kerosene in lamps? Diesel? How strange."

Maddie continued as they passed under one of the old humpback bridges. "It was the railways, Fenella, and their huge growth as well as the roads which put the carrying of cargo on canals slowly out of business and so the boat family way of life also ceased, many, many years back. Those engines also went into carriages to make them horseless too, carrying goods and people. These days, in England, horses are raised for racing and general pleasure riding but not manual work."

"My goodness. Belle, what are you doing?"

"I'm taking a photograph of that barge. Here, let me show you and you can do it," Belle replied, showing off her new iPhone as Fenella, trembling, held the device carefully towards the ongoing barge and tapped the screen.

"But photographs took so long to make and they were black and white. This is instant and in colour on a kind of screen. Is this a camera?"

"Sort of. You remember the telegraph?"

Fenella nodded. Occasionally she had to go to the post office and pick up long messages for her grandfather, always in an interminable queue.

"Well," Belle replied cheerfully. "Eventually, telephones which you speak down were invented to replace the telegraph and now they work without wires using invisible electric waves through the air, so this is a phone and a camera all in one with a little battery inside to power it."

Fenella examined the iPhone carefully. "Would I be able to have one of these?" she asked excitedly.

Abby laughed. "Yes, I'm sure we can get you one in due course, but as Victoria wisely suggested, one thing at a time. You must walk before you can run."

"Of course," Fenella replied, blushing. She was being too forward and presumptuous and her mind raced with new ideas and experiences, something her grandmother had drummed into her daily never to do.

Abby continued. "Can you remember, Fenella, why you were at Orsbrick Hall in the first place?" deciding that relaxing out on the canal bank was a good place to find out precisely what sort of scenario had been planned for James McKenzie and Mauveine to confront way back in 1865.

Walking slowly along the towpath, Fenella continued to admire the occasional, traditional pleasure boat moored alongside the bank. Burscough remained an important staging point for modern boat travellers and she realised the barges still looked so similar to what she was accustomed to in 1865, although the paintwork seemed much better quality and the colours very vibrant. She began to recall her last memories and talked non-stop when the next humpbacked bridge where they would come off for the George appeared in the distance. Two paired white swans were following alongside hoping for titbits.

"My grandfather had taken me in our best carriage for the first time to Orsbrick Hall, early in the morning. It was quite a long drive. I had been told the truth about my real heritage on the day of my eleventh birthday because rumours emanating from below stairs had suddenly begun to circulate throughout the household. My grandmother had become anxious I would find out from one of the servants. Up until then, I believed I had been taken in with my older sister, also called Madeleine, as babies of a widowed aunt who had died. It came as a huge shock to know who my father actually was and that my benefactors were, in fact, my grandparents. But quickly I rationalised the situation and desperately wanted to see the home of my real mother, Lady Morag McKenzie, who died giving birth to me, especially as I had inherited her gift of mathematics and love of science, which nobody else in the household seemed to understand. I had become very lonely after my sister, who I now know was my half-sister, died when I was ten and she was twelve of scarlet fever. My time was spent with intensive learning all day, every day, surrounded by female chaperones, governesses and maids as well as my grandmother, who fussed incessantly about my behaviour. I very rarely left the estate but I did have a secret boyfriend once when I was sixteen for a few weeks."

Fenella stopped to catch a breath and reflected with a sad smile. "Harvey, he was the head coachman and stable manager, very handsome and knowledgeable of the world, much older than me, but somebody saw us having a harmless picnic in the woods and told the governess and the next day he was gone. I cried for weeks. I never saw him again but he did kiss me once under the giant elm tree at the back of the barn."

Abby glanced at Victoria and smiled, rubbing Fenella's shoulder as they walked. "Don't worry, we've all been there and got the tee-shirt but lived to fight another day."

"Sorry, I don't understand?"

"My mistake. I'm sorry, just another saying of the present rather than the past—it means we've all shared the same experience. Do please continue with your fascinating recollections, Fenella," Abby replied, gathering the discourse systematically into her mind. The others walked alongside quietly but listened equally attentively. So many people around

Fenella's short and restricted life had sadly died. It was little wonder she was lonely.

"I had so many questions when I found out about my true heritage. My grandfather is a taciturn man and was very sparing with detail and reluctant to talk about what really happened. But I was tipped off by one of the servants. One night, I stole off quietly to a cottage out on the edge of the estate to meet the elderly head maid of my grandmother's sister, who had retired from service due to bad arthritis. She blamed it on cleaning out too many latrines. Her name was Agnes."

Victoria was admiring the intricate paintwork on the Jupiter, a renovated traditional canal boat moored on the near bank, the owners sitting on deck and drinking tea in the sun, whilst a large black dog snoozed alongside. She turned suddenly from her distraction. "We are aware of an Agnes who was head maid to Lady McKenzie ... err ... from old diaries of that period stored in our library," she cried, before immediately gathering her senses. Madeleine stared, alarmed, at her mother. This was no time for time-travel snippets.

Fortunately, the message was received and Fenella continued, unfazed. "How interesting, I would love to look around the Orsbrick Hall library sometime. Yes, I can confirm she was the very same Agnes who, despite her infirmities, was keen to talk and tell me everything she knew, having been sworn to secrecy all those years since my grandfather brought her with me to the Kirkby estate, which is even bigger than Orsbrick. Agnes looked after me apparently as a baby then was moved to Aunt Catherine's manor house, where she stayed for the rest of her tenure."

"What about the other servants? Was there only Agnes?" Madeleine asked.

"Yes. Apparently, a Mr Williams, head butler, and his wife the cook also left Orsbrick Hall a few months later. The two were distraught with the death of Lady McKenzie and went to manage a public house in Ormskirk, somewhere called the Red Lion. A horrible man called Rimmer, so Agnes said, took over as head butler and brought in new staff to look after James and Ellen, my half brother and sister."

Abby, walking behind, glanced over at Victoria and rubbed her finger quickly across her lips. "Actually, Fenella, I own the Red Lion with my husband Lynton who you will meet too at the George."

"The Lord God in Heaven above, what a remarkable coincidence," Fenella cried, turning to Abby, who smiled back, nodding. Fenella continued. "Anyway, I was taken away immediately by my grandfather because his son, Emmanuel, my father, who was a doctor in the village, was inconsolable over the death of my mother and in no fit state to look after a newborn baby. It appears that my mother and father had secretly married on the Christmas Day in Liverpool and a legal deed was drawn up that their baby, me, was to share the Orsbrick Hall estate equally with children Ellen and James, with one-third each. I would be entitled to residence and my rights to the estate would have priority over James's future children, unless he had a male heir. My grandfather, Lord Kirkby, had no idea until Agnes revealed this and in a short time, he located the solicitor, by the name of Green and Burgess. The deed was pulled from their archives and shown to him. My grandfather was now prepared to go to court and reveal publically, to see the deed enforced if necessary. Only Lydia and Mauveine, a bastard child, had been born and James's wife had died years before so there was no male heir. A meeting between my grandfather, James, Mauveine and me was to take place today to discuss the existence of this deed and unveil my presence, neither of which is known to them. That's why I was at Orsbrick Hall, waiting outside beside the canal for my grandfather who had just entered the house, when next minute I went dizzy, fainted and found myself here."

Abby pondered the second equally peculiar coincidence of the law firm involved. Green and Burgess had been the original name of Lynton's business when Victoria and she had first set off together from Rotterdam to Liverpool to meet him and find out about the mystery of Victoria's unexpected inheritance of Orsbrick Hall. She decided to say nothing. Peculiar could not begin to describe how she was feeling inside. A glance at Victoria showed that she too had picked up the inference immediately, although Maddie and Belle would be unaware as they were not even born then.

"Can we just stop here for a minute," Abby said, pointing to a couple of wooden seats conveniently sited for enjoying another lovely view across the flat fields to Parbold Hill. A former flour mill and now a heritage centre, complete with its original huge chimney, dominated the landscape on the other side of the bank. "What happened to Ellen and also Lydia who you mentioned? Were they not going to be present as well?" Abby asked, being careful not to overtly display she knew more, lots more. Fenella was turning out to be highly astute.

They sat down and drew breath. It was very warm in the spring sun. "No. Lydia had evidently left home and was studying art in Manchester and totally uninterested in Orsbrick Hall. Ellen, also an artist but now a widow had disappeared to France to live and paint and had no intention of ever returning. The matter of my status and rights concerned only my half-brother James and his illegitimate daughter Mauveine. But the meeting will have not now taken place. I wonder what has happened to Mauveine who I never met?"

Victoria, sensing an awkward moment, instantly distracted the conversation when another pleasure boat chugged past speeding onwards to the next lock further up, the two families onboard waving madly. This was not a moment to bring up Mauveine, especially if they are to discover her imminent resurrection later at St John the Baptist Church. How much did Mauveine know about Fenella? Questions to be asked and answered before either of them met. They turned the corner with the main Burscough Bridge in their sights, intending to walk off there and head quickly down to the George public-house, only to see an array of flashing police and ambulance lights on the bridge. People rushed about on the bank, a number of whom, soaking wet, had been in the canal. Someone covered over was put onto a stretcher and promptly carried up the slope to the ambulance.

Fenella started wide-eyed. "Those shimmering bright lights, what is happening? I think a person has just been pulled out of the canal."

They walked quickly, Maddie and Belle ran on ready to help but it appeared to be too late. Two policemen approached whilst paramedics were placing blankets over two shivering passers-by, an elderly man and a young woman.

"Move on past please," the burly police sergeant ordered, waving the five impatiently towards the bridge exit. "Incident is over."

The woman was crying bitterly. "I couldn't save her. I tried but she kept going under the water, my best friend. All because of that bastard boyfriend."

"Rowena?" Belle shouted across, recognising one of her sixth form friends at Cradwell Girls' School. "What's happened?"

"It's Elspeth. We were walking to the cafe for a chat. She was feeling really bad, having broken up with that philandering idiot Dennis Deakin. All of a sudden in the middle of the bridge she climbs onto the wall and jumped straight in before I had a chance to stop her. She must have hit her head on something, I tried so hard to pull her up, I really tried." The young woman burst into tears.

"That's enough Miss, move on now, I must insist," the sergeant reiterated loudly to Belle, very crestfallen. Victoria intervened. "Come on Belle please, we really must go. Sadly there's nothing you can do, you'll have to leave it to the police." Victoria turned to the girl shivering under a blanket. "Rowena, Belle and Maddie will phone you tomorrow and arrange to meet up. We're so sorry all this has happened. I assume your parents are coming for you?"

"Yes, they are. Thank you, Mrs McKenzie," Rowena muttered, shaking with shock and cold and trying to compose herself. She had to make a statement down at the police station immediately. "That would be really good, I'll phone you, Belle, thank you so much," she replied, blowing her nose.

Quickly they moved onwards back onto the road and headed straight down to the George public house, the distinctive white building finally coming into view amongst the trees near the church. Fenella put her arm around Belle, still visibly distressed. "That's so very sad. I do understand how you feel. The same thing happened recently to my younger cousin, Lucy. She jumped into the River Alt and drowned after my grandfather banned her from riding with Lord Hesketh's son,

Rupert, who she had fallen in love with. She was only sixteen. She couldn't swim with the weight of all her heavy clothing."

Belle smiled back, always the rationalising one in times of stress. "Thank you Fenella, I really appreciate your concern. I must just take a deep breath, for now, this has been a tragic accident, sadly. Shit happens as we say. I'll speak to Rowena tomorrow and see what I can do. Maybe you'd like to come with me. But first, we have to introduce you to the rest of the family."

"And," Victoria replied sternly, stopping everyone before they walked through the door. "Remember the story we've all agreed on. I hope, Fenella, you can play along with that at least until we know and understand why you are here."

Fenella nodded solemnly; there was so much to understand around her, let alone why.

The lounge was remarkably quiet for a Saturday lunchtime. Maddie strode towards her father, propping up the bar with Lynton. Both had started their second pint of beer. Abby was already organising everyone else around a large table near the window and glanced at the bar. Plainly, Lynton hadn't eaten either and from his ruddy face and irksome beaming expression had probably downed a few whisky chasers too alongside his favourite pale ale. Fenella sat down quietly, absorbing the surroundings and the horseless carriages through the window coming in and out of the car park, intrigued how they worked.

"I see you've brought Abby's friend with you. I must say, she almost looks normal out of that Victorian dress. Where on earth was she going?" Julian began, glancing across whilst a barmaid took over some menus.

"Dad, she's *my* friend actually, or should I say ... err ... well more like Janine's. It's a long story and Mum has said that Fenella can stay for a bit."

"You mean she's American?" Lynton interjected, putting down his glass. "Fenella? Unusual name, she looks very Romany. So where is she actually from, Maddie?"

Maddie took a deep mental breath. Explaining away Fenella was not going to be as simple as she thought and the more she dwelt on her concocted story the less she liked it already. "Actually, Fenella's from Ireland, but she was brought up in an extremely sheltered environment by a strange sect, confined inside a remote County Cork convent and has ..."

"Yes, I know, Maddie," Julian said, cutting her short. "Issues I think you were going to say. Definitely, for sure, that was obvious from the moment I walked in and she took me for a man of the church."

Lynton roared laughing at that God fearing concept, about as far from reality as one could imagine. Everyone was looking and Abby glared across. He looked well on the way to being thoroughly pissed and it was only early lunchtime. This heavy drinking had to stop ... alcohol was worryingly taking over his life. Abby thought instantly back to the grotesque Dr Lynton Grey character of 1841 she had just left behind and shuddered. Perhaps what she had met then was not so unreal in 2026 after all, a kind of ghostly vision of the future from the past; so very Charles Dickens. She marched over, just as Maddie was adding the defining descriptor.

"Dad, when I said sheltered I really meant confined totally, not just from the outside world but the outside time. Fenella and other girls with her were brought up as Victorian aristocrats. You know Janine's parents are senior Democrat senators? They used their Irish-American contacts in Dublin to force Fenella's release and bring her straight here as I'd offered Janine to try and rehabilitate Fenella to normal life."

Lynton sighed and shuffled on his seat seeing, across the bar, the fast approach of a thunderous-looking wife. Julian, meanwhile, had slowly removed his glasses and began to rub then vigorously with his handkerchief.

"Darling," Lynton began. "I'm coming over. We've just learned of Fenella's unusual and disturbing background, so anything we can do of course we must and help the poor girl adjust, she must feel totally disorientated."

"How much have you had?" Abby barked, deciding she was taking no prisoners. The day had all been too much already.

"I went for a run along the canal before meeting Julian here and changed in the toilets. This is my first and only pint honestly ... need to quench the thirst a bit, not quite in tip-top enough condition yet. I really meant it before, I mean about getting fit again and cutting down the drink."

Abby looked down. His designer gym bag was indeed on the floor, pushed to the back of his stool. His red face and sweaty appearance appeared to be genuine physical exertion rather than a paralytic proxy. "Okay, you're saved by the skin of your teeth this once, I believe you even if thousands wouldn't. Grab the specials menu please and come and meet Fenella," she replied, forcing a grin and grabbing his arm.

Watching Abby and Lynton wander back to the table hand in hand, Maddie and Julian, now on their own, smirked. "Lynton always plays close to the wire," Julian began quietly. "But he does really mean it this time. I'm surprised though he's decided to wind down the legal activity and join me on managing our expanding Orsbrick estate, a legacy which your mother and I shall, of course, be happily leaving to the four of you one day."

"Yes, Dad, but who would be the actual owner and inherit the title?" Maddie blurted out, her head still reeling from Fenella's revelations.

"There is no title, I thought you knew that. There was one once two hundred years ago but that was lost then and you four, as immediate siblings, would inherit and share ownership equally. What on earth is going through your mind, Maddie?"

Maddie immediately focussed her brain. She was wandering, so unlike her. She smiled. "Sorry ... I was thinking of something else altogether. But you and Mum will tie it all up watertight and legally won't you? The thought of the four of us squabbling in the distant future over the rights to own and live in Orsbrick Hall doesn't bear thinking about."

"Yes, of course, the document is already done. Green and Burgess have a deed drawn up with such provision if any eventuality happened to your mother and me. I know we should talk about it as a family soon and we will, I promise. I can see you're edgy. It's that young woman, Fenella, isn't it? Look, Maddie, this is between you and me. You've created a marvellous story, and I know more about story-telling than most but it's just too incredible, even for me. I can see through it a mile off, so what is actually going on?"

Maddie baulked inside. Shit, hell and damnation all in one. Her father was always too smart and streetwise by far. "Dad ... look, I just want to say for the moment, it's complicated ... Can you trust me for now? Fenella will be fine with us, I promise."

Julian took her hand for a discrete fatherly squeeze. "Yes of course I do. I can see she's complicated and I know, ever since you were a child, how your concern for other people's troubles and disadvantages can take over sometimes. You and Abby share a lot in common. Your mother has always been much more dispassionate, the dominant scientist in her I expect. I just don't want you getting over-involved right now in someone's difficult life, especially as you'll be heading to Harvard soon and out of our hair and Fenella's."

"Thanks, Dad, I'll keep everything organised and balanced like I always do, I promise. Belle and I just want to help her that's all. Harvard remains my priority and possibly Belle's too if her exams come off as she wants."

Julian laughed. His daughter, predictably, had everything worked out as usual. "Okay, deal. The sceptical inner me will remain silent and buttoned up, for now anyway. Come on, let's go and eat. Time for me to meet Fenella properly and dispel her of any notion of my giving sermons on Sundays. Do you think she'll like the George curry and chips special?"

Maddie laughed. "I'm sure that will be quite a unique experience but actually it's what I quite fancy myself."

Victoria closed the cover of her Blackberry phone after quickly glancing at the pinged message. "Can you also add two giant cheeseburgers and French fries to that order, please … oh … and two glasses of shandy," she said to the barmaid taking the food orders, before turning to the others. "Ned and Zac are ten minutes away. It appears they won the snooker doubles competition, would you believe?"

The pretty barmaid, Adele, laughed out loud. "Shandy? Ned always likes a few pints of Guinness on Saturday lunchtime," as Victoria looked up sharply and Adele realised out of the corner of her eye that Lynton was slowly shaking his head. "Sorry Mrs McKenzie, I'm muddling up everyone as usual, wrong Ned. I'll just get your food started, shouldn't be long."

"Good, I'm glad to hear it," Victoria replied, peering again at her phone. Adele had headed off quickly to the kitchen.

"So, what are you glad of? The food or the mistaken Ned?" Julian uttered with a grin, whilst Maddie and Belle giggled quietly.

"Both," Victoria replied, still concentrating on her phone, absorbed momentarily with a radical dye structure discovered in Germany.

Fenella was trying very hard to understand the nuances of the conversations. On this, she miserably failed. What on earth was Guinness? But she did like the unexpected warmth and friendliness of the McKenzie family around her. Everything felt so different from the unwavering upright, all proper and pious atmosphere of her grandfather's house and indeed when she was originally at Orsbrick Hall for that matter. Another major cultural difference between 1865 and now. She had to try and adjust but was already feeling much more pleasantly relaxed.

"Well Fenella, I understand that you've led a very sheltered life in an Irish convent. Would you like to tell us more about it? Being a writer I'm always looking for a new story angle," Julian suddenly interrupted, to a startled look from Abby. Maddie gazed narrow-eyed at her father. He had that mischievous look again and was never happier when being subtly or not so subtly provocative.

"You're a writer, Lord McKenzie? How wonderful. Pray, tell me what inspires you in your endeavours?"

"Please just call me Julian. I'm no Lord of the realm, sadly. That very title vanished from the McKenzie family a long way back. My wife, Victoria, is a true McKenzie, keeper of the genuine aristocratic bloodline, which is why she opted to keep her name when we married as have all our children. I'm a mere Endersby-Finnis, the family interloper. I write historical fiction if you know what that is, or I did should I say. I've just retired from a lifetime of all that, but I must insist. None of my books

39

has ever had a religious theme. I'm still intrigued why you called me Reverend when we first met in the house."

"I love fiction, Julian. Have you read any books by the Bronte sisters? Very popular now, they suffered such tragic deaths and at such a young age. I've recently read Jane Eyre, Wuthering Heights and Agnes Grey and enjoyed them all. But what an interesting coincidence ... I mean your surname. When I first saw you, I thought you were my close childhood confidante, Archibald Endersby, son of my grandmother's goddaughter, Lady Caitriona Endersby. You are both so alike. He took orders and has become the new vicar of the Burscough and Lathom parish church ..."

Fenella suddenly stopped. She realised too late for the second that she was still speaking in the present of 1865. She had to concentrate. "Perhaps Archie is a distant ancestor and you are not such an interloper after all."

Julian stared over, rather too thoughtfully for Victoria's liking who felt the hackles on the back of her neck rise. This conversation was sounding like they had never left their 1841 time travel. She caught Abby's stern gaze and watched her leg twitch. "Mmm ... perhaps you have made a valid observation, Fenella, but we will never know of course," Julian replied, more sanguine than calm. A distinct blush of red crept up his neck and spread to his cheeks.

Victoria decided to immediately change the topic. Now she was convinced that Julian has secrets and a past she has never been privy to, tied likely to that unknown period in London he never discussed except in brief, meaningless generalities. "Here comes the food at long last, I hope Ned and Zac will be here ..."

"No worries Mum, the smell of Katie's burgers were unmistakable before we even hit the front door!"

Everyone turned. Absorbed by the interplay between Julian and Fenella, they had failed to notice that Ned and Zac were already stood covertly behind the pillar, clearly stationed there for some moments by the manner which Ned was avidly eyeing up his sister's new friend from every angle. Zac had already whispered a warning a few minutes earlier when they spotted the family clique in the corner that Nancy would have his hide if Ned even remotely dared to suggest anything. They had, in the shadows, caught the ensuing conversation including Maddie's introduction of Fenella and her potential stay at Orsbrick.

"Any friend of Mad's hanging around is a friend of mine," Ned declared. "I'm cool with all of that. Hi Fenella, I'm Ned and the unsociable person gazing simultaneously at his new reality film tablet and the Liverpool-Everton derby match is my nerdy little brother, Zac."

He held out his hand, displaying his most versatile come-on smile, which always made Maddie and Belle wince and this occasion, was no exception. Fenella, however, was not only unsure what to do except smile, but was absorbed by the other person still lurking in the shadow and tapping furiously on his screen … He was doing the usual Zac, ignoring and shutting out all around him whilst concentrating on the search for some data or other which had immediately caught his imagination.

"Hello Ned, I'm pleased to meet you," she replied, still staring at the screen-tapper, who remained blissfully unaware of his surroundings. "Maddie has kindly explained about her brothers, you and Zac. I can see you are both twins too … Victoria, may I please go and see what Zac is doing?"

"Of course you can. Will you remind him that his food is about to be served, and I would like him to get Abby and me another gin and tonic, preferably Hendricks, if they have it." At least that suggestion persuaded Abby to smile again. Lynton had sidled back from outside and gave her a quick, reinforcing cuddle and kiss.

Fenella stood up and walked casually over to Zac who finally peered up from his endeavours and smiled awkwardly. "Hello Zac," she said softly. "May I introduce myself? My name is Fenella and I'm a friend of Madeleine. Your Mama wishes you to acquire a couple of gin and tonics for her and Abby."

"The usual request," he muttered. "Come with me to the bar, Fenella, and I'll buy you one too."

She hesitated. "But I don't know whether I should, is that not alcohol?"

"Time to live dangerously, at your age it's allowed don't worry."

She grinned mischievously and followed him to the bar. Abby had organised the pulling of tables together as food and initial drinks were placed down and everyone shuffled about into a seat.

Lynton couldn't resist the obvious quip. "Looks like the famous Ned chat-up methodology has failed miserably on this occasion, methinks. I rather speculate that Fenella prefers your little brother I'm afraid, Ned. This time Nancy won't have to give you a roasting."

Everyone laughed, jokes at Ned's expense happened frequently enough but he was scowling badly. He always hated being the butt of Lynton's sarcastic humour, aimed too often at him. But his turn would come.

Belle, coughing as her drink went down the wrong way, spluttered out loud. "The so-called 'methodology' is sadly only inside Ned's head. My friends at school actually think quite the opposite."

That quip set off more noisy hilarity alongside the loud clattering of cutlery and a further tray of drinks being offloaded causing Ned to grimace harder. But nobody was watching the unfolding of something else further away, an unexpected happening between two people in the mix of turmoil emotions and unexpected interplays that had progressed all morning. For one participant, the immediate emergence of Archibald had been experienced exactly as she remembered at sixteen when her passions had risen to their highest and her understanding of herself sunk to their lowest. She had to know the truth. The resemblance was so stunning it was tearing her mind apart. Had Archibald also passed forward in time to be with her?

She shook inside.

As for the recipient, invariably underestimated and taken for granted, the harmless nerd of the family occasionally irritating with his self-centred tech-mania, Zac was never perceived to set the world alight with intellectual prowess like favourites Maddie and Belle. But the moment he entered the George with Ned and carefully observed her mannerisms, caught her conversations in the shadows and then listened to the way she constructed her speech, there was only one clear and obvious conclusion, confirmed on his tablet. And the whole family had to stop playing games with one another, especially the nonsense which Maddie had cooked up for the consumption of their father, Lynton and Ned.

But one other person had quickly caught up, astutely analysing the giggling at the bar and watching Fenella gaze in raptures at her tall glass of some blue coloured cocktail which the barmaid was mixing. "Ned, tell me something," Maddie began, as she forked into her steaming curry and rice. "Is it true that Dottie and Zac are breaking up? I heard a rumour the other day at school. He hasn't said anything and neither has she."

"Sadly, they already have as of yesterday," Ned replied, swilling down a large mouthful of burger and beer. "Dottie wants some space and she's going to Uni next September of course, like my oldie sisters here. It's sort of mutual. Zac has been drowning his sorrows in his iPad, but they're staying good friends and have agreed to see how it goes."

"Really?" Victoria commented, looking up and following Maddie's quiet gaze towards the bar as Zac and Fenella, now in some animated conversation over something on his tablet, were heading back for their food. "I'm surprised. Although to be fair, both of them have plenty of time. They're still only young, plenty of fish in the sea as my mother used to say."

"That's the first time I've heard you use your mother as a benchmark, Vikki," Abby cried out with a giggle, "But I agree, so what about you Ned?"

"Me and Nancy are going to open a veterinary practice together after Uni, she's got it all planned out. Until then we keep chilled out, take each day as it comes ... Hey here's Sabrina. I wondered when she was going to leave the snooker hall."

"Snooker hall?" Julian said, cynically. "Really? What, dressed like that? Doesn't appear to be very suitable, leaning over a billiard table."

"The punters loved it and so did she," Ned replied, laughing. "She thrashed Jimmy 'Spot the Ball' Smith, the local singles champion with an amazing show all round. I'm sure you agree Lynton, don't you? Budge up. Sabrina will want to sit next to you ... for the electric socket of course, she needs to recharge after all that exertion," he added slyly, to giggles from his sisters again who had immediately cottoned on to the not so subtle nuances and guessed what he was alluding to.

Lynton reddened and shuffled along the bench seat with Abby quietly glaring again. She did not like the allusion one little bit.

"Fenella, sit here please next to me," Victoria shouted over the growing din as the pub was filling up fast. "I've ordered you a chicken curry too, the same as Maddie and Belle. I hope you like it." She looked sharply at her son. "I see Zac has treated you to a rather showy cocktail."

"With responsible low alcohol content Mum, much more lemonade," Zac replied cheerfully.

"Thank you, yes I will I'm sure," Fenella replied, carefully putting down her blue curacao and soda drink, known locally as a Boatman's Sling. "When I was a little girl, my grandfather used to buy the hot yellow powder from the British Raj he visited once in Bombay, curry has become very popular since Mrs Beeton added it to her recipes ... and ..."

Julian and Lynton looked up puzzled. Fenella was supposed to have come orphaned from a convent? She glanced at Zac, also sat down and hungrily tucking into his giant cheeseburger and went quiet, cursing herself again ... But Zac understood and she knew. Somehow she didn't care anymore either.

Fortunately, attention was diverted to Sabrina who slid gracefully into Lynton's prepared seat space and plugged herself into the wall socket, pulling down her short skirt which had ridden precariously over her thighs. She smiled. "That is so refreshing, especially when the voltage fluctuation varies 0.2% from the maximum amplitude, providing very pleasing sensations." Julian spluttered into his beer. She was waving her new polymer hand which had come in the post and was clearly overjoyed to be back to normal.

Fenella stared mesmerised. The peculiar and provocative dress sense was unfathomable to her and why had she wired herself into the wall? Who or what was this individual Sabrina, she had met first at the Orsbrick Hall front door and made her feel like she had descended down the rabbit hole in Alice in Wonderland?

Sabrina began again, with everybody's attention now focussed on her. "I had an unusual encounter first thing in the supermarket buying food. I asked a pleasant man who was leering at me if he would like to have sex in the aisle as I am programmed to experience something called orgasms but have not yet had the experience. But he ran off out of the shop very upset and alarmed? What did I do wrong?"

Lynton and the boys roared with laughter and even Victoria tittered but Abby and Maddie were distinctly not amused. Belle came immediately to the rescue. "Sabrina, this may not be quite the correct moment to be discussing this issue. Maddie and I will have a chat with you later on the topic when we get home. Is that alright?"

Fenella suddenly giggled and stifled her laugh genteelly with her handkerchief. She had come late to the irony and joke but was gradually beginning to understand twenty-first-century humour, a far cry from what she had been used to during her strict upbringing on the Kirkby Manor estate. But wonderful Archibald had always been a great counterbalance and taught her much of the real world when they were alone together, aside from the dour seriousness of the usual dinner table conversations of her grandparents and visiting aunts.

"Of course, Belle. Exactly as you wish," Sabrina replied, casually. "Anyway, I'm just working out my snooker moves because Ned has challenged me to a 'grand finale' on the pool table in the bar when you've all finished lunch and I'm fully charged up again."

"Fenella," Zac began, turning to her. "Let me explain in very simple terms about Sabrina."

Quickly, with a masterful technical summary carefully articulated to be understandable for her ears only, he finally dispelled and clarified the difference in Fenella's brain between a rabbit and a robot as she gazed at him, entranced.

"That was a very clear and succinct explanation, Zac, I'm suitably impressed," Victoria interjected, to soft claps from everyone. "Seriously, you should definitely think about teaching or lecturing one day, I believe you have a natural talent."

Ned laughed stupidly. A more incongruous thought could not have passed by his brain but then his little brother always surprised everyone when they least expected it, which did irritate him sometimes.

"Yes, I agree too," Julian said, but Zac, ignoring everyone, had sidled up into Maddie's empty seat as she went outside to take a phone call and was showing Fenella more robotic examples on his tablet.

Fenella suddenly looked up as Maddie came back. "Excuse me Victoria, but may I ascertain the location of the privies?"

"Toilets here, Fenella. I could see by the way you wolfed your food down, you were both hungry and enjoyed the curry. Maddie will show you the way."

Standing up to follow, Fenella smiled warmly for the first time. Both statements were very true. She had been ravenous. Travelling into the future had oddly boosted her normally poor appetite ten-fold or maybe it was because the food seemed more appetising.

"Given how she started off at the front door, Fenella seems to be settling down remarkably well, don't you think?" Abby quietly remarked to Belle and Victoria as they disappeared through the next bar towards the other end of the George.

"Okay everyone, I have something important I think needs to be said whilst I have the chance," Zac suddenly announced, watching Sabrina, unplugged, saunter off to the billiard table to have some practice.

"No need bro, I can see you fancy our new guest and she definitely has the hots for you. Must be that repressed convent background," Ned chortled, nudging Lynton but nobody else felt especially humoured with him at that moment.

"For f ... goodness sake Ned, will you please shut up for once. What do you mean Zac?" Belle asked, feeling a sense of something alarming. She always knew Zac better than anyone.

"Well go on then," Julian added impatiently whilst Zac silently drew his thoughts together and looked around. Most people were in the bar watching the start of the Arsenal football match on the giant Sky hologram TV.

"I think as a family ... we should be ... well ... united. I worked it out very quickly a minute or two after I saw her, it was so obvious. Fenella is a spook isn't she, like Mauveine but real and somehow travelled into our time-frame from the mid-1800s. I'm cool about it. As a family we have a special capability to participate in all of that psychic journey stuff, although I wish I could remember more like Maddie and Belle, especially at the Priory last summer."

"Yeh ... and I still remember nothing and see nothing, luck of the draw for me," Ned chipped in. "Only ever seen one spook, Isi, burning down the barn, so another around me, well I'm cool with that too. Zac's right. Maddie's amazing story line is fine for outside consumption but for all of us, like family, including Dad and Lynton, we should be on the same hymn sheet with this."

"What on earth are these two talking about Victoria? What Priory?" Julian said softly as three people walked past. "Has everyone gone crazy today and I'm the only sane guy standing and Lynton of course? I knew immediately that Maddie's explanation of Fenella's unusual convent background was a smokescreen for something and I was happy with that. I trust her ... but are you really saying that Fenella is a disembodied spirit, like Mauveine and Isi but here with us in real time? That's absurd."

Victoria remained silent, her fast brain weighing up a suitable response. These revelations were unexpected right then but perhaps it was indeed time to be open, in fact, the whole thing would be a relief. Obviously, the previous summer 1665 escapade at the Orsbrick Priory had been shared amongst all the children. But she was confident that their recent travel adventure back to 1841, the complicated interaction with her ancestors, Lady Morag McKenzie and son James, and the hilarious socialising with Ada Lovelace was known only by her, Abby and the girls. That secret and their return to 2026 normality needed to stay that way for the time being, especially from Fenella, until she understood what had happened since they returned. There were mind-boggling loose ends unravelling to solve first.

Abby was staring hard at Lynton. They had shared a few prism of purpurine secrets too, a while back after a passionate morning after when she was still drunk from the night before. But Lynton had already made a solemn marriage pledge to love, honour and obey her and her psychic, come what may, and he'd honourably stuck to it and had been remarkably relaxed.

He already understood that Abby was special, sharing the same powers as his daughter, so nothing new for him either.

"Actually, I didn't want to say before Julian, but I'm afraid I agree with Zac, and we must do all we can, as a family, to help Fenella," Lynton uttered confidently.

Abby smiled. Occasionally her man wasn't such an idiot after all, but like the good lawyer he was, could sense the inevitable as she was doing too and hopefully Victoria.

"Good God, Lynton, you're in on this too? I'm supposed to be the fantasy writer of steampunk and nineteenth-century nonsense fiction but it appears that I'm way behind all of you. Victoria?"

She drew a deep breath. "Stay calm Julian and just listen, you're usually good at that. Yes, Zac's right. From a family perspective, we need to be on the same page about Fenella. Maddie was doing her best to create a feasible narrative in a very short space of time this morning but events are moving on quickly. And yes, Fenella or should I say, Lady Kirkby, is not of this time but has travelled from 1865 to now, by a means and for a reason, we have no idea about. You know and have accepted right from the moment we met that our family has certain capabilities, and you too have seen Mauveine and Isi once. This is all tied up with it."

"Okay, I've no problem with that. But Fenella doesn't look like a ghost, she's all flesh and blood so to speak. And what happened last summer?"

"Let's leave last summer for when you and I are back home. She's not a ghost in the literal sense of the word but early this morning, in 1865, she was sat outside Orsbrick Hall, by the canal, waiting to meet my great-great grandfather and Mauveine, then she fainted and discovered herself outside Orsbrick Hall in 2026. We found her and you suddenly appeared for a beer. That's why I wanted you out the way. It was all way too complicated."

"That's fine, I get that too, I'm a storyteller for heaven's sake, but this is amazing. Zac, how on earth you worked all this out in an instant is beyond me. Forget teaching, you're a future novelist. Does Fenella know you know?"

"Yes of course … she kept initially calling me Archie at the bar and I told her I knew where she was from … and she told me quickly, Mum, what you just said. I like her and her quaint way of talking. She's really fast at maths too and wants me to teach her computing."

"Listen up everyone, Maddie and Fenella are coming back," Ned interrupted. "Mum … you need to tell her now that we're all relaxed on her true identity but we keep Mad's story intact for outsiders. That shouldn't be too difficult."

Victoria looked over at Abby who nodded as did Belle. "Okay, agreed. Thank goodness it's quiet now in here. Let's get this over with but one thing I want all of us to agree on; no questions yet. Fenella must not know about Mauveine, as Abby and I think there may be more surprises to come from her and Isi. Julian and Lynton, you have to be prepared for more questions than answers at the moment …"

"Yes, of course, Victoria, I've come to expect that over all these years," Julian replied, resigned but enormously relieved that however bizarre, some kind of truth and family unity with no fibs, lies and stories was taking shape, which was much more important to him.

"Now that's sorted I'm going to thrash Sabrina, err … not literally Lynton," Ned said smirking, striding off with a fresh pint of Guinness and his championship cue in hand whilst Abby rose promptly from her seat.

Chapter Three

April 20th, 1841. The rectory, parish church of Burscough: familiar clattering of cutlery resounded through the scullery along with a pleasant wafting of beef stew in the air that made the Reverend Thomas Langton smile for the first time that day. Struggling with his sermon for Sunday on the avoidance of sin and sifting through the large seventeenth-century Bible for suitable quotations from Leviticus, at least his decision to appoint Martha Butterley from Newburgh village as visiting cook and maid was already paying dividends, despite initial opposition from Alice, his wife.

Martha, best friend of Agnes, the head maid for Lady Morag McKenzie, had arrived highly recommended from Lord Ottersburn who had been forced to reduce his staff after recent investment losses. Order and sanity were already materialising around Reverend Langton. Running such a large house alongside helping him in the church and parish were proving too much for Alice, although she was reluctant to admit it. But they had to remain vigilant when Martha was around. It was fine when they were relaxing alone and could revert to their true identities of Mauveine McKenzie and Isi Fazackerley as they always did with Victoria, Abigail, Madeleine and Annabelle when they were together.

Contemplating their situation with despondency, trapped in an unfamiliar time-warp back in the year 1841, Isi was pleased that they had collectively ensured that Morag's son, James

McKenzie, would survive his disastrous typhoid malady. Such achievement would ensure all McKenzie descendants should now follow the correct pathway towards the future existence of not only Mauveine but also Victoria and her daughters.

But despite incessant nightly musing over all possible scenarios, neither he nor Mauveine was any closer to understanding what would enable them to return back to the time they had come from or how. Surely, as Mauveine strongly hinted, they didn't have long? The temporary rift in the psychic time-barrier could likely soon close up and he and Mauveine, as well as Victoria, Abigail, and the two girls, would be trapped in this period and never exist in their own futures again. He had to fight his doubts and keep them to himself. There really had been some strange and unexpected outcomes, not least the appearance of manifestations of Julian and Lynton, belonging unequivocally to this time only and not the future. Was that a mistake or some form of diversion? On a bad day, he still vacillated over the wisdom of triggering this McKenzie family time-reversal in the first place but Mauveine always remained calm, steadfast and unwavering. Logically, she was absolutely correct. There had been no other option but to return to 1841 and ensure the correct destiny of Morag and James and he was hugely enjoying the bonus of his unexpected status as the local vicar, an occupation that he found a natural leaning towards. Yes, their duty had to be done but emotions about the consequence of failure perpetually dogged his inner mind. He felt like the Lord's disciples at the Last Supper, perhaps another theme to embellish and take up at the pulpit.

A rattling of the front door opening and a loud squeak of the ancient hinges made him smile. He immediately arose to greet his wife. Mauveine was back from her flower arranging in the church. The regular parishioners had already been highly complimentary, saying nobody previously had ever taken as much effort to make the ambience inside so welcoming, but they didn't know Mauveine. Being a highly organised scientist, her laboratory had always benefited from the same orderliness. A pleasant and tidy environment aided her thinking to work creatively.

"My dearest Isi, your familiar smile has finally returned. It's never been like you to be gloomy. And by the smell of that lively beef stew, it isn't your sermon which is cheering you up either. On this decision, I accept you were right to employ Martha. I can see the difference already and I feel much less of a stress in the mind."

"Good," he replied giving her a loving peck on the cheek. "I see you have some letters already. I didn't hear the post-boy. Shall we have lunch and find out what news prevails today?"

Martha suddenly appeared from around the corner carrying a small tureen of stew and potatoes. "Lunch is ready Mrs Langton. I can serve it immediately if you wish?"

"Indeed, if you please, Martha," Mauveine replied, placing her hat and coat on the stand and gathering up her long skirt. "These boots you bought me from the Ormskirk market when you met with the Bishop last week fit beautifully, Thomas. And Martha, I assume you are undertaking all my instructions and that you have made a portion to eat for yourself too?"

"Yes I have, Mrs Langton, thank you so much. I am not used to … well being treated so generously. I don't know what to say."

"It is as the Lord would wish, the sharing of food and drink is fundamental to our beliefs," Isi replied gently. "We would not want it any other way, and you may eat with us now and at any time in the future."

"Thank you, Reverend Langton, I would be honoured to join you but I can see that you and Mrs Langton have much private business to discuss with so much post to open. And my friend Agnes is coming very shortly with some advice and our weekly chat in the scullery as I need to understand more things about my employ functions, which are much wider here than previously. Agnes has so much experience."

"Then you must share lunch with Agnes and join us for dinner tonight," Mauveine replied, thinking immediately that cultivating a hospitable environment for some likely gossip about the happenings inside Orsbrick Hall may well be advantageous. "Don't worry, we will serve ourselves today, the stew smells delicious."

Martha blushed and with a quick curtsy headed down to the scullery, expecting Agnes at the back door any minute.

Mauveine began opening the mail carefully with her brass letter knife. "More bills, dearest, from the florist, the grocer and also the graveyard gardener, Luke Melling. He writes beautifully, I'm amazed he is literate. Looking and listening to him you wouldn't believe it. Don't we pay him directly from parish expenses?"

"Apparently his family were wealthy boat-builders in Wigan and they paid for him to go to a church school as a child," Isi replied, spooning out the stew for both before it went cold. "But his family threw him out, why I don't know and he wouldn't say. He's dug graves and tended churchyards ever since. We'd better eat our food. Is there anything from the Bishop?"

Mauveine had all the letters laid out in front of her and after ladling out the spring carrots began to read the rest, Isi now cheered by such a splendid meal. "Well," she said. "Despite your forebodings, the meeting with the Bishop went better than you thought and he has instructed the commissioners to ensure you receive a special monthly stipend of ten guineas and that all the rent is to be paid annually … Your worry about organising proceeds from the old parishioner tithe is no longer required. They have approved this new system with immediate effect and have paid retrospectively. Five pounds is enclosed from the Arthur Heywood and Sons bank. We have some legitimate funds at last. I was increasingly worried that the money box left by your previous incumbent would be bare by next week."

"Ahh … the Lord be praised," Isi replied, his mouth full of stew. "That private bank is used by the cathedral of Liverpool and presumably the Bishop, himself. Anyway, with some luck, assuming Victoria and Abigail have made continuing headway with Morag and James by means possible with the healing dye solution you all made, we should be returning to our time very shortly. Although how we do that still eludes my intellect greatly. Whatever is the matter Mauveine? You have suddenly gone quite pale. Is the food disagreeable? Are you unwell?"

Mauveine had gone deathly quiet, staring at the last letter and pondering intensely. "No, no, the meal is excellent. Isi … you know you say constantly you are enjoying the role of parish priest? You must listen carefully as I read out this letter. It is from Morag, written early today."

Dear Reverend and Mrs Langton

You will be pleased to hear that Doctor Emmanuel Kirkby, or Manny to his patients, has finally arrested James's symptoms of cholera with an experimental saline solution administered rectally. The fever is now subsiding dramatically and I pray fervently to the Lord that he will be well again quickly. The experience of near death has changed him overnight and he is now most keen to learn science which Manny will personally oversee, especially as I too have decided to reapply myself to chemistry and dyes again and forgo forever my unfortunate dalliance with natural philosophy and electricity. Manny has convinced me wholeheartedly that much money could be made by linking my researches to the growing needs of the Lancashire textiles industries. The blacksmith and his family have suddenly vacated Cinderblack cottages and have gone to live in London with his sister and I have offered Manny the premises for his new surgery to support the sick in Burscough, Orsbrick and Lathom, a welcome gift from me, in thanks for his perseverance and diligence curing James.

"Heaven be praised that is excellent news, my dearest," Isi responded enthusiastically. "Victoria and her children have succeeded with of course your invaluable help. Their future and our future are secured but how do we all now return to a more congenial period of time? Strange isn't it that Morag hasn't mentioned Victoria though? I thought James had symptoms of typhoid. That was very clear when I was called to administer the last rites. Why does she now say cholera?"

Mauveine looked up, her eyes sad and her expression fixed. "If I read the last part you may understand the answer to your question, my darling Isi."

I hope to call at the rectory in the next few days. You have shortly so much to organise at the church and I would like to help and pay my good fortune back to the Lord above.
With best wishes
Morag, Lady McKenzie of Burscough.
Oh before I forget, Dr Kirkby has also offered to help find a suitable governess for James and Ellen, a near-relative of his I believe, and something I have needed for so long.

"Mmm … makes no sense to me," Isi replied casually, digging a knife into the apple pie and cutting off two large slices. "I'd better head over there this afternoon, minister our sincere congratulations to Morag and then quietly have a chat with Victoria, to find out what is actually going on."

Mauveine stared at him, unimpressed. "You know Isi Fazackerley, sometimes you can be so incredibly wise, unworldly and trusting, excellent qualities for a parish priest, but at other times you are simply plain stupid," she cried pointedly, her voice cracking. It had taken her a nanosecond, as ever, to work out what had happened at Orsbrick Hall.

He looked up sheepishly. He'd missed the inference again; his wife always saw the wood whereas he remained content with admiring the detail of the trees. Despite her volatility, he had never lost his temper with her, ever, no matter how cussed she sometimes addressed him. Remaining calm and focussed in adversity was his strength and he could tell by her expression that moment had arrived again. "Please explain my dear," he replied slowly.

She began her analysis, slowly and carefully so that Isi could ponder on the life-changing implications. She had realised in an instant that a psychic cataclysm must have taken place at Orsbrick Hall and that Victoria, Abigail, Madeleine and Annabelle had returned back to their own time. She was certainly aware, from the comments Victoria had made a few days earlier, that a showdown had been building up with Morag over some issue, likely Morag's jealousy over the brief affair Victoria had undertaken with Michael Faraday. Or maybe Morag was sensing that Victoria possessed unknown scientific capabilities and knowledge which frightened her and she reacted badly. Morag would undoubtedly have been torn between her gratitude to Victoria for saving James's life and her personal vitriol for a mere governess proving so intellectually capable. But what had triggered the cataclysm? Tragically, she and Isi will never know because the space-time rupture and repair meant, as ever, that the existence of Victoria, Abigail, Madeleine and Annabelle never happened. History had already been rewritten around Morag who had stated in her letter that she never had a governess. Also, her cousin, Abigail, would never have appeared either. But the painful conclusion was she and Isi hadn't returned to anywhere. They were stuck, mortal flesh and blood in 1841 time, to live out the rest of their lives as they are.

Isi remained calm and pondered long and hard. He could see that Mauveine was taking this situation emotionally badly. The embarking of a time return was always a potential risk but he never expected this to happen like it did. However, the logic of what they should do was clear to him and laid out before them. "We shall carry on taking care of this parish that we have always loved and I shall continue enjoying my life with you as the vicar," he said slowly and quietly. He rose from his chair and put his strong arms around Mauveine, holding her tightly as she sobbed.

But at least they were still together. If they had been split up that would have been a tragedy she could not have coped with. She pulled herself away tenderly and looked into his deep blue eyes. They had been through so much together already and reluctantly she would support him completely as she always had before. It could have been worse and they had already garnered much respect from the local parishioners and church congregation. Besides, there may be another opportunity to return … although what would they return to? Ghosts? She hadn't thought that through properly, maybe that was why they had remained. They were likely forbidden by complicated laws of space-time interactions to cross the barrier back to anywhere, including their original lives.

Isi was planning ahead, thinking through what may make life more bearable for his wife. "Dearest Mauveine, we have two large cellars under this rectory and there is only so much wine I can store down there. I think you should build yourself a new laboratory and continue your research secretly on dyes, perhaps collaborating with Morag. I'm sure we could work out a suitable story to explain your knowledge. That may facilitate a future second chance for you and me to follow Victoria."

Mauveine held him tight. "Mmm … just like when we first met, Isi Fazackerley, you always think calmly ahead when a crisis takes hold. I rather like that idea."

They kissed gently. "Anything to see you smile again. Besides, at least we can bask in the knowledge that Victoria, Abigail and families are back and their future secured again and James has been saved."

"I agree and I do feel very happy for Victoria. But what is James saved for? Presumably not as my father. There are complex things we need to ponder carefully, dearest. Anyway, Agnes will be back soon to clear the dishes … shame to waste this lovely apple pie and cream. Let's finish off our meal then you have a sermon to finish and I must get back down to the church and meet Morag. We must now become independent beings in this created universe we have facilitated. Let's make the most of our new lives, especially as we are still with each other."

Mauveine did very quickly set up her secret laboratory and returned to researching the antibiotic dye, xanthene, which had saved James. The link between dyes and medicines would be a fruitful line to follow and perhaps alter history again. Having quickly acquired a couple of Morag's redundant Bunsen batteries and copper wiring, she managed to create a workable but crude charging up current for her old iPhone and revelled in the memories and pictures still on it; one small and secret piece of twenty-first-century time which could be cherished. She was resolved to her future existence of not being born and to enjoy what they now had together.

Chapter Four

Early August 1852: 6 Great Cumberland Place, Marylebone, London.

A still and deathly hush permeated the early morning air. The usual noise of clattering carriages had unexpectedly abated. Even the ubiquitous street-sellers, out and about to catch the early morning trade with a few boxes of matches here or some pots and pans there were noticeably absent. The tall, well-dressed male in his pale grey morning suit, sat quietly in the sleek, two-seater brougham, gazed through the carriage window and pondered the strange solemnity of the environment around him. It was, he concluded, not a good omen, like the foretelling of an imminent funeral. He really should have made more of an effort during the last six months to have visited his old friend and collaborator. Perhaps it may already be too late. He had been so busy writing papers, doing talks and redesigning his project, but that was really no excuse.

The carriage drew up outside a magnificent five storey townhouse, huge marble pillars encasing the double-door front entrance with a splendour and individuality which indicated immediate wealth and status. So, he thought wistfully, this was the new London residence of Lady Annabella Byron. He should not have been surprised reflecting on her idiosyncrasies, although on a personal level he had kept very much at a distance from the ramifications and unhappiness projected towards all who had unwarily crossed her path.

Drawing a deep breath, he alighted briskly from the brightly coloured carriage and thrusting a note into the driver's hand, asked that the man wait discretely down an adjacent side street. An immediate return home almost as soon as he arrived felt a distinct possibility. The grey and unwelcoming ambience provided no encouragement that this would be a positive visit, purveying a reinforcement of the dreadful rumours that had recently come his way.

The heavy, oak doors opened slowly as he approached and a maid stood quietly at the entrance to escort him inside. He glanced down at her features and his fast brain immediately ran through his repository of known people. He still retained an excellent, almost photographic memory and she seemed familiar. Then it came to him instantly. Of course, it was Lucy, the former personal maid of his good friend. He had last come across Lucy eleven years ago when he and Faraday called on his friend's equally splendid town house in Mayfair. But Lucy, much older with sunken cheeks, lacked the former sparkle and vitality in her eyes of those fun, collaborative visits and exchanges which the three of them regularly indulged in, especially on his Friday night science soirees and the Royal Society lectures. Why was she not living there now? This did not bode well whatsoever.

"Good morning sir, may I please take your hat and coat."

"Of course. Lucy, isn't it? I do remember you from a long way previous. Are you back in the household employ?"

"Indeed sir, the Countess requested me to return personally a few months back. I was, by then, far away in the service of Lord Londonderry in Portsmouth, but she found me, how I still do not know, and I came immediately by the night sailing of an oyster cutter. Now, I must escort you quickly to the Countess's room as Lady Byron has gone out to the new Wandsworth prison. She is petitioning for improved conditions for the inmates. We are not sure of her return and the Countess prefers that your meeting remains strictly private."

"Of course, I do understand."

They walked down a long, well-lit corridor and up a set of sweeping stairs to the first floor, encountering a closed door at the end. Nobody else seemed to be around, no other servants or the usual butler. On knocking, a faint but familiar voice replied and he walked in as Lucy went off to fetch some tea and cakes.

A tall and opulently dressed woman, staring out of the window, turned to greet him, her smile genuine but clearly, she was in great pain. Her face and her hair, swept into a tight bun, were made up as eloquently as ever and her legendary composure was equally evident, but an inner alarm swept through him immediately; she had become so thin and pale. He took in the rest of the room instantly. A combined study with her old desk and masses of bookshelves lined the walls as expected, but a large four-poster king-sized bed was also prominently situated and a fancy dressing table stood alongside, piled up with all kinds of potions and medicines. Evidently, she needed long spells of rest in bed during the day. He must not overtax her.

"My dearest Charles, how wonderful to see you and I have so much to share on the Engine. The most amazing ideas have been pouring from my brain onto paper. Pray, do not look so glum. Since when did the irascible but suave Mr Babbage ever be nothing but cheerful in my company?"

Babbage moved forward and held her gently in his arms. "Oh Ada, and since when did my amazing enchantress of numbers ever stop being uniquely innovative and creative? I

64

apologise profusely for allowing such a long period of time to elapse since our last discussion, a pressure of work and family matters."

She withdrew and giggled coquettishly, exactly as she used to when they argued over mathematical proofs and she was inevitably always right. "That last discussion entailed a long walk along the Sussex downs as I remember—oh I wish desperately we were there now. Anyway, I want to imbibe your great mind with a follow up to the Menabrea notes, we published on the Analytical Engine. I have had further deep and constructive thoughts around non-numerical calculations and have sketched out a paper outlining how the Engine could be programmed to compose music—a mechanical rival to Mozart. So, what do you think? Is this not as revolutionary as Napoleon Bonaparte himself?"

Babbage frowned. She was again over-taxing herself and seemed particularly excitable, even for Ada. This was not a good activity, given such clear indicators of a serious illness. She had to concentrate on getting well. "My dearest Countess of Lovelace, I am sure you have been producing original thoughts but I would not wish you to overexert yourself on my behalf …"

She stopped him immediately and grinned. "On both our behalves Charles, my angel. I confess I have not been too well of late, my usual stomach pains again. I'm under treatment by my mother's top physician, she insisted vehemently but already I'm feeling great improvement with the medicine prescribed, now enhanced ten-fold by seeing you today."

Walking to the desk, Ada picked up a large folio sheaf of bound papers which she placed carefully inside a leather pouch.

"You used a strange expression a minute ago, the word programming?" Babbage said. "What so this usage? I assume you mean executing the processes to capture the end from the means?"

She smiled inwardly. Yes, she had deliberately used that word because she had remembered its origin and in particular from whom. All the while, for all those years since 1841, she knew something significant had happened and fortuitously, her illness had facilitated the roadway which convinced her she was absolutely correct.

"I would describe my new word programming, Charles, as the means of instruction to tell the Engine what to do and how to produce the results you want."

Babbage grimaced. Ada's thoughts were well in advance of his own, where did she get her bizarre ideas from? He dreamed only of more efficient mathematical calculating but her concept of the Analytical Engine was way beyond anything he could comprehend right then. In fact, so unique were her concepts they felt desperately unreal. He remained very sceptical, especially given Ada's latest state of mind and health. She was bordering on complete madness. He had to discourage her, for her own sanity— and maybe his.

Ada continued. "Here is the paper. You will need to take this away and digest it carefully. There are many novel ideas alongside a rather clever notation I have invented to facilitate the processes of setting out the iterations and calculation. It is a little crude presently but I believe will have merit for refinement given the usual deep analysis from you."

Babbage took the pouch and placed it inside the small carrying case he had brought in. Undoubtedly this would end up on the fire but he had to listen to her as best as he could.

Ada had begun to decant a couple of glasses of red wine, as he watched her pour a milky concoction from her array of medicine bottles into hers.

"What is that potion you are about to consume?" he asked, curious.

"A unique mixture of chloroform and laudanum, dearest Charles, which has been greatly relieving my pain and also stimulates my mind at the same time. A pleasing combination don't you think?"

He shuddered inwardly. Such usage was prescribed only for terminal patients when a stupefying addiction takes hold and the patient subsequently leaves this world in a delusional hazy fog of euphoria. This was worse that he had first realised. Heaven's above, may the Lord be merciful with her so her pain does not endure much longer. And yet, despite the increasing failure of her body, her mind would not let go. She worked incessantly, night and day as much as she could.

"Come," she said, "we may not have the Sussex Downs at our disposal but we do have my mother's beautiful rear garden to chat further and it is such a lovely day, a great shame to waste the opportunity. But before I do, I wish to give you this other letter; I must insist it remains confidential. I have thought long and hard about such matters and I wish only you to be my future executor on my death, which I'm sure, will nevertheless be many years off yet. I have decided so many things, including burial with my father at Newstead Abbey. You will appreciate my mother will not be agreeable, so please take legal advice on my behalf immediately that my request is lawful, which I believe wholeheartedly it is. Can you hand me my walking stick please"

Carefully hiding the envelope behind her papers, they walked slowly down the corridor and stairs. She held onto him tightly with her other arm.

"Tell me, Ada, why are you staying here, in your mother's house? I much prefer your residence in St James Square; it has a distinctive and congenial atmosphere? Is William happy with this arrangement, if I may ask?"

She breathed in deeply. She must be honest with him. "My life became rather complicated, I'm afraid. Unfortunately, the mathematical betting formula I was working on for the last four years did not bear sufficient fruit and I'm afraid I lost some money, which I couldn't really pay back. William told my mother immediately, why I still cannot comprehend. I begged him not to, he could have simply helped me through my difficulty, I wouldn't have repeated such a stupid error and I had apologised so much. You know how moralistic and dominating my mother is and she has never liked William, always viewed him as spineless. His wealth was his only marital asset in her eyes. They fell out so acrimoniously. It was unbelievable hell, the vituperative recriminations that were bandied back and forth. My mother will not speak with him, ever again. He became intolerably angry and has disappeared back to the Sussex estate, ignoring my needs totally. And so my mother decided to take charge of my welfare, especially with my latest illness bouts."

Babbage stared. He knew she had been gambling but had no idea of the extent, but there had been rumours. More often he chose to ignore them, but the rumours were not only about gambling. His dearest Ada had gotten herself into a wholesale and terrible personal mess.

"I'm so sorry to hear of such troubles, please forgive my impudence but how much is your debt? I shall take it upon myself to clear it immediately."

"That is so kind, my dearest Charles, but there is no need. I pawned some fabulous family jewellery which William had given me. The experience was heart-wrenching and my mother, in the end, also agreed to pay half, as long as I cease all immoral and degrading activity, in her eyes, and obey her wishes completely, to be secured on a righteous path out of the arms of the devil. The total debt had accumulated to around three thousand two hundred pounds."

Babbage's eyes narrowed. Such a vast sum, how could she have been so stupid and reckless? Obviously, she had been egged on by that irresponsible egomaniac, John Crosse, that she was rumoured to be in cahoots with on the race course and off it.

Ada's eyes suddenly flashed with a look of her old defiance and independence. She clung hard to his arm and quickened the pace as they walked down the long garden towards a pretty summer-house at the bottom, shaded amongst some tall elm trees. "However," she whispered, gaily. "I can admit in your ears only, seeing as you have known me so well for so long, that piety and discretion can so easily be faked. And the faking art form is one I have perfected very well, especially with my mother, who I never wanted back in my life. But on a good day, she is becoming more pleasant company ... as long as I don't mention men, especially my father. Most importantly, darling Charles, I have my mind, which is fired and blazing again with so much that the top of my head could burst wide open. But I must reconcile with William. It is unfair for him to be so hurt and angry ... I have decided to confess ... my ... former ... err ... friendships ... and seek his forgiveness, with abject apology and remorse, if he will only come and visit me."

They sat on the long bench which had been laden with soft cushions by Lucy along with a large plate of cold beef, cheese and cut bread. A jug of her favourite lemonade and a couple of cut glasses stood alongside with a tumbler of laudanum, which she swigged down immediately, breathing an instant sigh of relief.

"I would counsel against your confessional plan," Babbage cried, alarmed with the thought, pouring out two glasses of the lemonade. "Let the past be gone and sleeping dogs lie. You must look only to the future now and recover from your malady. Especially, do not mention that scoundrel John Crosse. His reputation in polite society has been most suspect. I cannot see what benefit such news in William's ear will do ..."

Ada cut him off gently. "No, on this action I must do so. My mind is made up. I have to cleanse my wrongdoings once and for all and regain William's trust. Hopefully, he will then move to bring me back into our London home away from my infernal mother. Please, let us talk no more of such matters ... I wish instead to enlighten you on researches into my fascination with manned flight, which I have recommenced after all these years. And I know how the Engine could solve some difficult differential equations of fluids which have emerged from my concentrated thought." She looked at her pocket watch and smiled. "Mother will not be back for a few hours. I have paid the coachman to enact a little diversion to ensure she is kept away, so let us tuck into this splendid food."

And thence they talked and talked and Babbage listened hard, mesmerised with the power of her thought and originality, delving with abandon into concepts and related unknown mathematics which he had never conceived of. It was clear to him that she had deliberately been shutting down her ailing body so that all her energies could be concentrated in intense and pure mathematical thought, doubtlessly aided by the effects of the laudanum which she admitted was mixed with a little opium to maximise strength. The situation was tragic. Ada, the Countess of Lovelace, clearly had so little time left in this world but was fighting her departure with all the iron will and strength of spirit a human being could possibly muster.

However, time as ever passed by, its sleek arrow seeming even quicker than usual and he sensed her concern that she should return to her room. Then he would depart immediately by the back way and seek immediate counsel on her wish for him to be her legal executor.

"There is one last thing," she whispered. "I wish to confer with you something else, in strict secrecy before you go. For a long time, I have been studying the discipline of mesmerism extensively, fascinated by its power and the revelations of hidden rooms inside the mind, and have quietly engaged with a practitioner, regularly over the last four years. For too many years I have been continuously troubled in my subconscious by a past stupendous event which I have not been able to recall. However, on my last two visits and under the catalytic encouragement of ingested liquor of wild forest mushrooms, I spoke and my words were secretly recorded. And now I finally remember in my conscious mind, at long last. I have recalled a strange encounter and an angry altercation with Lady Morag McKenzie at Orsbrick Hall in the spring of 1841 involving her governess Victoria, Victoria's young daughters, Madeleine and Annabelle and Morag's cousin, Abigail, a fine artist. Victoria and her daughters had returned in time from the year 2026. She was a direct McKenzie descendant, a future relation of Morag and an accomplished scientist and mathematician who described how computation of the Engine was driven one million times faster through electricity rather than mechanical means and that serious illnesses like polio and smallpox had been completely eradicated from the world as well as an array of other amazing things such as horseless carriages and machines which flew effortlessly through the air from country to country."

Babbage listened gracefully. Poor Ada had clearly been especially high on a cocktail of hallucinogenic drugs; this outpouring was just too fantastical for words. He actually knew Lady McKenzie had never employed a governess before she tragically died giving birth, but Ada fervently believed it was true and real so he would give her the benefit at this moment. He sat patiently as she continued.

"Morag went completely hysterical, and began stupidly screaming about the arrival of Satan but I had already rationally deduced the correct conclusion from Victoria's behaviour over the previous weeks. She clearly knew things which had not been invented yet and I was calm and so excited inside, realising this would be the greatest discovery the likes of you and I as scientists could ever encounter. How we could have moved on in society, technology and medicine with such knowledge. But before I could intervene further, there was a tremendous explosion and they vanished, and I remember nothing further. I must now find out the truth. Can you recall anything at that time?"

Babbage breathed in quietly. He had to respond with something without giving the game away that her imagination had been severely distorted and warped, although he did admit the vision was totally fascinating and in line with Ada's futuristic leanings. This compounded further his feelings of pending and imminent sorrow and tragedy of her plight. "That period was such a social whirl at the time, I really can't recall a governess but I do remember Lady Morag McKenzie though. She came to a number of Faraday's Royal Society lectures; they seemed very close at one time."

Ada grinned … the gossip and titillation over Morag's affair amused her once more.

Babbage continued. "Something I do recall though. A woman called Alice Langton who I had met at Morag's funeral, wife of the local vicar who conducted a beautiful service. She too had a deep knowledge of science, quite remarkable when we chatted, given her vocation. Maybe Mrs Langton knows more? Anyway, I think it's time I went. I don't especially wish to meet your mother, Lady Byron. I have had too many altercations in the past."

Ada laughed. Inside she was already calculating a tactic in her fast brain. Of course, the rather mysterious Alice who she remembered a little of but had never actually met … But Victoria had once mentioned that Alice Langton was her sister! She turned to Babbage affectionately. She knew he didn't believe a word she had said, but that didn't matter anymore. "Thank you, Charles, that is very helpful. Lucy is waiting at the top of the garden with your hat and coat; she will lead you through the back door."

He was about to stride off when suddenly he turned and held her tightly again in his arms. Lucy looked the other way. "There's something I want to tell you, Ada Lovelace. I love you and always have … The biggest mistake of my life was not asking you when I could, I wish we had married." He kissed her on both cheeks gently, anything more would be too improper.

She blushed and gave him her old dazzling smile which always brought men of every type, background and intellect eventually into her domain of dalliance and flirtation.

"I know," she whispered. "I just wish you'd told me sooner. Apart from you and despite all that you may have heard, I only ever loved one other man with all my heart in my short life, and that was Morag's blacksmith who turned out to be an even worse philanderer and liar than my friend Caitriona, his half-sister. But that dalliance was over many years ago, almost indeed as quickly as it started, but I confess he was the impetus for my over-indulgence in gambling and racing.

Charles Babbage frowned momentarily, forcing his quick mind back to those early social interactions in the early 1840s with Lady Morag McKenzie, but try as he did he could not remember such a person.

"What was his name again?"

"Julian, my dearest Charles. But pray, you have no need to fret. The rogue vanished as quickly as he came and I have loved you solidly for twenty years and more and I love your Engine almost as much as you!"

He laughed heartily. "Our Engine, don't ever forget. You remain as incorrigible as ever, my dear Countess, but now I must fly. Lucy is beckoning hard, her ladyship must be due. I have some business in the north to undertake over the next month or so but I shall visit you as soon as I am back, and to hell with your damned mother!"

"That's the spirit—now go quickly," she replied, grabbing his head and kissing him briefly on the mouth, to his astonishment but delight.

In a trice, Babbage was gone. She listened contentedly as the clattering of his brougham disappeared into the distance and her mother's two pet chows, barking loudly, romped through the open double garden doors and tore down the path, chasing each other, almost knocking her for six. Her mother had definitely returned. Ada removed her hip flask of laudanum and took another large swig. The pain was returning at more frequent intervals but her mind remained clear. She had to lie down first for an hour, rejuvenate her mind and then she would return to her desk. There was much work to do.

A mere ten days had passed and Babbage was already returned home from Leeds to face the most distressing news which he had hoped could have been forestalled. His lawyer had already warned him that Ada's executor letter was unlikely to stand up in court if challenged and wholeheartedly challenged it was. In her time-honoured manner, Lady Byron had browbeaten her daughter into confessing that she had requested Babbage to take charge of her affairs on death. Immediately, using her influence and the highest level of contacts, Lady Byron had put in charge one of the best barristers in the land to refute any legitimacy of Ada's request. William once again stood aside, refused to back his wife, in fact, refused to do anything.

Babbage, sipping claret in the dull gaslight of his spacious and elegant drawing room, read Lady Byron's threatening letter with deep sorrow. It not only confirmed that Ada's original letter did not give him executor authority as he had feared from the outset, but he was ignominiously barred by court order on the grounds of being an undesirable moral influence, from visiting the house at Cumberland Place. He breathed in deeply and heavily. The consequences of all this stupid vituperation and misplaced hatred by Lady Byron were too much to bear. He knew instantly that he would never see Ada again and wept inconsolably, an act he had only once succumbed to previously, when his beloved wife, Georgiana, died suddenly in 1827 along with his newly born son, Alexander Forbes.

Ada, however, remained stoic, continuing her mathematical researches, but by the end of August, her condition had begun to worsen. Apart from Ada's children, Lady Byron would, by then, neither permit any other visitors nor allow Ada to leave the house. And to make matters even more difficult, Ada's quiet confession of indiscretions to William resulted in his final departure in a wild rage, and she knew she would never see him again either. She sought solace in her work, resting often during the day, with the ever present Lucy remaining her sole and valued companion and carer. Her doctor had readjusted the proportions of opium and laudanum and the effect dramatically improved the pain relief and unpleasant bleeding.

Day after day, Lady Byron would visit Ada's room extolling her daughter to repent her moral decline and sinful activity by accepting a complete religious conversion and embrace the will of the Lord in all His Glory. Ada fought, every minute, every hour, every day, with as much will as she could muster but it was hard and unfair, ultimately she would have to succumb to her mother's relentless will ... when, in the middle of yet another pounding sermon, the front doorbell could be heard to ring.

Lucy had discretely appeared at the open bedroom door. "Please excuse me Lady Byron but there is a visitor for the Countess and he insists he has your blessing and an invitation."

"Nobody, not anybody, is to pass over this door, and I would never give such an undertaking." Lady Byron screamed, indignant and angry that she had been so rudely interrupted just when she was at last beginning to break the will of her recalcitrant offspring. "The man is a rogue and a charlatan; dismiss him at once, that vile Mr Babbage."

Ada quietly rose from her chair. She had an idea who it might be and had quietly plotted with Lucy to get a written message sent out, difficult though it was with her mother and the personal servants constantly watching her for the mildest of transgression. "Lucy, please explain, who is this visitor?"

"It is Mr Dickens, ma'am, Mr Charles Dickens the famous writer and he has come specially to read to you."

Ada looked at her mother who was for a moment uncharacteristically dumbstruck. Was her mind also in decline?

Lady Byron could not recall permitting his visitation but perhaps it may not be such a bad idea, a respectable and highly sought after person in the best of upper-class society, and certainly, Charles Dickens and Ada had indeed been friends for many years. She could not bring herself to make any further objection, but this would be the last outsider.

"Mama, it would make me feel so much better to see Mr Dickens—he has a unique ability to raise my spirits with his gentle voice and far-reaching words of prose on the desperate plight of the poor and destitute, a cause equally close to your heart too. Please pass me my favourite of his novels."

Lady Byron decided to relent and walked over to the large bookshelf near Ada's bed. "Of course, my dearest, but not too long if you please. You must not over-task yourself today." She handed Ada a copy of 'The Old Curiosity Shop'. "Lucy, please cover the bed with the yellow and green throw and bring Mr Dickens upstairs with some tea and cakes. I shall retire to my quarters but I wish him to be gone in one hour." She marched out promptly as Ada winked at Lucy behind her back with one of her mischievous grins.

Accompanied by a trolley of freshly baked apple doughnuts and a large pot of tea, Charles Dickens was soon sat alongside Ada on her comfortable giant sofa, quietly reading with his deep sonorous voice, excerpts of Ada's favourite chapters from his chosen novel. Before pouring the tea, Ada surreptitiously unlocked a small cabinet door and brought out a hidden bottle of her best red Merlot which Lucy ensured was replenished regularly and two large glasses. Tipping in a dose of laudanum for her, they clinked glasses and laughed as they always did. She was immediately feeling her old self again, an island of uplifting relief from the deathly sermons of her mother. Charles Dickens was one of her oldest friends and he had done so well, as she predicted when he first published Oliver Twist all those years ago. She had not seen him for a long time and was fascinated to hear about his recent American tour and his experiences on the lecture circuit, replete with tales of amazing adulation and crowds nobody had ever seen for a writer and journalist. How she would love to visit America too, with Charles Babbage and to lecture on the Engine. She simply had to fight even harder and get well. She asked after Mr Dickens's growing family but, despite his wealth and fame and beautiful house in Kent, detected that his relationship with his wife was not going so well. She changed the subject back to his writings and his deep convictions of the need for fundamental changes in the care of the poor and needy in society.

But she had one task, a vital endeavour which she must not forget, and interrupted him part-way through his reading and handed him a secret letter with instruction to ensure it reaches the intended receiver. She had written the letter in anticipation that he would come, her only guarantee of ensuring its posting because Lucy was watched day and night and accompanied everywhere outdoors by Ferguson, the butler.

After her last meeting with Charles Babbage, she had managed one final secret session with the mesmerist and dosed herself heavily with chloroform, which seemed to provide the necessary gateway into her deepest inner subconscious. This session enabled the potential completion of her plan. She had remembered everything in vivid colour and sound. Not only did her hypnotised mind confirm that Alice Langton had been described as Victoria's sister but she could even recall one chance meeting with Alice, the day the boy James McKenzie had made his miraculous recovery from typhoid, all due solely to Victoria's diligent scientific intervention. She had witnessed all this with Victoria in James's bedroom, having first called into Orsbrick Hall with presents for everyone after a successful betting session at the Aintree races with that damned rogue Julian Fazackerley. She and Alice had passed and smiled at each other in the hallway, just as Alice was departing back to the vicarage, oddly with some flasks of a bright orange chemical in her hand. It was then that Victoria had explained. Alice also had a science background in chemistry and had been crucial to assist with their medicine making. It wasn't Victoria's attempts at rather over-doing the explanation then which had set off questions in her mind, but being naturally inquisitive, she looked hard into Alice's face that was not only extremely like Victoria's but even more markedly almost a double of Morag's former mother-in-law, a formidable and clever McKenzie matriarch. All that had elicited a sharp tingle of even more curiosity up her spine.

Sitting quietly that same evening in Orsbrick Hall, having enjoyed the intriguing company of Victoria's adolescent daughters, Madeleine and Annabelle, and sipping through a bottle of Morag's best burgundy wine, she had reflected long and hard, creating scenarios in her mind to fit the facts. She was by then convinced as there could be no other rational explanation for that cumulative set of actions and behaviour over the last few weeks. Victoria and her daughters were somehow not of that time but bizarrely of some distant future, wild though that concept was. In which case Alice was also not of that time nor was Thomas Langton, her vicar husband. But Alice's day to day living as Victoria had described, her clear dress sense and ease of fitting in with the local community indicated a time for her much nearer to 1841 than Victoria … And why the obsessive, almost fanatical interest in ensuring James's survival? The death of children was a sad but regular occurrence in this age of poor medicine and even more hideous doctors. Perhaps that was the answer all along. Why Victoria and Alice had, by whatever miraculous means, crossed time barriers from the future back to the past ... to ensure James's survival and hence their own future. If he died they would not exist.

Now, nine years later, Ada was convinced as she intensely mulled over those past thoughts once more, alongside the information which Lucy had quietly brought in with her favourite evening meal of freshly made shepherd's pie and a half-carafe of red wine. Ada still had important contacts at the new government registry office; the present Director's wife was an old childhood friend, Lady Estelle Castlewood. After her meal, she rummaged through the swathe of papers she had received from Estelle whilst Lucy prepared a warm bath, following line after line of every McKenzie in England, registered in the births, marriages and deaths every year since 1841, being so fortuitous that all such recording had to be done by law since the act of 1837 introducing the system. She knew this was a long shot, and tedious. There was a fair number with that name, and the task was far less exacting than calculating and analysing the iteration results of Charles Babbage's formulae for the Engine. And the present year was still only 1852, but amazingly, standing out clearly, she spotted one strange item which caught her eye instantly, registered in the first quarter of 1849, Burscough, Lancashire. A summary of information had been specially attached for each entry to cross reference against the existing certificate in the file, in this case, a birth certificate ... Undoubtedly, they were efficient in the national registry office. She owed a large debt to Estelle having persuaded her curmudgeonly husband to provide all this. She read it all again carefully:

Recorded by the formal notification of James McKenzie of Orsbrick Hall in the second quarter of 1849, a Mauveine McKenzie in the district of Burscough and Lathom, Lancashire. Born on the seventh of January, 1849, on a packet barge of the Leeds and Liverpool Canal. Mother recorded as Henrietta Gibbons. Father recorded as James McKenzie.

Ada drew breath and scrambled on her reference bookshelf for a French dictionary for that word, clearly Gallic in origin. What a strange name but the translation as she speculated indicated a vivid colour of purple? What were the meaning and relevance?

She swigged another glass of wine plus a thimbleful of her opium concoction and lay back on the bed, letting her mind swirl into the usual dreamy hallucinations which always meant bridging her imagination with the sequencing of logical, timed events. And the deductive solution came analytically quick, effortlessly and clear.

'*Morag …Victoria … dyes … Alice … flask of bright chemicals … purple … mauveine … James, his bedroom recovery conversion to study the chemistry which saved his life …*'

Of course. Alice Langton had indeed returned and she was Mauveine McKenzie an illegitimate daughter of James McKenzie, by her appearance and age from the future 1860s. Probably she had followed her father into science and dyes. Mauveine was itself a future dye which James must have been associated with. Hence it was not at all surprising that Alice had accommodated into an 1841 life far easier than Victoria could.

Ada recalled again the moment Victoria vanished and how she awoke in a dream-like state with Medora nearby. That cataclysm happened when she had pressed Victoria about the date of her own death. Victoria became instantly alarmed and unduly reticent then bang ... whatever mechanism had enabled transport across time there were obviously laws and rules. The process had fragilities and disclosing future events was clearly one of them and forbidden. But Alice Langton was still there. She was not present at Orsbrick Hall, but not yet born ... a bizarre confluence of situations that in itself should have been a displacing point back to her own time. But Alice may likely know her own date of birth and the date seems to have passed without change ... because nobody had told her, and because nobody knew, as the facts didn't historically exist.

Except Ada had indeed now told Alice or would very shortly ... She had written all she knew down in clearest exposition inside the envelope Lucy handed to Charles Dickens, with a simple request. To return a letter back with her, Ada's, death written inside, which with luck and fortitude Alice may already know. Then a joint trigger could be released, like igniting two metal psychic cylinders of gunpowder with a voltaic battery, the very act enough, maybe, to rupture that time barrier again and release the trap for Alice ... And what did she, Ada, have to lose? She knew in her heart of hearts that she didn't have long to live.

She smiled and lay back in a haze on her bed, her brain shutting down in vivid dreamy colours. Little did she know until they woke her the following morning surrounded by an army of doctors and nurses that Lucy had returned, and finding her comatose, thought her mistress was dead and departed. The wine and medicine had been overdone, but Ada awoke smiling. Her mental constitution remained strong and it had to be ... because Alice, she hoped, would receive her letter in the following few days.

Saturday, early October 1848 at the Burscough rectory:

It took a little time, but the Reverend Thomas and Alice Langton did establish a disciplined and regular routine for work and reflection which suppressed further thoughts of depression and a hankering after their former existence. One characteristic that stayed with them throughout their marriage was a strong, unbending work ethic and a firm belief in their value to science and the community. Their predicament had been opportune to draw on such source of comfort and stability once more. Isi made Mauveine laugh one day in early 1842 when she was flagging with effort and harbouring severe doubts they could do this for much longer. "We survived being ghosts for one hundred and sixty years," he remarked jauntily, "so this episode will be a breeze, a strange phrasing as evinced by one regular church goer, a Richard Patterson, head of the largest boat family in the parish, with, would you believe, twenty-two living children and three barges to house them all!"

And whilst not always a breeze, the Reverend Thomas Langton, assisted by his industrious wife Alice, had decidedly gained a strong following over the previous seven years, of genuine devotion and admiration from their flock of regular worshippers at the church. Baptisms, especially amongst the boat families, were markedly up as were marriages. Burials had encouragingly declined, particularly after Alice had instituted Sunday classes for boatmen's wives, to improve hygiene and cleanliness in their cramped and overcrowded canal living quarters. She even had them using carbolic soap, by-products in plentiful supply from the thriving Burscough town gas works, a godsend for those unfortunate to be carrying regular loads of human excrement from Liverpool to farmer's fields in the parish. The other activity Alice was especially proud of had been the establishment of twice-weekly mixed education classes for the young children of boat families and farm workers, the vast majority of whom were illiterate. She made use of the large, unused barn at the back of the rectory. Both she and Thomas had always valued education, given the progress in life that such learning and knowledge had provided them. They were totally committed to the embrace of reading and writing as the best means available to pull their parishioners out of systemic poverty and make the most use of their capabilities. She also taught them art and science and was amazed at the latent abilities of some of the boat children, who clearly had the academic potential to rise to university. Reverend Langton began persistent discussions with the Bishop of Liverpool and agreed in principle to the setting up of a special annual church scholarship fund for the three best pupils of Alice, to support their continued education and upkeep at the Bluecoat School in Liverpool. Albert Claiborne, an unlikely scholar of outstanding mathematical ability from one of the most destitute of canal boat backgrounds, would be the first nominee. His family were proud of his achievements and eternally grateful to Alice Langton for enabling Albert to step onto a ladder of potential opportunity and prosperity, something they could only have dreamed about. Every evening, once alone after dinner, they reverted to their true identities of Mauveine McKenzie and Isi Fazackerley and reminisced about their former past lives, speculating and debating how Victoria and her family were progressing.

Regular as clockwork, they awoke at six am on the crowing of the cockerel to their usual Saturday routines. Feed the chickens, prepare the sermon for Sunday, organise the agenda for the afternoon women's fellowship group and do some dye work in her cellar laboratory. But unease had recently occupied their recent evenings relaxing by the fire after a long day's work. And the ticking time bomb was now approaching, visible on the horizon … the looming date of Mauveine's birth on January the 7th 1849. Of course, Isi's birth date in 1840 had already passed before they found themselves back in 1841. Somehow that hadn't mattered because he was in theory already born and the psychic time travel frame had accommodated around an accepted contortion of space-time warps and bends. However, her birth date was in the future and they both had concerns how that could be reconciled. Would it be cataclysmic and hurl them back to where they had come? Or perhaps the event would leverage even more dire consequences and annul her existence totally, leaving Isi on his own … The thought of forced separation, forever, was hard to bear for both of them.

A knock on the door took Alice away from trying her new dye concoction for blacking the grate, which could potentially be sold commercially to raise parish funds. The post boy had arrived early, handing her numerous church related letters for Isi and a large brown envelope for her. She didn't recognise the handwriting. But it was time for breakfast and a delicious smell of bacon and eggs prepared by Martha was wafting down the corridor as she turned and followed behind her husband, who had been chopping logs in the yard for the fire. It was becoming a decidedly chilly autumn already. The brief summer seemed to have hardly impacted on them, having endured a long and wet spring.

Isi, wolfing down his substantial breakfast, was busy reading his letters whilst pouring out a large mug of black coffee each, definitely an acquired exotic taste following the appearance by the gardener of a number of large containers, found in the graveyard under the elderly yew tree. No doubt they were part of a 'lost load' from the canal which had been hidden by a boatman for a more opportune time to retrieve. They took one jar and Alice donated the rest to the women's fellowship, a gift from God. Every little helped in times of hardship.

"My goodness, dearest," Isi exclaimed. "The Bishop has not only authorised the three fellowships to Bluecoat but has sent the agreed funds already for the first year by cheque. It appears a generous donor associated with the new Albert Dock in Liverpool heard about the scheme last weekend in the Cathedral and has contributed immediately. A certain Philip Hardwick, one of the architects. I must write to …"

"Never mind that for the moment Isi. Please listen, very, very carefully."

He looked up sharply. It was unlike Mauveine to speak so. She was concentrating and re-reading the long letter again and finally put it down carefully on the table in front of her. "Have you any idea who this is from?" she cried, distressed. "More importantly the contents are so incredible as to defy the most complex of the Lord's deepest puzzles and mysteries."

"God in heaven above, Mauveine. Pray, please explain clearly in the manner you are so wanton to provide better than anyone I have known."

Mauveine began, her hand trembling holding the letter. "It is from the Countess of Lovelace, you will remember her, a good friend of Morag? Also, in that short time in 1841, she became close to Victoria. I met her once in Orsbrick Hall and her eyes flashed instantly with a depth of acumen and mental power, unlike anyone I had ever encountered. I understood immediately why she and Victoria found so much in common. Cultured, fabulously rich and a natural revolutionary against the stifling patriarchal society of the present, she was fighting hard to uphold the rights of women to pursue science and mathematics and to be permitted to have a university education. Ada Lovelace is a well-connected aristocrat and mathematics savant who was intent at the time on opening doors for Victoria and the girls, having been enchanted with their company down in London."

Isi pondered and stroked his heavy beard he had grown quickly to ensure fitting in with the fashions of the time and his status. "Yes, I recall Ada now, although I never actually met her … Oh, of course, no, I did meet her. She was introduced by Lord Ottersburn after the service I gave at Morag's funeral. You were very busy with Martha, tending to the guests and ensuring everyone had sandwiches and a glass of wine but I did point you out down the end of the church hall. Yes, you're right, a look of intensity crossed her face and she smiled like she was making connections to something, but never said."

"She did the same when I met her. I suspect her sharp mind had figured out I had more than a passing resemblance to the immediate McKenzie family and she was characteristically putting two and two together. Victoria said one afternoon, whilst we were waiting for James to recover, that she was embarking on some kind of an affair with Julian, Morag's blacksmith. Victoria hid her upset very well, with a high degree of nonchalance, and looked relieved when I said that the 1841 versions of Julian and Lynton which your unfortunate actions had brought into the mixture, really had to be discounted from her mind as they were an irrelevancy to the bigger picture of ensuring James became well, which of course he did. Thank the Lord for His merciful action."

"So what does Ada say?"

"A lot but let me summarise in a nutshell. Ada was present when the psychic rupture occurred and Victoria, Abigail and daughters vanished and unbelievably she has recounted the scene in great detail. For everyone else, including Morag and all associated with Victoria's presence in 1841, the giant wave of warping space and time which we are now very familiar with, wrapped itself over their worlds to rewrite history so that Victoria, Abigail and family never existed."

Isi sat up straight, his face darkened. "Yes, of course, which is why it's been so hard to try and piece together any logic or conclusions for us and to plan where we go, except to live day-by-day in the service of God. No doubt, as always happens, Victoria, her daughters and Abigail will remember their experience, wherever they are, but Ada is not immediate McKenzie family. How does she remember such an event and more importantly what has she concluded?"

"It appears she is seriously unwell with a stomach malady, although from her description I would concur it is likely a bad and terminal cancer, similar to Lady Beveridge in Newburgh, God save both their souls. She has, for some time, been taking large doses of laudanum, chloroform and opium for the pain giving her hallucinatory experiences. With the help of a mesmerist, memories of Victoria from her deep subconscious have somehow been drawn out over a period of the last few weeks," Mauveine replied, picking up the final page with the word 'proposal' written in large letters.

"This is quite unbelievable," Isi exclaimed. "It means that she must have some kind of deep, perhaps hidden psychic abilities too, with a frequency and wavelength in harmony with Victoria and Abigail … That will also explain why they all got on so well."

"Yes, dearest, I agree, but here is the bombshell. Ada has also been reminded by her collaborator, the scientist Charles Babbage, that I was Victoria's sister. Ada Lovelace has a powerful mathematical brain and she has cleverly, as I had once suspected, not only researched but put together all the logical pieces including who I might be and has even found my date of birth in the government registry ... she knows I am Mauveine McKenzie. She had noted my resemblance all those years back to Lord Malcolm McKenzie's mother, my great grandmother."

Isi gasped. "But that's not possible. You haven't even been born yet, how can she do that?"

"Because the stated date on the letter is August 26th, 1852! We have gone into the beginnings of some kind of localised time warping, probably because Ada has formally predicted my birth, ahead in the future, generating a potential trigger to instability, likely heightened by the closeness of the actual date coming. She has worked that out too. Ada and we must be living in parallel universes, both functioning at different times. It appears Victoria triggered the space time-rupture in response to gross insults and raging from Morag that Victoria was Satan in disguise who had come to destroy the family. Ada had already concluded, excitedly the day before, that Victoria was from the future and Victoria then admitted it during the blazing row ... and that her true living time period was the year 2026. Immediately, dark clouds and a great ball of light enveloped them, a rupture took place and the rest followed the expected pattern, except for this turn of events now. Ada insists, I quote, that 'I write back to her with her date of death, as this may have a further beneficial effect. She would be very comfortable with the knowledge.'"

Isi was reflecting deeply. "When did Ada pass away? Can you remember? She was famous of course as the only legitimate child of Lord Byron. Not far into the future by the sound of it. And I have a hunch."

Mauveine shook her head, annoyed with not knowing, then her eyes flashed wildly as something else passed across her fast brain. "Come dearest, down to my laboratory. You recall I managed to charge up Abigail's old iPhone, I purloined during our former ghostly incursions. I have no idea why that came with us but the device has provided me with happy memories. There is some kind of an encyclopaedia on it which I have never used but which may provide us with answers."

Martha began clearing up the breakfast dishes and Mauveine went quickly but patiently through the necessary ongoing routines with her for the rest of the day. There was extensive washing to be done of Isi's service attire after being covered in mud, slipping over at yesterday's funeral, fortunately not into the grave thanks to a helping hand. Once Martha had departed to work they opened the hatch and went down into the deep cellar, igniting a couple of gas lights. Mauveine unlocked a drawer and took out her iPhone, carefully connecting it up to the voltaic cell and pressed the start button. The old and familiar screen lit up as she searched adeptly through the applications until she found the offline application which also contained key facts and biographical information on the arts and the sciences. She scrolled through to find the science section and searched Ada Lovelace. Immediately, a brief biography came onscreen, including stunning pictures of Ada in her prime wearing the most beautiful dresses … and finally her date of death: November 28th, 1852.

Isi drew breath. "I think my hunch is correct. It's normally you, dearest, who is quick off the mark on these things. I would hazard that the period between now and your date of birth is exactly the same as the period between the date of Ada's letter and her actual death. This disjuncture of time and space we now find ourselves in is distorted for a reason, to ensure both dates occur simultaneously and trigger a full response. Ada was buried with her father in Nottingham at Lord Byron's once stately home. You must send that date and that letter to her now Mauveine and light the long fuse as it were. I think the

Countess of Lovelace has correctly concluded the same. This may be our only chance to escape back to our time?"

She looked at him hard. They had adjusted well to their new lives and roles. She followed his logic perfectly but one key question lay in their path. What was their time? "Do you really want to do this Isi? We are now happy with our lot here, I have adjusted to an acceptable compromise and you love your ecclesiastical way of life, you were born to it. We don't know how this may end, it could be eternally catastrophic."

He studied her thoughtfully and then held her tight. She was as ever absolutely right. But they had taken the risk to come back to 1841 and the task, to ensure James McKenzie's future be put back on track, was successful. James had recently worked his way through Cambridge University and was planning an industrial future for Orsbrick Hall including work and shared prosperity for the local community. Already they were within some warped space-time anyway … they had to see this proposal through. Ada's actions were part of the process of potential completion.

"We must complete what we started and leave this time, Mauveine, it is not ours to linger any further. And we must do this together. I have total faith in the Lord above to carry us safely through our next journey."

She looked into his dreamy eyes and smiled warmly. "And so do I. Now when is the next post?"

Isi began walking up the steps; he had a sermon to urgently finish. She watched him go contentedly, visibly relieved for the first time in many months. They had made a decision to take back control of their destiny, what could be better. Picking up her iPhone to disconnect it carefully from the battery, an irrational, silly thought passed through her head as she glanced again at the apps on the screen. It was never going anywhere but it made her feel good as she sent a tweet to Abigail and Annabelle, the only addresses in her list.

Chapter Five

Glancing through her iPhone emails, Maddie screwed up her face with annoyance. There was nothing from Janine despite the peculiar message sent earlier in the afternoon whilst at the George. And Janine wasn't answering her phone either; she should surely be awake by now. Maddie decided to keep her thoughts to herself for the time being. But at least she had some good news arrive in the post.

Abby was out in the garden, plucking off spring-flowered dead heads from a giant camellia bush near the window which had blossomed into its annual gorgeous red. She peeped through, immediately sensed that Maddie had something on her mind and opened the patio doors.

"Your mother and I are walking over to the rectory shortly. Neither of us can bear the suspense any longer … we need to find out what's going on and if our fears are justified. Ever since Fenella knocked on that front door, something just doesn't feel right to me and I wish I knew what it was. I don't have any psychic imbalances but … well … it's sort of instinctive, I suppose. How about you?"

"Yes, I'm uneasy too but I really want to help Fenella to adjust and I'm determined to try. Where's Mum?"

"She went out to get some ingredients from Waitrose. We decided to make an apple charlotte, something Fenella said she really missed on the way back. Actually, I can hear Vikki's car, she's back already. Is it only Fenella worrying you?"

"No, I'm fine," Maddie said, cheerfully, but Abby remained unconvinced. However, whatever it was could wait.

"But you won't have very long to spend with Fenella. Your course at Harvard starts in six weeks. Where is she?"

"Up in her bedroom, settling in with some thick science and art encyclopaedias from Belle's bookshelf. She wants to do some intensive reading for a few hours on her own. I'm sure she'll have a snooze, she looked worn out."

"That's understandable. I believe your father has already found a temporary furnished flat through one of his publisher contacts in New York to see you through for the time being until Belle finishes her final exams and school in the summer, then you can both look seriously for something permanent."

Maddie brightened up. "Really? Gosh, so typical of Dad, he never said, but I suppose this entire Fenella thing in the last day has dominated everyone. I know Belle will get top grades. She's waiting for the results of her application for medical school. And I've got some news that will please Mum too."

A loud voice resounded out from the patio. "Good, I need something cheery and normal please, Maddie. So what news have you got?"

They turned to see Victoria breezing through the door followed by Sabrina, carrying two large shopping bags full of groceries.

"I have scanned through the appropriate cookery books and I believe my memory circuits will allow me to extend my cooking skill from reactionary running dog bacon and egg for Julian and Lynton towards sophisticated preparation, which of course I understand is expected behaviour after the latest television bake-off show," Sabrina announced before heading off into the kitchen, singing some variant of a North Korean folk song.

Victoria shook her head as Abby and Maddie giggled. "Whoever programmed her still has a lot to answer for. So?"

Maddie handed her mother the brown envelope. A giant smile drew across Victoria's face once she read the contents, and beaming proudly she gave her daughter a giant hug. Abby looked on, intrigued.

"Not only have you passed your Cambridge examinations with top grades," Victoria cried excitedly, "You also came top in the mathematics scholarship paper and Trinity College have offered you an unconditional place to study natural sciences with a mathematical physics speciality. Ada would have been proud of you. I'm so pleased that your backup is in place. What is Harvard saying now? Shouldn't you have the admission details?"

"I'm really pleased too, Mum, all that hard work finally paid off. I'm still waiting on Harvard but there's time yet and I have had the place offer," she said whilst Abby followed on with another giant hug.

"Not long, anyway," Victoria replied, changing the subject. "Abby and I are going to the rectory shortly. Want to come with us?"

"No, I'll catch up later, if that's okay. I want to keep an eye on Fenella for the rest of the day; everything has been sort of intense."

"I'll come with you though," a voice cried out, as Belle suddenly breezed in with giant wolfhounds Jeb and Kai in tow, their coats gleaming having had a good brush down. "Ned and Zac have gone out on their bikes to see Ade; they won't be back until dinner."

"Mmm … fine," Victoria said, quite surprised that Maddie had chosen to opt out, but decided from her demeanour not to ask any questions … It had been a tough day for all of them.

Walking briskly along the canal bank towards the rectory, Abby wasn't convinced that knocking on the door was such a good idea after all, especially because they had no idea what to expect and even less what they were going to say. Victoria, however, briskly dismissed any foreboding.

"Given what we've just been through and come out of and the fact that Mauveine and Isi were an integral part of our successful return, then, quite frankly, there is no other logical and sensible action. And if they've returned to our time, albeit as vicar and wife, well, they had a good ecclesiastical apprenticeship in 1841, didn't they? Being with us again has got to be better than floating about Orsbrick Hall aimlessly as disembodied spirits, although they did possess interesting attributes, like peering into the future and the past. That skill didn't seem to be in evidence when they were in the flesh, so to speak. This space-time distortion is a peculiar phenomenon and I'm convinced it's all linked with dark energy at the heart of the connecting wormholes. I'll get to the bottom of it one day."

Abby scowled. "Put like that and obliterating all my arguments in two sentences then we don't have any option do we, especially, Vikki, as you have your serious face on."

Belle intervened, taking a selfie photo of them on her phone in front of a gaily coloured traditional barge moored near their exit path. "I agree, Mum, but I'm really surprised that Maddie didn't want to come. I would have thought she would have been first here, given how close to Mauveine she became."

"What's the matter with Maddie, Belle? Something seems to be bothering her?" Victoria replied, opening the rectory gate carefully. "Now, remember, whatever the reception, not a word about Fenella. We need to engineer that bombshell when we ascertain any more information, with of course some judicious questions."

"Mmm … sort of like, did you find Fenella after all, Mauveine?" Belle responded. "Yes, something is bothering Maddie, but despite her being my slightly older by five minutes twin sister, I haven't got a clue."

"I'm sure whatever it is, Maddie will work it through," Abby said, reassuringly. "Both of you have so much more sense and maturity than I had at your age. I was an emotional mess at Art College, wild and crazy."

"Hey, what's changed?" Victoria cried with a grin, as they walked slowly up the path.

Everywhere around was deathly quiet; not a sound from inside the building and even the popular church, stood stark against the sky through the extensive graveyard, was oddly devoid of outside visitors and walkers. Victoria walked up to the door and rapped hard on the unusual decorative brass knocker, exactly the same one as in 1841 although much more worn. Silence continued. Victoria knocked again and finally the familiar sound of the stiff inside door bolts unlocking could be heard and the large, heavy oak door creaked open slowly. They peered into the gloom … but couldn't believe what they saw. It was decidedly becoming an occupational hazard arriving at this particular door.

Uncharacteristically, Victoria stood silently, her mouth gaping open, alongside Abby and Belle equally dumbstruck.

"Don't look so surprised, Victoria," the person behind the door cried, wearing a pair of smart, skinny black jeans, ankle boots and a woolly yellow jumper. A large smile emanated from her radiant face. "I'm your new curate, Elizabeth Milbanke at your service," she continued, opening the door fully so they could see properly.

"Ada? I don't believe what I'm seeing. Is it really you? But how?" Victoria blurted, still overawed by such an unexpected encounter. "You have a famous history, a lifetime sadly shortened from what it should have been, but mapped out extensively until your death in 1852. You're buried deep in a vault with Lord Byron near Newstead Abbey in Nottinghamshire, I can't recall the village."

"Hucknall is the place, quite near the Abbey, actually. I did so adore that beautiful, ornate period property of my father's and those wonderful gardens. Sadly, I only visited once because of my awful, obsessive mother. But that is in the past, to be forgotten, as of now." She looked furtively back inside. "Now listen carefully, all of you. Where's Madeleine? From now on, there is no Ada, never was and never will be. I'm Elizabeth and I like it long, not foreshortened."

"You mean the name, Elizabeth?" Abby replied with a knowing smile. "The humour hasn't changed. Yes, we've got the message, all understood."

Victoria, a few deep breaths on, had raced through a myriad of psychic scenarios in a few micro-seconds but couldn't make any rational connection. "I do like your name. The occupation amazes me, but these days we should cease being amazed. Milbanke, I seem to recall, was your mother's name before she married Lord Byron, wasn't it?"

"Yes, such a beautiful irony. Now, whatever you do act normally." Elizabeth turned and footsteps could be heard walking slowly from the kitchen down the inside corridor and two shadowy figures, both dressed in black, suddenly appeared into the light. "May I introduce the newly appointed Reverend Thomas Langton and his wife Alice. This is Lady Victoria McKenzie of Orsbrick Hall, her daughter Annabelle and her … err … cousin, Miss Abigail Warren."

The second opportunity for incredulous expressions and open mouths arrived quickly, but hiding the disappointment was extremely hard. They were not looking at Mauveine and Isi but two completely different people, both of them elderly, short and stout. Something very peculiar and unforeseen had happened.

Reverend Langton held out his hand. "I'm so pleased to meet you, Lady McKenzie. Your name has been mentioned enthusiastically a number of times over the last week at parish meetings. Like our new curate, Elizabeth here, who we've just appointed, I'm afraid that Alice and I have to get up to speed quickly, there is so much to take in." He laughed loudly but then coughed raucously with what sounded like an ominous chest infection.

Victoria, towering over both of them, shook hands warmly. "How nice to meet you both, I hope you're gradually settling in. Sorry, but I must make a few corrections … err … I'm not actually Lady McKenzie. Just plain Victoria will be fine. Titles in my family died out in the mid-1800s, I'm afraid," she said awkwardly.

"And I'm Mrs Grey, but everyone calls me Abby. Warren was my family name although Victoria and I have a very distant cousin relationship."

Elizabeth, holding a few sheets of paper, grimaced. "I do apologise, I was reading some notes left by the previous curate, which appear somewhat dated. But Mrs Grey, you are a local artist though?"

Abby laughed. "Yes, that aspect is correct, although I must confess; I haven't been near a paint brush for years. I own and manage a gallery these days, buying and selling artworks from around the world."

Belle came forward. "I'm pleased to meet you both too. Please call me Belle. My twin sister Maddie should have been here today, but something urgent came up."

Reverend Langton smiled. "I understand, not a problem. Now, how can Alice and I help you all? Unfortunately, I'm afraid Alice and I have to fly … we must get to a meeting with the Bishop of Liverpool, but please do come inside. It will be a good opportunity for Elizabeth to hear more about the parish and she and I can converse later. I do apologise for having to leave you so abruptly."

"Don't worry at all, Reverend Langton. We only popped over to introduce ourselves," Victoria replied. "I'm sure we will have an opportunity to catch up soon … by all means feel free to knock on our door at Orsbrick Hall any time." She was making every effort not to sound stiff and formal. This was a major shock.

"Excellent. Ahh … there's our taxi coming. Aggie, our housekeeper, will make you all some tea. Come, Alice dear, we must make a move. Goodbye then, see you all soon," Thomas replied. Both of them walked stiffly to the taxi parked on the road.

The three turned to see another short and plump, smiling woman appear at the door, with a large apron wrapped around her. But the face of Agnes Speed looked all too familiar, clearly a distant relative of the very same Agnes who had been Morag's excellent head maid. What was going on?

"Good, now we have an opportunity to talk properly. In you go," Elizabeth murmured, chivvying them through the door. They headed for the familiar sitting room, replete with modern decoration and lighting but still possessing the welcoming ambience and even much of the same old furniture which Mauveine had once chosen. "Tea and your lemon drizzle special please, Aggie," Elizabeth shouted into the kitchen. "Have to save the hard stuff for another occasion," she added softly, grinning mischievously as Victoria, Abby and Belle sat down in the comfortable chairs.

Aggie immediately reappeared with a large pot of Earl Grey tea and huge slabs of welcome lemon drizzle cake on a tray. She left and discretely closed the door.

"So, where do I start?" Elizabeth mused whilst Abby passed around the cups and plates. "With myself I think is probably best and how I ended up here. Something has unfortunately not gone right. I can see that neither you, nor indeed I, expected this particular Reverend Thomas Langton accompanied by his mouse-like companion Alice, but I am sure Victoria, like you, I will patiently wait, think deeply and put as many associations as possible together once they unfold. How I wish there were some proper mathematics books in here. What I would like next, if you can indulge me for a minute, is for me to do all the talking, I know, nothing new there, and be patient until the end with questions."

Victoria glanced surreptitiously at Abby who stifled a mild giggle with a cough but not quick enough for Elizabeth to shoot across a mild glare.

"Abigail, no sniggering please or I may ask for my winnings back ... at present day value!" Elizabeth said, pointedly. "At the end, I propose we try and draw some logical conclusions as to what may have happened to the former Thomas and Alice Langton who we all admired, especially you, Victoria, being, of course, Alice's sister."

Victoria gulped. The Ada Lovelace of old, teasing and stirring controversy, had definitely resurfaced in the resurgent Elizabeth Milbanke of 2026 ... and her memories of their 1841 experience seemed as powerful as ever. But why? Elizabeth wasn't a McKenzie. Why had that sudden rupture in the space-time not erased Ada's history too and how had she got here? From her comment on the Langton's and her expectation there must have been a more direct relationship between Ada and Mauveine, but when and what? … Too many questions and no clear answers as yet. They all had to listen.

Belle had run through a similar mental argument but was never one for constant questioning. She always preferred to draw the strands of the problem together into practical tasks and remove emotional clutter that stood in the way. Belle knew her strengths, unlike her sister. In this, they were quite different, but she desperately wished Maddie was there.

Abby took a different line and had immediately come to a simple conclusion … Ada must have not only been psychic but on a similar wavelength to them, although not a McKenzie and certainly not a Warren. Probably, more like Judy, tuned into their space-time history by chance. But Ada had been manipulative, extraordinarily clever and ultra-determined. Abby realised that something significant had happened later, following the time rupture cataclysm, which had enabled Ada to psychically connect up, probably to Victoria, and perhaps then remember what had happened that fateful afternoon in Morag's drawing room, with her, Victoria, Maddie, Belle and of course Ada's half-sister, the lovely Medora. Pity Medora hadn't come over the time divide too. But if this was the case, were Mauveine and Isi left behind? Locked into the 1840s period forever until they died? But Victoria was here; she had been born and had lived … none of this conundrum was making any sense. Then Abby felt a sharp palpitation. Victoria probably hadn't yet realised. If Ada … no, she must get it right, Elizabeth, remembered all of them, did she also remember

Julian? Hellfire and damnation … a massive big shit-storm to come … fuck.

For once, everyone remained uncharacteristically silent as they tucked into tea and cake and waited patiently. Elizabeth stared silently through the window, gathering her thoughts in succinct order when a loud banging on the outside door made them all jump.

Elizabeth smiled her mischievous grin once more. "A revealing knock, I do declare. I think I know who that is likely to be, the prodigal daughter returned?" She sprang forward and promptly opened the drawing-room door, shouting down the corridor. "I'll answer the front door Aggie, I'm expecting a visitor."

The rapping continued and Belle turned to Victoria and Abby. Do you think it's Maddie? How does Ada, sorry Elizabeth know? I must remember to use the right name."

"Yes, we all do," Victoria replied quietly. "This situation is as overly peculiar as it comes. What with Fenella and now our so called Elizabeth, I'm really worried about Mauveine and Isi. Are they still trapped in 1841 time or in some disconnected nether world? I know Ada died in 1852 so what date is it now for Mauveine and why is Ada here in our time?"

"November 28th, 1852, to be precise," Belle added, peering at her smartphone.

Abby interjected with a loud whisper. "Look on the positive side. We're all born and alive in our own time and with memorable histories. So what we set out to do by going back to 1841 was achieved. Listen, there's a lot of talking and laughing going on out there so it can't be Maddie, and hopefully not …" Abby immediately bit her lip and would have liked to slice her tongue off too. Why didn't she think before she talked?

"You mean Julian don't you, Abby," Victoria cried, her eyes flashing wild. "You don't think I didn't think of that immediately we set eyes on her? I'm going to have to be pretty forthright on that issue immediately. Hands off or face the consequences …"

"Come on Mum, Dad?" Belle intervened. "You must be joking. Not because he's past it but you know what he's like. Loyalty to you and our family is always the most important thing to him. Those gross manifestations in 1841 were not the same people and we agreed all that. Remember Lynton, Abby?"

"Don't I just!" Abby replied with a laugh. "A more disagreeable human being would have been hard to find. So keep the shotgun bolted to the wall, Vikki, at least for the time being and smile, please. We need your logical wits right now more than ever."

Victoria visibly relaxed. "Okay … yes, you're right Abby, and at the end of the day, we did all like Ada, I mean Elizabeth, me included, so one step at a time. Hey, the visitor is coming. Sit up and look normal."

The door opened and they gazed, mouths open, as Maddie breezed in with Elizabeth alongside, like bosom pals from yesteryear.

"Gosh, why are you all looking so … glum and tense?" Maddie muttered. "I had to come because I just knew Ada was here. I'd been feeling odd all day. When I opened my tablet her picture was on the screen and then her biography fell off the shelf. Elizabeth has filled me in quickly about how she thinks she crossed space-time. I feel so much better now, and it's wonderful to be reunited. We've been discussing calculus and computer programming already. But Mauveine and Isi are missing?"

Elizabeth smiled. "Ahh ... well, that bit of the mystery is solved. I wondered what Mauveine's husband's real name was. Isaac, I assume. Victoria, don't look so perplexed. A long time further on from 1841, when I suddenly recalled our final Morag departure calamity, I also remembered your sister, Alice, and the Reverend Thomas Langton. They performed a wonderful service at Morag's funeral. With the help of some opium and laudanum to quell my awful stomach pains and my personal mesmerist, I gradually put the logical sequences together, including why you were present in 1841. The almost maniacal focus on James McKenzie's wellbeing triggered my conclusions. I saw him recover too, remember, and both I and my husband directly received the backlash from my Harley Street physician of the time who thought you were a maniac needing immediate incarceration. The coup de grace came when, using my London network of friends, I researched the new government birth registry and found a Mauveine McKenzie registered by father James McKenzie, born January 1849 and then, as they say, the guinea dropped. I had long realised the subtle differences between you and Alice, who was plainly much more comfortable with our period of time encompassing the ghastly early Queen Victoria, and both of you were a dead ringer for Malcolm's mother, a dear friend of mine when she was alive ... Sorry, I've been watching this fabulous television technology. I'm already picking up the crassest Americanisms, such fun. So, back to the logic, Alice had to be Mauveine, a French dye name, who also had returned to 1841 and you are a descendent of her. You both returned for a defined purpose, Victoria, to ensure the legitimacy of your futures. James could not be allowed to die. So, are you all impressed with my logical detective work?"

Stunned silence could not do justice to the atmosphere in the room. All that could be heard was a song thrush, singing his heart out on a tree branch outside. Maddie was the first to speak. "Ad ... Elizabeth. You have the most brilliant mind I have ever known, except Mum of course. Gosh, I am incredibly impressed and so pleased you're here."

Everyone laughed, even Victoria. Elizabeth beamed. She always liked, no she needed compliments. It felt good to be back to near normal already.

"I have to say, I agree with Maddie on every point," Victoria jested, now smiling rediscovering her 1841 admiration for Ada and her stunning analysis, despite the blacksmith faux Julian episode which wasn't truly Ada's fault. He was consistently, throughout their time, an unscrupulous con-man.

Elizabeth looked around the room and began opening cupboards. "Hell fire and damnation, oops ... better curtail my swearing with this dog collar on ... there must surely be some communion wine in this righteous abode to celebrate with," she murmured, finally finding a bottle of unopened best port and clean glasses. She pulled off the cork hastily. "This will have to do, nobody has gout do they?"

Abby, however, remained ruminating over Elizabeth's remarkable deductive capability. "You said you researched Mauveine's date of birth, so presumably that day must have happened. When did all this revelation take place? We're so worried about Mauveine and Isi ... Where are they and was Mauveine still trapped when her own birth date arrived? If so that would likely have triggered a violent rupture in the psychic space-time."

Elizabeth poured out a glass each of the deep red port and handed them around. "Would be nice to have some Stilton with this. Well, good health, prosperity and fortune, everyone."

They clinked glasses, such a peculiar situation. "I'm glad you said psychic," Elizabeth replied. "I am a total believer in such a state of being, following unexplainable experiences since my childhood. Now, to try and answer your astute question, Abigail. We are talking about my epiphany arriving in the autumn of 1852. I was feeling increasingly ill and frail again and had become reconciled to an imminent demise, despite a pleasant short revival a few months before when I saw my good friend, Mr Charles Babbage. The more the laudanum increased, the more I remembered about Morag and all of you. Some days were lived in a complete delusional haze and I felt so depressed because my mind was relentlessly churning out idea after idea on the Engine, I had so much still to do. So I wrote everything I knew into a letter, secretly forwarded to Alice Langton by my other good friend, Mr Charles Dickens, and asked her to write me back my date of death, figuring that such a revelation might create the same convulsion that propelled you back to 2026. It was that exact knowledge you refused me Victoria, then the world fell in. I also thought such an act would do the same for Alice and said so. Clearly, she was still at the rectory after her date of birth. Why or how that was possible I can't explain, but a letter did come back. My hypothesis was correct. I lay in bed very weak, the letter arrived in my hand and I began reading the crucial date, the 28th of November, 1852, which was that very same day. Instantaneously, the bright lights began again, the swirling void set in and my mind disappeared. I found myself standing inside a decimated room of my virtually unrecognisable home in number twelve, St James's Square."

Victoria turned to Abby, Maddie and Belle. "The process of Ada becoming Elizabeth has been through the same splitting of time transformation as Mauveine to Alice but in reverse. Whereas Mauveine went backwards, Ada instead came forward, but their past histories remained intact. That, at least, makes some sense."

They all nodded.

"But what we don't know or understand is what happened to Mauveine and Isi between January 1849 and November 1852," Maddie cried. "They may be in limbo or inside another universe."

"Or they may be ghosts again … is that not the same thing?" Belle replied, trying to make sense of the impossible.

"Again?" Elizabeth interjected, quizzically.

"A long story, Elizabeth," Victoria replied softly. "Another time, I suggest, when we can explain more."

Elizabeth sighed and grimaced. She may, in consequence, have been responsible for such a calamity. "Mmm … a complex interaction. One other possibility, however, from what you have said about moving through universes, is a time delay."

"I think we have to hope that may be the case," Abby added, despairing over Mauveine and Isi's fate. "A ghostly existence seems wrong somehow … we had all become so accustomed to being real in each other's company in 1841."

Belle was idly flicking through her phone. "Gosh, would you believe, I did get a @missdyehead tweet earlier, so they must be somewhere whatever form that is, and sent from your old iPhone I reckon, Abby," she suddenly added, cheerfully.

Abby grabbed her own phone from her bag, almost tearing off the cover and peered at the app messages she hadn't looked at for a week. She never normally bothered with Twitter. "Hey, me too … looks like it was sent a few days ago. There may yet be hope. Whatever, they won't be back as Alice and Thomas Langton though. There's not much we can do, is there, except wait, listen and gauge any changes."

Victoria was impatiently feeling a strong urge to move on. She had already come to that obvious conclusion some time back. "Yes, agreed, Abby. Now, for part two of this mystery. Elizabeth, you were starting to recount arriving at number twelve, St James's Square. Can you continue so we understand how on earth you ended up here as a curate? Not by any wildest hypothesis would I have guessed that outcome."

Elizabeth laughed and poured out another port for everyone, finishing the bottle. "Me neither. Better hide this in the outside bin. At least there's another one at the back there … I'm sure the doddery Reverend Langton has no idea. They are both teetotal, heaven save their souls."

The irony made Maddie giggle out loud, but she decided to decline the second glass as did Belle. Elizabeth continued to recount the bizarre moment when she awoke from a deep sleep and found herself in another world, time and place inside her former loved residence at twelve, St James's Square, when she needed all her sharp brain, wits and analytical skills to extricate herself from the odd looking policemen in unfamiliar uniforms and sit outside in the almost unchanged Square Gardens to think hard what to do. They listened intently whilst Elizabeth told her next story …

Back in St James's Square: Elizabeth hurried from the building and stood quietly on the pavement, perusing the peculiar environment she found herself in. She worked her mind furiously to orientate every experience into recallable patterns and lock them rationally inside her head. Her grand plan, hatched desperately in haste, seemed to have miraculously worked. The last thing she remembered was lying in bed feeling tired and ill and Lucy, her face grave, handing her the letter from Alice Langton. Struggling, she had propped herself up on two pillows, gulped down a large dose of opium tincture and read the pages assiduously, noting it had been sent on the 28th August 1852. Alice had highlighted her death, exactly three months from that date, but why had the letter taken those exact three months to suddenly arrive, then? She lay back to contemplate an answer and the whole ceiling began to spin, faster and faster in a complex vortex, huge, transparent worm-like creatures wriggled in front of her eyes and the room became intensely bright as she rose up from her bed into the air … then she opened her eyes and there she was, back in number twelve, staring out of a window but everything around her, even the clothes she wore, were so unfathomably different. And she felt well, very well like she was a young child again. Outside, the horseless carriages, painted metal boxes of some kind on rubber wheels which people drove and steered, fascinated her, although she noticed some which seemed to drive under their own volition. How was that possible? Did they have some kind of brain? She looked down and saw that the road was no longer the familiar slippery old stone cobbles covered in horse dung, just a smooth and black shiny surface. Pillared metal barriers, erected to stop the carriages from going further, rose up from the road and a paved area had been constructed where people walked around, which continued further down towards Pall Mall. She walked carefully along this paved area in her heeled shoes which felt quite strange but were rather nice, an expensive brown leather in appearance, to join the throng of shoppers. How simple, clothing had become for both men and women, still fashionable in a sense but which she needed to get used to very quickly. She was pleased she was not walking in a cumbersome long Victorian dress and felt distinctly liberated. Realising she had a kind of diminutive watch on her wrist with no winder, she perused the digital display. It spelt out 11.50am on the 10th of April 2026. She smiled ... success!

The pleasant greenery around the Square still seemed remarkably familiar. She was convinced that some of the old trees were the same as when she lived there, especially the gnarled oak tree on the corner with the gigantic trunk and huge umbrella of leaves just coming into full leaf. Elizabeth sat down on a bench in the Square gardens and perused the statue of King William III erected originally in 1818. Heavens above, that monstrosity was still there but looking somewhat worse for wear. However, the familiarity was comforting as she continued to casually take in the bewildering sights and sounds, but no longer any bad smells of sewage in the air, thank goodness.

A young office worker, dressed in a pretty cotton summer dress, had popped out in the warm spring sun for her lunch and sat next to her, eating a burger and sipping a can of coca-cola. A strange ringing sound made Elizabeth jump and she turned to the woman who pulled out a mobile phone from her bag and began to answer a call from a friend she was meeting in fifteen minutes to shop on Jermyn Street.

The mention of shopping in one of her favourite locations raised Elizabeth's curiosity and she turned to the woman when the call had finished. "Excuse me, pray, may I ask where I may purchase one of those devices in this vicinity? Is that a particular type which you might recommend? I do apologise, I'm recently widowed. My husband took care of all day-to-day needs; in fact, he took care of everything."

The woman stared at Elizabeth momentarily but could see that she was dressed very expensively and spoke with an impeccable and distinctive accent, presumably a rich aristocrat who had lived a sheltered life, now fending for herself out in the real world without a clue. The woman moved closer and handed the smartphone to Elizabeth, opening the cover so that a bright array of applications against a blue background could be seen through the glass screen. Holding it carefully, she immediately worked out the icon for calls, some others could also be logically deduced given a little playing around, noting the time and date again. This must the electrical wireless speaking telegraph which Victoria had screamed about in Morag's house, probably powered by a small battery of some kind, and a prediction Victoria had made to that idiot Faraday in one of the lecture evenings, who scoffed rudely at her.

"My name's Geraldine, I work around the corner, doing virtual events. Haven't you seen a smartphone before? Actually, my best friend who I'm meeting in a minute bought this Samsung in John Ferguson's over there, the small shop lit up with the garish flashing lights. They've got a sale on this week. One payment and you can buy the phone bundled with a year's free calls and unlimited messaging plus two terabytes of data a month, a real bargain and everything is set up for you."

"Why thank you, Geraldine, that is truly most helpful," Elizabeth replied, her brain churning over at warp speed trying to work out the unfamiliar accent. A Sam…Sung phone? Mmm … the manufacture sounded Asian. A talking device without wires you carry around portable, she had to have one. Elizabeth closed the cover tentatively, such a strange material and handed the phone back.

"Thanks," Geraldine replied, warmly. "To be honest I used to work on these devices at one time. I was a Google engineer, trained in America for highly paid employment in the UK and then, three years ago, I was made redundant overnight along with a thousand others. My job has been replaced by robots, produced happily by the same company I worked for, would you believe? Artificial intelligence … a blessing for some but a curse for many already. Even skilled professionals like me are being put out of work at a fast rate. I was lucky to get another job. Fortunately, I'd done a Masters in marketing at Oxford University."

Elizabeth stared wide-eyed. "You were an engineer? You mean you were allowed to practise such a discipline as a woman?"

Geraldine laughed loudly, incredulous that anyone could be so out of touch, obviously, such people were still around, amazingly. "I can see you have lived ... err ... quite a ... protected life. Lots to catch up on I'm afraid, but a smartphone will help you. This is what I call good AI, tailored information at your fingertips inside your own little personal computer, technology at its best, so to speak. Anyway, I must fly. Only half an hour for lunch and we have evening dresses to buy for a wedding."

Geraldine stood up, shoving her lunch remains into a waste bin. She carefully readjusted her short dress, and then suddenly pointed in the direction where Elizabeth had come. "That building over there, number twelve, has a blue heritage plaque over the door commemorating where Ada Lovelace, a Victorian mathematician, once lived. She was the very first computer programmer although she never knew it at the time, such incredible foresight of the future, and a real inspirational heroine of mine. Ada would have had a field day now with smartphones and the internet of things."

Elizabeth smiled and felt a warm glow suffuse through her entire body ... one hundred and seventy-four years on and she was actually remembered in the street as a pioneer, a role model even? She'd missed the plaque. She had done something remarkable and special after all, despite the suffocating and constant paternalistic battles of the time. "I'm sure you are absolutely correct about Ada, Countess of Lovelace," Elizabeth replied, her eyes flashing with pleasure and the thought of also shopping for evening dresses. "She will indeed have a field day. Thank you so much, Geraldine, I would suggest Harrods would meet all your couture purchase needs in one visitation. They cater for all formalities."

Geraldine laughed loudly. What a strange way with words this intriguing woman had. "I'm afraid that department store is well out of my pay grade nowadays. But I can see you enjoy going there by the look on your face. Ahh … there's Eliza. Bye and have a great day."

In a moment Geraldine was gone, lost in the crowd of shoppers. Elizabeth continued to sit for a few more minutes, flushed with delight, but pondered desperately over how to learn and absorb the immense amount she needed in a short period of time. At least she had ascertained rather cleverly that Harrods still existed and so it should, this was still England. The first task was to buy one of those phones, but how? She needed money. Walking across to the shop, she noticed a small queue of people outside a building, shoving cards like hers into a square opening in the wall and tapping at buttons. She watched discretely, dumbfounded to see they were walking away with notes, presumably cash out of an electrical dispenser. What a fabulous concept. Waiting until the queue had dispersed, she rushed over. There was a name, Gurney Bank, over the top. She remembered the name, a financial institution popular in that lovely city of Norwich when she had visited the Duke of Norfolk with William her husband in the 1840s. She took out her Coutts card, read the screen and inserted it, following the instructions carefully. Bank balance first but what is this four digit PIN? A number? She would have to guess, mindful and anxious there was a queue building up, but after numerous mutterings and grumbling behind her, they dispersed to the next two machines leaving her on her own. The screen also stated she only had three attempts and the machine would lock up her card. Lord in heaven above, this was like going back to the Aintree racecourse again, but she realised she still enjoyed the idea of a punt and the logic, as a mathematician, would be something she could relate to. Unfortunately, neither the constants 'e' then 'pi' worked, leaving one shot left on this money roulette game. She racked her brain. What was she working on last before receiving Alice's letter? Of course, Bernoulli numbers again: she had refined the set of instructions for the Engine to post to Charles ... Maddie and Belle had used the phrase 'computer programme' after she plied them with copious red wine that evening in Orsbrick Hall, which became the convincing moment when she knew both they and Victoria could not be of that time. This must have been what the woman on the bench, Geraldine, had meant she had been remembered for. Amazing ... the iterative process was so mathematically obvious to do and yet she was the very first person to document the process. She smiled inwardly. Poor Charles Babbage, such a sceptic, but he never could conquer his inner battle over the fact she was both a logistical mathematician and a woman. She must find out whatever became of him and the Engine.

"Hey, lady, are you using that fucking machine? If not then move on will you, we're in a doggone hurry."

She was shaken out of her delightful reverie by a completely unfamiliar southern American drawl from a very rotund male behind wearing a peculiar wide-brimmed hat and bulky Hawaiian shorts. She turned to face the hideous sight. Never one to suffer idiots gladly, she unexpectedly found herself thinking what Julian would have done. Uttering a put down in her best accent would be a good start. "My suggestion, oaf, is to park your loathsome fat body elsewhere or I shall scream assault for a policeman to arrest you."

The aggrieved man blinked aggressively but before he had time to react his pink-haired female companion hollered a loud guffaw. "Say, Drew Boy, this crazy woman has sure got the measure of you. Hey, get on that other machine over the road for fuck's sake and leave the mad bitch alone. Ain't worth heading to the slammer for, we've gotta plane to catch."

They slunk off grumbling as she thought Bernoulli sequences again; B2 equals one-sixth ... turn into a decimal, first four numbers ... and she entered 1667, which worked. She was on the right side of the gambling angels for a change, a good omen. Check the balance. Good Lord—£434,600.97, eighty-two times the five thousand three hundred pounds which Julian had last banked into Coutts before he could get his hands on it. They were meant to share the spoils. Now she had all of it and a deep satisfaction ran through her body. A goodly amount to play with. She definitely admired the inflation effect of one hundred and seventy odd years on. Noting the quaint decimalisation of money, she drew out five hundred pounds and walked immediately into the phone shop.

The friendly and patient young sales assistant explained the workings of the Sam...Sung instrument and the mysterious, invisible wireless network pervading the air, called the 6G mobile internet, which provided unlimited access to incredible knowledge and information through the screen icons. Perfect. She secured the deal exactly as Geraldine described and using her Covent Garden Market bartering skills, even bargained off ten percent for cash at exactly one hundred and eighty pounds. She decided to walk to her favourite shop, Fortnum and Mason, to see if that existed and browse once again as she did weekly in

116

the early happy days of her marriage to William, but passed an old period restaurant in Jermyn Street en route. She decided to have an early lunch, perhaps steamed mussels and fresh salad, try the phone and call Orsbrick Hall … She could be there by the evening if trains still existed, and she would also pop into Harrods after buying a guide to London and a Times newspaper on a pavement stand. London in the year 2026 was almost home from home and infinitely cleaner …

The sudden glare from the sharp lights made her blink repeatedly. A gentle voice was ringing in her ear. "I'm sorry Miss Milbanke but I'm afraid I have to wake you, we are closing in fifteen minutes."

Elizabeth opened her eyes fully. For a second a feeling of terror enveloped her; where was she? Then immediately she realised with the well-dressed, uniformed waitress standing over her that she was still in the restaurant. A glance at the wall clock was quite a shock.

"I must have been asleep here for nearly three hours. Such irresponsible and appalling behaviour. I do sincerely apologise, I hope I wasn't snoring," Elizabeth replied, looking around fearfully but everyone had gone.

The waitress, with a Miss Estella Havisham label on her breast pocket, smiled warmly. "No, you were exceedingly quiet. It was evident you must be exhausted from a long journey into London so we left you. Are you travelling onwards far?"

"Mmm … yes, it was rather a long and eventful journey I must confess," Elizabeth replied, smiling inside. "Tell me, have you read Great Expectations by the wonderful Mr Charles Dickens?"

The waitress laughed. "No, I really should, everyone says that. My father's family did come from the East End of poor London though, sometime in the nineteen hundreds."

"Likely your family was an inspiration to Charles, an unusual name. I have a signed first edition. When I return home I shall send it to you here, I have no need of the book now."

"Really? Gosh, your family must have once been close friends with Mr Dickens."

Elizabeth beamed. Little did Miss Havisham know. "Yes, you could say that, quite intimate even. Anyway, I must pay the bill ... now where is?"

"I put your debit card back securely in your handbag, Miss Milbanke; you had it in your hand when you dozed off. Can't trust people these days, especially with contactless payment up to one thousand pounds. That's how I knew your name. The Milbanke family were very well-connected aristocrats in the Victorian period, also an unusual name. Are you related?"

Elizabeth laughed. "Yes ... rather distant cousins many times removed, you know how it is. I'll just pay the bill with my card," she said, waving it over a reader as other customers had been doing. Now tell me, Miss Havisham, can I still get to Parbold station from Euston by train?"

"Parbold station? Where is that?"

"Lancashire, not very far from Liverpool and the racecourse. I am seeking to get to the village of Burscough."

Miss Havisham smiled. "Of course, sorry, there's no station at Parbold but there is one at Burscough but not for the main intercity train. I know that area quite well, my sister lives in Ormskirk. Yes, a fast Maglev train departs every hour from Euston to Liverpool which takes about fifty minutes, and then you catch a local train to Burscough, via Southport.

"Excellent. Can I get a tube from here or would it be just as easy on a bus? Although I suppose I could get a taxi, one of those electric driverless things. I have an electro-uber app on my phone, haven't had a chance to use it," Elizabeth replied then stopped suddenly. Why was she saying things she didn't know?

"The uber, definitely, I always use them, they're here in half a minute. Since driverless has taken off, the traffic jams of old in London have halved, you'll be there in no time."

"Thank you Miss Havisham, I must fly, some shopping to do."

Elizabeth decided to walk to Harrods, have a cream tea and jam scone and reflect very hard. Her mind felt oddly different, relaxed, open and normal, as she looked around and ran through what had become familiar. Carriages were cars, the dispensary was a chemist, wool and cotton became a wide array of artificial textile fabrics, wood was plastic, and she now knew what these things were. She switched thoughts to advanced mathematics and her mind tumbled through an array of calculus and formulae she never knew before but understood easily now, and creating iterative instructions were indeed about writing code in a fourth generation computer language called Ruby, which she understood totally. The instructions for Bernoulli numbers that she had toiled over for years, she could scribble in a few minutes, which she did on the bill. In fact, her mind was getting to grips with so-called sixth generation languages to use with quantum computers and solve problems through a machine billions of times more powerful than poor Charles's Analytical Engine. If only he were here. Spooning into her clotted cream, she opened her phone and knew instantly how to use it and what all those mysterious icons were … She decided to find the rectory first in Burscough where logically, Alice Langton should be, and travel there as soon as possible. A Google search quickly revealed a phone number …

Maddie was listening, wide-eyed, to this effusive explanation and her fast mind had homed deep into the last statement. She was first off the mark with a comment. She couldn't hold it in any longer. "So, whilst you were dozing in that restaurant, your brain had begun some kind of realignment. The space-time transition into the future recognised that you could never acquire one hundred and seventy years of advancement and evolved your mind to match the future during your first sleep cycle, a logical survival process. I'm sure I experienced the same thing too going back to 1841, except there is less to learn in many ways as we already knew much of the past through history knowledge, so the experience would be less severe. I realised on that last day when you and Medora came, whilst I was sitting on my bed with Belle. A week had gone by but my mind and outlook all at once seemed remarkably at ease with understanding everything around me. It didn't make sense. Now it does totally."

"Gosh, Maddie," Abby cried. "I never understood either how I could blather on to John Ruskin about art which I never really knew beforehand, the words just came out but I never thought about it that logical way. We must all have had the same experiences and never realised, a kind of gradual filling up of the brain suitable for the time, relevant to us as individuals."

"But in your case, Elizabeth, moving into the future is a far more severe jolt with no history to inform you; everything has to be in stark newness," Belle added excitedly, really warming to the theme.

Elizabeth grinned. Maddie and Belle were as sharp and interesting as ever. "Exactly, except it feels smooth and natural. And I've been here ten days and each day has changed when I awoke, with more perspectives initially exponentially filling up, but this phenomenon has flattened off. I think I may, as it were, be there, at the level of what my natural knowledge, given my innate mathematical curiosity, should be at. And I still remember everything about 1841 too."

"As we did about 2026 in 1841," Victoria cut in, understanding perfectly. "Evidently the space-time transfer, using dark energy, is governed by a set of laws which we have just observed, like the second law of thermodynamics, a sort of built-in memory entropy."

"Actually Victoria, I believe this process is linked to a necessary equivalence of quantum gravity, using the medium of dark energy solely as a transfer communicative channel," Elizabeth began, before Abby decided to change the direction of this conversation. The scientists were taking over again and in their enthusiasm, they were forgetting one crucial thing. Where was Mauveine?

"So how did you end up here as a curate and realised Alice and Thomas Langton had not followed the journey?" Abby interjected.

Elizabeth looked at the clock. "They may actually be back shortly so I'll be quick. A most peculiar turn of events, I must hasten, even for me. Well, I phoned the rectory with, I may say, some anxiety using that wonderful device, my Sam…Sung, for the first time. The moment an elderly female voice answered, I knew something was decidedly wrong, especially because she answered as Alice Langton. I had to think on my feet, so I asked if I could speak to the Reverend Thomas Langton but before I could commence some searching dialogue, he immediately began by hoping I was calling about the post of curate. They had received no applicants and he was desperate. Had I any experience? In a moment, after reorientation from the shock of women curates, I thought this may be a better way to safely explore the finding of all of you, and at the same time give me some purpose whilst I worked out … well … what I'm going to do in 2026. Don't forget, I was imbued, from childhood, with a deep understanding of religion and all its formal manifestations by my mother. We had numerous curates from the high church which my mother embraced, coming and going regularly to our home so I was confident I could do it. So I rattled off some suggestions to his questions and I was given the job to start immediately! I kitted up with new clothes in Harrods and bought a nice suitcase, made up some tale of having been abroad administering to the poor in Paris and arrived by train in the evening, helping with the service the following morning to the Reverend Thomas's great delight."

Victoria laughed. "You never ceased to amaze me in 1841, old habits definitely die hard. May they continue as robustly as ever, but Abby, quite rightly, has drawn us all back to our mutual dilemma. What has happened to Mauveine? I suppose all we can do is wait for anything to materialise."

"I don't feel anything psychic either, same as Abby," Maddie exclaimed. "I don't know whether that's good or bad but I agree, we need to be patient. Anyway, Elizabeth, in the meantime I'd like to talk to you about artificial intelligence when you're not busy."

"Excellent, Maddie and I've already started," Elizabeth replied, cheerily, picking up a thick tome on introducing artificial intelligence off the table which she was halfway through. "This, I believe, is my natural area of work to continue from where I left off in 1852, given a little progress in between!"

They all began to laugh again and relax when Belle interrupted. "I can see a taxi pulling up down the path, I think Alice and Thomas are back. We'd better go, mustn't overstay our welcome. We hope to see you at Orsbrick Hall soon, Elizabeth."

Victoria stared hard at her daughter. Normally she thinks before she speaks but the impact of meeting up with Ada again had made her forget ... or maybe it was deliberate. She reflected in an instance and decided, as Abby and Maddie both glanced over anxiously. Bold was always her modus operandi, so to hell with any further caution. "Yes, that would be nice. I'll send you a formal invitation to dinner in your role as the new curate. We have a visitor staying for a while I would like you to meet."

"That sounds intriguing I must say," Elizabeth said, in a hushed voice.

Abby silently drew breath. Was that such a wise idea of Victoria?

Victoria continued. "Finally, something I wanted to ask. Do you still remember Julian by any chance? We all wondered how you two ... err ... got on in the end?"

Maddie glanced hard at her mother. Why was she raising the issue of Dad when they had already agreed all that disgusting behaviour in 1841 had been some manifestation and certainly not Dad whatsoever or indeed Lynton.

Elizabeth's face turned a shade of crimson ... anger mixed with a tinge of regret but times had changed dramatically. "That piece of horse shit? The minute he got to his sister, Caitriona, in London, he vanished for good and out of my life, despite all I'd given him. Julian was a con-man of the worst kind. Well and truly forgotten, in fact, I hate men."

Victoria smiled. "Good. You know, Elizabeth, we felt exactly the same way, all thoughts have been vigorously expunged.

Right everyone, let's go now and sneak out via the back door, I suggest. A pleasing walk back along the canal will clear the mind."

Abby, however, had resolved to have a long and personal discussion with Victoria quickly. Whatever obscure tactic was in Victoria's head was not one she had been sharing. But Abby missed Elizabeth's quiet smirk as they gathered their things to leave. A delicious factor of wavelength equivalence had not been lost in the respective forward time transfers of Elizabeth and Victoria. Subtle irony had been a shared and enjoyable characteristic between the two. Elizabeth knew an emotional message had been transmitted and greatly anticipated discerning the true meaning, although she had good intuition what it was likely to be.

However, walking back alongside Victoria, something else was quietly bothering Abby. And she had no answers to that conundrum either. Further ahead they turned into a partly concealed short lane leading to the back of Orsbrick Hall, where a bright onslaught of yellow and red flowers dominated the view over the style towards the main road. A confluence of hanging laburnum blossom hung a heavy scent in the air, the trees interspersed amongst a group of huge camellia shrubs, bursting into bright red flower. The shrubs formed a pretty boundary for a small clump of birch trees behind, rooted inside a circular dip, demarcating a small and rather green, algae-laden pond.

Walking ahead, Maddie and Belle turned, indicating they were going to investigate the pond habitat's biology, never having previously spotted that area despite all the years they had lived nearby, and dived over the style, laughing and giggling.

Abby finally faced Victoria, both in a contemplative and sombre mood. "Are you thinking the same thing that I am?" she said quietly.

"You mean about our visitor?"

"Yes, something doesn't quite add up."

"Mmm, perhaps ... let's see how things transpire in the next few days. I suggest, for the moment, we keep this to ourselves. Something tells me we should have a tactical chat back home, before Lynton and Julian return. I'm so glad Claire and Danielle are back from their holiday. Despite Sabrina's impressive dexterity and willingness to learn, there seems to be an inbuilt electronic barrier in her wiring towards cooking variety ... even Lynton is tiring of the rotating three from five combinations of bacon, beans, sausage, egg and chips for dinner. Heaven knows what Elizabeth will make of Sabrina ... that should be a fun encounter."

"Definitely," Abby responded, smiling. Both trudged silently onwards leaving the girls to their own devices, oblivious to what Maddie and Belle had instantly spotted on the grass down the dip. Two people were lying amongst the wild flowers having an amorous cuddle, oblivious to whether anybody was around. Perhaps it wasn't so unexpected given the obvious signals earlier. Maddie nodded quietly to Belle and they tip-toed away unobserved, to be analysed and discussed later, strictly between the two of them only.

Chapter Six

Orsbrick Hall, one month on:

Thrashing about in his sleep, Ned woke up in a lather of sweat. Peering out from under the duvet to a blaze of light through a gap in the thick curtain, his mind raced uncontrollably. He rubbed his eyes and squinted at the alarm clock. Still only six in the morning. He'd had a most peculiar dream, floating out in the middle of the River Mersey on some boat, wearing weird clobber with a large rubber tube attached to his chest and about to dive into the water. What the fuck? Either that cask beer in the Ship Inn was off or the late-night curry they ate with Zac and Fenella had disagreed with him. Normally he could manage anything and the hotter the better, although maybe insisting on mixing chilli and ginger together with the chicken vindaloo was not such a good idea. And what was that massive weight draped over his legs? The quiet, deep snoring answered that mystery. Remonstrating loudly, he shoved off the great carcase of wolfhound, Jeb, sprawled over the bottom of the huge bed, who sloped away begrudgingly to the far corner of the room to lie next to his brother, Kai, still fast asleep.

"Hey there, magical lover, what time is it? Bloody hell, it's still early, can't you sleep? You're a bit sweaty, what's up?"

He turned and wrapped his arms around Nancy as she cuddled closer to his warm body and he kissed the top of her head gently. "Bit of a nightmare, probably ate too much curry."

Nancy sighed heavily. "Balancing on the railing of the landing stage after six pints of beer wasn't exactly a brilliant display of sense either. The water was really rough. Fenella got quite hysterical. You don't have to show off to her just because she eyes all over Zac day in and day out."

"Doesn't bother me, although only my little brother could pull a classy bird a hundred and seventy years old."

Nancy raised herself up and pulled the sheet around her, eyes narrowed. "What exactly do you mean, Ned McKenzie?" she whispered.

Ned had to think quickly, he'd well and truly put his foot in that one. They had all promised to say nothing about Fenella outside of the family, although Nancy was family in his eyes. With Zac and Maddie's help combined with her voracious reading, Fenella had normalised amazingly well. "My offbeat, cynical sense of humour that's all. She was apparently raised in some Irish convent by crazy nuns who brought her up very strictly like a Victorian child."

"Really? I never knew that. Probably explains why she's so shy. She was completely mesmerised by the bus ride into Liverpool. Anyway, the six pints didn't seem to affect the great Casanova for a change, you were quite ... how shall we say ... frenetic last night."

"Mmm ..." he replied playfully, pulling the sheet over her head. "Fancy an encore? Then I'm going to get up and have an early Sabrina-style Sunday breakfast, I can smell cooking."

Nancy giggled and laid right over him, pulling his chest hairs gently. "Your Mum is really cool about you and me being able to sleep together in your bedroom. I think she's pretty amazing actually, a role model for us go-ahead career girls."

Ned laughed. "She's not so cool about Zac and me going out on those electric scooters that Dad bought us. Ade's just got one too; he saved up from his night work job at the mental hospital. Just have to remember to charge up each night like Sabrina does. Oh shit, I nearly forgot. I said we'd all meet up later to celebrate Dottie's birthday with lunch somewhere. I like the Liverpool pub scene these days, the George has become really boring, so I suggested we head on the scooters to the Black Anchor on Dale Street. Ade can take Dottie on the back and he's offered to pay, a first for him … He won the hospital weekly lottery draw and got a hundred quid, and I'll keep strictly off the booze this time. I'm not totally irresponsible, just like a little fun now again," he whispered, kissing her hard.

"Hang on," she spluttered, pushing him off. "You mean Zac, with Fenella and Dottie, together? Isn't that a bit toxic after the monster breakup?"

"Naah … Dottie knows about Fenella," Ned replied calmly. "She's perfectly fine, quite happy for him. Apparently, she's seeing some older guy, a mate of Ade's brother and as you know is also heading for Uni soon. She and Zac are still good friends. It's all very grown-up, the usual rational Zac. He works out the logical steps and programmes his brain to be Mr Reasonable."

"Mmm … okay, if you say so. Victorian women weren't always shy and demure. A few became famous serial killers."

"Oh, yeah, sure … like Jacqui the Ripper you mean?" he jested, gripping her close again.

She laughed and nudged him. "That cooking is making me hungry now. You'll have to be quick, I'm afraid."

"Speedy is my middle name …" he replied, chasing off Jeb again who was attempting to crawl back onto the comfortable, warm bed.

Maddie was pacing around the pond, alone and in turmoil about what she had just received. Ponds always made her relaxed. She needed to focus because the decision she would make could affect the rest of her life. And she was determined she would come to a decision herself, no badgering from her mother, advice from Abby or even kind words from her dad, all of which were welcomed but she was an adult now and had to face difficult things directly and exercise her own judgement. She stopped and sat on one of the log benches that her father had cut, fashioned and varnished many years ago before she was even born, but they were still like new. She stared blankly for at least ten minutes into the blue and almost cloudless sky. Inside the perimeter of the tall reeds, copious amounts of frogspawn moved about with black wriggly bits, the emergence of the tadpoles imminent and a duet of croaking ensued as two large brown frogs, jumping after a small green specimen into the water, made a loud splash. She noticed a few familiar carp swimming near the surface and wondered if the twenty-pound pike which Ned had caught in the canal and released into the pond last year was there, maybe basking in the shallower reeds which he liked to do. But she didn't spot him that time. Distraction felt good. Her subconscious was still busy weighing up the pros and cons but the most important factor had been determined. She was not going to Harvard in two weeks time.

Dashing a yellow wash over her pencil sketch of the Red Lion but distracted by an array of irrational thoughts, Abby's large diamond ring caught the paper which ripped right through. "Fuck everything," she screamed and kicked the leg of her easel which toppled over sending paint and water flying across her cherished oak floor.

Down the corridor watching the highlights of last week's football on their wall TV, Lynton heard the commotion and rushed out towards Abby's studio then slammed his head into the door, turning the handle. It had been firmly locked.

"Jesus Christ, Abby, are you all right? What's happened? Why on earth is this door locked?" he shouted through.

Abby was sobbing. "Yes, I'm fine. You can't come in. I'm doing something special and I don't want to be disturbed, especially by you."

"Darling, what's the matter? Tell you what, I'm heading to the sitting room and I'll fix us both a nice gin and tonic each. I won't try and come in … promise. I was concerned hearing all that racket. I thought you'd collapsed or something, you've been a bit quiet lately and peaky too. I was worried that's all."

"As if you care. Too many other important things fill your life these days. Anyway, I'm still here alive and kicking you'll be displeased to know."

"Bloody hell, Abby, what on earth has got into you? What have I done now? Listen, I'm going to make a double gin. Promise you'll come down and let's talk it over, we've never kept secrets from each other, you know that."

"No, not until now … okay … I'm sorry. I'll be down in a minute. I need to clear up first, had an accident. I don't want any ice, just lemon."

Taking a deep breath, she heard Lynton wander off towards the other end of the corridor and sat down. She really was edgy and decidedly off-colour which was never like her. But this unsavoury business with Lynton couldn't carry on any longer, it was time to face the facts. She'd really had enough of the continuing innuendos and sniggers and Victoria, as usual at the wrong time, had been emotionally defunct and blissfully ignorant. Grabbing a cloth out of the sink, she carefully wiped up the mess. Fortunately, it was only a light shade of lemon yellow and being water based, the paint did no harm to the polished wood surface, although the edge of the easel falling had taken a chunk out of the wall plaster. Damn, she'd have to fix that later. No good asking his majesty outside. Do-it-yourself was decidedly not his forte. In fact, what was Lynton's forte these days? Despite unexpectedly deciding to give up the day-to-day management of the family law practice and volunteer to work with Julian on managing the expanding Orsbrick estate, he hadn't actually done anything apart from watch the television all day and drink more profits out of the pub whisky stock. Was this all a manifestation of a mid-life crisis, happening later than everyone else? Perhaps Lynton's lack of general interest in life was the reason the other thing had been going on? Or was it going on? She had to find out once and for all.

She unlocked the door and walked quietly towards the sitting room. At least, a big gin and tonic would be welcome. Then she could go back later and restart her picture. She had decided to paint again after all those years managing her successful gallery, but work in watercolour rather than oil, inspired by that burst of creative activity when she was cavorting, in 1841 time, as Morag's distant cousin ... the so-called talented artist inspired by Constable. At least John Ruskin had found her inspiring. Maybe she should have stayed and married him ... no, she really had to get that silly thought out of her head. This was the year 2026, the here and now was back around her but her marriage may genuinely be in trouble for the first time. Perhaps she should have had a chat with Maddie first, but Maddie was only just eighteen and had a lot still to learn about relationships despite her maturity.

Entering the room, she looked about and felt a feeling of relief come over her, provided entirely by the environment. She loved this room, her favourite in the entire Red Lion building. A large and airy ornate ceiling, the gnarled beams peppered with original woodworm holes, and the ornate covings and lime plaster painted lovely pastel greens and yellows, draw her gaze every moment she entered. Matching antique furniture complimented the ambience. The sofa and chairs she had recovered herself in an original Georgian pattern to match the special wallpaper bought from and made by a student design company run by the Liverpool College of Art and Design. The high sash windows directly overlooked the Leeds and Liverpool canal and she spent many a happy hour with a glass or two of red wine, watching the pleasure boats cruise past and imagining the nineteenth century days of the ubiquitous boat-families managing their slow, horse-drawn barges fully laden with coal, cotton and tobacco. She drew a deep breath. This was finally truth time, but why was Lynton sitting at her piano, a shiny, black Baby Steinway which he, at great expense, had bought her for their tenth wedding anniversary?

Her double gin and tonic was standing on the coffee table. She grabbed it immediately and took a large swig. Fortitude was called for and she decided to lay into him, immediate and direct. There was going to be no beating about the bush.

"Lynton, look at me," she yelled. "I don't know why you're sat on that piano stool but I've finally come to the end of the road. All the sniggering and the not so subtle joke innuendos from the rest of the family, which I don't find in the slightest bit amusing, along with your fucking awful, uncommunicative behaviour over the last three months. Okay, I can understand you've been under some stress, winding off the running of the law firm, but for Christ's sake, you own sixty percent of the shares so you can keep on taking a nice chunk of profits for occasionally showing your face whilst Reggie and Ronnie, as I call them, do the real work. But this bizarre love obsession with Sabrina has finally worn me down. She's a robot for heaven's sake, so why the fuck are you shagging her? The thought is disgustingly gross, beyond even my wildest imagination, and I have had just about enough ... I'm off to an apartment in Southport this evening that I've agreed to rent."

He looked up startled and his face turned a deep shade of crimson. Large beads of sweat poured down his forehead. He realised she had been edgy lately but had no idea she had garnered any inkling of Sabrina and him.

Abby's face was contorted with an anger never displayed in all their years together. She shook with rage and the acute disappointment that their relatively good marriage, despite the ups and downs, had come to this ignominious conclusion. She shuddered inside thinking that she would become the first person in the world to cite an affair with an autonomous female robot as grounds for divorce, and she had made up her mind too. Every last penny and minutiae of asset he legally owned she would take half of it and more if she could. She would fleece him rotten, the bastard. Independent, with financial means and spirit, she had always wanted him for the rest of her life but now she didn't need him. However, she would grace him with hearing what he had to say before she departed for good and a new life. Already, his odious level of discomfort confirmed serious guilt at a one hundred percent level. But as usual, everybody else could see the car crash coming except her. Why did Victoria engage in a conspiracy of silence and say nothing to her? She was even more disappointed with her best friend.

A long silence engulfed the space between them. She sat down and took another swig of her drink, whilst Lynton continued to stare out of the window in deep thought. He had been so stupid. He should have told her from the beginning but had been trying so hard for months to work out what was the matter with his life and why he hadn't felt fulfilled and contented for years, if ever, certainly with his career. He never really liked the law profession. Yes, it had given him an excellent income and he and Abby had been able to live a life free of money worries, but now he was at an age where he could reconsider everything and fulfil his childhood dream. This was what he should have done from the beginning but had been thwarted at every turn by his domineering father who insisted on micromanaging both his childhood and his pliant mother who had zero understanding of his real needs. After all those years, Sabrina had enabled the rediscovery of who he really wanted to be and he felt a huge relief, a massive weight off his shoulders for the first time. But he had to try and explain this tumultuous change to Abby. There was only one way, which had to be now and direct. "You've realised, I'm sure, that I haven't been myself for a long time. I tried drinking my way out of it which of course is stupid and only ruins your health. I've had to reach the depth of the problem of keeping my genuine self well-hidden for many, many decades but by sheer chance, Sabrina helped me find the way."

"What? By having an affair with a piece of sex-crazed plastic?" she screamed loudly. Now her deep frustration had to come out. "You really are out of your mind, Lynton. I should have left you years ago. I always suspected you had a roving eye but chose to disregard it because so much of our life seemed to work fine anyway. And I've had plenty to keep me seriously challenged, especially building up my gallery business. I really thought you enjoyed all our art collecting. Obviously, buying and selling was just a front for rampaging around Europe seeking fresh female challenges. Why, oh why, have I been so foolish?"

Crestfallen, Lynton looked over her … and felt utterly devastated that he had inculcated such a bad impact on Abby and their marriage, clearly for far longer than he ever realised. The last five years had been passing in a secret haze of daily whisky and lager, only forcing him to moderate whenever he was in her company. He pulled the stool closer to the piano. "No, Abby, your accusations are completely wrong. The hours spent secretly with Sabrina have been about this."

Unexpectedly, he began to play softly, his fingers rapidly moving up and down the keys like a seasoned professional. Lynton demonstrated the same ease with the piano as if he were the great Oscar Peterson, running through a rapid sequence of intricate jazz pieces, one of which he had recently composed. This was the secret passion he shared with a robot. Sabrina provided something he never dreamed possible, a reawakening after all those long years of a natural talent, present since a small child, but lying dormant and repressed because he had been petrified to 'raise the devil's sin' his father thundered and indoctrinated into him when he was a terrified little boy. Equally, for opening his eyes and his mind, Sabrina had asked him to provide something in return … there was a quid pro quo but a timely intervention, fortunately, changed that dynamic in the end.

Abby sat in amazed dumb silence. The perfectly executed modern jazz pieces flowed from the keyboard as effortlessly as water from an emptying canal lock. Her Steinway possessed the most beautiful tone and Lynton made it sing heartily, in a way she would never have dreamed of. He had shown zero inkling of musical talent before. Yes, he genuinely enjoyed her piano playing and singing and always, to be fair, had encouraged her to practise regularly. But she never needed to and anyway, her creative heart was always immersed within her painting and art. But Lynton had a deeply creative capability which he had kept hidden from her and the world all those years they had known one another, a talent seriously repressed and bolted down inescapably inside his head, never to take root and blossom forth until now, of all times. She still couldn't believe her ears and pinched herself in case she was back in 1841 or some other silly scenario.

Lynton stopped after an idiosyncratic rendition of 'Fly Me to the Moon' one of her old and favourite Sinatra pieces, whose words she was unable to resist humming along with. Her mind raced wildly with the idiocy of the situation. She was supposed to be clearing off for good within the hour and now discovers that her husband is a jazz genius. "Okay, Thelonious Monk, please explain," she thundered, totally disorientated, with a whirlwind of resounding dilemmas flowing around her head.

Lynton sat back and took a small sip of gin and tonic. "I've cut back hugely on the booze … a while ago I made a few visits to Alcoholics Anonymous in Southport. The experience scared and jolted me back to reality. I was on the cliff edge of self-destruction looming fast, this, incidentally …" he said, holding up his glass, "… is mainly tonic. I'm afraid yours is mainly gin … you looked like you needed it."

She laughed. One thing definitely hadn't changed. Lynton's usual crassness when a crisis occurs. "Go on then, so which part of your ego, or otherwise, has Sabrina been expertly massaging? And since when could you play the piano or anything musical for that matter? Even with her supercharged circuits, you must have had some serious musical technique taught to you beforehand, although by the way you stroke those keys you've always been able to play, haven't you."

"Yes, correct, I was a natural from the moment I could climb onto a piano stool, but buried my talents beneath a great wall of childhood repression, physical pain and frustrated will. My father was a horrendous, overbearing tyrant who viewed all music as a nasty perversion that had to be eradicated at any cost and by all brutal and physical means necessary. My mother was the genius from whom I had inherited the gift … she had been a budding concert violinist before she met my father. I never understood why she fell in love with the monster although he was very rich, gorging on inherited pickings from ancient nineteenth-century cotton trading. Their relationship never ended well. He became lazy, corpulent and alcoholic and my mother spent much of her equally short life locked up in an asylum. That was why I was brought up by my grandparents on a country estate. Simply listening to you play and watching you perform so well was sufficient for me. But that suddenly changed. If you'll let me, I'll try and explain."

Abby, sipping her gin, sat down quietly on the large sofa with Lynton perched at the other end. She waited for the revelations, although the first sensational scenario had arrived, delivered by two hands and ten fingers. Now she understood, for the first time, why Lynton spoke very little about his childhood, a reticence neither she nor Judy, his daughter, could effectively break. He, when confronted, merely repeated the same variant of old mantras that his early years were spent happily on his grandparent's estate in Cheshire and that his parents had sadly passed away when he was a teenager.

For the next half hour, Lynton poured out the true nature of his secret assignations with Sabrina. Their musical affair started by accident when she visited the Red Lion, one day, in the self-drive car of Victoria's. She was carrying a large house plant, a present for Abby who was away working, but on entering the grand sitting room became immediately drawn to the Steinway piano. The moment Sabrina sat on the stool and tinkled at the ivories with the skill and dexterity of a modern jazz virtuoso, Lynton, shocked and astounded, was hooked. Not, he emphasised for Sabrina but simply by the amazing playing along with the lost inspiration he found welling up again inside. Quickly they attempted a Herbie Hancock duet and he realised his piano capability, although dormant since the age of eleven, was capable of coming back to life, with practice, despite his father having beaten the crap out of him and forced a final cessation after Lynton had dared to improvise his secret hero, Oscar Peterson. And Sabrina equally felt compelled to show him all she knew. Unknown to Julian and Victoria she had been programmed to play and teach jazz by her creator, Professor Ash Kolinsky, Julian's friend at Stamford who was a jazz fanatic and pianist. But this aspect of Sabrina's robotic cognition had not had the opportunity to come to life until that moment in the Red Lion ... although she did admit an urge to play the baby grand piano in the Orsbrick Hall ballroom, but it was kept locked and hidden beneath a heavy dust sheet.

"But why, Lynton?" Abby wailed, moving her suitcase to the back of the room. "Why did you keep such a gifted musical talent bottled up inside, especially knowing my enthusiasm for singing and playing? I would have understood, clearly, I would, and encouraged you. I certainly wouldn't have been jealous or threatening."

"I know but I can't explain. I simply had repressed the experience totally, right through the rest of my schooling, then university law school, my first marriage, Judy's childhood, the family business and finally you. It was too deeply painful to revisit. Why my father treated me the way he did over a harmless style of music, I never found out ... something awful must have happened to him in his youthful life but then he was so extreme, started drinking heavily, had various women in tow and my mother finally left him for good when I was thirteen and I went to live with her and her parents. She was still only young, coming from a wealthy family with a huge estate in Cheshire and my grandfather effectively brought me up, especially when my mother, a couple of years later, had a violent, suicidal breakdown which she never recovered from and she had to be incarcerated permanently. The family law business was actually his, not my father's. Soon after that calamity my father left in a small boat from Weymouth across the Channel for France and was never heard of again, presumed drunk-drowned and dead."

"So what magical stardust was a North Korean female robot able to sprinkle over you, which was beyond the rest of us mere mortals and awaken the latent genius? Sorry, I sound ultra-cynical … didn't mean it to sound like that and I very much sympathise with the trauma your childhood must have been. But hey, let's be honest, I am ultra-cynical, that's my Abigail Warren nature. So did this amazing electronic generosity, shared between like-minded musical souls if a robot has a soul, not come with … well … mutual expectations, you know … traditional jazz accompanied by modern benefits?"

Lynton blinked, he was treading on thin ice in that area. He knew exactly what Abby, straight to the point and quick as lightning was getting at, the totality of which lay at the very heart of her deep unhappiness with him. He wasn't going to lie but neither was he prepared to embellish the entire reality … known only to him and Julian. "No, no, absolutely not. The thought which you've been screaming blue murder at me for the last half hour is as repellent to me as to you … it never crossed my mind, nor was it implied. That sort of behaviour is

139

for … I don't know … weird perverts, the kind of losers who turn to animated dolls for emotional comfort. I was, as usual, too stupid or inwardly fixated to realise that there were innuendos flying about the family. Doubtlessly, my affection and admiration for Sabrina potentially changing my life was misconstrued. Even Judy, not known for subtleties, was saying some odd things that made no sense. I'm really, really sorry Abby. I should have told you from the beginning. I don't want you to go and end our marriage, it's devastating. I love you as much as ever." His eyes filled with tears as the enormity of everything coming to a head came crashing down to hit him for six.

Abby was still not convinced. But she was prepared at least to give him a chance. The situation was so bizarre but it now seemed the sensible thing to do …

"So, Lynton. I've at least put my suitcase down. Where do we go from here? And what do you want to do with your life? I thought you were going to become Julian's assistant and run the Orsbrick estate?"

He stood up, pondered and went to give Abby a hug but she backed off … feelings remained raw, not yet. They sat down again on either end of the large sofa.

"To be brutally honest, much as I love and admire Julian I don't want to do that whatsoever. The law firm will run itself under Charles and I've given him and Rupert a twenty percent stake each to incentivise them. As you observed, I or should I say we, hold the remaining sixty percent, because a number of years ago, I altered that shareholding for both of us equally. I've put your dividends, which have amounted to quite a lot, into a special savings fund in Singapore in your name … for a rainy day, so if I ever drop dead you have a large chunk of ready cash to cover anything you need so you would never have to borrow off Victoria. It's in my will."

Abby stared at him in disbelief. What could she say? They never discussed such matters. He had a track record for peculiar ways of doing things ever since they started dating back in 2010, so she shouldn't be surprised. But to be fair, his generosity had never wavered and remained true to this day. Why had she prejudged him so harshly? She certainly hadn't been herself either, that's for sure. "But why didn't you tell me, you idiot. I do earn my way and more these days from the gallery, although I must admit I do like to spend and indulge. Saving for rainy days has never been my strong suit. Any other surprises lurking?"

"No. Now that I've finally broken the barrier, late in the day though it is, I've decided to pursue this lost dream. I'm going to consider performing around the UK and composing and I've decided to turn the large outhouse building out the back into a state of the art recording studio. I'll still help Julian out of course, as ever, but I was never drawn to become his apprentice estate lackey, despite his obvious desire to shove me into that role. You, my music and the grandchildren will be the focus of my life from now on. Decision made. I caused this fucking mess so I'll pay the lease charge for that apartment if you decide to stay with me."

Abby picked herself up from the sofa, threw the remaining gin and tonic down her throat and laughed. "Okay, deal accepted, but there's no need to shell out any money. I never signed anything formal. The place happens to be a seafront holiday bolthole offered by one of Carol's London friends, no formalities … in fact I'm sure Carol will be quite relieved I don't take it up."

"So you're staying then … with the new me?"

"I think you'd better give me that hug, new you …"

A couple of hours later, Abby prised herself out of bed, took a quick shower and wrapped her fluffy dressing gown around herself. She gazed at the semi-slumbering naked form under the sheets, still not bad for his age despite the paunch. It had been a very long time since they had indulged in pleasant daytime sex or any sex for that matter. Perhaps playing jazz does, as they say, act as an aphrodisiac, in which case she should go out and buy him a dozen Thelonious Monk albums. Creeping down the stairs, she stole out into the corridor, keeping out of the way of the kitchen and front of house staff who were readying the pub for the onslaught of the evening hordes and the weekly quiz. Business at the Red Lion had been looking up over the last six months, especially from the increased number of pleasure boaters who moored at the large landing stage Julian had skilfully constructed out of old railway sleepers and the remains of a discarded wooden bridge left to rot up the canal.

Once inside their kitchen, she closed the door and briskly made a couple of black coffees from El Hombre, a favourite obscure Columbian blend which Lynton had covertly imported. She decided she ought to reassess the wronged Sabrina who may have actually cyber-rescued her marriage from permanent destruction. Gazing nonchalantly at the wall clock, she jolted out of her afternoon reveries remembering she had an important appointment. Shit, she had to get dressed and get a move on.

"Perhaps a bit of this in-between your future composing sessions wouldn't be such a bad idea," she purred, kissing his sleepy head as he came back to life. She handed him the mug and sat cross-legged on the large bed, both sipping their hot coffees. "Darling, I forgot, I must make a move and see the doctor. To be fair, especially over the last month, I haven't been feeling myself whatsoever with these waves of feeling queasy on and off every day. I hope I've picked up a bug which that new antiviral tablet they've released will sort out, or maybe it's that early menopause thing again. I should have gone to the surgery last time that happened … this unwell feeling hasn't helped my mood and made me short tempered and snappy, so it hasn't all been one-way on your part. I reckon I could do with a tonic."

He patted her arm gently and pecked her cheek with a light kiss. "Probably a good idea, I knew you weren't yourself. Perhaps some iron tablets will do the trick. They helped me last time, combined with vitamin D, although the best cure has been cutting off the booze. Hopefully, the pot belly will go down too, especially with the daily gym I've started."

Abby had thrown on her jeans and a top and was ready to fly out of the door. She felt miles better already but decided to keep the appointment anyway, if only for a tailored tonic from the nurse after she had a quick blood sample instantly analysed. "Okay, see you later. Are you continuing with your robotic music lessons then?"

"Yes, but only once a week. I think I'm ready to fly my wings now. It didn't take long for the magic to return, that was the amazing part of the whole story."

She kissed him gently. "I rather like the magic new you already. If you suddenly decide to change back to a lawyer, talk to me first will you," she jested.

"No chance of that. Yes, see you later, darling. Don't forget we're supposed to be going to Orsbrick Hall for an early dinner at six. Judy is coming with all the children and Victoria has apparently asked Claire and Danielle to make some special treats, it will be quite noisy and lively I expect."

"Gosh, I'd forgotten actually. I'll see you there then. I'm going to call in on Carol at the gallery after the doctor's appointment to tell her I'm not leaving you after all and sort out the no-longer-required apartment with her friend."

In a flash, Abby was out of the door and jumped into Lynton's Mercedes. He had gone as far as a compact new hybrid car, very electrically green rather than the large and particulate belching diesel he always used to have.

Lynton lay in bed for a while longer and pondered his near escape from disaster. Lesson truly learned. He would faithfully discuss all issues with Abby without fail and not let them fester. Why had he been such a fool for so long? He still couldn't fathom that one out but perhaps his late mid-life crisis was finally over. He felt an indescribable relief disperse throughout his whole body. However, he still felt marginally guilty for not revealing the whole truth about Sabrina to Abby. But then, sometimes a little obfuscation, especially in this type of situation, was wise. As a lawyer, he could always justify it. Besides, Julian had fortunately sorted that problem.

There certainly had been a quid pro quo agreed after all … jazz lessons first in exchange for sex lessons later. But in the end, when he could no longer put off the necessary deed, he confessed to Julian. Julian had immediately contacted Kolinsky who typically found the whole business highly amusing. Kolinsky admitted he had programmed Sabrina to gradually become sexually aware, a fact the rest of the family had embarrassingly begun to notice and which fuelled the flames of innuendo with Lynton's over-enthusiasm for Sabrina's company. Apparently, if she ever achieved an orgasm, certain parts of her anatomy would glow a full spectrum of colours, blinking like a beleaguered belisha beacon, another of Kolinsky's weird, so-called humorous add-ons. Julian had found the description hugely amusing but saw that Lynton was not only seriously unamused but in a decidedly difficult pickle. So Kolinsky finally agreed, after pleading and threats from Julian, to send a new programmed charger by next day delivery. Once Sabrina plugged in for her nightly charge, the computer chip responsible for Kolinsky's fetish feature would be deprogrammed. Julian secretly exchanged the chargers and Lynton subsequently breathed a sigh of relief, but it was close, far too close for comfort, just like this very day when Abby and he almost wound up their long relationship for good. Had he been tempted with Sabrina? Nobody would ever learn that particular secret, although Julian was convinced of knowing the answer.

Chapter Seven

Walking into the sitting room, Victoria decided to have a long and solitary contemplation. Day by day, over the last month, a general unease had inexorably crept upon her. So many things were not where they should be, so many imponderables had reared their ugly heads with insufficient answers, starting with Mauveine and Isi, and a lack of purpose reined, always anathema to her well-being. At particular times in the day and night, she lurked around parts of the manor house where there might be a semblance of a sighting, perhaps a sign, maybe the return of Vultura, the black crow, at the telescope room window, something which indicated that life had returned to a previous existence when Mauveine regularly projected her ghostly presence to her and Abby.

Inside Victoria's mind, she was hankering after life like it used to be. But suppose, in the end, that Abby was right. Mauveine and Isi had also moved on since their combined 1841 return and expecting both to manifest their presence as old ghosts of the past was in many ways completely incongruous. Yet a scientific investigation was worth pursuing. The results were zilch, not even a feeling of misapprehension except from her, and Abby felt nothing amiss whatsoever in that psychic head of hers, reluctant though Victoria remained to accept a psychic persuasion. She thought about what Elizabeth eloquently voiced before they were interrupted by the actual

Langton's return and pencilled in a time in her diary to do some serious research on the physics of quantum gravity and dark energy, wormholes, parallel universes and time travel in relation to many-dimensional space … all difficult concepts and her maths was not in as good a shape as she would like. After all, she had spent a lifetime at the forefront of dye chemistry, not topological geometry. She thought again about Elizabeth, who undoubtedly wished to engage in such difficult mathematical research, but who had been avoiding the invitation to come to dinner since they had been to the rectory. Had the mention of Julian and the subtle aside which Victoria knew instinctively Elizabeth would understand, really put her off coming to Orsbrick Hall? Certainly, there had been plenty of good and legitimate reasons around the onerous duties of Elizabeth's curate role, which Reverend Langton had insisted were to be energetically undertaken in order to clear up the diocesan mess which their old friend, Reverend Welly, had left in the wake of his sudden departure to climes hippy and eastern.

Claire gently knocked on the door and came in with a welcome giant teapot and a piece of moist carrot cake which Danielle had made earlier.

"The treats for the children should go down well, Victoria," Claire began, beaming. "Danielle pulled out an old recipe from the library for a Victorian children's party, and she found a number of old moulds for jellies and cakes in one of the attic trunks, so we're going authentic tonight. I'm just putting up some streamers and I found an unused box of Christmas crackers in the pantry too and we've got balloons and small presents. To top it all, Danielle has been to the fancy dress shop in Ormskirk and got hold of a set of Victorian children's costumes, so they can have real fun dressing up … for three-year-old Toby he's going to become a pickpocket urchin out of Oliver Twist and we'll blacken his face a little with artificial soot. They'll have so much fun. I hope Judy will be pleased."

"Gosh, Claire, how thoughtful you've both been. Please thank Danielle for me, you really shouldn't have gone to so much trouble but, I must admit, I'm very pleased. We could do with something to cheer everyone up."

"Yes, I have noticed a certain glumness about the house. I didn't like to say, Victoria, but Abby especially has not been herself the last few weeks, decidedly disengaged and short of patience which is not like her. Is she alright?"

"Good question, I don't know is the short answer. But you're right, there has been rather a lot going on this year with one thing and another, making everyone unsettled. I'm looking forward to going to the States soon with Maddie, Belle and Abby. We'll make this a proper holiday too, that should bring a summer smile back to their faces. I must find Maddie, I think now we should take Fenella too."

"I'm afraid to say," Claire began, hesitantly but continued. She had witnessed a disturbing incident. "I'm not one, Victoria, as you know for telling tales, but Maddie and Belle have had an almighty row, which is so unlike them. They are so close. In fact, I've never seen such a thing before whilst I've been here. Maddie is in her room crying."

"Oh no. What on earth has gone on? ... I know Maddie has been especially edgy of late but she wouldn't say why. I'd better go and find both of them and try and sort it out."

"I'm afraid Belle has left in a temper ... she went off to follow Ned, Zac and Fenella apparently to Liverpool along with Nancy, Ade and Dottie. They're having a birthday lunch somewhere. Belle's friend, Lucinda, has driven her in apparently. The others have gone on the scooters."

Victoria sat for a moment fuming, annoyed with Maddie and Belle for arguing and especially with Ned and Zac as they had been warned explicitly not to go to Liverpool on those damned electric contraptions. She would first talk to Maddie and find out first-hand and then phone Ned. But before Victoria could start, she and Claire were disturbed by a loud banging of heavy doors outside and muted voices.

"What on earth is that truck doing in front of Julian's workshop? Good God Almighty!" Victoria exclaimed as Claire looked through the window wide-eyed, neither believing what they were seeing.

Julian, outside and looking distinctly shifty, was opening the rear doors of a refrigerated lorry as two men in white coats came out of the workshop, one holding the head and shoulders and the other the legs of Sabrina in a most undignified manner. She looked quite inert.

"Excuse me, Claire, the world is going completely bonkers today," Victoria cried, before rushing out of the back door. She shouted down the yard also noticing Maddie staring forlornly out of her window. "Julian, just hang on one minute, please. What the hell is going on here?"

Julian looked up sharply. A hasty expression of alarm at seeing Victoria passed across his face but he realised he couldn't carry on secretly as he had hoped and tell everyone without fuss later when they realised Sabrina was gone. By then, the two white-coated, Asian individuals had placed the lifeless looking Sabrina inside, slammed the doors and jumped in, revving up hard and driving off in a blur of spraying gravel.

Victoria ran across the yard and caught up, breathless, with Julian, still stood there with welding glasses around his neck and a very large spanner in his hand, now himself quite miserable.

"I'm so sorry Victoria. Everything happened in the last half-hour, I had to act."

"What do you mean everything?" she screamed out uncharacteristically but she was as much on edge as everyone. "Where has Sabrina been taken? Who were those unsavoury looking characters? This was like watching something out of a James Bond spy thriller. Has she been doped up? Sorry, robots can't be doped, what was wrong with her?"

"Kolinsky had to reclaim her right away," Julian replied solemnly. "I'm sorry I had to do something immediately. I went to the workshop to find her. Earlier, we had agreed to both go over to the solar farm substation and fix one of the heavy power inverters, a faulty system code had come into her computer. When I went into the workshop, she was slumped over my bench, lifeless and immobile as it were. I phoned Kolinsky there and then. He had been expecting the call. Apparently, the other two robots, Adam and Jenny, earlier versions from Sabrina, one based in Australia and the other in South Africa, had done the same thing yesterday. Then a couple of hours later they had autonomously revived and gone berserk. A servant in South Africa has been killed and the farm owner, an old colleague of Kolinsky got badly injured before they smashed Adam up with a JCB digger. Jenny's head blew up as she was about to strangle her owner, badly burning her. Kolinsky was confident he had ironed out that potential bug with Sabrina but had already put a contingency emergency plan in place, locally here, but I called him before he called me. He wasn't going to take any chances. He thinks the key part of her hybrid brain, which is a bio-electronic replica of a human brain but twice as powerful has possibly degenerated instantly, far quicker than planned."

"You mean like an accelerated robot Alzheimer condition?" Victoria queried, suddenly intrigued by the advanced biochemistry of this artificial intelligence creation.

Julian laughed. "I suppose so; immediate retrieval seemed a better option than her going berserk. Good job I had this heavy spanner in my hand."

"Anyway, the good news is Sabrina or a safe version three of her will return sometime in the future. I hope it is Sabrina. She's become part of the family. We'll miss her in some way. But I must admit she was developing some peculiar character traits lately."

"Yes, I don't think any of us could fail to notice the increasing signs of AI nymphomania. It appears Lynton was not one to be deterred by her … err … demands?"

Julian felt alarmed. He was hoping that unwanted issue had gone away and out of mind, clearly much more talked about than he had realised. But then he'd been so busy lately with the estate, he'd failed to notice. "No, no, it's not what you and Abby think, all quite different actually."

"Like what sort of difference? Fifty Shades of AI?"

Julian normally found Victoria's occasional bucolic humour amusing but he didn't feel in the slightest bit comically aroused.

"No, Victoria, trust me. It's for Lynton to explain what he was up to with Sabrina, not me … he'll probably clarify that tonight."

"And does Abby know about this great love-in between man and machine, especially as it's her man and our machine?"

"I just wish sometimes you wouldn't be so cynically clever by half. I expect by now she does. Okay, yes, she does. I've had a text from Lynton."

Victoria sighed. "Okay, Mr Man of Mystery, we'll wait until later. At least the children will be having fun and I'm sure Judy will, especially with all the treats and games Claire and Danielle have prepared for their party tonight. You haven't forgotten have you?"

He had but this was not a good time to admit it. "Err, no. I'll fix that inverter tomorrow with Ned and Zac. More importantly, I heard Maddie and Belle having a real ding-dong row before. Something about America but before I could find out what, Maddie had shot into her room and Belle disappeared with Ned and Zac and then I find a dead Sabrina. Would be nice to have a quiet day occasionally, wouldn't it?"

"Yes, you bet, definitely," Victoria said, despondently. What was the matter with Maddie and Belle? Leaving Julian to tidy up, she went back inside, feeling already a little sad too about Sabrina who had proven, albeit a challenging concept, very useful around the house. She had to agree with Julian's quaint observation that strangely, Sabrina had become part of the family. How should she tell the others? 'Hey guys, our robot's died' seemed a little callous but then Sabrina was only a hunk of metal and plastic. Had she been a true sentient being in the normal human sense? In many ways probably yes. She very much had autonomous volition but the drivers had been carefully pre-programmed as far as Victoria could tell, although to be fair to Julian's friend, the inventor Kolinsky, the boundary of that distinction had become very blurred. But she could see the value in so many areas for more AGIs as Maddie described Sabrina technically, especially in areas such as health care where the continuing social crisis of supporting elderly people was now beyond normal government taxation levels to solve equitably. Society had decidedly polarised even more inequitably. If you were rich enough you would and could fund your own social care help. The McKenzie family were privileged but then they had worked hard since their early years of marriage for their amassed wealth, which in Julian's case had admittedly been more luck than design, writing something which became a hot bestseller, one subsequently following after the other. But wasn't that always the case with writers? Enough of philosophising …

She headed up to Maddie's room, everywhere deathly quiet and a knock on the door elicited not even a muted response to come in, so Victoria entered anyway, hearing a faint soundtrack of something classical in the background.

Maddie was sat silently and cross-legged in the middle of her bed with a pair of virtual reality glasses on, a Christmas present which had certainly been value for money and into which Maddie would escape when stressed or needed thinking time. Victoria turned down the music streaming to her headset, distracting Maddie sufficiently that she stopped and removed her glasses, immediately seeing her mother at the end of the bed.

Victoria could see immediately that Maddie had been crying, her eyes had tell-tale black rings around them and she looked very miserable. "Sorry Maddie, I heard the music so I knew you were in here. Do you want to talk about what's happened between you and Belle? It's not like you two to fall out, is it?"

"Where is Belle, Mum? She was so insanely angry with me, I've never seen her so annoyed and it's really not my fault. The whole thing's just happened out of the blue. I hate myself for upsetting her like that. I don't think she's ever going to forgive me."

Victoria gently stroked Maddie's long hair. Being tactile, affectionate and comforting was never her style, it always made her deeply uncomfortable inside, a dark hangover from that insane childhood, but this rift was so unusual between the twins. "What's been going on, Maddie? This will strictly be between you and me if that's what you want. Better to share a problem. We scientists always resolve tricky issues that way, don't we?" Victoria sat down on one of the comfy chairs and Maddie slunk off the bed and slouched into the other. "Belle has apparently gone off with Ned and Zac to Liverpool for the day. Your father is also very worried as he heard you both rowing."

Maddie began to relax, but deep down she wished Abby was there. Sharing problems with Abby had always been so much more natural. It had never been easy talking to her mother but Maddie drew a deep breath and assembled her thoughts in order. Yes, this was a major setback but there would inevitably be other alternatives, but what and when? She was so confused but concluded that her mother had one key skill better than anyone in the house: solving tricky problems dispassionately. Sometimes, mothers and daughters needed each other and this was probably one of those times for her. She decided, as was always her way, to dive in at the heart of everything.

"I'm not going to Harvard next week, Mum. I had a letter a few weeks ago. They were reviewing the course, possibly for a September start; why was not explained. Then I had an update email yesterday. They were very apologetic but they've decided now to close my program altogether. It appears the University is undergoing a major review of its financial and ethical commitment to artificial intelligence teaching and research. There is something politically difficult happening over there, I think, and higher education is being drawn into some major bipartisan battle over whether the US should start collaborating again and come out of the last ten years of inward introspection and the America First mentality. This is probably to do with the election of the new Democratic President, Kelly-Ann Watkins, who has made a serious commitment to revitalising all education in the US. I'm so disappointed."

Victoria kept her gaze focussed on Maddie and thought quickly. More than Victoria realised, Belle had obviously set her heart on the Harvard medical school and if Maddie wasn't going there then Belle concluded that neither could she. Technically, that didn't matter. There were no reasons, financial or otherwise, why they couldn't go to separate institutions in different countries but there may likely be an emotional wrench from being parted which neither of them could reconcile presently. So Belle, taking the easy pathway, became angry and blamed her sister totally.

"Okay, I understand this is a setback for you Maddie," Victoria replied calmly, "but let's work through some logic first. You've passed your exams with top grades and you've also been accepted at Cambridge, admittedly not for an AI course, but it is the mathematical physics course you had your heart set on beforehand. And they do offer postgraduate research at the cutting edge of AI which is as well respected as Harvard."

"Yes, I know you're right Mum, and Cambridge is located in the UK and not far-away America ..." Maddie replied. "I agree in principle and I'm so glad I listened for a change and did those entrance exams. I haven't rejected their offer yet. But ..."

"Excellent," Victoria interjected not giving Maddie a chance to reflect further. "Then you can call them tomorrow and accept your place, can't you. However, I can still read you like a book ... It's not so simple is it and I think I know why. But don't tie yourself down to a relationship at eighteen. They will come and go, believe me. Studying for a top degree and your future career is far more important."

Maddie looked hard at Victoria ... who did exactly that when she was eighteen, tied herself down with Eva not exactly practising what she was preaching but Maddie was determined to rise above bringing that delicate point up. What would it resolve? She knew her mother meant well but other factors were also on her mind and she was adamant that relationship decisions were solely hers to make, whatever. "It's not about Janine. Actually, I had a quick phone call from Abby earlier. She told me about what Sabrina and Lynton have been getting up to, which is quite incredible. I suppose that now puts to rest all the snide comments and gross innuendos which Ned kept making. One day, way in the future, he may just grow up a bit."

Victoria stared and her eyes narrowed, incredulous that Abby had confided yet again in Maddie and in something extremely personal and sensitive. Why hadn't she and Abby had that conversation first? "Sorry, but whatever 'that' entails is news to me. I just don't know what's happened to Lynton these days."

"No, Mum, it's not at all what you've been thinking. Sabrina and Lynton have, unbelievably, been playing secret jazz piano together and she's unleashed his inner creativity, or words to that effect as Abby put it. Music is what he always wanted to do, apparently and he's a natural, quite brilliant. It all came as a bit of a shock to Abby. I think we're going to be treated to a musical demo tonight and hear the full story ... but keep it to yourself. I can't wait to see Dad and Ned's face. So what on earth has happened to Sabrina? I saw Dad carting her off into a white van ... where's she gone?"

"My goodness, the Lord above save our souls, as one previous Orsbrick occupant would have said, I'm sure that revelation was a real shock. I can't quite believe such a thing either, which makes it doubly sad that Sabrina is with us no

156

more, a total circuit burnout. Lynton will be understandably upset too. Actually, I think Dad already knows. He alluded to as much before Lynton confided with Abby. Ned's face we'll all love to see."

Victoria realised she was being cleverly diverted off the topic of Maddie by Maddie. She sat down and explained briefly what Julian had been forced to do. Maddie straightened up, her mind focused sharply.

"I agree, Mum. Sabrina shutting down is a definite shame, but her demise reinforces something I've been thinking about for some time. I'm not sure I'm that interested in the technical aspects of artificial intelligence and robots to be fair. What I'm really keen on is the ethics. Sabrina was a clear case in point. Her interaction with Lynton demonstrates that with clever programming she was becoming culturally sentient and thinking creatively with Lynton, man and machine in harmony. So what happens with the next generation which can then think through and devise their own culture within closed robot groups? Will there or should there be robotic art, literature, films and feasibly, stuff we have no idea of or relationship to? And, most critical, could that culture form a civilisation clash with humans? And what can we do about it if anything? That's just one issue amongst many which trouble me hugely now I've quietly studied much of the development of artificial intelligence in preparation for Harvard. The singularity, when robotic intelligence overtakes humans, which we are getting closer to exponentially, is enough of a concern. Even if we do manage to agree on built in off-switches which humans control, and that is debatable, there will always be rogue players who will want to do otherwise for their own evil ends. It's a bad world out there."

"You mean like the old 1990s film 'The Terminator', that type of scenario?" Victoria said, warming to Maddie's thought out academic arguments, something stupidly she had not really thought hard enough about when it was so obvious.

"Absolutely. When entertainment, fiction and daily reality are no longer distinguishable. Is this why Fermi's paradox is evident?"

"Fermi's paradox?" Victoria asked puzzled. "Connected with the atomic bomb?"

Maddie was enjoying, for the first time, outdoing her mother on science. "Not nuclear physics. No, Fermi in the 1950s, not long before he died, made the observation that statistically there should be billions of solar systems with planets around distant stars and that some of them could easily have evolved much earlier than us. After all, the universe is thirteen billion years old and the sun has only been around for the last four of those. So why haven't we encountered any aliens? Or even any artificial intelligence for that matter? It's not mathematically congruous that we are the sole inhabitants of our massive expanding universe with millions of galaxies containing billions of stars each. Perhaps when life eventually evolves to a certain technological level anywhere in the universe, then it self-destructs as alien finally battles robot in Star Wars type scenarios. Our astronomical observations confirm billions of earth like planets in their own solar system safe-zones where liquid water and potential habitable life could exist."

"Or maybe, Maddie, these different life-forms inhabit billions of different dimensional universes, and the only way of intercommunication is to jump through space-time like we've all experienced," Victoria said, keen to even up the debate. "Or maybe aliens simply aren't psychic like you and Abby."

"And you. Gosh, Mum, that's an awesome concept, which is why I want to study AI ethics and philosophy, certainly as a post-graduate option being developed at Cambridge. Harvard is more hard-core programming. At first, I fancied the tough challenge and still do to an extent, but like Belle changing her mind from computing to medicine, I'm doing the same. Perhaps this Harvard course glitch was genuine serendipity as Abby would say. I haven't confided in her about any of this, you're the first."

Victoria felt a warm glow inside. She wasn't competing with Abby for Maddie's attention but it was good to realise that their mother-daughter bond still had its unique strengths too. "One constancy in all this deep mind stuff is your love of maths and physics … starting that as a first degree, then looking at option modules, including AI or maybe cosmology and astrophysics, or even quantum theory could be a very sound basis."

"I've been coming round to the same thing, especially since Ada, sorry Elizabeth, came into our lives. She is so incredibly inspiring … but Belle is hugely upset and angry that she can't go to Harvard now. She's hasn't said it to anyone only me but she's been accepted by the Harvard medical faculty, Mum, on the strength of her school reference and her expected grades."

"Belle is as bad as you … why does she think she can't go? If she wants to she can. We'll support her exactly the same way we were going to for you."

"She has it in her head that you and Dad expect her and me to study and live together conjoined and that my choice, being the older twin, will always be the paramount direction she has to follow, so my not going to Harvard messes up her life totally. You mean to say neither of you would mind if we split up? We would be happy together but also we are very different in other ways. It's not such a big deal for me."

"No, of course, we wouldn't. Both of you are old and mature enough to strike out separately if you want to. I didn't fail to notice those differences during our fated voyage on the Queen Lusitania and the subsequent consequences, 1841 style. We've all been so terribly preoccupied and with everything that's happened lately, your father and I have seriously neglected sitting down with both of you and having a frank and open discussion on all this. You are each so independent that we've defaulted and left you to it for far too long. Summer resolution, I promise. Tomorrow we all sort this properly ... Belle is going to Harvard if that is what she wants. Goodness me, what on earth is that racket downstairs? Someone at the front door again? That antique brass knocker your Dad put on last week resounds all around the house. Are you expecting anyone? I'd better go and answer it."

"No, I expect Claire has gone, now we have no Sabrina. I can hear her coming up the stairs already."

A swift knock on Maddie's door was followed by a breathless Claire. "Maddie, there's a young woman outside asking for you. She seems rather distressed. Victoria, she's arrived by taxi and doesn't seem to have any money. Shall I pay the driver, he's still waiting?"

"Of course, take it out of the housekeeping money. I've got to go to the bank later so I'll replenish it. Maddie, who on earth is it? You'd better go and see."

Claire turned as she departed. "Oh, I almost forgot, I think she's American."

Maddie turned to Victoria with her hands in the air when it suddenly dawned on her. Her American acquaintances and proper friends were not that extensive. She didn't count Facebook but there was only one person who knew where she lived. No, that was not possible.

But as she approached the front door, hearing the taxi drive off, Maddie could see the rear outline of a well dressed, tall, slim female with long dark hair and tight blue jeans wearing a dark green outdoor jacket, a white woolly hat and high-heeled ankle boots. A large backpack lay at her feet. "Janine? Is that you?"

The female turned around and smiled warmly, as Maddie stood open-mouthed. "Gee, Maddie am I so darned glad to see you. I have had a terrible journey over here, not least getting through your immigration because I had no visa. But it appears our President and your Prime Minister have just signed an agreement revoking the need for US-UK visas so they let me through … one of the first I think. I took a cab from that John Lennon airport but I had no cash and those taxi guys don't use contactless, the first I've ever seen. Sorry for the bill, I'll pay it back somehow."

"Never mind the money," Maddie replied, stunned. "It's fantastic to see you in the flesh, you look even better than on Facetime. But what are you doing here?" They embraced in a passionate hug followed by a long kiss, as Claire, taken aback, looked the other way and set off quietly back into the kitchen, closing the door behind, having just paid out two hundred pounds. Victoria watched discretely from the top of the stairs. She had not really wanted to admit that Abby was right and wasn't even sure why she felt so uneasy, given her own ambiguities before she met Julian. Somehow, observing her own daughter following in the same footsteps, made her distinctly uncomfortable. But she decided to immediately subdue her innermost mindset alongside that irrational feeling. Maddie, as they had just agreed, had her own life. Without a doubt, Janine turning up was going to potentially complicate matters on a number of fronts. Victoria could see and hear that

Janine was a young and determined woman with a strong mind of her own like Maddie and would be arriving unannounced on the doorstep for a good reason. None of it gave her any confidence that the ramifications would be straightforward. The heavy rucksack indicated Janine was here to stay for the time being. A good job they had such a large house, which was beginning to feel like a grand hotel of late. Closing Maddie's door with a loud clunk, Victoria began to walk down the stairs, her heels clacking on the marble.

Alerted, Maddie and Janine withdrew instantly from their embrace seeing Victoria descending. Maddie could feel an embarrassed and unwanted blush come over her. Her character was such she never wanted to flaunt her feelings publically in front of her mother but Janine remained calm and unfazed. Realising instantly from the likeness that this was Maddie's amazing scientist mother, Dr Victoria McKenzie, with a profile on Google as long as your arm, Janine put sensible discretion into high gear and stood well apart, smiling warmly as Victoria approached.

"Hello Janine," Victoria said softly, holding out her hand. "From your accent and your appearance, Maddie has shown us endless photos of you, I don't think I'm wrong. It's a pleasure to meet you at long last. I'm Victoria, Maddie's mother."

"My pleasure, Dr McKenzie," Janine replied, shaking hands warmly, whilst Maddie looked on, not sure what to expect. "And I recognise you too. I looked up your profile on SciDat. It's a real honour to meet such a distinguished academic on dyes and polymer chemistry."

Victoria smiled. Her spot-analysis from a corridor distance appeared correct. Janine had an abundance of confidence and an innate air of privilege, but then again her Senator parents were each from old established and wealthy influential

American families and both were alumni of Yale University, her father being on the governance board. "Victoria will do fine please, Janine. We can reserve formality for academic occasions. I assume you have had a long journey and will be staying so I'll ask Claire to make up a room for you." She turned to her daughter. "Maddie, the nice one opposite Fenella's with the ensuite, I thought. Is that acceptable?"

Maddie glanced over coyly at Janine and finally smiled. "Thanks, Mum that would be great. Is that okay Janine?"

Janine instantly relaxed. She had been constantly worried how turning up out of the blue would go down, not just with Maddie, but especially her parents, but she had no choice but to leave home. "Thank you so much, Victoria, I really appreciate that, and I apologise for such short notice coming ..."

Victoria cut her short. "I'm not sure we had even a microsecond notice, but that doesn't matter, Janine. Make yourself comfortable. We'll be having dinner around seven, a bit of a family gathering has been arranged, I hope you'll like that. Anyway, Maddie will show you around. I'm sure you both have lots to talk about. I have to get to the bank."

"That's wonderful," Janine replied. "Being an only child, and my parents are always busy as you probably know with being senior politicians, I rarely experience family things. Gee, that sounds great. The last part of my journey was the trickiest actually. The taxi got lost, going round in circles because his satellite navigation was broken but some old guy near the woods, carrying a large wrench and what looked amazingly like a high voltage insulator, helpfully gave us directions."

Maddie laughed out loudly. "Oh my God, Janine, I think that old guy was my dad?" she exclaimed, Victoria looking very po-faced.

"Really? The famous steampunk author, Julian Finnis? Oh gosh Victoria, I do apologise. He wasn't that old really, in fact, he was very good looking for his age and …"

Victoria smirked, she was, as her regal counterpart in 1841 would have said, highly amused. "You have to learn, Janine, when to stop digging that deep hole you're in," she said with a laugh. "Don't worry. Julian is an old geezer sometimes especially with those trashy overalls that he always insists on wearing. Look, Claire is taking some tea and cake into the drawing room for you. I'll see you two later … Gosh, Maddie, there's Abby outside stepping out of her car now. Why is she going around the back in such a hurry? Sorry, I must go and find out before I do anything else."

As Victoria headed down the other corridor, Maddie picked up Janine's rucksack and put it on her back. "This is some weight, what have you got in here? Come along, English afternoon tea, an old aristocratic tradition in here," she giggled. "Then you must tell me absolutely everything, no secrets allowed."

"Promise," Janine replied, "But may I ask? Who is Fenella? I thought you only had one sister, Belle?"

"It's a long story, you first," Maddie whispered, closing the drawing room door quietly.

"Why are you skulking around here Abby? What on earth is the matter with you?" Victoria hissed, grabbing a startled Abby by the arm and pulling her into the boiler room entrance.

"I didn't want anyone to see me, only you. I was intending to creep in through the kitchen and catch you in your laboratory. You said you'd be working in there this afternoon. Something dreadful has happened."

"I was, but now I'm here. A lot has been going on this afternoon that's for sure. Sabrina went into a catatonic state and has been taken away by persons unknown, Maddie and Belle have fallen out big time, and to crown it all, Janine from Boston has turned up looking like she's run away from home. And before you start, I know something has gone on between Lynton and Sabrina although Julian assures me it's not what everyone has been thinking, thank goodness. So it can't be that bad can it?"

"Oh never mind about that, this is far worse ... I'm pregnant would you believe."

Cutting the air with a knife along with the deep profound silence did no justice to the stilled atmosphere around the pair. Victoria stepped backwards sharply, almost tripping over a pail of coal she had been experimenting with. "Pregnant? Are you sure? But how? Sorry daft question. But that can't be so terrible surely? Look, I know how you felt in the past about babies, but Lynton, I'm sure, will be over the moon with the news, and you are really good with children. Let's face it you had plenty of practice with my four over the years. Shall we go down to the lab and sit around the coffee area, out the way. Julian is working and apart from Maddie in her room with her best friend, the rest of the family and Fenella are in Liverpool somewhere celebrating a birthday."

They walked down into the refurbished and modern laboratory environment of the old cellar and Victoria began to make each of them a strong coffee.

"No, not for me, better be weak tea," Abby began. "No coffee, please. Yes, of course I'm very sure. I went to the doctor earlier. You know I've not been feeling good lately, tetchy with everyone, sickly in the morning. I thought it was stress, especially with Lynton's antics and I was a bit run down. I went into the clinic asking for a tonic and came out booking an appointment with the midwife. Actually, your first comment about how isn't so daft."

Victoria stared puzzled, uncomprehending why Abby was so agitated, although at forty-five Abby would admittedly have to take more care and will become one of the increasingly older mums. It was common for professional women to start a family in their forties but at least the health service was finally gearing up to that social reality, although Abby would surely go private? She had the means and between her and Lynton, certainly enough assets to enjoy the experience of motherhood without any financial worries, unlike many. But Victoria's subconscious had mulled over Abby's throw-away comment when her fast brain suddenly clicked … and she felt a pale chill creep down her spine. Surely not that? It couldn't be possible. She looked across to Abby quietly munching a digestive biscuit, gazing into space and slurping her tea of old, looking for that instant very contented.

"Tell me," Victoria began, hearing her own voice strained, which she was trying desperately to avoid. "Abby, you're not really trying to say … no, surely not. That couldn't be possible."

"Oh it can, Victoria, believe me, there isn't any other explanation. In that period of five days of ecstatic madness, I was even willing myself to conceive. I so much wanted a baby, and now I'm getting one. John Ruskin is going to be a father, sadly one hundred and seventy-five years too late to enjoy it."

"No, Abby, totally unbelievable. That process simply couldn't transfer. Think about it, we were temporary manifests in another space-time universe, an illusion built up as false reality but we returned as whole and complete as we left … Anyway, haven't you and Lynton … you know … been at it? How long gone are you?"

"A month and a half, the timing is spot on. You're sounding your usual techno-science babble self again, convincing both of us of an unassailable logic but you've forgotten what Mauveine said. We were constantly careful about what we ate, hygiene, safety etc. Why? Because all of us, including her and Isi, were mortal and could have lived or died in 1841 just like everyone else. And as for Lynton? Yes, we celebrated the day we returned, the first time for six months. I wanted to know if I felt the same after ... my experience. But he had some local difficulty which he's come up against for some time. If I was going to become pregnant I would have done many years before, when both of us were in better shape as it were. Vikki, do I need to spell out the mechanics in gory detail, why Lynton can't be the father?"

Victoria patted her hand. "No, sorry, of course not. I get it but it may still be possible. Conception isn't all about volume; I assume that John Ruskin didn't have ... err ... the same problem?"

"A fit man of twenty-five and I was at my cougar best? I mean, come on, what do you think?"

"Okay, point taken. Shit, Abby, this is a situation beyond bizarre and baffling. For once I don't know what to say."

Abby, seemingly far more nonplussed now than her tongue-tied best friend, poured out another tea and grabbed a slice of leftover cherry cake, as Victoria looked on, an exasperation of helplessness creeping over her fast. "Mmm ... one of my favourites, baking in here has become quite top notch again," she said, stuffing her face with a huge bite. "I'd missed lunch, have to eat for two now."

"So what are you going to tell Lynton and when?"

A protracted silence filled the air as Abby continued to chew blissfully. "In-between the medical centre and here I took a diversion, drove up to the top of Parbold Hill and pondered for a while over the fantastic view. Then I decided to call in at Appleby Lodge. I still miss Aunt Eveline so much, especially her wise counsel. I thought maybe being there in person would impart some wisdom?"

"And did it?"

"It was a strange experience. I've not been to the Lodge since she and Gerald died and how long ago was that? Donkey's?"

"Me neither. Pardon? ... Donkey's?"

"Never mind, I think I'm going native Mancunian again, a maternal need to revert to my roots with my new baby."

Victoria sighed. Abby was over-compensating as well as acting oddly, letting the enormity wash over her to stay sane because some of the most difficult decisions she may ever have to take were looming fast.

Abby continued. "So, against my better nature, I knocked on the door, which was answered by a Colonel Blenkinsopp, in charge apparently since Betty Grable retired."

"A military man? What, running the care home?"

"No, Colonel Anita Blenkinsopp, ex-special forces, not that you would have known by her appearance but you could see immediately the place was run on highly organised lines. In the orangery, all of Eveline's tapestries were still hanging on the walls and admired daily; it felt cathartic. Anita even showed me Eveline's old room, now converted into a new art studio in her memory but looking just as grand and splendid. Her fridge, full of special paints, was still there amazingly. When I left after twenty minutes and an online donation to the artist materials fund, I felt immediately uplifted, as if I had been speaking to Eveline herself again. Maybe psychically I had been, but I became crystal clear what I am going to do."

Still pacing the room silently, Victoria sat down again, her mind running through every angle. "Which is?"

"I will tell Lynton I'm pregnant tonight after we return home. I know what you're thinking, Vikki, I can still read that holier-than-thou face of yours and no, I am not contemplating such an awful thought, rational and sensible though it may be in your head given the circumstances. Lynton will become a proud father again and the real truth will stay locked in my heart and your discretion forever. Is that a deal?"

"Yes, of course, that goes without saying, Abby. Let's face it, you and I have too many secrets running back too many years but you know how it is in this family, a plethora of over-smart and inquisitive people especially my daughters who may have other conclusions about the truth. And, we have the time-travelling and socially reconstructed Elizabeth Milbanke around with an extremely long memory."

"You mean Ada knew about my secret fling with John Ruskin?"

Victoria roared laughing. "Abby, everyone knew of your fling. You were the talk of London society in that short blitz of ardour. You didn't exactly make discretion your top priority, did you."

Abby laughed loudly, forcing her to cough as she swallowed her tea down the wrong way. "No, I suppose not, but fortunately no one is alive to tell the tale except the redoubtable Elizabeth, through her laudanum, absinthe and opium sozzled last few months when our escapade of 'back to the future' returned into her mind. Probably it excluded little old me."

"I wouldn't bet on it ... but you can always rely on Elizabeth's legendary discretion."

They both giggled with the comical irony followed by more fits of laughter, Victoria taking turns to grab a glass of water.

Thank goodness, Abby thought, she could assume a state of light-heartedness once more with Victoria and likely Elizabeth in due course.

"To be honest, talking this through with you has properly orientated my thoughts. At the end of the day I don't care, Vikki. I just want Lynton to be happy as I will be when this little event sees its way through … and that's it. We've got plenty of money and time to enjoy parenthood and I really want it to happen now. Simple isn't it."

"Yes, if you say …"

But before Victoria could finish, a familiar voice rang out and footsteps on the old, creaking wooden staircase echoed around the laboratory. "What is it you want to happen, Abby?" Suddenly Maddie's smiling face appeared into view before she stopped at the bottom and looked up, waving her arms.

Victoria glanced anxiously at Abby. Maddie, on cue, was always guaranteed to appear when they least needed it, but Abby was ahead of the unexpected interruption and replied immediately. "Something exciting, Maddie, shared between Lynton and me which will be revealed over dinner, and not even your mother knows despite all her cunning to try and wheedle it out of me. You will all have to wait."

Victoria breathed a sigh of relief, and that was at least true. She had no idea what Lynton had really been up to with Sabrina's help.

Still waving her arms and staring up the stairs, Maddie chuntered back. "Excellent, I always love family dinners and the emergence of yet more secrets, it's what makes we McKenzie's and Warren's tick. Come on down, everything's fine."

A second clatter of feet on the bare wood sounded as person two descended the stairs quickly. Once the pair stood side by side, a smiling Maddie pointed warmly to her friend. "Abby, can I introduce you to Janine, my best friend from America, who just arrived an hour ago. I've been taking her around Orsbrick Hall. Janine will be staying for a while. Aren't you just a little bit impressed with the pad, Janine? Just look at Mum's laboratory."

Abby said nothing momentarily but stared hard at the two of them standing side by side and pondered; her artist's eye had caught the obvious immediately.

Janine promptly walked over and shook hands warmly. "I'm so pleased to meet you, Abby, Maddie never stops talking about you. Sadly, my artistic talent is near zero. All my brain seems to have gravitated around theoretical physics."

Abby laughed. "I do love your accent, Janine. Is it Brooklyn, New York by any chance?"

Janine smiled back. "Sort of, I was brought up there in New York as a child until I was eleven when my parents moved to Boston for the politics. You know your American accents well. Nobody has said that before so accurately."

"We Brits are more international than you may think, Janine, well at least some of us are. It's great meeting you so unexpectedly and what a lovely surprise I'm sure for Maddie. But aren't you supposed to be studying hard for your finals at Harvard?"

Janine shot a glance awkwardly at Maddie as Victoria carefully weighed up how much they had chatted about since Janine arrived. "Actually, I've already graduated," she said calmly. "My last six months were project based and I submitted my final thesis before Easter, early, and it was accepted unreservedly, so I've got my GPA grade. I've been graded 4.285. I've been told I'm getting a magna cum laude award."

Abby frowned. "Sorry, that means nothing to me ..."

Victoria intervened promptly, not only impressed but amazed. Janine really was as outstanding a student as Maddie. "It's equivalent to a very good first degree, almost a one hundred percent grade. That award is a great honour, well done. Were you top of your year with those marks? When do you start your postgraduate program, or maybe you have started?"

Janine blushed. "Actually, yes I was top, Victoria, sorry Maddie. I didn't want to appear like I was boasting …"

"But that's wonderful, Janine," Maddie said and gave her a congratulatory hug. "No need to hide your light under a bushel in this household, as we say, but perhaps you'd better tell Mum and Abby now."

"Tell us what?" Victoria replied, a mild glower beginning to emanate. She just knew all was not straightforward.

"I'm … err … well, I've kind of left home and Harvard and not started a post grad course. When I heard that Mad's course had been dropped, I realised she wouldn't be coming over so I contacted Cambridge University and had a long chat with the Dean of Trinity College, a kind of hero-worship place for me here in England. When the Dean heard what I'd achieved and studied she was very interested in my application, and Mom, despite my father's reluctance, has agreed to fund me if I got accepted."

"Have you fallen out with your parents, Janine?" Victoria continued. She had guessed that likely scenario from the outset of Janine's unexpected and flustered arrival but was surprised at the resourceful fallback which Janine had arranged so quickly. No wonder Maddie was looking five hundred percent perkier.

"Janine also has savings to use from when she was teaching first year students," Maddie added, "but she can't access them until she's set up a bank account which I said I would help her do tomorrow so I've lent her some of my own money, Mum, to tide her over, I hope that's okay. But I think you'd better tell Mum the rest of the story, Janine, don't you?"

"Rest of what story?" Victoria asked, suspiciously. There was too much happening here for her liking. She always had an innate dislike of change and disruption, but on the other hand, could see immediately that Maddie was back to her old self.

"Let Janine tell us, Vikki. This all sounds interesting, grab a seat each of you. I can see you're both bursting with something exciting," Abby said, sensing the usual Victoria stiff and formal reaction showing its head, never happy letting Maddie off her leash.

Janine smiled taking an immediate liking to Abby and pulled up the two chairs which she and Maddie plonked into. "What the Dean told me is that Cambridge and Harvard are collaborating on a special artificial intelligence project with Eratosthenes, a joint spin-off company of Google and Space Ark who are building autonomous robots for inter-planetary travel."

"Mmm ... finding an algorithm for prime numbers, I like the historic Greek name," Victoria muttered, finally listening properly.

"What are you on about Vikki?" Abby said, screwing up her forehead.

"The Sieve of Eratosthenes. Oh, never mind Abby, please continue, Janine, precise and to the point please."

Janine took a deep breath. She was trying hard to be concise, having got the measure of Victoria, who had less patience for waffle than even her own mother. "They are planning to land on a near-Earth asteroid next year and bring a sample back; a Mars moon will be next. The eccentric CEO of Eratosthenes, a young guy called Kit Astenbaum, is a former star Cambridge postgraduate, a Brit and originally from this region somewhere, a place, I think, called Tarleton? And he is apparently very keen on finding a site in Lancashire to develop a research institute, kind of in the spirit of bringing the next industrial revolution back to where it first started. Cambridge has finally agreed because research and development space around there has now become so oversaturated and there's no decent local housing availability. I told Mom who is still on the Harvard governing board; Daddy resigned a while back. She's spoken to the Director who is also keen to create an elite graduate teaching facility, sponsored through Eratosthenes and to offer joint degrees with Cambridge, a partnership never done before. When I told Mom I was heading here she asked me to check out anywhere suitable. In summary, if it gets off the ground there's a research place for me and I'm sure one for Mad too."

Maddie's eyes lit up. "I've had a mind-blowing thought, which Janine and I have just chewed over. Why don't you and Dad offer the land, now you've bought all that extra acreage, especially around where your old cottage used to be? There's the spur to the motorway nearby being built. Wouldn't you fancy sponsoring a new, prestige institute like that?"

Abby clapped enthusiastically. "What a super dream idea. Victoria, cheer up, it's an amazing proposition to facilitate a cutting edge research and teaching centre in artificial intelligence. You and Julian have the land that's for sure and the means. I'm sure you'd get local planning permission, given the debt they owe you with your factory in Burscough and the amount of employment you provide. Full marks for entrepreneurial spirit, Maddie, once again the McKenzie's are in the vanguard of the next industrial revolution, well digital revolution I suppose, in keeping with family tradition."

Victoria's thoughts were circulating around at speed. It wasn't the concept, so out of the box and unexpected. She could see the logic and all manner of spin-offs and Maddie would be around a lot longer. She was not looking forward to such rapid nest-fleeing of the children if the truth was on the table, but Abby knew that instinctively. Both had a desire to remain close to Maddie. However, something else bothered her, more of an instinctive feeling; she had no precise idea what unusually, but the something was decidedly Janine. "The idea has merit but I would need to have your father onboard. I'm not so sure Julian would be supportive, he probably has other ideas about the estate and …"

"I can confirm that Julian is very much onboard. I can't think of a better idea for those ten acres of scrub and spent heathland," a deep voice resounded from the stairwell. They looked up to see Julian coming down the steps, still in his old overalls with oil over his face. "I've just finished. I caught those last sentences of Maddie and Abby. Don't know what you're talking about but in principle count me in anyway. Hello, Janine, I assume it's you … Claire told me we have a new visitor. I think we met earlier, a close encounter with a lost taxi. I'm Julian Endersby-Finnis, Maddie's Dad."

"A pleasure to meet you Mr McKenz … sorry Mr Finnis," she replied, weighing up just how old he was, certainly older than Victoria.

"Just call me Julian, a lot less complicated," he replied with a grin. "I'll see you all at dinner later and then you can both tell us more. I have to get changed and walk the dogs seeing as Ned and Zac aren't back yet as promised. Where are they, Maddie?"

"In Liverpool somewhere, the Black Anchor I think," Maddie replied, watching her father dive back up the stairs. She turned, concerned, to Victoria. "Mum that reminded me, there was something else I came down to tell you. I've tried calling Belle and also Ned and Zac on their mobiles and I've texted but it's really odd. No answer from any of them, not even a voicemail response to leave a message, the phones just ring and ring. And Dad's right, they should be back now. Fenella is with them too but the phone that we got her is still in her room."

"I wouldn't worry," Abby said, comfortingly. "They're probably in a dead zone. There are still some notorious ones in Liverpool, despite the so-called ubiquitous 6G. Dale Street, where I think The Black Anchor is located from ancient memories, has a couple apparently. I expect they've forgotten the time, celebrating. Anyway, Janine, do you like cooking?"

"It's a real hobby of mine, particularly spicy Mexican," Janine replied, intrigued.

"Good, because I assume Maddie has missed the kitchen completely which I shall personally show you, as I'm a fellow cook too unlike the rest of this household. Victoria has a kitchen to behold planned by yours truly, me. If you both go up, I'll follow in a second."

"Janine, I never knew you were a culinary geek?" Maddie chortled as they both headed off.

Abby turned to Victoria once they were out of earshot. "You haven't noticed have you?"

"Noticed what?"

"Who does Janine remind you of?"

Victoria stopped. "I don't know, okay enlighten me?"

"Think, the picture in the hall, admittedly a more modern version with a wholly different style but some of the facial features are very similar even in the year 2026."

Victoria stared, and her eyes narrowed. "Eh? Sorry, I still don't get it, Ms Picasso. You do too much painting for your own good and see things no one else does. But I do agree that

Janine has sharp, distinctive features quite like Maddie and is very confident and determined. Too confident, I would say, for her age."

"Yes, just like you and Mauveine were. Do you see it now? Oh, never mind, we clearly need to give the Victoria brain more time to digest the obvious. I tell you, Vikki, dinner at Orsbrick Hall hasn't lost its ability to remain unfailingly illuminating, and we haven't even started with Lynton's escapade yet, let alone Judy, progenitor extraordinaire. It appears the twins are actually triplets, so she has just texted. How could they have missed one extra? So much for the restructured NHS maternity service, I'm going private."

Chapter Eight

With crowds of people propping up the bar in the lounge of the Black Anchor, Ned pushed forward to order the next round of drinks. True to his word, he was sticking to soft drinks but was increasingly concerned with Ade and Zac piling on the alcohol. Lunch, consisting of fish, chips and mushy peas all round courtesy of Ade's hard-earned bonus, followed by homemade apple pie and custard, went down very well, especially with Fenella, who not only was enjoying a new social experience but had become the unexpected centre of attention. Increasingly less shy, she dominated the conversation with witticisms and jokes, now much more at ease picking up what was talked about in order to develop an interesting discussion. She demonstrated a prodigious capacity for nightly reading from her iPad tablet which Zac had bought her, absorbing enormous amounts of information into a sharp and highly capable brain. Over a month, Fenella had transformed from being an odd, shy spectacle, totally out of her depth in a world she unwittingly entered, to become one of the crowd, overtly enjoying the unending adoration of Zac, despite twinges of discomfort from Dottie on the other side of the table. Nancy and Ned, knowing Zac had zero sensitivity when it suited him, had agreed a plan to distract Dottie as much as possible, by engaging her to talk about her new course and her plans for University in the coming autumn. Also, Belle and Dottie had increasingly become close friends, having finished their exams and effectively left school for good.

Ade, watching Ned at the bar struggling with the drinks, nudged Zac and they headed over to help. Over the chatter between the other girls, Fenella silently watched Zac depart and then suddenly turned to Belle, who was continuing an animated conversation with Nancy and Dottie. "So, you'll be heading to Boston and Harvard on your own to do medicine? Do you not find the prospect daunting, leaving home and Maddie behind for the first time?"

Belle looked up sharply, disarmed for a moment by the uncanny and bold straightforwardness from Fenella. How did she know that? Belle was certain Maddie had not spoken to anyone whatsoever, not even Abby, definitely not their parents and most certainly not Fenella. This major fallout was between only her and her sister and no hint of anything amiss to the rest had been given during the day. Still agitated, Belle had no idea what she was going to do next. Taking up the offered place at Harvard Medical School was simply not going to be an option if Maddie wasn't going. That was the way things were and her mother would be appalled by the very notion. No, she would likely have to apply late to Cambridge instead, the same as Maddie, and pray that her predicted top grades would sway the tutors to offer a place, if there were any left. Medicine was booming again now the government had removed all restrictions on doctor training and offered substantial bursaries to every successful applicant. Two years previously they also barred ninety percent of foreign students from the European Union and elsewhere entering Britain.

Ned was the first to return with his tray of drinks followed closely behind by Ade and Zac.

"Listen you two," Ned called out to them. "I really think this should be your last pint. Getting caught riding those scooters back is decidedly dodgy. You don't want to lose your electric licence because that will mean you'll not be eligible for an ordinary full licence for ten years besides an extortionate fine. And the girls are riding on the back. It ain't responsible, dudes." He turned to the girls, deathly silent. "Hey what's wrong with you four, like you've all seen a ghost?"

Fenella laughed loudly, everyone staring at her. She stopped, seemingly embarrassed and spoke softly. "We're all waiting for Belle to answer my question, Ned."

"What question?" Zac interrupted, intrigued and vaguely uncomfortable seeing his sister looking forlorn suddenly.

Ade sat down and turned to his sister. "Dottie? What's going on?"

Belle had now composed herself. She had no intention of talking about her and Maddie to anyone until she calmed down and decided what to do. Besides, they both needed to talk to their parents who had their hearts set on the whole Harvard venture. Belle assumed it was highly likely that Maddie had already spoken to their mother anyway by then and they could all have a mature discussion tomorrow. But for some bizarre reason, Fenella had let the cat out of the bag and raised the issue in a very condescending way, as if both she and Maddie were childish simpletons and not mature enough to influence their own lives, which wasn't true.

"Come on then, Belle, come clean. What has Fenella asked you?" Ned began again, grinning stupidly, sensing his sister was in a pickle so that he could make some kind of joke about her as usual.

"Okay, seeing as everyone's listening, it's very simple," Belle began, sick of Ned as ever. "Maddie isn't going to Harvard for reasons unknown. Her course has been suddenly cancelled, so all the planning, buying a flat as well as my medical course are off too. I only heard this morning and flew into a rage. Coming out with you guys has been a good safety valve to calm down and get my act together."

"Whoa, hey Belle, that's a bit of a bummer. I'm really sorry for you, I know you were so looking forward to it. I could tell something was up," Zac chipped in.

"Actually," Belle replied calmly. "Fenella seems to know already and she asked me how I'll feel about going to Harvard on my independent own; as if that preposterous prospect would even vaguely materialise. You know how Mum and Dad are."

Ned said nothing but nodded in agreement. Not a good time for doing his usual cynical jesting at his sister's expense. There were umms and ahhs of sympathy from the others but Fenella sat and said nothing until they changed the subject and began to pick up their drinks.

"But you will go, Belle, I know these things," she said in a low voice, followed by the faintest of smiles. Belle stared at Fenella but made no comment, a private unease wafting around in the back of her mind.

"Anyway, enough serious stuff, I'm sure it'll get sorted, Belle, knowing you," Ade said jauntily to his former girlfriend, trying to push the conversation back to normality. "I think we'd better put Ned out of his misery, don't you, Zac?"

"What misery?" Ned fired off, indignantly.

"This," Ade and Zac responded, downing their pints of lager in synchronised large gulps as Ned gazed forlornly at his fizzing glass of Coca-Cola. "Next one already I think Zac, your shout."

"I can't believe this stupidity ..." Ned began, horrified, as Ade and Zac laughed loudly and the girls looked on, mystified.

Ade started to explain. "In half an hour, my loony brother and his weird girlfriend, Esme, are coming here with her horse box and them-there scooters will be heading for a safe passage home alongside Bozo, the randy stallion. We'd better get Ned a proper drink or maybe two to make up for lost time," Ade continued. "Don't worry everyone, we're booked in here for the night to sober up. Boys share one room, girls the other two, although there is always scope for a bit of mix and match," Ade continued, staring lustily at Belle again who glanced away, unimpressed.

Ned laughed heartily and stood up, waving his arms about. "Get them in, Zac, my boy. Make mine a flagon of their special brain-blower, have to make up for that lost time."

Nancy glared in disgust.

Suddenly Fenella interrupted and they all turned. "No Ned, I don't think so," she said in a soft, deep voice. "You're going to be needed sober and definitely not drunk."

He moved behind her, his large hands on the back of her chair ready to make one of his classic jests when a loud whining sound suddenly permeated the entire room, growing louder and louder, distracting everyone. The bar immediately filled up with a glaring bright white light, throbbing with a blinding intensity, forcing them to cover their eyes. A deathly silence filled the air for a few seconds then intense screaming started from the corner and Ned felt increasingly dizzy. The room was swirling in an eddying orange blur in front of him, he could barely stand and the noise escalated in intensity and frequency. He clasped his hands around his ears and shouted for all he was worth. "What the fuck? Run Nancy, all of you, run for your life now …" before falling, entwined around Fenella, down and down into a vortex of black, swirling mist. The last thing he saw was her face, eyes blazing, and a wide smile drew across her mouth. She had clasped him tightly in a full embrace, her hot breath pouring over his mouth, all encompassing as her red lips pressed hard and deep into his …

A loud screeching filled Ned's ears. He was struggling to wake from the deepest of deep sleep, his head pounded and throbbed mercilessly and a thick satin quilt was half-pulled over his face. He was lying in a hard bed of some kind and tried desperately to open his eyes but they stayed well shut, almost like the eyelids had been glued down. He needed to come alive gradually. How much had he drunk? The screeching stopped momentarily but then started again when he realised he was listening to seagulls and the bed he lay on was gently pitching about. Voices and noises could be heard somewhere in the distance.

One eye began to slightly open and he looked up, blurrily, at a wooden slatted ceiling. A tiny window was letting in daylight at the side and he could see blue sky and white clouds. Was he dead and staring at heaven? His mind tracked immediately through final recollections in the Black Anchor, the dazzling lights, painful siren sound and finally disappearing into some swirling void with Fenella wrapped around him. What the fuck was happening? He realised he was stark naked and slowly lifted himself up from soft, deep scented pillows and opened his eyes fully, staring out of the window at endless white foaming waves undulating off into the distance He was in some strange ship's cabin out in the sea somewhere, and he could see endless rope rigging outside. What?

"Glad to see you've finally woken up at last," a soft voice sounded. "That was quite a performance you provided me with last night. Now you know why I needed you relatively sober, although the bottle of whisky we consumed together was sufficient to loosen the inhibitions but not dampen your ardour. Shall I get you some breakfast?"

Ned turned towards the other side of the room, his mind reeling. He had zero recollection of what he'd been doing but wished otherwise. Nor could he believe he was looking or rather squinting at a familiar and very beautiful, tall, long haired woman, who wore only a semi-diaphanous, knee-length silk crème nightdress with a revealing split up the front. She stood purposefully and unabashed before the open wooden door, in the direct glare of the sun's rays pouring light in. Never in a million years could he have imagined who he was staring at. His eyes were playing tricks.

"Fenella? I don't believe this. Is it actually you? What's going on, where are we? More to the point, who the fuck are you?" he croaked, already desperate for water. His throat felt parched and dry, probably from excessive alcohol and he was certainly starving hungry. She picked up a rough-looking pitcher from the floor and poured water into a large clay mug which he gratefully took and guzzled down the lot. It tasted odd.

"Welcome to my ship, Ned," she replied confidently. "Ahh, here comes breakfast. Sorry, not quite what you're used to, your meal is salted bully beef and some stale bread but we will get fresh supplies soon. However, we do have coffee, my one expensive indulgence. And, to answer your first question, yes I am Fenella but my men here call me Fanny. But we'll wait until you've eaten before we explore the rest."

Behind her, a short, slim man appeared, holding a wooden tray with a plate piled up high with something. He deferentially touched his cap. "Madame Captain, here be the food you requested," he said in a peculiar accent. "Is it for the renegade here? He isn't tied securely. Should I get some rope and lash his legs to the hooks?"

Ned stared, mystified, at the man's apparel, trying hard to get his slow and fuzzy brain into gear. This guy was obviously a sailor but wearing the most unusual clothing. The only item vaguely familiar was his brown, wool knit cap. Over him, he wore a dark blue and single-breasted open jacket with a matching high neck vest under a blue and cream checked shirt buttoned up; not cotton but maybe linen? What did he know? The trousers looked like brown army canvas but hung very wide and bulky, reminding him of old pictures of men wearing loons in the nineteen-sixties. And those black pumps on his feet? Why no decent boots? The man's hair was very short at the sides but tied back in a small ponytail. All a bit retro but smart. Where on earth was he?

The sailor handed the tray to Ned who snatched the plate and fork and began eating voraciously. Salty the food certainly was but surprisingly tasty, and he'd had worse bread. But then he was so ravenously hungry that dead dog would have been tempting. He had to survive, first and foremost, and try and work out what to do next.

"Merci, René, mais non. L'homme ne se rendra n'importe où il sera ici."

Fenella and the sailor laughed heartily. Ned stared at his pock-marked and weather-lined face. He was probably only in his early twenties but looked like shit. Ned knew Fenella had spoken French but hadn't a clue what she said, obviously something that amused them both. The sailor handed her a couple of mugs of a dark, steaming liquid and vanished. A couple of other guys similarly dressed walked past outside, stared at him briefly and also laughed. Fenella quietly closed the door on a crude latch and handed him one mug … of what was presumably the hot coffee but looked and smelled like black tar, not exactly the same as Abby's best barista mix in the Red Lion.

"That was René, he is my personal servant. Like half the crew here, he's French. The rest are local seamen enlisted from Liverpool."

"How come you're captain of your own ship, women just don't …" he blurted stupidly and wished he hadn't, catching the immediate disdain. He should know better not to act like Ade, given Nancy's strong views and he had the bruises to show for it.

"I still need to dispossess you by whatever it takes, of some unsavoury, antiquated views. Some women do, Ned, and I'm one of them," she said menacingly, holding an antique pistol pointed alarmingly to his nether region. This was certainly not the shy Fenella of old.

Finishing off the food and now very weary, he put down the plate and shivered. His bare chest was feeling the chill. Fenella opened a wooden trunk in the corner and pulled out a grey shirt similar to what he had seen on René. "This should be the right size for you, I must admit it was difficult finding one big enough from the stores. The rest of your clothes and an outdoor coat are inside. I saw you admiring his dress … smart isn't it. I had their apparel specially made, exactly the uniform worn by the elite British Navy. The deed took some doing and the usual bribery, but it's amazing what a few hogsheads of fine Jamaica rum will get me."

She tossed the shirt to him and he put it on readily, but it felt very rough. They both sipped the hot coffee in silence. Feeling much better, he tried again to marshal his thoughts into something sensible.

She pointed to a bucket under a sink at the other end. "I think you can guess what that's for. There's cold water in the barrel. You will be pleased to know that as my special guest you won't be sharing a cabin, unlike the others. This one will remain yours and mine is next door … you only have to knock lightly," she said, giggling, and rapped the wooden wall. She threw a dressing gown around her. "Now, I'm afraid I have work to do. I must plot a new course and quickly check that our other guests are not too uncomfortable. You'd better get your clothes on, René will be back for you, we need to get you trained up and acclimatised." In a moment she had the creaky door wide open again and sharp sunlight filled the cabin.

"Wait," he cried. "Fenella, you said the others. What's happened to Zac and Ade and Belle and the girls? Are they on this ship too? Surely you haven't forgotten Zac, my little brother, after all he's done and felt about you?"

Ned was desperate for a glimmer of sense. Maybe some appeal to Fenella's former reasonableness was all he could hope for but this wasn't the same Fenella they knew yesterday. She was a different person, a polar opposite of the shy and retiring girl who appeared from nowhere into their lives at Orsbrick Hall. But then it struck him. What Zac had purported to have worked out about her, all the psychic time travel crap of Maddie and Abby again and that mumbo-jumbo of Fenella being a back-to-the-future throw away from Victorian times. In reality, it had washed over him like the rest of the spook stuff, that nonsense was their turn-on. None of it had any effect on him but he went along with the story to keep the peace and nerd Zac had almost turned human as a result of the subtle wiles and demands of his new friend, Fenella. But the environment surrounding him and what had happened the night before was massively weird. He had no explanation and here he was on an ancient looking ship, he could even smell the salty air. What if, he reflected, his mind focused back on the sailor dress? What if Zac's rantings were true and he was now the one passing through time and going backwards? He'd almost forgotten, he'd just asked Fenella a question.

Fenella laughed quietly. "Yes, poor old Zac. I was cruel leading him on, but the tactic was necessary. I wanted you from the moment I entered Orsbrick Hall, but I knew quickly my desire was not possible. You were not attuned to me ... or anything else much, except beer and that half-wit girlfriend of yours, Nancy."

"What do you mean necessary? ... And where is Nancy? I hope she's safe, otherwise ..." he began, anger burning as he jumped aggressively out of bed, still naked.

Interrupting him, Fenella smirked again. "There is no otherwise Ned, especially looking like that. I'm afraid you're with me for a purpose as well as the benefits. Okay, you'll find out shortly. Zac and that great big imbecile Ade are here too, but alas, learning their new job. Admittedly, it took five of my best men to hold Ade down and teach him a lesson, not that he was going anywhere out in the middle of the sea, but a persuasive good kicking did the trick. He's cooperative now, especially as the well-being of quiet and cerebral Zac depends on him behaving."

Ned felt some sense of relief; at least his brother and Ade were nearby. "So, where is Nancy?"

"I'm not a totally cruel person, Ned. You'll be pleased to know your irritating sister Belle, half-wit Nancy and dull Dottie remain happily in the Black Anchor."

"Really? So they are safe?"

"Mmm, safety is a relative terminology. You may like to know that the hotel now isn't quite the same Black Anchor, a somewhat earlier version you might say, the authentic Black Anchor, full of rough sailors with pockets of flowing money and wanton women. By the way, all women in there are wanton by expectation, exceptions being those serving behind the bar. Life can be tough in these times, can't it, especially for females unless they create their own independent destiny like me but I'm sure Belle, Nancy and Dottie will never be on the wrong side of the divide. You get the gist, Ned?"

He stared, puzzled, what the hell was she talking about? Then the penny dropped. "What date is it today?"

Fenella smirked again. "Getting around to the obvious has taken you an inordinately long time. I see your subconscious will fight anything you don't want to accept. Well, the date is exactly as you left yesterday, Monday, the 8th of May but a slight change of year, my favourite seeing as I fortuitously departed it. We are in 1865, isn't that wonderful? I hope I haven't made a bad choice with you, Ned, but I did watch you swim, sans pantaloon across the pond, a source of inspiration in many ways ..."

Inside a dank room, swells of dirty water glistened on the blackened and cobwebbed ceiling. A drip-drip plopped monotonously from various cracks above onto the slippery red-tiled floor. Belle gazed up, alone and frightened, desperately trying to find her bearings, thinking at first she was in some horrendous prison. She shivered in the cold, then realised why after seeing what she was wearing ... a long, green cotton dress, made of one type of thin fabric only, probably cotton with some frilly lace on the sleeves and a leather apron tied around her. What had happened in the Black Anchor? A shaft of light struggled through the rusty bars of a slatted open window behind a wooden ceiling hatch at the other end, through which a draught of cold, salty air blew over her face. She was standing next to a wooden tray holding metal tankards, on top of a hewn trestle. In front, a huge barrel rested on the wet floor and she could smell beer, although it wasn't especially pleasant. She was down a pub cellar somewhere. Was it inside the Black Anchor? Surely not this decrepit?

Suddenly she heard voices and someone clattered down the rickety steps behind her. She swallowed hard on seeing his dirty face, covered in a thick bushy beard. The well-built man was wearing a grey cloth cap and a dirty waistcoat over a very grubby shirt, with brown corduroy trousers and heavy black boots. The aroma of body sweat almost overpowered her as he approached, a pipe puffing in his mouth.

"Well, young Annabelle, my son said you were down 'ere. Name's Henry Abbinant, owner of this fine establishment the Black Anchor, which goes back many years before you and me I daresay," he said, in a funny accent, half Burscough and half Irish. "And I understand you've experience behind bar, but seeing the way you're a day-dreaming I got my doubts already, lass." Breathing heavily, he banged his pipe gently against the barrel of beer and a large blob of tarry remains dropped to the floor. "Aye, this cask be full, right enough. Well then, fill some of them tankards, my girl, I need to test quality. If it's as shite as the last lot from Thannets, that crook Arthur Jones will be back pronto like, if his fucking old horse doesn't drop dead beforehand." He laughed and then coughed, a horrible guttural racking sound, followed by a large spit of phlegm in the corner. "Apologies my girl, this bronchitis hasn't shifted since Christmas, despite eating a damn hundredweight of these new fangled Fisherman Friends." He popped a large, purple coloured sweet from his pocket straight into his mouth.

She now knew for definite, the 1841 escapade had been seared evermore into her psyche. Somehow she was back, back in time again but when? How or by what means would have to wait but just as before, she needed to get her act together and fast. Survival was critical. At least she didn't feel overwhelmed and unsure like the last time and would try and play it well and play for time. Clearly, she had some sort of history again or would need to make it up, probably both. Where were her glasses? She was struggling a little.

It was true, she did have some illegal bar experience. Three months back undertaken behind the bar of the Rushton Arms in Scarisbrick, a favour for that creep landlord Jason, one of Ade's brother's friends, desperate during a week when his barmaid and girlfriend had gone absent without leave. Her parents never knew of course and Maddie was typically offhand and prudish but likely envious that she, Belle, had been asked first, and the jealousy increased when she became good at the job.

Belle stared at the wooden tap near the bottom of the barrel. At least someone had put that in, likely the son, whoever he was. "Straight away, Mr Abbinant, you can call me Belle, most people do," she replied, jovially. "Hopefully, this will be nice and clear and sweet-smelling of course with the hint of a head." She carefully poured out the large tankard until full and handed it to him.

"Heaven's above girl, you really are posh with that plum voice of yours. I didn't believe Ernest, the fool doesn't know what posh means. Run away from Lord and Lady Muck have you? We don't ask in this house but you'll be a nice novelty for the scum we serve in here. At least you look presentable. Pour yourself one too, I want you to try it first and tell me what you think … And if you drop dead I'll have to change me supplier!" He laughed again but stopped this time just before the cough was about to start once more.

Reluctantly, she poured out half a tankard but then had a sudden brain wave. She remembered Abby sucking through a box of Fisherman's Friend last autumn for a racking cough, in her case after she had resumed smoking for a month but then Abby stopped thank goodness. That stuff was historic medicine and had been invented by some quack pharmacist in 1865. Was that the time period she was in? Henry Abbinant certainly looked mid-Victorian with the full beard, short hair and dress, lots of men's fashion had changed since 1841 and the clothing, dirty though it was, looked far better made, likely by machine. Belle looked into the tankard. The dark brown beer was crystal clear with a dainty head. She gently smelled the aroma ... mmm ... very pleasant. She took a few sips trying to look confident, taking heed that beer was often preferred to water as more safe and sanitary, centuries back, and smiled. The beer was actually very good, genuine cask ale of old, and far better quality than the manufactured keg crap which they had in the Rushton.

"I take it that barrel is satisfactory then, young lady?" Abbinant said, smirking and downed his tankard in one. "Yes, truly excellent, I'll get Ernest to connect up the pumps. Reckon that'll be gone in two days. You're hired I do declare, now where are you from ..."

Before the conversation got any further, racking her brains for a credible story, they heard loud yelling and screaming going on above. "Better see what that idiot son of mine is up to, come on."

He bounded up the steps as she followed warily, hitching up her long skirt. They immediately entered into a fulsome bar area which led to the main corridor, without doubt now in her mind, mid-Victorian surroundings, to see a young woman, sporting a mass of bright orange curly hair and dressed in a gaudy, long red skirt and flowery, white blouse, being dragged kicking and screaming out of a nearby room by presumably Henry's son, Ernest. He was short and stocky, about eighteen, also with curly hair, but quite ugly, Belle thought, and stupid looking, wearing a checked flat cap and a blue, long sleeved shirt with rolled up sleeves. Over the top, dark blue dungarees were hoisted up precariously with red braces.

"What on earth are you doing lad? Bring 'er in 'ere for fuck's sake. Who is this girl?"

Still shouting, the person shoved Ernest's hands off her arms and then pushed him with such force he stumbled against the door post, banging his head hard much to his father's amusement.

"Lass has a feisty temper and is a strong 'un. Can certainly make the better of you, yer damned fool," Abbinant cried out.

Belle stood quietly and stared wide-eyed as the girl turned, her bright red face distraught and eyes wide and frightened. They looked at each other. It was Nancy, Jesus Christ.

But before anything was said, Ernest, rubbing his bruised forehead, began to speak in a high-pitched, squeaky voice but distinctly Lancashire. "Annabelle, yon cousin Nancy ere ain't no good as a whore, despite her wholesome looks. I should have listened to yer, she be arguing straight off with the client, she did." He turned to his father. "Mr McKenzie, he wants a virgin as usual and he says she's been fucked more times than a bitch on heat and got reet angry he did, stormed off, saying he was going t' Pump House on docks."

Belle shuddered and didn't dare think what had transpired but clocked in her head the client name ... coincidence or what? She had to ask, her sharp brain simultaneously running through her ancestry maths. She stared at Nancy, now silent, and wiped her finger across her mouth a few times, a makeshift sign ... to keep quiet for now. Nancy, fortunately, took the hint and stood sullen and uncommunicative. Belle then asked. "Mr Abbinant? Was Mr McKenzie by chance a Mr James McKenzie, master of Orsbrick Hall?"

Muted silence filled the air. Nancy stared hard, her own quick brain whirring. She was totally in disbelief and denial this was reality around her and remained convinced she was caught inside a bad dream but felt much relief seeing Belle. But why were they both wearing Victorian apparel? And who was James McKenzie?

Henry Abbinant was taken aback at first, but being quick on the uptake fired back. "Indeed Annabelle, he was for sure, but 'ow do yer know that, young lady? You his bastard daughter then?" He laughed and coughed violently once more. Belle grabbed a box of Fisherman's Friend on the bar and handed him one quickly with a cloth, but she had to stay clear. That cough may be tuberculosis, although she saw no blood come out.

"I see at least you're brought up well, my girl. Thank you sincerely," he said softly, wiping his sweating brow.

"I'm no relation, sir, but I knew Mr McKenzie's daughter well since childhood, she taught me to read and write. I lived in a cottage nearby on the estate with the village blacksmith. My mother was off the boats. Never knew her or my father. And to answer your question earlier, I had to leave. The cottage burned down."

Nancy stared silently and pinched herself but didn't wake up. Where was Belle getting this story from or was she making it up as she went along?

Henry smiled. "Aye, that makes sense. His daughter taught thee to speak proper too no doubt. McKenzie, rich bastard aristocrat and arrogant, never did like him. The Pump House are welcome to his custom. He mentioned a daughter once come to think of it, Lydia be her name. Studied painting, he was reet proud of 'er."

Belle nodded … Shit, Lydia was around Orsbrick, but no mention of Mauveine, but then she hadn't been formally recognised as his daughter until later.

Henry continued. "As too, I think I would be proud, Annabelle, if I had a daughter like you, reet proud I'd be. Instead, I have an oaf for a son. But he's not always as daft as he looks. So, Ernest, what do you propose we do with Nancy 'ere? Be quick lad, we must open shortly, only closed the doors temporary like whilst that bastard McKenzie were indoors."

"Nancy says she's very experienced with horses, Father, and Rory is desperate for help since his brother, Frederick, did a bunk, so she can help in the stables at back. Also, I got other bar covered too. Found a girl this morning wi' head in her hands, sat on the step staring into distance down Dale Street at the carts and mumbling about where the others in the bar had gone. She looked presentable so I asked her if she was 'ere for the job and could she pull a pint handle? She said yes. She's been busy sorting out snug since, done a reet good job already."

Ernest turned and shouted down the corridor. "Hey Peggy, get in 'ere will you and meet my da."

Nancy and Belle turned to see a neat woman, hair in a tight bun, wearing a long brown corduroy skirt and soft linen shirt, well protected by a large clean apron. Their mouths dropped instantly … Dottie had appeared and she undoubtedly looked the part of an efficient barmaid. How come Ernest was calling her Peggy? Dottie looked eerily at ease with the predicament, almost as if she had worked it out already. Just not possible Belle decided quickly, thinking about what happened to her previously, although Dottie was very bright and street-wise. She had secured a scholarship to study English Literature at St

Hilda's College, Oxford University in September. Maybe Zac had spilled some family secrets which wouldn't be surprising given how close he and Dottie had been before the breakup, especially after that strange incident she and Zac experienced involving Isi and the burning barn, a trigger of the original time return to Orsbrick Hall and Morag in 1841.

"Shall I take them to the room in the attic?" Ernest ventured, looking towards his father who peered at his pocket watch. "Lizzie has done cleaning and sorted out blankets and sheets and their bags are up there now too."

"Yes. The old suite your grandmother had before diphtheria took her seems appropriate," Henry replied. Nancy grimaced. "There's a single and a double bed in there. You girls can fight over who gets to sleep alone. We open in one hour and work starts then, three bob a week, board and food included. Take it or leave it."

"Thank you Mr Abbinant, most generous, we'll take it," Belle said gratefully, staring hard at Nancy and Dottie who both nodded. A moment later they walked up the four flights of creaking dark stairs, carefully missing the rotted one near the top and were finally left alone inside a very large but spotlessly clean attic bedroom, with one dormer window looking out over the busy main road. A small grandmother clock, its heavy pendulum ticking slowly on the wall, showed three-thirty. A couple of old bags were lying on the floor. They had an hour to talk and Belle knew she had to explain as much as she could very quickly and succinctly, although she had no idea why, how or what the consequences might be. But at least they would know when. Belle took the day's two pence copy of the Liverpool Mercury from the hotel lobby on the way up, dated May 8th, 1865.

Nancy couldn't hold in the questions a second longer. "So, have we managed to get onto some crazy reality TV show, Belle? 'Live like your Ancestors' theme or something? You can spill the beans now, I must admit the cameras are well hidden down there. All those weird effects last night made me dizzy, although I know I had a lot to drink. Next minute, I'm standing in a room with this Victorian dressed toff who's ranting on about me being damaged goods, although the stream of obscenities from his mouth I wouldn't want to repeat. It scared the shit out of me until I saw you two. Where are the boys? Nice clobber the production team provided us, although I can't for the life of me remember getting into this lot, so ..."

Belle intervened before a bigger hole was dug. "Just hang on Nancy, I'm going to have to explain actual reality and you may find it a shock, so brace yourself." Dottie, in contrast, stood silent and remarkably nonchalant, almost amused by Nancy's outpouring. Belle was certain now that Dottie had figured something out, or at least the time travel part, and was already playing into the role well. "Let's sit around that small table. The housemaid has left us some tea, thoughtful."

Nancy poured out the black tea into the three old cracked mugs. She grinned. "Go on, I'm ready for anything you know me."

Belle handed her the newspaper. "Look at the date, Nancy."

Nancy stared at the peculiar typeface up from the headline that a woman had drowned in the Albert Dock and perused the old sepia photographs of sailing ships unloading cotton bales into barges heading for the canal. "All very authentic, including the year of 1865. Props are superb. Sometimes, I wish I'd gone into media and not veterinary ..."

"Stop Nance, please," Belle whispered softly. "There are no props. This, I'm afraid is our reality. We're living it."

Nancy looked up bemused. "Come on Belle, I don't know what you're on but you know that's not fucking possible so stop the charades now and let's agree how we do the next scenes. I really wish I'd done more acting at school …"

Belle could feel a severe frustration building up but had to persist, however painful. "No, Nancy, it is possible and I'm telling the truth and the quicker you get your head around it the easier it will be for all of us to survive the next hour, day, week or whatever. We are genuinely living in an 1865 time. We've travelled back through some explosive discontinuity in the interconnected warp and weft of past, present and future time, space and gravitational fields, through from our 2026 universe, which happened in the Black Anchor last night. Why or how I don't know, but there will be a purpose for this and our priority now will be to play along, act these parts we've taken on as best and as carefully as possible, and gather information covertly and quickly. Tell her Dottie. I can see you already know. Presumably, Zac told you about the weird psychic capabilities that seem to be an inherent feature of our McKenzie family passed on through generations past."

Nancy gazed incredulously at her two friends. She couldn't believe her ears, this nonsense was inconceivable … but then she recalled that strange fire disaster at Orsbrick Hall and the oddly dressed man she saw running out of the burning barn at the start and Ned talking stupidly about the first time he had seen a spook. Nothing had been said since. He often talked daft and she hadn't asked but that experience had rested uneasily in the back of her mind.

Dottie smiled. "Yes, I'm sorry but it's true, Nance. Zac swore me to secrecy about things which have happened within the family, including to him … Only Ned and Julian seem unaffected by this psychic teleportation and Belle, you've been in this situation before haven't you, which is why I assume you're so calm. I worked it out the moment I sat on the step outside the Black Anchor … I was obviously in another world, there could be no other logical explanation. Zac explained, Belle, how you, Maddie, Victoria and Abby survived when you found yourselves back in Orsbrick Hall in the 1840s. We need to do the same I assume, survive and work out how to get out of here and forward to our own time. Belle is right."

Nancy turned pale, the inevitable conclusion had rapidly suffused her brain. "Fuck it all," was her initial response as they each quietly reflected before she continued. "Okay, I think I'm going to have to believe you both, massively hard though it is. I admit, everything we've just been through is far too authentic to be anything but the reality you've described … Jesus Christ, why did this happen to me? I'm not even a McKenzie and what if we can't get back to 2026?"

They began sipping the hot and incredibly strong tea. Belle continued carefully. "For now, we have to live in this time because this is our life now, whether we like it or not. We must be careful what we eat, take care with cleanliness without arousing suspicion and avoid getting ill or catching things. If we die, we die, end of story. Yes, I was here briefly before as Dottie said, in 1841 and living in Orsbrick Hall with my ancestor, Lady Morag McKenzie. Maddie and I at the end of that week had put plans in place for how we would carry on and make our way in the high society of the time. We had become disillusioned that anything would happen to disrupt the space-time again, but it did, unexpectedly in Orsbrick Hall when my mother lost her temper and admitted to Morag she was from the future. Ordinarily, Mum would have been locked up as a lunatic but a coming together, by chance, of knowledge and people who were not allowed to know that fact had assembled in the room that night. There and then, Maddie, Mum, Abby and I returned, in a kind of reverse sequence to what we three experienced last night in the Black Anchor bar. Certain space-time physical laws cannot be broken, it seems, and mixing past and future together seems to be a key violation as this potentially triggers an explosive disruption and changes the universe and the family history to accommodate the new space-time distortion. Sorry, Nance for sounding almost as nerdy as Zac."

Nancy laughed. "Actually, I quite like these cool clothes and this wild hairstyle, obviously my inner rebelliousness has been captured for the time. No way was I going to be a whore though. I slapped that lustful idiot, James McKenzie, hard across the face. He immediately backed off, shocked. I must say, he seemed quite a gentle, thoughtful soul and very good looking for his age. Jesus, Belle, is he really an ancestor?"

Belle had been thinking about that strange encounter. Somehow, James McKenzie's appearance may be part of the secret purpose. Two things were now clear to her. "Listen, we're going to have to get back downstairs shortly for work and we have to unpack our things, whatever they are. Collective eyes need to be peeled and ears pinned back. We must try and find out where Ned, Zac and Ade are. If we three are here the chances are high so are they. And we have to try and escape and make our way to Orsbrick Hall, which I believe will be the key to everything, in particular the purpose why the six of us are here. Orsbrick is the logical focal point where this space-time distortion comes together each time, inwards or outwards. The weird thing is that apart from James McKenzie, Mauveine, his daughter, should be there too, now we're in 1865."

"What? The ghost who haunts the place?" Dottie replied.

"Haunt isn't really the right description, Dottie," Belle said. "Helpfully oversees our lives is more apt. Besides, neither she nor Isi are ghosts anymore."

"You're serious?" Nancy intervened. "How come or should I say what are they then?"

"It's complicated Nance and a long story. But now you've mentioned it, neither would it make sense for Mauveine and us, well me especially, to engage. Too much of the past, present and future might come together ..."

"To create that explosion and then get us back to our time?" Dottie cried. "I reckon that confirms we definitely need to head towards Orsbrick Hall, but how?"

"Possibly by train," Belle said. "By 1865, excellent train services were well built across the country. Even Burscough by then had a station, on the same line from Liverpool to Manchester. We must save our wage if possible. But let's not get ahead of ourselves. We need to try and find Ned, Zac and Ade yet, although how heaven knows."

Nancy was already rooting through the three large, old leather duffel bags. "Bloody hell, what's this doing here?" she said, pulling out an iPhone. "No way is this phone going to work. Belle, it's yours isn't it?"

Belle grabbed it, looking furtively at the door. Nobody must see this, least of all Henry, Ernest or the housemaid. The battery was still full as she'd charged up in the pub the previous night. "It might be useful but later, don't ask, we'll get to that. Twitter has occasionally crossed time barriers, would you believe. I'll have to hide this somewhere."

"You must be joking. I hate Twitter, all crap and noise," Nancy cried. They laughed and Dottie turned round having pulled out and waved a nice yellow dress from her bag. "Belle, we've forgotten something. You said six of us before but there was seven remember, including that cow, Fenella. Why isn't she here with us?"

Belle stopped and thought hard. They had been so wrapped up in the present and the here and now they had totally forgotten about Fenella, before it struck her forcefully and clearly. 1865 was the year Fenella had arrived from, the day she turned up at their doorstep. Was there a link and more to the point, was Fenella connected to the reason this has happened? If so, where was she? "Quite possibly, Fenella may be a key part of all this but again, why or how, who knows. She is related, a half cousin six times removed …"

"Hang on," Dottie said, her brain stirred by that revelation. "You mean Maddie's weird friend is a McKenzie? But more to the point, she's from the past? All that crap from Maddie about being brought up as a Victorian in an Irish convent by crazy nuns. I never did believe it but I thought what the hell and it makes Zac happy, so what. So is she from this time period, Belle?"

Belle drew a long breath and sighed. "Yes, I'm afraid so. She arrived as an aftermath, like a blowback from our former 1841 experience. But will Fenella make an appearance as a benign friend or an evil adversary is a good question."

"I know where I'm putting my money," Dottie replied firmly, her face screwed up.

"No, Dottie," Nancy said. "If she turns up we must give her a chance. She was friendly and tried hard to fit in and was doing well until …"

"Not convinced," Dottie said with a resigned smirk.

"Me neither," Belle added. "The only other person who will probably know what this is about will be Mauveine. But where she is I have no idea. Finding her at Orsbrick is our best shot, despite the risks with me. I just hope back in 2026, someone is trying to find out answers. After all, we'll be reported as missing. They must be going frantic by now, but nothing we can do about that."

The three sighed and looked glum. There were more consequences than they wanted to think about. Nancy finally broke the silence. "Okay. Look, let's get a move on, first unpack your things. No need to toss that old penny coin, Belle; Dottie and I will share the double bed, we're used to it. Don't you dare smirk, Miss Annabelle McKenzie, 'thee better not be thinkin' of us as two lezzies, we be just very friendly lasses' …" she cried, mimicking Ernest superbly and causing them to laugh until their sides nearly burst. They desperately needed a return of some lightheartedness in this dire predicament. "Anyway, I have to find those horses and the stable hand, Rory. You never know, he may be a dashing Victorian lothario. Horses can have quite an aphrodisiac effect on men, all that jogging up and down and the things they watch."

Belle and Dottie grinned. Nancy was getting back to her usual lively self.

"Ned won't be very happy about your wandering eyes though, Nance," Belle cried.

"What the eye doesn't see the heart won't fret over," Nancy replied, her eyes dancing mischievously.

Putting her apron back, Dottie headed for the door and stared down the long corridor. "You two will have to wait, I spy a water closet opposite. If my history is right, they had sewers built here by now, especially down Dale Street, although God in heaven knows what the Mersey must look and smell like. Environmental regulations were not exactly foremost in 1865, but at least the loo has a big chain from a tank and a wooden seat. That's promising and I can see a huge porcelain sink with one tap. Catch you both later; I've got a bar to run. More fun, I hope, than the George ever was."

Chapter Nine

Walking down the deck with René alongside, Ned decided to remain calmly cooperative and not upset the apple cart. He needed his wits about him more than at any point in his life. Besides, the guy spoke pretty good English so couldn't be that bad. He'd studied at the Sorbonne and was four years older, almost twenty-two. Ned didn't often dwell on his sisters but fretted over Belle alongside Nancy and Dottie. He hoped they were all safe. Zac's psychic freak show stuff was spot-on; it took a nanosecond to realise. Looking around he saw another world and definitely another time, so he had to take crazy Fenella at her word. But how the fuck did she do it? He was stood on the deck of a medium-sized and relatively fast clipper, normally filled with passengers but modified with creaky looking cranes and ancient rope winching gear. Why was he here? Like the replicas he had visited many times at school in the Albert Dock Museum, this ship was wind powered, with three masts, loads of complex rigging and even a high crow's nest lookout. Another person, dressed in similar clothes to René, was precariously perched up there, gazing about with some kind of crude binocular. As he peered harder, he realised that person had long brown hair tied back in a ponytail and looked uncannily like Fenella. Shit, how did she get up there? What sort of woman was she? Nothing added up.

"I see you admire le Warrior Queen, Monsieur Ned, a fine ship, of Mademoiselle Fanny, non?"

"Warrior Queen?" Ned looked up at the smiling Fenella who waved. He was duty bound to wave back and laughed, the ship's name seemingly very apt but preposterous.

René continued. "You will shortly meet your friends when we turn around this corner. Do not be surprised by what you see. But I will leave you for a few minutes to, how you say, reacquaint? Then we must start work exactly as the captain requests."

"Nothing surprises me anymore, René," he replied glibly before drawing a hard, deep breath at the strange sight towards the stern end of the ship. Sure enough, he recognised great hulking Ade, a good head and shoulders above the burly sailors guarding him, a sturdy leg iron keeping him tethered to a huge ring hammered into the side. Ade looked very much worse for wear, decidedly bruised and battered but cocky as ever with an air of defiance. It would take more than a few French sailors to keep him down. And there was Zac, stood in the sea breeze with his shirt off, the sweat glistening on his chest. He hadn't realised his little brother had gained some very credible muscles since Dottie had left him, from the working out in the gym. Zac looked less nerdy than Ned had ever seen. It was what they were doing which mystified him more than anything. Each one was stood at the end of a long handle which they were pulling and pushing for all they were worth, attached in the middle like a see-saw to a peculiar contraption. A long and flexible pipe, difficult to tell whether made of rubber or leather, led to the side and dropped down into the water. The effort required to pump the handle up and down was considerable.

Ned gazed around. He realised they had dropped anchor and were way out at sea, but if he strained his eyes through the haze he was certain he could see an outline of land in the distance, including sand and what looked like sandhills and a visible tall landmark. Were they off the coast and out in the Liverpool Bay at the mouth of the River Mersey, in almost spitting distance of the beach around Hightown and Formby?

Ned walked across the deck smartly. Zac looked up and spied his brother with a smile, saying something immediately to Ade who looked across and grinned inanely. Momentarily they stopped pulling and pushing the see-saw handle to release an immediate tirade of shouts and abuse from the guards, one of whom pulled up a whip and gave Zac a sharp lash over his bare back.

"Aucun arrêt vous ne doit pomper dur plus rapidement," the whip sailor screamed loudly. They had to carry on pumping harder.

Wishing his French was better, Ned winced for a second but saw his brother brush the blow amazingly aside and start again, both pumping faster and faster. A creaking winch was being turned slowly and Ned could now see a rope drawing up from the sea as a commotion gathered. A group of sailors, leaning over the side, were hauling something up out of the water. They dragged it over, roughly onto the deck and Ned gasped. He could see a person, a man dressed in peculiar and bulky leather apparel with a metal helmet over his head, attached to a breastplate on the suit. The pipe could now be seen visibly attached to the back of the helmet. He ran over to join Zac and Ade, just as other crewmen were tearing open the suit, from which an enormous amount of water gushed out, visibly draining down through the man's glass visor on the front.

René joined the melee but immediately shook his head. "Cet homme est très mort, get rid of the body, fast."

Zac and Ade watched, horrified, as four crewmen picked the bloated corpse up and unceremoniously carried him away, to be likely thrown into the sea at the other end. Ned walked up to them immediately. Zac was the first to happily holler.

"Bro, are we glad to see you safe and sound. What the fuck have we landed ourselves into?"

They embraced and Ned then gave his best friend, Ade, a gentle hug, mindful of the nasty bruises over Ade's arms and face. With the disturbance and a dead man surfacing, the three were left on their own; all overseeing activity had stopped.

"I've worked it out," Zac blurted hurriedly. "All very obvious since our family, care of Maddie, has won the 'been there and done it' tee-shirt. So, I've explained the essentials of time travel and disruption to Ade quickly before those sailors kicked more crap out of him. Although I must say, it took six of them to hold him and three now have half their teeth missing. He's more of a sceptic than you, brother. But we've been cooperative since and were forced into this hard labour, pumping air into diver's suits all day long although what they're looking for down there we haven't a clue."

Ade looked down at Ned and pulled himself to his full six feet-seven-inches height. "Do you really believe all this psychic time travel shit? I must say though, I can't figure out a better explanation. We've definitely gone back a hundred years or more. But why us? And where are the girls?"

Ned looked around, the other sailors remained distracted. "Yeah, even I'm in on this one with Zac and I'm zero-psychic, unlike my weird sisters and Aunt Abby. We're on our own, it seems, the girls remained in the Black Anchor. Wish Abby was here though, she always knows what to do. Look, this situation has sort of got complicated ...," he began, when he noticed Zac suddenly glance behind him, his eyes on stalks, and Ade was muttering profanities softly into the floor. Ned stopped and turned, to be confronted by his earlier nemesis wearing a long weather coat, tight trousers tucked into high black boots and a souwester hat, her long hair trailing over her shoulders.

"Don't you think *I* know what to do, Ned? I thought we'd demonstrated that beyond any doubt last night." She laughed and kissed him delicately on the cheek as he stood immobile, trying not to react. She focused her attention on the other two, now speechless. "Zac, I'm really sorry to have missed you and Ade earlier but I see Fillon, my first mate, has already tasked you both in productive work, excellent. Do you like my ship?"

Zac finally blurted out, disbelievingly. "Fenella? But why?" However, any exhortations from him fell on deaf ears as she clung fiercely onto Ned's arm and stared provocatively into his eyes. Ned stood there mute, not knowing what to do except blush a deep and involuntary red. He gazed back at Zac as innocently as he could muster, pleading silently that this turn of events was completely out of his hands. His brother took a less favourable view and his face turned into an angry matching crimson.

"I can't wait again for tonight, can you Ned darling?" she murmured softly into his ear, mischievously pitched loud enough for Zac and Ade to catch unequivocally. That was the accurately despatched flame to light the emotional tinder. Ade, quick off the mark, grabbed Zac in time as he swung a heavy punch towards his brother who backed off fast but was caught slightly on the cheek. Fenella looked on amused to see the warriors scrap.

"Whoa, Zac, cool it," Ade shouted, tussling for a moment before he held on tight to the puce-faced Zac. "This is not all it seems and we need to keep a clear head and stay calm. Right woman, wrong time period, remember? Whatever time we're in."

Fenella decided enough was enough for entertainment. She had important work to get on with and the three would need to cooperate. "Dearest Zac, I am impressed as ever with your huge deductive brain, it always inspired me. But your friend Ade, who I thought an ignorant oaf and I take that slur back too, is absolutely correct. Things have moved on now we're in the year 1865. You have to grow up Zac and learn. Women can be terribly fickle over men, even little me. I'm so sorry you had to fall in love but you'll get over it and maybe forgive your brother for seducing me." She giggled stupidly as Zac struggled again in Ade's strong grip. He needed to lay his brother out, he felt so enraged inside.

"Listen to Ade and Fenella bro, this is no time for you and me to fall out, you understand that don't you," Ned said softly. His eyelids subtly twitched in a sequence, like he had grit in them, a childhood secret communication they shared whenever there was a confrontational misunderstanding at school, which decoded as 'chill and I'll explain later'. Fenella missed it, but Zac stopped wriggling. He was taking in the significance of the year 1865, took a deep breath and nodded. Ade slackened off his grip. The other crewmen had returned including René and Fillon, who appeared to be the only two amongst them to speak reasonable English.

"Madame Captain," René began. "The men are bringing out the other sea-suit. I am afraid we have now buried Stefan, the Dutch diver, in a fitting way and I said a small prayer to help him on his way to paradise."

"Thank you René, you may finish the day's log now. I'll take over here." Fenella turned to Ned, still standing silently as a group of men struggled towards them carrying heavy apparel along with other paraphernalia and tools. "I have had the good fortune to do business with a very clever engineer down in

London, a certain Mr Siebe, who has made significant improvements to the latest diving apparatus. This suit is made from a new weighted and waterproof canvas and the helmet has a built-in valve to regulate air pressure, so a diver will be more stable and breathe easier whilst walking around. Sadly, Stefan drowned when he overbalanced on the seabed and his helmet filled with water. The Warrior Queen will, therefore, have the honour of being the first vessel to test out this new contraption. And you, Ned, will do the testing." She looked up at the weather and pointed to Fillon and his crew. "Get all his clothes off and fit him into the suit, we have no more time to waste."

Ned blanched. He had undertaken a little diving in the Mediterranean on their last school holiday and was told he was a quick learner and strong but this proposal felt a step way, way too far. "No chance, Fenella. This gear is crude and rudimentary. I ain't going anywhere near that water."

To the first sailor approaching, Ned slammed a hard punch, one-two in the face and he fell unconscious to the floor. The others instantly moved en-masse to ensure another beating exactly like they had done to Ade, as Ned squared up. He would take as many as he could … but Ade jumped between them.

"No, Ned, we have to comply and do as we're told, you know that. Your brother and I will look after the pumping," he shouted, nodding to the right. Ned turned and his heart sank. Fenella was stood next to Zac, held firmly by two burly crewmen, holding a large, gleaming pistol pointed at his head.

"I'm impressed with the fisticuffs, Nancy said you could look after yourself, I can see that, very nice indeed. But this is becoming boring, Ned. Do I really have to blow Zac's brains out because of your silly pride?"

Ned threw his hands up in the air. "Okay, you win. I'll get into the fucking suit but I have no idea what you're looking for or what's down there."

Fenella smiled and put down the pistol. "Excellent, I knew you'd see sense and I'll make it up to you tonight," she purred. "And when we land later I shall acquire fresh chicken and cook you a strong curry, like old times. The job is very simple but requires skill and strength, Ned, which is precisely why I chose you. I don't want treasure, not from here anyway. Down below us is the wreck of a large sailing ship called the Mountain Moon. In early 1841, she set sail from Liverpool for America but only reached the mouth of the Mersey when there was a mysterious explosion and she went down with the loss of all crew and passengers. You must look for the captain's cabin amongst the debris and inside there will be a sealed oak chest. It will have the markings of a black falcon painted on the top … that is what I want."

Ned smirked. "What's inside the box to make you want to go to all this trouble? Maybe not the usual sort of treasure but something valuable? Lots of money, jewels?"

Fenella appeared angry momentarily but quickly regained her composure. "Yes, Ned, there is something valuable, but it does not concern you," she replied sharply. "I will be back in ten minutes and I expect a start to be made." She shot off watched by everyone, clearly agitated.

Ned, down to his boxer shorts, was quickly inside the large canvas suit with weighted feet, which fitted him remarkably well. The air tube was connected to the back of the new helmet and bolted securely onto the breastplate to make a watertight seal. Zac and Ade began slowly pumping in air to test the mechanism, including the valve, as Ned attempted to breathe. The contraption almost felt like a modern diving suit that he had tried out in the Mediterranean last summer, walking on the seabed for the first time. What he had learned then was how difficult it was to both walk and keep balanced and having seen the fatal effect of falling over by Stefan, the previous diver, he hoped this new design was robust enough, but he would still need to take great care. His greatest concern was how he was going to see, down there in the murk. No battery powered halogen lights around to guide him. Hopefully, the water was not too deep so enough light could reach the bottom. They reckoned, pulling up the dead man, that the wreck below was around twenty metres or about sixty feet down. He would need to be very dependent on feeling his way around, but at least the sun had come out and it was a sharp and bright, blue sky afternoon.

Following instructions on how he should jerk the rope tied around his middle to trigger if he needed to come up and also indicate any success, he watched as the other rope with a weight on the bottom for hauling the wooden chest to the surface was lowered down first as a guide. The weight hit the bottom at exactly twenty-two metres, around seventy feet. Tying his rope to the jib of a crude crane winch, he was swung out into the open sea and gently lowered until he just entered the water, not perfectly calm but less rough than he expected. His heart was beating fast. He wasn't scared but definitely apprehensive, looking through the glass visor, held in with thin metal bars across his view and not exactly providing the most brilliant vision, however, he had no choice but to get on with it.

He peered up to see Fenella back on deck and watching carefully, her face drawn. Perhaps she really was genuinely concerned about him going down into danger. But he wasn't going to hold his breath over that remote possibility or anything else right then. Zac and Ade continued pumping slowly, his lifeline, and their diligence would be vital. The air was coming in okay and the ongoing exit of stale air seemed to be regulating fine through the valve. He could hear the escape and hiss and hopefully, the mechanism sealed as it had been patented to do once he was in the water, but he would jerk the rope straight away if it didn't. The plan was to lower him down about ten feet first, to test the new suit and helmet was working satisfactorily and then proceed after he jerked three times.

Ned felt his body immersing under the water. He slowly descended the first run jerkily which finally stopped at the designated ten feet. Only fresh air was coming in and as he exhaled the bubbles emerged continuously—a good sign. No water was entering the helmet, so far so good. Everywhere inside the suit felt reassuringly dry. Down below, the murk was clearer than he expected and underneath him, he could see a large dark shape some way further down, presumably the Mountain Moon. He pulled three times and slowly began the final descent.

As he was lowered further his chest began to tighten. He knew this was likely with the increased pressure and pulled a series of jerks to indicate for Ade and Zac to pump harder, which they did. The light diminished considerably and a variety of silver fish swam past as he indicated to slow down. He was approaching the shape of the wreck and struggled to see where he was. Two of the tall masts were broken at the base and lying flat across the deck whilst a third had split off half way and was sticking up dangerously. He had to go carefully now and felt his feet touch on something hard. Peering down into the gloom and being ultra-careful to try not to stir up too much debris, he realised he was standing on some kind of upper deck. Now he had to find the captain's cabin. He remembered from his visits to the sailing ship museum in the Albert Dock that this area would be at the stern end and would likely bridge the full width and be fitted out quite luxuriously in its day, although, down at the bottom of the sea, much of the lavish infrastructure would have rotted away.

He peered further into the gloom where a shaft of light came through from the surface, just sufficient to allow him to get his bearings. He needed to walk slowly to his right and began perilously as clouds of debris swirled up making it much harder and far more dangerous. Inch by inch, he made his way along what was left of the main deck, dodging various obstacles including muskets, cannons, barrels, swords and other objects typical of their time. Keeping upright and dragging the heavy rope behind him, he could make out a silhouette of the earlier weighted rope through the haze which he shortly passed hanging down and logged the key location in his head. He could not be far from the stern when a further deck loomed up out of the hazy blackness. He was tiring already. The pressure was noticeable on his chest but the air kept coming well, Ade and Zac must have been working hard. He felt the vertical edges and sensed windows and a door which he pushed and it fell off its hinges inside, creating an unwanted cloud of muck and debris which forced him to wait to clear. This search was now becoming very difficult. There was barely enough light to see anything, although the cluster of windows around the rear provided a sufficient backdrop of faint illumination to work out this was a vast room with all manner of furniture and clutter lying about. Then he noticed a cupboard which had fallen over. The whole ship was lying at an angle of about twenty degrees which he could gauge looking at the splendid, intact floor boarding. Suddenly his heart pounded. A white skeleton, its arms and upper torso covered in bits of blue uniform and even a hat perched on the grinning skull was

215

poking out of the end of the blackened cupboard holding it down, and a great jagged hole was visible at the far end, through the entire wall of the ship. Alongside could be seen the possible site of an explosion. Twisted debris and broken pieces of furniture were scattered everywhere. Had the fatal event happened inside the captain's cabin? And was this indeed the captain? Highly likely, Ned deduced. The uniform, despite the obvious deterioration underwater, looked smart. Struggling, he carefully pulled the rope and manipulated the air piping so he could stand further inside, feeling the floor under the mess. Something box-shaped caught his attention as he ran his hands along the perimeter; this may be what he was looking for.

He grasped the side as best as he could and pulled and pushed. The object wasn't too heavy, fortunately, but he needed to drag it out into the better light and see. It was a trunk, definitely, but he saw no falcon design on the lid. Shit, he was getting tired and it was time to go up. He'd been down long enough and was now feeling the cold through the canvas. He would have to resume tomorrow, not something he relished at all. But what was inside that was so secretive and important to Fenella? He pulled the loose lid up out of curiosity and looked in amazement. Inside, at the bottom, he could see and feel a much smaller box, buried amongst a pile of rotted clothing which spilled out, streaming weirdly through the water. The inner box, made of a very dark wood, maybe ebony, displayed a distinctive but unclear marking on the top. This could be the prize. He pulled carefully and the small wooden chest, probably eighteen inches square, came neatly out as one side of the rotting holding trunk collapsed off its screws. With much effort, he pulled the box slowly along the deck towards the hanging rope and into better light, finally looping and tying the end securely around with a crude harness.

He really had to get to the surface fast. He was totally exhausted and his chest and lungs were hurting badly with the breathing effort. He watched initially as the small chest slowly ascended towards the top, pleased with himself for achieving success on his first dive. But something felt wrong. His body was feeling not just cold but wet as he looked down and saw a small tear in the canvas suit bubbling out air, probably done when he struggled to get through the door into the captain's cabin. Shit. He was filling up inside with water and felt cold terror with the thought of following on from the previous drowned diver to be the second person that day, ignominiously buried at sea. He had to hurry but couldn't be too quick either or the bends might kick in, that decompression sickness when gases dissolved in the body under pressure come out too fast giving the diver extreme pain and serious permanent damage. He knew that had been a huge issue for the early pioneering divers who also inevitably struggled with ruptured ear drums for the rest of their lives, and he was now one of them. Making a rough calculation of how long the water inflow would take, he reckoned he could just make it by going steady and tugged three times on the rope. Immediately, he felt the force pulling him up into a slow ascent but halfway up, the motion jerked to an abrupt halt. He waited for ten seconds, still no movement and his legs had already filled up, and the more water that came in the faster it seemed to be happening. Panic set in. He tugged again on the rope numerous times but no response.

Unknown to Ned, up at the surface, the ascent rope had tangled up around a stupid metal spike just below the surface. The crew pulled harder but nothing moved, and they became concerned that too much force could snap the rope altogether.

Fenella, standing alongside the sealed chest now on deck was watching the ensuing panic with alarm. She shouted immediately to Zac and Ade. "Both of you, for heaven's sake get down there immediately, untangle that rope and save your brother and your friend. We'll tie another rope around each of you." She shouted to the crewmen to fetch more rope and tackle whilst Zac and Ade were relieved of the pumping by four other well-built sailors.

Ade blanched. "I can't go down there, I can't fucking swim. I'd be next to dead and useless," he cried out, storming about helplessly as he looked at Zac. Everyone knew from the coded last tugs that there was something badly wrong and Ned needed to be brought up promptly.

"I can't dive," Zac shouted back. "I hate seawater and putting my head underneath. It makes me panic and I never could even master scuba."

Fenella spat over the deck and screamed angrily. "You make me sick, Zac. I don't know what I ever saw in you, a huge disappointment if ever there was. If Ned dies I shall personally have you strung up naked on the yardarm for the seagulls, make no mistake."

She knew she had no trained divers amongst her crew and that she had to act fast … when a short sailor, stood at the back, stepped forward and motioned for the rope to be put around him immediately. Fenella turned and grimaced. This was not her expectation but she had no choice, the emergency had to be overcome and Ned rescued. René had arrived from his quarters alerted by all the shouting and volunteered immediately. He had in a short time grown to like Ned and he knew how to dive and was not frightened. He turned to Fenella and smiled. "Les Anglais sont vraiment une nation de commerçants, nous aurions dû les détruire en 1815."

Fenella smiled and nodded. His sharp humour, parodying Napoleon, as always honed accurately towards the occasion.

"What did that fucker say?" Ade whispered in Zac's ear.

"Haven't got a clue mate but going by Fenella's face it wasn't a compliment aimed in our direction."

Down below, Ned had gone into total panic and tugged again and again at the rope. The water was now up to his waist inside the suit and the air was no longer circulating properly through the valve. He was going to drown, suffocate and likely die horribly of both at the same time.

But unknown to him René, securely tied and held by five men, was already on the sea surface, a large knife and mallet wedged in his belt. He took a deep breath and dived under the waves. He quickly found the rogue spike and hammered at it hard, moving it slightly, but he had to resurface again and catch his breath once more. Three times he went down, digging hard into the wood with the knife and hammering frantically with the mallet until on the fourth attempt they pulled again on deck and the spike yanked itself out, falling deep into the murky depths. Rene resurfaced, triumphant. "Allez, allez, remonter le plongeur maintenant, vite, vite!"

Zac and Ade took over the pumping again with more assistance as the effort was becoming harder and harder. Ned finally felt movement and the ascent slowly restarted. He knew he didn't have far to go and much of the gas probably had been dissolving out of his bloodstream whilst he was stationary, so he pulled hard to indicate he was ready for a faster lift. The water was up to his chest and he could hardly breathe when he felt a rip below. The weight of the ingested water inside had split the original small tear wide open. Immediately, with not a second to lose, he breathed in as deeply as he could and held his breath as the water flooded inside, air bubbles escaping everywhere. Up above the pressure dropped dramatically.

"Stop pumping," Rene shouted, back on deck. "The suit has burst, just pull, pull, pull." Zac and Ade took hold of the rope too and everyone heaved hard. Rearing upwards out of the froth, Ned's lifeless body was hauled into the air and swivelled back on the crane. Immediately on deck, René took charge and with Ade, they tore off the remains of the suit and quickly unbolted the helmet, water pouring out everywhere. Ned had been completely enveloped and had drowned, his body immobile and his breathing stopped. Zac looked on, his face grey and ashen. What was all this about? He gazed around for Fenella but she had disappeared back to her cabin with her beloved box that Ned had died for retrieving.

But René was having none of this acceptance of such a décès, death … he saw a foot twitch and began to push at Ned's bare chest, nothing. But this was Ade's cue for action … he had done a lifesaving certificate at school.

"Move aside, Frenchie," he yelled, "this is my gig now," shoving René hard to the side.

Zac, distraught and angry, had quietly sneaked off in the pandemonium and headed for Fenella's cabin, a curved dagger in his hand. Revenge would be sweet, they'll hang him anyway.

Ade instantly moved into the proper sequence and rhythm and pumped hard a number of times, water pouring from Ned's mouth. This was followed instantly by a loud cough and violent spluttering as Ned lurched back into being, he was still alive. Ade turned him onto his side to allow all the water to escape from his lungs and mouth. A few more heady coughs and Ned raised himself up, smiling, to the accompaniment of loud cheers and clapping.

"Hey guys," he muttered, hoarsely, "you didn't think a bit of water's going to finish me off, do you? Where's the rum?"

There was a great roar of laughter as René handed him a hip flask. As Ned guzzled down the strong nectar, at long last a proper drink, he spotted Fenella at the back of the crowd looking strangely stiff and awkward with Zac directly behind her seriously stressed out. Unknown to everyone, she was being held firmly by her belt and a dagger stuck hard in her back. But both seeing Ned alive, they reacted instantly. Zac let go and Fenella ran forward deliriously to hug him, which she did to more cheers with Ned waving the flask about in bravado style as normal. Zac quietly shoved the dagger under a tarpaulin and moved forward to join Ade.

"What the fuck's happened?" Zac whispered. "I thought he was dead. I was just about to gut the bitch in front of everyone when exactly like Lazarus, my brother rises from the dead, thank God."

Ade was beaming. "Looks to me like the same old Ned is back in town. Just needed some proper resuscitation. That fucking life-saving certificate came in handy for once; I only went on the course 'cos I fancied Ellie Mills the teacher. But Zac, my old friend, let's face it; the real hero was actually that fop, René, who saved Ned's life jumping in that crappy water. We were a pair of useless shits at the end of the day."

Zac nodded. What severe punishment was Fenella going to dream up for him? A cat of nine tails lashing at the least but in a moment she was stood next to him and smiled. "Thank you Zac for alerting me to Ned's predicament," she shouted loudly over the din. "I had no idea inside my cabin. I'm so pleased he is now alright. You're forgiven your little transgression."

Zac took the hint; it was his lucky day too, clearly. He stepped forward and hugged his brother.

"Big bro, I really thought you were toast, but fair credit must go to this man, he saved your life freeing the rope under the water," Zac said softly in Ned's ear and pointing to René. "Admittedly, Ade finished off the job by belting shit out of your chest to clear that water from your lungs. Me … I did fuck all I'm afraid."

"One thing I can see you've been doing is thinking, Zac. I can see by your expression. Only I know that look. And that's what we're going to desperately need next, your brains. Down there with Neptune, I've thought up a plan," he whispered back quickly.

Zac had indeed been thinking hard, off centre beam as they said on-board this vessel exactly as his nerdy reputation dictated. When he found Fenella in her cabin, she was completely engrossed, peering over a dirty parchment which she'd already extricated out of Ned's seabed treasure box retrieved from the Mountain Moon. What exactly it said he didn't have time to see, but he reasoned the parchment was likely connected with 1841 family issues as it had a prominent 1841 date and seal on the top. He was now convinced, joining up the dots, that the adventure back in time to Orsbrick Hall which Maddie, Belle, his mother and Aunt Abby had found themselves embroiled in was likely connected too. But how? What was Fenella's relationship to that year in 1841? Had she been lying about her age? She looked a lot younger than she said, so was 1841 her actual birth year? Shit, that would make her twenty-four or five. He'd been cavorting for the last few months with an older woman. At least that achievement made him smirk. And what was so special about a sailing ship sinking in the mouth of the Mersey, en route to America? Why was that box in the captain's cabin marked with a falcon's head? Was there someone important on-board who Fenella had some relationship with? And finally, was this all connected with Orsbrick Hall and their ancestral McKenzie family? One thing was becoming clearer by the minute. They had to get off the Warrior Queen fast and head for the family home to find answers which may spur them back into their own time as happened with Maddie and Belle. Knowing Ned, he was probably working out how to escape. But they needed a plan from there. Zac was significantly heartened when he retrieved the dagger from out of his bag on the way to Fenella's cabin. Because under the mess of clothes he'd found something else unexpected. His iPhone ... fully charged. Weird it may be, but more importantly the question was could he actually produce a connecting communication through the space-time they had come through, back to the year 2026 and Maddie? Also, in all this peculiar set of events, they still didn't know where the girls were. Had they also been transported back here in 1865? Ned didn't think so but he was not convinced. Fenella had mentioned to Ade they would anchor nearby for a couple more days whilst the weather stayed calm and clean up the items in the hold which had been salvaged a few days ago off Birkenhead by the dead diver they threw in the sea earlier. Then the Warrior Queen would head for land to conduct some business and replenish supplies before returning for Ned to salvage more valuables from the Mountain Moon. A window of escape opportunity might arise then. He, Ade and his brother had to talk.

The moment sunrise filtered through the morning haze, noise and clatter instantly disseminated up and down Dale Street. Horses and carts of all shapes and sizes were busy everywhere and a general hubbub of activity started up, mostly centred on the docks and port arrivals. Fishermen and seamen were busily embarking and disembarking from ships up and down the estuary. Belle, Dottie and Nancy were about to wake and start their third day. Sufficient time had elapsed to adjust to a routine with their new jobs and even enjoy some downtime for an hour the afternoon previously, when they decided to traipse along Water Street towards the familiar Pier Head area, taking care to dodge the copious horse muck and mud in the furrowed road.

Comparisons between their existing 1865 time and 2026 were foremost in their minds, having wandered down the same street before that fateful evening and made fun at Ned and Ade's antics on the landing stage. Already, that felt a long time ago when they were together as a happy group. Where had the boys disappeared to? Watching their footing on the slippery cobbles, they crossed Water Street, dodging the many hawkers with large carts on the pavements and side of the road, their smelly, dirty horses chewing at bales of hay thrown on the ground. Vendors pushed their wares vociferously, clearly bartered for resale from disembarking ships. Many street people appeared very poor, wearing ragged old clothes, accompanied by barefoot children needing a good wash, with father and son sporting the ubiquitous cloth caps and corduroy dungarees whilst mothers and daughters, dressed in bulky long dresses, helped out or ran stalls of steaming food, including whelks, crabs and mussels for hungry sailors walking up and down. The air smelt strongly of the sea and fish, mixed with a never-ending whiff of raw sewage. A number of factories belching smoke could be seen in the distance.

Liverpool was bustling and thriving. A throng of well-dressed professional men, resplendent in smart three-piece suits and top hats, many with thick beards and moustaches, walked in and out of the tall, four and five storied Georgian buildings, still familiar but a lot sootier. Or they were jumping into or out of a horse-drawn brougham carriage, sometimes accompanied by equally fashionable women. These people appeared more wealthy, middle class and professional, perhaps merchants, lawyers, office managers, sea captains. Belle remarked that such people didn't frequent the Black Anchor whatsoever, clearly not their expected establishment, which catered solely for seamen and labourers. Where the rich and wealthy went would be useful to find out. That could be a means of making contact with or finding out more about Orsbrick Hall. Suddenly, halfway down Water Street, Belle pointed out the picturesque silhouette of the tops of ship's masts with furled and unfurled sails, prominent in the distance.

"Gosh," Nancy cried excitedly, "that view looks just like the 'Tall Ships' extravaganza every summer when they all congregate and sail off out to sea up the River Mersey. I always watch them from Hightown beach."

But Belle and Dottie were staring over the other side of the road at a row of shops, more upmarket and extending up a couple of side streets, including a popular bakery with large loaves of dark brown bread steaming in the window. Occasionally, larger and more opulent carriages could be seen been driven up and down, as very well-dressed and refined gentleman and lady upper-class couples of leisure, usually accompanied by a servant, would stop and alight at this specific row of retailers, with a dress shop being notable for their immediate attention.

"Look, there's a proper tea shop," Dottie said, pointing to a cafe with seats outside in the sun. "Very popular they were in the mid-nineteenth century. I've had a sub on my wages from Henry so I'm going to treat you."

"Oh, yes?" Nancy asked smirking. "And what has tight-fisted Henry had in return for such a magnanimous gesture?

Anyway, I thought we mere women were banned from those male bastions of idle pleasure."

They all laughed. They still had almost an hour and a quarter left of their break too. "Never mind about Henry," Dottie replied. "Perhaps instead it's time to hear what you and the delectable blond Rory have been getting up to in the hay shed?"

Belle interjected. "Listen, you two, no time for your usual trivial sex banter. More importantly, I'm formulating an actual escape plan, so a good opportunity here to plot. And Nance, it was coffee houses in the sixteenth and seventeenth century which banned women. Once tea suddenly became popular in early eighteen hundred, tea houses replaced them for all of society including we frail members of the opposite sex. In fact, women tend to be the big users, especially for afternoon tea. I don't know why they never lasted. We're just in time, as you can see. There's a table free, next to that aristocratic-looking woman in the light-blue dress and matching hat. Good job we're well scrubbed up and got our best frocks and hats on. I've an idea so try and look and sound posh … like me."

Dottie and Nancy groaned. They carefully crossed the street, with Nancy pulling Dottie away from the lure of the prominent window dresses of Miss Carter's Couture shop next door. That would be inspected after tea.

They sat down briskly and a young and presentable waiter approached immediately from inside whilst they perused the menu. "Good afternoon ladies, tell you what, I do recognise you three. Didn't I see thee all in Black Anchor Hotel with old Henry Abbinant the other day?"

Nancy, her mane of red hair billowing under her hat and over her shoulders, immediately brushed it back flamboyantly. Feigning opprobrium, she protested. "Absolutely not. I think, sir, you are very mistaken. That disgusting abode is an establishment for harlots only," projected in a loud and put-on voice. She always liked the opportunity to play-act. "Now, may we please order three Earl Grey teas and a slice each of your best Victoria sponge cake? *We* are celebrating the publication of my writer friend's *new* novel," she continued emphatically, looking mischievously at Dottie. It was about time Dottie's so called superior English literature was put to the test.

The waiter, surprised for a moment, stood silently and blushed then murmured an apology before shuffling off with the order. Belle grinned, it was her turn. She had already clocked the aroused attention of the lone rich woman next to them, quietly reading a large book over her refreshments.

"So, Ottoline," Belle began, staring at Dottie; her natural voice was posh enough without trying too hard. "Have you had an advance already? In which case, I declare treats are on you today, don't you agree Violet?"

"Yes, I have Virginia," Dottie replied, easing herself in confidently and putting on a very affected accent. "No need to dig into that measly allowance of yours today, I think it's time you started writing too or swap that miserly cotton merchant husband, more interested in business than having fun."

They laughed discretely when the lady in blue suddenly interrupted. "Pardon me, do please excuse my intrusion but I couldn't help overhearing ... I do so love the challenge of a new book. When will it be for sale?"

Dottie turned and smiled. "Oh, next month, entitled 'Notes on Love' but written under my pen name, of course, Miss Vita Sackville."

Belle coughed and took a sip from a glass of water on the table. Thank goodness Dottie's nom-de-plume had not even been born yet. The waiter arrived and began sheepishly setting

227

out the dainty porcelain cups and saucers, plates of generous cake and a large pot of tea. "Would you like fresh milk, madam?" he said to Nancy.

"Yes please."

He placed a jug carefully next to her then vanished. Belle turned back to the woman. "Would you care to join us ... err?"

"Yes, that would be most pleasant. My name is Lady Fox, Mary Fox. Please call me Mary. I spend many afternoons here whilst my husband occasions himself with necessary business; he imports wine, for pleasure and investment."

Belle indicated to the waiter to bring some extra tea and another plate of cake but Lady Fox declined the cake. "I eat far too much, I must watch my waistline carefully," she said smiling, her voice soft and clear but very definitely plum upper-class. Her clothes were exquisite and expensive as she carefully laid out a pair of white silk gloves on the table.

They continued chatting, first about books and then onto clothes whereupon Lady Fox highly recommended the select second-hand clothes section of the next door couture shop. "One has to ask discretely," she whispered as the three gathered closer. "They are kept in a special room at the back, invitation only. There are a small number of fickle ladies of wealth I know who regularly discard all manner of gowns, dresses, shoes and other accessories there after only one wear and many times brand new, but one buys them at a tenth of the original cost. Ottoline, if you wish to indulge, do mention my name." She handed Dottie a small, embroidered card. Dottie passed it to Belle who immediately noted the address: Haddersby Hall, near Scarisbrick. Belle had heard of that place, a former stately home but a hotel now for a very long time. But this wasn't the year 2026 of course.

Lady Fox suddenly pulled out a tiny watch from her leather handbag and picked up her red leather, first edition book of poetry by Elizabeth Barrett Browning. Dottie was sorely impressed. She had studied that particular writer extensively for her A-level English and used the knowledge in an interview for her Oxford scholarship she had recently won. Lady Fox sighed. She appeared tired. "I'm so sorry, I can't linger any longer. Thank you so much for tea, my husband, Charles, will be picking me up very shortly and I had better return to my table. He becomes angry if I socialise with other women, apart from his sister."

Nancy perused Mary Fox's face, which was expertly made-up and discretely powdered but could discern telltale bruising underneath. She was probably not much older than them. Bastard Charlie Fox, some old aristo-git, was regularly beating the hell out of her. Nancy, bursting inside with rage, wanted to get hold of him and apply some of her well known physical retaliation back but bit her lip quietly. She had to think rationally. They were not whatsoever in an emancipated environment for women which she, Belle and Dottie took for granted ... Women in 1865 were still fifty years from the vote, let alone equality generally.

Belle suddenly asked. "How do you travel back to Scarisbrick, by carriage then I assume?"

"Oh no," Lady Fox replied instantly. "Far too uncomfortable for Charles's piles. It wasn't that long ago that our manor house was surrounded by marshes of the Mere and the roads are still poor. We take a comfortable train these days, first class of course, which Charles and I catch from Lime Street to a little station called Heathey Lane Halt then our carriage picks us up. It really is too far to walk."

"I expect you're acquainted with Orsbrick Hall then, not that far away?" Dottie added, taking an additional cue. Belle looked on approvingly.

"Good Lord above, yes, the beautiful home of James McKenzie. Do you know the family? Charles, who is much more acquainted with the McKenzie's, and I, attend occasional social events there, although since his wife died some years back, smallpox I understand, the fabulous gaiety has abated. Orsbrick Hall was once the centre of social life in West Lancashire. We usually have dinner and play bridge with friends."

"And his daughters too?"

"Sometimes. One of them, Lydia, is often away studying serious painting, a very talented girl. I like her very much, lively and interesting and very beautiful and gifted. Tell me why do you ask?"

Nancy and Dottie went silent and looked hard at Belle. Her turn had come. She needed to say something. "I'm a rather distant cousin of Lydia actually," Belle said quietly "but I have never actually visited my uncle. We lived in Ireland until very recently. And is his other daughter an artist too? I don't know anything about her?"

"Heavens above no, she's quite the opposite, a strange individual, quiet and studious. Spends most of her time in a laboratory working with her father. Rumour has it that he found her as an abandoned baby and then adopted her. She possesses a strange name, I can't quite remember it. I only met her the once and even that was by accident."

"Mauveine is the name you require," a deep voice sounded. "I see you've made some new friends, my dear."

They all turned to see a tall man in his early forties, handsome with a bushy moustache and thick head of brown hair, very well dressed in a light brown suit and matching top hat. He had emerged from nowhere out of the shadows of the cafe interior behind them.

Lady Fox, alarmed, turned quite pale for a moment but forced a dazzling smile and picked up her bag carefully. "Why, Charles, my angel. I was just going to find you when these ladies asked me a question. I'm so sorry."

"I know, I heard," he said with a disapproving look that spelled trouble. "So, one of you ladies is related to James McKenzie then. An old acquaintance of mine but certainly not a friend, bit of a cad actually, has a predilection for other men's wives." He shot a glance back to Lady Fox who shuddered slightly.

Belle looked at Nancy, her face already thunderous and fists clenched, ready to do business once more. Belle groped under the tablecloth and felt her friend's leg hard, instantly relieved to hear Nancy take a relaxing, deep breath and hopefully say and do nothing. However that wasn't Nancy's style.

"From a woman's perspective, better I think a little covert seduction which is normally a gentleman's prerogative, rather than the other male preoccupation of wifely assault and battery, undertaken solely of course by disingenuous cowards. Wouldn't you agree, Lord Fox?" She held out her hand, accompanied by a glowing smile. "Violet Keppel is my name, and these are my friends, Miss Ottoline Morrell, an author, and Mrs Virginia Woolf."

Belle stared again. Nancy liked to ride the hi-wire with one wheel, including even nom-de-plumes. Charles Fox, thrown momentarily by the audacity, stared at the gorgeous woman with a gaudy green dress and wild mane of reddish hair. On the one hand, he was fascinated and entranced totally, a woman of daring and challenge, the complete opposite to his ever boring wife and on the other felt incensed to violence, but this was a very public place and too many people around knew him.

"I'm sure you ladies are all dedicated Jane Austin aficionados," he said sarcastically before turning to Belle. "If you decide to visit James McKenzie you may catch the same train but must change at the next station from ours, Bescar, to pick up the Manchester train and alight at Burscough." He turned to his wife. "Now my dear we must depart, please." He took her arm and hauled her up before whistling a passing brougham taxi. In a moment they were gone, Lady Fox did not look back.

"Fuck. That poor woman will get the beating of her life when she arrives home, I should have pushed his eyes out," Nancy said, fuming.

"I agree," Belle replied, "but just as well you didn't. Walton jail in 1865 would definitely not appeal, Nance. We did get useful information though, so a train to Orsbrick it will be. Now for the rest of the plan, I suggest we take a quick wander down to the Pier Head, explore the view and then, sadly, we'll have to get back to work for the next shift."

Turning the last corner at the bottom of Water Street and wending their way through a large outdoor market, avoiding the myriad of hens, ducks and pigs and even a monkey, wandering through the gangways, Belle pulled Dottie away from chattering to the squawking green parrot perched mournfully in a gilded cage.

"He's a striking specimen, wish I could take him back to the Black Anchor," Dottie wittered, walking away to a sudden parrot mimic of 'Fenella is a bitch … Fenella is a bitch, eey-aye-addio Fenella is a bitch,' the owner shaking his fist and shouting various obscenities. They dodged swiftly around the next stall and out of sight.

Dottie continued, still pondering their earlier discussion in Miss Carter's Couture shop. "I do like the concept, Belle, of you becoming a travelling aristocrat and me and Nance playing the part of your maidservants. Those second-hand dresses in there would be perfect to escape in and become incognito, first class on the train. That's the last place anyone searching for us would look. But how are we going to get the money for the great escape plan?"

Belle grimaced. She hadn't worked that one out. They could be around for months before they had enough between them. "I've got that covered, leave the money to me," Nancy suddenly whispered in a low voice.

Dottie stared, her eyes narrowing. "But how? Surely you're not going on the game, are you? I know you look the part but hey, there's a limit to what a girl should be doing …"

Nancy laughed. "Cheeky bitch. No, no, no … last night, as I was making a hot chocolate and you two were in bed, I spotted old Henry trying to count up the day's takings. He puts it all in an unlocked drawer in the Welsh dresser would you believe, probably banks it once a week or so. The pub takes a lot in the day, but let's be honest, despite the grime, the place is very busy and popular. There were notes strewn on the floor and all over the place. He didn't have a clue how much was there and just shoved it all in a drawer and staggered off to bed. Have you noticed how pissed each night he gets? … Certainly believes in having one with the regulars."

"Yes, that's true," Belle replied. "Henry must consume ten pints a night or more, let alone how much during the day. Probably a bit of an alcoholic sadly, but he does seem a nice guy underneath."

Nancy, glancing about furtively, pulled out a wad of notes from her pocket. "I thought I'd better even up his accounting properly," she said grinning. "And this was only off the floor and under the dresser."

"Bloody hell, Nance, how much have you got there? Shit, what if you get caught or he finds out?"

"Fifteen pounds. Once I double that, which I should do very soon, we'll have easily enough for those dresses, the train fare and more. Lady Fox threw away a used ticket from her bag as she left which I retrieved ... a single is two shillings and sixpence, first class. The quicker we head off to Orsbrick the better. I'm not sure how long I can fend off Rory though, he's becoming a bit persistent."

They laughed again, Dottie and Nancy cracking more jokes with each other when they heard Belle suddenly exclaim. "Just look at that. Would you believe it?"

The three stared, wide-eyed, at the myriad of masted sailing ships berthed along the quayside. A long loading shed stood in front, twin train tracks dominating the road area, with various goods being unloaded inside or piled up on a crude platform. A row of six-storey warehouses stood behind, heavy bales of cotton and large barrels being winched up inside by squeaky cranes. There was a lot of activity everywhere, loud shouting and horses and carts careering through, orchestrated by male dockers of all ages. Some seemed as young as ten and dressed in heavy dungarees and caps. Numerous couples, arm in arm, were strolling by and taking in the splendid view across the River Mersey whilst a group of dishevelled old women, pushing rickety prams stuffed with old clothes, stood gossiping on the other corner. This was certainly not the Pier Head they had been used to. The environment could not have looked more different.

"Of course, I've remembered," Dottie cried. "This part was an actual dock in 1865 … called George's Dock before it eventually was wound up and dismantled in the late eighteen hundreds and the more familiar Pier Head area started to be built. Apparently, George's Dock became too small for the bigger ships coming in as trade bound for Liverpool boomed. It all looks a bit cramped and crowded now, doesn't it."

"Hey, look over there," Belle exclaimed, pointing excitedly. "All is not lost, we have a floating landing stage, and I can see a boat coming across with a load of people on it. They must have a ferry going, to Woodside presumably. There are people waiting this side too, I can see them now."

"Ferry 'cross the Mersey, anyone?" Nancy exclaimed, waving a pound note.

"Listen, Miss Gerry Pacemaker, I think you've forgotten. We have to be back in fifteen minutes, work to do remember," Belle replied. "And you've got gorgeous Rory to placate."

"Hey, you girls aren't thinking of going far away to sea are you? Don't think you'll be allowed today!" a deep voice called out, followed by a raucous bellow of laughter. They turned around to see a small group of teenage dockers standing in front of a warehouse entrance, filthy dirty with what looked like flour over their clothes and aprons and going by the broken bags and sacks lying around that was likely what they were loading. One of them threw a paper bag full of flour at Nancy who quickly dodged out of the way with a skittish shriek to more laughter and inter-jostling. The missile burst open over a metal capstan.

An older male immediately emerged, obviously a foreman aged in his early twenties and dressed better, clean and wearing a smart brown leather cap. They stopped fooling about instantaneously and became deathly quiet. "Hey, Gilbert," he hollered out loud. "Why don't you fuck off inside you stupid idiot before I break your head open. And the rest of you, back to work, now."

The dockers ran off quickly into the next warehouse, as he strode over and headed straight to Nancy, already fluffing up her hair. She always had that effect on men.

"I'm sorry Miss, would have right messed up your good clothes that would. I'll skelp his backside that brother of mine when I get him home tonight. Are you ladies doing some sightseeing? There are some amazing ships in port this week as you can see, don't normally see so many at once. My name's Nathan, I manage this warehouse for my father who owns it."

Nathan had a dazzling smile, looking over each one in turn, but then continued staring at the fanciable Nancy. Belle, never to be outdone and observing that Nancy was, as predictably expected, readying herself to chat him up, immediately spoke first, putting on her best upper-class accent. "Yes, we're just visiting from the country, thank you, Nathan. No harm is done to my friend here. Is it true that there are no female sailors on board any ships then?"

Amused, he bellowed loudly, when a swarthy colleague, much shorter and older, thick stubble spread over his dirty face and very stocky, joined him. "Certainly not in these parts, Miss," Nathan replied. "The thought would give most of those old seadogs nightmares that's for sure. The only females they claim to see, after a night of rum, are mermaids."

Nathan's dishevelled associate smiled. "Royal Navy won't even allow nurses, right stupid that is in this day and age, especially after them lives were saved by Florence Nightingale in Crimea. There 'ave been the odd women, stole on board, dressed up as young boys and I heard a few captains have even allowed their wives with 'em but that is rare indeed, and only to my knowledge out in the Americas."

"Can I introduce you to Christian, my foreman, he's spent a lot of time at sea," Nathan said, waving his friend forward who, taking an instant liking to Belle stepped towards her and held out his arm to shake hands, sadly short and withered. But they were distracted by a loud bang near to the dock quay as a tall pile of barrels clattered over, rolling in every direction including into the water. Dockers and merchants ran from the shed to try and salvage their sherry stock, spilling out all over the roadway. Belle stepped back, looking at the unsightly pock marks on Christian's face, grateful for the distraction.

"Idiots, I told them earlier it was too unstable, I'd better go and help," Christian said, much to Belle's relief. "Mind you, Nathan, there is one notable and unique exception to the lady's question, isn't there. Think on, my friend." In a moment he was amongst the others, taking over and redirecting the retrieval efforts on the loading bay.

Nathan grinned. He had forgotten for the moment. "Of course, how could I ignore her ... owns her own ship she does. How she did that nobody still knows. Aye, I had a run-in with her one time too, real argumentative and can handle a pistol remarkable like. Fanny Kirkby is the name. She captains a large sailing ship, the Warrior Queen, very appropriate I do declare."

Dottie immediately looked up, now interested. "Have you seen the said Fanny lately?"

He pondered. "Aye, we did briefly now you ask. Ship had docked for a few hours for specialist supplies, oh ... must have been five nights back. Captain Kirkby searches for treasure, does salvage, around the coast, of old wrecks. A very lucrative business, I daresay, but hard to get a good diver. Government and the Royal Navy use most of them with any talent and pay

237

well, especially for coastal warfare and sabotage. I hear the Warrior Queen is out in the Mersey right now somewhere."

Nancy suddenly realised the time. They had to hurry. Being late meant docked pay and a good shouting. "I'm so sorry, Nathan, so nice to meet you but I'm afraid we have to go. We have work to do at the Black Anchor. Maybe we'll see you there later?"

He stared, taken aback. "The Black Anchor? You must be joking, Miss. A rough place for sure, I wouldn't be seen dead in there, real bad company. I much prefer the Horses Head around the corner for a pint in the evening and a pie. What do you do there?"

"Oh … I do farrier stuff, stabling, that kind of thing for the hotel clients, certainly not bar work of course. I'm an animal person. Well, maybe we'll see you here another day then."

"I hope so … err …?"

"It's Nancy, bye Nathan …"

Hurrying off, Nancy turned and waved back to Nathan as he walked into his warehouse. "Before you start Belle with that surly face of old, Nathan might be useful. He's fanciable and he has money and frankly, I don't care anymore. We might be stuck here for good. Okay, Dottie, back to business. Were you thinking the same as me? The bitch is back?"

"Fanny being a nickname for Fenella, I assume," Belle murmured, walking between them. "Seems plausible, but why is she here as the ultra-Victorian feminist? A female ship's captain, probably the only one in England, seems utterly bizarre in comparison to the Fenella we knew."

"Which is exactly the point, don't you see?" Nancy shrieked. "For someone who spouts on about logical scientific thinking Belle, sometimes you miss the wood and the trees. Captain Fanny is the real Fenella, swashbuckling away on the high seas in 1865. We've been experiencing a convenient diversionary tactic in 2026 by a … err … what's that name …?"

"Manifest," Dottie said forcibly.

"Yeah, manifest. What's a manifest for fuck's sake, know-it-all?" Nancy replied, grimacing.

"Manifestation to be precise is the correct terminology. It means a ghostly spirit," Belle added, with a faint air of smugness.

"Jesus Christ, I'm surrounded by two know-it-alls … I think I'll sign on to Fanny's ship and swell the ranks of women power by a hundred percent before she conscripts us too."

Belle suddenly went quiet. She was reflecting hard on that sarcastic comment and realised. "You're a genius, Nance, that's the real distraction, of course. Where would Fenella like to have three healthy, strapping young men who she knows well and could doubtlessly manipulate and dictate to because she has the upper hand? We're back, after all, in her time and comfort zone. Conscripted onto her ship for some nefarious activity. Is that where Ned, Zac and Ade are?"

"Gosh Belle, I take it all back, nice bit of logical thinking there," Nancy whispered. "I could buy that from the devious cow. We must keep our ears open and eyes peeled inside the Black Anchor, someone may know something. We've reached the front door already. See you all later, I've got hooves to clean and Rory to chat up once I get changed."

Two days of bobbing about on the edge of the Mersey, cleaning up the previous two week's salvage from a sunken seventeenth-century naval vessel off the Bootle shoreline, was driving the three conscripts to distraction, although the first mate had been generous with the rum. But if Zac saw another plate of salted bully beef he would throw up over the side. Ned was making the most of his own personal distraction by ending up the second night in the luxury of Fenella's personal cabin, a huge room which crossed from side to side on the boat, resplendent with expensive furniture, her personal bar and a huge antique desk, piled up with papers and charts. Zac had calmed down and accepted Ned had to do his duty. In fact he was missing Dottie again but the chances of her, Belle and Nancy turning up were zero. What he had done to amuse himself in the dim light of one miserly candle, alone in his hammock, was to secretly configure a new app for his discovered iPhone, downloaded from a special geek site on the dark web the day before their disappearance. This piece of software claimed to allow a phone to detect black holes in the nearest galaxies and pinpoint them on a sky-map through perturbations in background gamma radiation. The effect, which worked by simulating the phone as a black hole, was triggered by simply starting up the phone's Bluetooth so was independent of internet connectivity. He had plenty of charge left so if correct the software detector should work in 1865 too.

He suddenly remembered something Belle said before they set off for lunch on that fateful 'back to the future' day. She had been wittering on about their psychic experience being a space and time distortion of dark energy, whose properties little was still known about but at least had been proven to exist. Belle was reluctant to say where she had garnered that information from except the source was a credible and super-capable mathematician. Belle, too, had downloaded the app as had Maddie and both were going to play about with it because huge black holes had been the demonstration sites for the recent evidence of dark energy, owing to their intense gravitational attracting power and pulsating energy bursts from rapidly circling massive stars about to disappear into the black hole event horizon. Maddie was almost on a personal mission to research this psychic power hypothesis but the advanced mathematics needed was proving too much for her. In time though she felt confident, after more advanced study, the topic could be a future PhD topic. Maybe, Zac reflected, just maybe they could communicate over the time barrier using this black hole simulation. Firing up the app, he noted the sequencing of coloured buttons on the top, so far so good. He didn't know whether it worked but turned on the Bluetooth and a map of the northern sky overhead appeared and a few blinking flashes associated, according to the blurb, with a couple of significant galaxies less than fifty light years away. Mmm ... interesting. Quite spontaneously, he typed a concise message. 'Help us ... imprisoned on the Warrior Queen,' and pressed send. A silly move really as the two processes couldn't possibly connect, especially as the message would fizzle out on the Bluetooth carrier at fifty feet. Deciding to conserve charge, he picked up Moby Dick, which Fenella had kindly lent him out of her cabin library, supposedly one of her favourite books published recently in 1851. He'd never read it as a child. The book appeared more interesting than he thought and he had nothing better to do anyway.

Ade was still down in the hold, sat amongst the latest salvage with a dozen crew members enjoying a five-card stud poker match. With plenty of hard drink flowing and cigars liberally smoked, Ade was becoming pleasantly accustomed to this new lifestyle. He already knew how to play the game from his misspent time with his elder brother down at the social club. The rules and betting style hadn't altered in all the intervening years, except now he was playing literally for pennies. The three of them had been given a few pounds each in advance from the first mate, on orders from Fenella for their potential share of the sale of the salvage in Southport the next day, where they would be docking first thing in the morning. That would be their first experience on land at long last. Ade with his experience was on a winning streak and had extended his initial sixpence bet to a guinea's worth of stakes.

Soon, only a hard core of players continued in the smoke filled room and Ade's cash pile had risen to over ten pounds, far ahead of the others, but they were still determined to win back their hard earned wages.

"Hey, grand-homme, where you learn to play like this?" one unsavoury participant, his left hand replaced with a brass hook and down to his last shilling, demanded in a strong accent. "This game is nouveau, I am the first to bring it from Louisiana and the American civil war which only finish in January … and I leave original behind," he said with a grimace, waving his metal hand. "So I say you are despicable cheat!"

Fiery Ade, never the most even-tempered at the best of times, stood up and instantly grabbed the sailor around the throat and lifted him up into the air, one-handed, to his full six-foot seven-inch height, eyeball to eyeball, the sailor spluttering and coughing in Ade's iron grip. The other players scattered. They had seen Ade's fighting mode originally when it took six of them to hold him down and they'd all had too much to drink this time to try and repeat it.

"I don't cheat, arse-hole, I'm just smarter. We learned this game here in Liverpool and we do things better than Louisiana, got it?" He squeezed harder as the man reddened, before releasing him to drop heavily onto the floor. Instantly the man drew a large knife from his belt when a kick from nowhere sent it flying into the sacks of tobacco alongside.

"Non, Henri, vous êtes un imbécile, et le commandant de bord ne sera pas heureux avec vos menaces." René had quietly walked in, with Ned alongside, both viewing the altercation with some alarm. "Now, I suggest Ade that you call it a night for the gambling, you have won enough. Henri here cannot afford to lose all his wages. He has ten children to keep."

There was a silence as everyone waited. Ade, still feeling aggressive after too much rum consumed, caught Ned behind nodding. He held out his hand and pulled up the sailor by the hook. "Okay, my apologies, Henri. Here, now feed your kids, they deserve better." He threw down his winnings on the table, keeping a couple of pounds back as a grateful Henri scooped the lot up immediately.

"Monsieur Ade, you are a man with a good heart after all. I will remember," he muttered grabbing his knife and stomped off towards the sleeping area. The game ended, the rest of the men dispersed into groups to continue drinking and talking. It was soon time to rest up for all of them; they anticipated a long day in the morning.

Walking out quickly, Ned turned to Ade before climbing up the ladder, the air finally stilled and the ship calm. Earlier, the three had twice emptied the contents of their stomach over the side, much to the merriment of the rest of the crew, another reason why Ade was happy getting his own back by winning all the money off them. "René wants to discuss some business with us. We're going for a walk on the deck quickly."

"What sort of business? Anyway, I thought you were fucking the … err … in the company of Fenella tonight. What are you doing here? And where's Zac?"

"Zac is reading and playing with his whatnots … I mean thoughts."

Ade laughed but he got the message. They both knew Zac well enough. He was cooking something up in that giant nerd brain of his.

"Fenella was concluded earlier than expected and she's fast asleep now after half a bottle of Drambuie. I'll head back to her cabin in a minute."

In a few moments, Ade, Ned and René assembled at the bow of the ship, well away from prying ears. Ned began to explain. "Okay, tomorrow we disembark at Southport for the day and we four will be accompanying Fenella and the salvage swag to a dealer in the town centre. She genuinely wants us to enjoy some downtime. There will likely be a bit of a celebration in the Dog and Duck on the front."

"Fuck me, that shit-hole place? I hope it's better than it used to be when I was a nipper," Ade replied, grinning, but shut up when he saw the perplexed expression from René. "Sorry, had too much rum tonight, head's all mixed up. I've never even been to Southport. So what's the business then?"

"Very simple," Ned replied in a whisper, looking around furtively. "René wants out."

"Out of what?" Ade replied, perplexed.

"Sometimes, Ade, you can be as dense as those molasses in that barrel. He's had enough of a life of servitude with the all-demanding Captain Fanny, he has other plans. As do we."

Ade looked hard at René who then continued quietly. "We have, as they say, a mutual interest to help each other. Ned has explained your wish to escape so this is what we do. The crew will load the salvage into a waggon on the quay and return to guard the ship. I will drive the waggon with the four of us and the captain to the dealer's shop. He is a strange old man who talks oddly and has, I am sure, seen better days. I would say he is heading for senile but he has a grande connaissance of old antiques and paintings and always pays well to our captain. She trusts his judgement. However, on arrival and after unloading, I will engineer a diversion to remove the captain and take her away from the scene ... She will trust Ned to complete the deal, so you will need to be quick. Outside, once you have the money, around the corner another carriage painted in red will be waiting for you ... You split the proceeds and give half to the driver. He is my brother, Francois, unlike me, tall with a great red beard. The carriage will then take you along the coast road to a remote jetty ... a wherry will be waiting, loaded with cotton. You board, hide in the hold under canvas, which will take you around the coast towards Preston and then up the Ribble river to the small estuary of the River Douglas and onwards inland to Tarleton where you can then join the canal and take a packet barge towards your destination. Is that all clear?"

Ade grinned. "Completely clear, René my friend, yes we will go with that proposition. I wish I'd kept my ten pounds now. But what will happen when Fenella finds out we've done a runner?"

"You will receive a lot of money for the salvage, believe me, sufficient for your needs for a very long time," René replied, shaking both their hands to seal the deal. "The captain will be very angry, à incandescence avec rage, you get the meaning?"

Ned nodded sombrely. He knew this was a major risk. They had to convince Zac next but that should be fine as he too was desperate to escape and get to Orsbrick Hall again. Ade could be a loose cannon at times but seemed on board, without any doubts. This was their best chance otherwise they may never have another once they sailed off again.

René continued. "Captain Fanny will organise search parties for us all straight away. I will be on my way back to France immediately with my brother and out of the area quickly but you three will be more vulnerable. You must have a good reason to want to go to this Orsbrick Hall place. I do not ask, but you will need to take great care, not from the police, they will not be interested or involved, but from her underground network of dangerous, ruthless assassins. They are very formidable."

Ned nodded again. The risk was doubled because Orsbrick Hall, of course, could likely be guessed by Fenella anyway. They had to be prepared for the possible confrontation there and hope it would be in their favour. He and Zac needed to talk that through on the way, the second part of the plan. They departed immediately back to their beds.

As Ned crept back into Fenella's cabin, he could hear her sleeping heavily. A distinct chill filled the air and taking off his clothes he shivered violently before slipping under those thick cotton sheets and heavy blankets and wrapped his arms around her warm, naked body. The situation they were in was beyond bizarre and he reflected long and hard about Nancy and his guilt escaping. If she knew what had been going on here on the ship she would literally cut him dead instantly, but it was survival for the three of them on the line. He had no choice. Fenella, still half-asleep, responded with a pleasing moan to his caresses and pulled him tighter around her. He had to admit he was enjoying fucking and bucking her and felt very conflicted in too many ways about the escape plan the next day, all compounded not only by knowing and liking Fenella before but especially knowing and liking Fenella now, but there was no other way. They had to find some way of breaking out of this horrendous time warp they were trapped into and return to their own present and hoped that Nancy, Belle and Dottie would be waiting if that was ever going to be possible again.

Chapter Ten

Burscough: Down in the church rectory

There had been an expectation of a much longer settling in period. Elizabeth smiled, quietly picking up the brown enveloped letter in the muted light of a dimmed table lamp. Old habits of faint flickering candlelight still endured, as did staying up half the night reading and sipping red wine. She listened to the rattled snore of the vicar and his wife droning upstairs, one complimenting the other in an almost comic syncopation. They commendably drank very little. So what was it about old age which engendered a tendency to become noisier in one's sleep? But enough, she had more important and pressing matters to apply her intellect to. Her secret assignations with Madeleine on exploring advanced mathematics and accelerate understanding of this modern world she was dramatically thrust into, was proving highly productive, aided by her new phone-linked 'Sam…Sung' tablet. The vast intellectual storage inherent within the amazing internet of information, data and things had not ceased to amaze her … if she only had accessed such powerful tools in the 1840s, where would society be now. She was wholly impressed with Madeleine, rating her amongst the same calibre of natural talent and academic capability as her old friend and mentor, Mary Somerville. Back in 1841, the real differences between Madeleine and her gifted twin sister Annabelle were not clear when outside of the beady eye of Victoria, their mother. She had put both through their paces of rigorous mental challenge, admittedly lubricated by rather large glasses of her best red wine, to discern the truth of their origins. She achieved success in such speedy and frightening clarity. It was catastrophic that Morag McKenzie had to go and completely ruin the huge scientific potential unfolding with her manic and obsessive narrow-mindedness and lack of clear thinking. But quietly observing both sisters now in the context of their own time, it was patently clear that Madeleine was in a class of her own regarding mathematical aptitude and abstract thinking. Annabelle appeared to have all the makings of a future stellar career in medicine.

Elizabeth was pleased that Madeleine was sufficiently confident of their friendship to exchange confidences about her McKenzie family, but the bombshell about Julian Endersby-Finnis, her father, especially amused Elizabeth and also that peculiar art collector individual, Dr Lynton Grey, who now turned out to be Abigail's husband, clearly a foursome of long-standing friendship and shared life and marital experience which Elizabeth would have envied back in 1841. What a poor marriage she had endured, like most women then. And she was never really cut out for children but had been fascinated to follow her husband's and children's progress through life and death on the Wikipedia encyclopaedia, strange though it felt, like a ghostly voyeur. Later, when she had more time, she would trace any family descendants, alive in 2026, although on reflection that may not be a sound concept. Meeting such people could trigger a law violation of her space-time travel and send her ignominiously back to the past again. She shuddered. No, she would leave that task well alone; to what end would it serve except gratuitous and unnecessary curiosity? She rather liked the way her life was already panning out. Her memory of the short romantic period in 1841 spent with Julian Fazackerley was still sharp and intense, but time had literally hugely moved on, then and especially now. She had no feelings of love left for old Julian so would, in due course, be happy to meet new Julian without causing apprehension for Victoria and Abigail. She was grateful to Madeleine for being pre-warned discretely. Of course, this explained why Victoria had made those strange and esoteric comments on the first day they met at the rectory. To delay going over to Orsbrick Hall for dinner had been a sound tactic. Madeleine agreed too, on the grounds that so much needed to be done adjusting to her role as the new curate, which, most surprisingly she was actually beginning to enjoy and had an unexpected aptitude for. Probably, because she had always been interested in people from all walks of life, naturally curious and enjoyed gossip. How she used her time was working out nicely and her duties had become advantageously flexible due to the ongoing kindness of the eccentric Reverend Langton and his wife not wishing to exert too much pressure. Her accommodation too, whilst not palatial as it once had been in the old days, was very comfortable, warm and clean and the housekeeper was almost as good a cook as she had employed at St James's Square, so she was definitely not complaining about her new lifestyle, far from it. Moreover, she had the added comfort of remaining secretly rich, with a bank account she had full control over, which made her smile often. How she wished her mother could see her now. Likely Lady Byron would still be angry, manic and unrepentant of her sins of control and disdain of her only daughter and the vibrant memory of the father she never met, Lord Byron.

Working with Madeleine, a fascinating aspect was to reflect and freely generate ideas on the set of interrelated phenomena of space, time, dark energy, multiverses, and the psychic occurrences which she had become engaged with in the early 1850s. These were all formidable concepts which had been rigorously developed mathematically in the intervening one hundred and seventy year period and changed the face of physics upside down. If only dear Charles Babbage had been around to see it, he would have been just as ecstatic and approving. Understanding the necessary mathematics had been exceptionally challenging, but the grounding she had in those ancient quaternions, discovered by her good friend Hamilton and her advanced calculus and algebraic knowledge set her off quickly down the pathway of vectors, tensors and other necessary Riemannian topology tools. These enabled her to grasp the fundamentals of Einstein's General Relativity Theory and the implications of recent findings in 2026 still being assessed. Amazingly, somebody years back in the rectory must have been an ardent physics lover because there were varieties of old leather science books covering this topic which she devoured avidly over a few sleepless nights, especially the popularising space, time and general relativity book published in 1921 by someone called Arthur Eddington, supposedly the first person, immediately after Einstein to understand what he had accomplished. With Madeleine's assistance, she had short-cut through to the latest astrophysics research and was convinced, having devoured endless online papers on quantum gravity and black holes, of Madeleine's belief that a strange rippling of dark energy was correctly creating the space-time shifts and the opening up of so-called wormholes through different universes which permitted the experience of time travel they both shared. Although she showed Madeleine how it was mathematically possible, the key issue, with no answers for the moment, was how this event had physically happened. What were the exact mechanisms and drivers and what was so special about the McKenzie family to have this unique ability to engage the process? That was an experimental question and would have to wait.

Elizabeth realised that Madeleine had understandable knowledge limitations with the mathematics. Only diligent study would correct that deficiency. Madeleine was not able to enjoy the same 'forward into the future' effect of the peculiar time and knowledge compression adjustment which she, Elizabeth, had gradually acquired since arrival. That phenomenon, combined with her extraordinary mathematical abilities, had meant she could zoom along the advanced knowledge and applications curve at a very fast rate of knots indeed, a breathless pace for the very best mathematician to accompany and Madeleine would one day be one of those rare exceptions. Despite her age handicap, Madeleine was decidedly benefiting from the bumpy ride and clearly understood the principles of what they were analysing. Madeleine would have much to do in her future intended programmes at Cambridge University to continue this exciting research path.

All the deep personal reflection had halted Elizabeth's task in hand. Grabbing the letter opener knife, she slit open the brown letter. This communication finally may provide answers to the other personal quest she had quietly and assiduously followed up ... again with some assistance.

Stepping carefully up the stairs balancing a tray of soup and bread, Maddie remained extremely concerned about her siblings and her friends, Dottie and Nancy, plus of course Fenella. There had been no sign or sound from any of them and the time was creeping past six pm. Judy, her triplet bulge suddenly very apparent, had already arrived with all seven children and they were enjoying a rollicking jelly, cake and balloon party in the Orsbrick Hall dining room. Husband, Jarvis, was absent owing to evening mayoral duties hosting a delegation of visiting Chinese hoteliers in Southport, but Judy proudly showed off their new Mercedes electric mini-bus which they had bought. Scrupulous forward planning for the growing tribe was evident alongside a major rear extension being built to their large townhouse, increasing the bedrooms to nine. Victoria and Abby were conferring in the drawing room, joined now for a drink by Julian and Lynton. The intended large family evening dinner seemed increasingly unlikely as they debated what was happening. Victoria wasn't yet so concerned as Maddie but she was certainly puzzled … the lack of communication by her children was very unusual.

Maddie knocked quietly on the door and heard a muted 'come in' response. Janine had suddenly gone down with a bad stomach bug, vomiting embarrassingly in the scullery over the dog's eating bowls when they brought them in from a long walk. Jeb and Kai were unimpressed. Fortunately, their GP, Dr Jenny Lee, was out on call in the locality and managed to fit in an extra visit, immediately confirming, after an instant digital blood and saliva test, a US variant of norovirus compounded by Janine being overly-tired, heavily stressed, and not sleeping properly for weeks. Effectively, Janine was worryingly run down and needed urgent bed and rest for a few days, just at the moment when Maddie had become preoccupied with her sister's and brother's absence. Maddie pushed the door open to see Janine sitting up in bed, wearing one of her thick winter nightdresses and looking quite miserable.

"I'm so sorry Maddie, I feel dreadful; waves of hot and cold nausea and I'm so embarrassed puking like that in the kitchen. At least I missed the dogs, they moved fast. I don't know where

I picked up this bug but you'd better not get too close, the last thing I want is for you to catch it."

Maddie smiled and put the tray down on the bed. "Dr Lee said you were very run down and need rest, but it is important that you don't dehydrate and eat a little and often. I've made you some vegetable soup if you can manage that," Maddie replied, eyeing the bucket strategically placed alongside the bed. "Later, I'll bring you some boiled rice and a piece of banana."

"Thanks, I don't know what I'd do without you, you're a real love. I think now I can manage some of that nice soup, but I feel so exhausted, which isn't like me at all. My immune system must be down. Any news of Belle and your brothers yet?"

"No, and it's so unlike them to just go off the radar. I'm getting worried, to be honest. On the other hand, Ned is becoming increasingly belligerent with everyone and desperate to be more independent, although it's not as if he and Zac don't have any freedoms. Dad is very indulgent with the pair of them. It's Mum who continues to crack the whip with reasonable expectations, you know, like sensible behaviour and study. She hates it when Ned is always acting the fool; she's too serious for his character."

"Like her eldest daughter," Janine said, forcing both a smile and some spoonfuls of soup inside her. "Sounds to me like they've all been having great fun and simply lost track of time. We all do it and probably from Ned's perspective, deliberately, which is why they've switched off their phones. Are you going to tell me more about the intriguing Fenella? You've been rather coy about your new guest. Is she a rival for my affections then?"

Maddie blushed. Janine was always so direct, whereas she still felt hesitant about being overt with her feelings, especially in her own house. "No, of course not," she whispered in a low voice. She had to reflect fast. There had been no time for thinking through and rehearsing detailed Fenella explanations once Janine turned up out of the blue. All Maddie could do was go with the same broad flow agreed by the family for outsiders. "Fenella is a distant cousin who had a very difficult childhood brought up in care in a weird convent in Ireland so, as a family, we're helping her to get on her feet and normalise, which is why she's staying here for a while. When they get back and I introduce you, I think you'll like her a lot. Fenella has a sharp mathematical mind and has taken to computing amazingly well with Zac's help. She's a natural programmer. And she and Zac seem to have become a bit of an item now as a result, so the answer is a very big no. But you'll have to get rid of that awful bug before your next kiss I'm afraid!" Maddie added, laughing.

Janine grinned. "Okay, fair enough. I'm done in," she said, handing the tray and half-finished soup back.

"Have a good sleep now, I'll love and leave you and see how you're doing later," Maddie replied, blowing a kiss and walking towards the door. In one important way, she was glad Janine was temporarily out of it. She needed to pop out and make a visit. Unlike her mother and Abby who seemed deliberately oblivious to deeper thought, Maddie was far more fearful of the reality of what might be happening to Belle and the others and she needed to test out her ideas with someone else who would understand.

The moment she walked into the drawing room to rejoin her parents, a loud knock on the door began, drawing protestations from Victoria who was tiring of unannounced visitors that day. Maddie hoped, above all else, that it wasn't the police and peered through the window. An old, white transit van had parked outside and a woman in her early twenties with long, red hair was sat quietly in the passenger seat.

"I'll go. Claire and Danielle will be busy with the children," Maddie said, remembering suddenly on the way to the door, whose van it belonged to. She eased back the heavy bolts and pulled the old, oak door open so see Ade's brother stood there quite agitated.

"Jonny, I thought that was your van," she said warily, unhappy with his expression. She knew he had an even shorter fuse than his younger brother when the mood took him. "What are you doing here? Ade is out with Ned, Zac and the girls."

"I know," Jonny said, looking about fearfully. They're not here then I take it? The thing is Maddie, I'd arranged after a call before lunch from Ade, to head into Liverpool and pick up all the scooters so they could carry on, have some drinks through the evening and not worry about riding back pissed. It was going to be a surprise. Ade intended to treat them all and cheer up Ned who was getting grumpy being teetotal all day, you know how he is. Then they'd do the club next door for a quick disco and come back on the midnight train. Well, me and Esme got to the Black Anchor …"

"The Black Anchor? Is that where they went … on Dale Street?"

"Yes, why?" Jonny replied, his eyes wide. "Didn't you know?"

Maddie felt an unaccountable iciness trickle down her stomach and that odd pounding in her head suddenly set off, but just as quickly the pain stopped. She hadn't mentioned it to anyone but Fenella had talked about the Black Anchor a lot in the first week when she opened up about things she had enjoyed in her childhood. Apparently, her grandfather, Lord Kirkby, was a frequent visitor there for his import business and used to take her in his carriage. Often they would walk down to the George's Dock as it was then because she loved the tall ships, always berthed on the quayside. "No reason. Belle never mentioned it before they left. So what happened down there?"

"Well, that's just it. Esme and I get there, find all the electric scooters in the car park and load them into the van. I had a plank with me to push them in, fortunately. Ade had unlocked them ready when I sent him a text to say I was almost there. Then I go into the pub to get the keys and say hello but there's not a sign of them anywhere and nobody in the pub seemed to have either seen or heard of them when I asked the landlord and a couple of people at the bar, really weird. They've vanished. No answer from their phone, no anything. That's why I came here. Couldn't think of anything better."

"Oh, hello Jonny, we don't see you here often," a voice behind Maddie sounded. Victoria had come to the door to see who it was with Abby right behind, joined a moment later by Julian and Lynton. Jonny turned to the van and waved his girlfriend, Esme, to join them and prompted by Maddie, he relayed the story again. Esme then added to the mystery, having picked up a small brooch off the bar floor … a distinctive item which Maddie immediately recognised as the one she and Belle had bought for Fenella from the market earlier in the week.

Julian, as ever the quiet oasis of calm and rationality, came forward and intervened the moment Jonny said he was going immediately to the police. "I would suggest we give them the benefit of the doubt … at least for the next twelve hours, Jonny. It's not yet seven pm and the plan, clearly, was to continue celebrating and come back by public transport later. It appears to me like they've all gone somewhere else … I'll guarantee our lot will be severely grounded when they get back for causing so much anxiety. I'm becoming quite tired of Ned and his rebelliousness. He and Zac are only just seventeen; they have to start to toe the line more."

"I agree with Julian," Abby added, also walking outside as did Lynton to join Victoria. Maddie remained standing by the door, ignored by the elders but observing and very curious. "They've obviously switched off their phones deliberately so we won't be able to interrogate where they are, down a nightclub I expect where they shouldn't be by the sound of it."

"Also," Lynton added, "let's be realistic. The police won't want to know, at least not yet as Julian says. Belle and Fenella are over eighteen as are Dottie and Nancy now. In theory, they're adults. Only Ned, Zac and Ade are seventeen and legally underage for pub drinking which will create a likely fuss, especially after the latest crackdown. Abby and I know. The Red Lion has been swarming with undercover police and black market identity cards are thriving of late. The hefty fines are becoming a good income earner for the local police commission, any excuse."

"What do you think, Victoria?" Julian asked, rubbing his glasses carefully with a handkerchief.

Victoria pondered for a moment. "This is certainly out of character for Belle, Ned and Zac, although Belle had left in a foul temper and Ned has been getting on all our nerves of late pushing the envelope of unacceptable behaviour, but we shouldn't rush to judgement yet. I propose, Jonny, we give them until nine am tomorrow morning and if they're not back or there is no communication by then we'll go to the police together. How does that sound?"

Jonny nodded as his girlfriend squeezed his hand. "Yeh, fair enough, thanks, Mrs McKenzie. I'll also give Ade a good bollocking when he comes home too ... sorry about the language."

They all smiled and began chatting. Lynton suggested he and Julian help Jonny offload the scooters into the secure workshop. Victoria suddenly thought and turned back to the front door. "Maddie, does that seem sensible to you too?"

But there was no Maddie, she'd vanished. In all the intense discussion nobody had noticed that Maddie, hugely frustrated having made up her own mind from the obvious evidence staring her in the face, had exhausted her patience with the tin-ears of her mother and Abby and slunk off quickly. It was now a matter of urgency and she needed help. By the time they noticed, Maddie was already out the back and cycling down the canal towpath at a fast rate of knots. But she did find time to send a text to Abby … to try and jolt at least her into a right frame of mind again.

"Where's Maddie gone?" Julian blurted out. "Is she upset with what we've just suggested?"

Abby felt her phone ping in her jeans pocket. She took an instant peek. "No, no, Maddie has just gone out quickly to check with a few mutual friends of Belle and Dottie, see if they've picked up anything."

"Okay, good," Julian replied. "Jonny, if you drive your van around the side over there, Lynton and I will push those scooters into my workshop, where they'll be safe. Thanks a lot for bringing them back, much appreciated." He fished inside his wallet and pulled out three twenty pound notes and shoved them into Jonny's shirt pocket. "For the petrol and your time. Can you pour some more gin and tonic, Victoria? I think we could all do with one … back in a minute."

Victoria grimaced. She disliked his ordering of the servant tone of voice but conceded that a stiff drink was a good idea. It reminded her. She still needed to confront Julian about his nebulous London past which had been nagging in her subconscious and find the truth. Does he actually have a secret sister named Caitriona? Going by the racket and the shrieking

258

at the other end of the house, the children's party was still in full swing. Everything was beginning to give her a pounding headache.

Back inside, Abby almost shoved Victoria into the drawing room and closed the door immediately, causing Victoria to hit back. She was irritable and annoyed with Maddie's attitude for disappearing like that, without even a by your leave and Janine lying poorly in bed upstairs too.

"Jesus Christ, Abby, has everyone gone completely bonkers today, even you? What's the matter? Why all the pushing for fuck's sake?"

Abby was already pouring out the gin and tonic, a large one each. "I want you to read Maddie's message," she said sombrely, handing Victoria her iPhone. "And the tweet she's forwarded. Now is the time to stop having cloth ears and bandaged eyes."

Victoria read the text and blanched. Her mind instantly worked through the logical evidence that both her and Abby were studiously avoiding. "Shit, she's gone to find Elizabeth and confer. Maddie is convinced it's happened again and Belle, Ned and Zac and the other girls have gone back in time, back to Fenella's time! And what on earth is the Warrior Queen?"

"Let's be honest, Vikki, neither of us were happy about the sudden appearance of Fenella, nor the tale she told, convincing though it sounded. We've been taken in, conned by a subtle and effective rehabilitation into our time and deep inside we all wanted to believe it, seeing how well Fenella was adjusting and becoming part of the family. All very cosy, almost mind-numbing. Maddie and Belle contented, Fenella and Zac being good for each other in what appears to be a normal relationship, everyone getting along. Whereas, clearly, quite the opposite was being plotted ... Fenella is someone or something quite malign, thrown up out of the distorted space-time disruption that we became part of in 1841."

Victoria looked hard at Abby. Was she right? If so this was serious. Where was the evidence? Maybe Zac had been playing a practical joke, all part of their sudden disappearance. A prank to show the adults that they can be in charge of their lives from now on and certainly for her, as their mother, to be less demanding with conforming. Even Belle was getting uppity. "How can we be so sure we're not being taken for a ride by some concocted escapade, a charade to force Julian and I to lighten up a bit, especially me with Ned and Zac?"

"Oh God, Vikki, here we go again, never trust your instincts always demand the hard-scientific facts. I know you're never going to change but this time, trust your daughter. We know how attuned Maddie is and I believe her, despite the fact I feel no psychic imbalance whatsoever. I'm mildly disappointed that she's chosen to confide in Ada first, sorry, I mean Elizabeth. Maddie must be in turmoil particularly as we've ignored her and the obvious signs since the phones went dead. We've even left her to get on with looking after her sick friend on her own. I haven't been up there to see how Janine is and neither have you and you did display a level of haughtiness with the girl which has likely added to uneasy mistrust by Maddie. I've said it before and I'll say it again, let her work out her emotional feelings and her identity in her own way, just as you did once upon a time. You really do find that hard to accept. And I haven't told Lynton I'm pregnant yet, nor am going to until we've worked through what the hell is going on around us."

Victoria took a deep breath. Harsh words from her best friend but she needed the jolt. "Yes, as usual, you need to put me in my place at the necessary time. Let's go over to the rectory, four heads will be better than two. I have a sneaking suspicion that, like 1841, time is not on our hands. Fuck it all, Lynton and Julian are coming back in … this is definitely not the time to reveal anything."

"I agree," Abby said as the door swung open and the smiling pair entered, immediately focused on the drinks trolley, despite Lynton's earlier reassurance that he was giving up the booze entirely.

"And, what do you agree about, dearest?" Lynton remarked, heading straight for the gin bottle which Abby snatched away. Smiling weakly, he nodded and poured out a straight tonic.

"That you and Julian can entertain the children now with lots of games, stop them from being bored. You're good at that Lynton. Abby and I have to go out, we'll explain later."

Screwing up his eyes, Lynton looked up. "Eh?"

Julian had decided on a bottled beer and yanked off the cap. "The strange machinations of the female mind in evidence once again," he said in a droll voice, shaking his head. "Yes. I'm sure we can relieve Judy and Claire. I'll just fetch that box of party games the kids used to enjoy years ago out of the cellar."

"Excellent, we'll catch up with you both later," Abby said. "If you feel peckish later just help yourself to the chicken tikka and basmati rice that Danielle has prepared, which will be keeping warm in the oven. She's also done some aloo gobi. Family dinner is off tonight."

Lynton perked up. His favourite curry in the oven, which he'll wash down with one, but only one, of Julian's beers, once Abby was out of the way. "Okay, I'll be magician in chief. I used to be good once with those tricks … we could do with a rabbit in a hat …"

But by then Victoria and Abby had disappeared out the door, heading quickly down the canal towpath.

Peering through the Georgian windows, the rap-rapping on the outside door brought her a feeling of self-satisfied justification for the intense work she had been doing. Once again, the imminent appearance of who she expected proved her instinct correct. She knew from Maddie's pained expression that this was not a social call or a working session to discuss mathematics. Just as well the Reverend Langton was over in Ormskirk visiting their sister church of St Peter and St Paul to see the unique dual steeple and tower. His wife, as was often the case, had gone to Liverpool, shopping with friends. Elizabeth suspected Maddie's visit required both privacy and strict confidentiality, but in her view, a question only of when not if. Something had arisen which brought their mutual interest together to elicit the truth … the conundrum of missing Mauveine.

Maddie was soon seated in the large rear drawing room which the vicar had effectively provided Elizabeth for her sole private use. A tray brought in by Agnes greeted them of a huge pot of tea and a plate of Elizabeth's favourite Chelsea buns, made to the original 1701 recipe, a small reminder of home as it used to be.

"I think I know why you're here," Elizabeth began. "I surmise that both of us are compelled to discover the whereabouts of Mauveine and her husband. On my part, I need to know if they too were able to jump through your history cosmos when I did. I owe Mauveine and Isaac a great debt of gratitude for my resurrection in good health. Now, are you going to tell me your precise reason for needing to find her? Take your time Madeleine."

Maddie blinked. Elizabeth, as before in 1841, retained that sharp forensic intellect and uncanny foresight. She just wished her mother was half as sensitive and worse, why had Abby become so weirdly distant lately? Tears began to roll down her cheek, thinking of the dilemma Belle and her brothers must be experiencing if her prediction was correct. She wished wholeheartedly there was an alternative explanation but all the signs pointed exactly to what she didn't want. Her siblings were trapped in time but where, when and for what reason? And what was the connection with Fenella? She took some deep breaths and forced her emotions back inside her mind; now was the moment for clear thinking. Her fast brain began a concise summary and she held out her phone for Elizabeth to read. "This message has come from Zac, my brother, via a special astronomy application which targets black holes and potential dark energy perturbations."

Elizabeth read it and pondered, cutting a Chelsea bun in half. "I assume your inference is not that Zac is thirty light years away in another far-off galaxy, but instead, given our recent and credible musings on dark energy, black holes and theoretical time travel, that he has disappeared back in time?"

"Yes, along with Annabelle, my brother Ned and their friends, Ade, Dottie, Nancy … oh and Fenella. They vanished at lunch time from an old Victorian public house in Liverpool called the Black Anchor. Mauveine is our only hope of identifying where, how and why and trying to get them back. I must find her urgently."

Elizabeth was reflecting deeply and suddenly remembered. "Mmm … may I ask? You separated out Fenella. Was that because she is different from the others? Who is she?"

Maddie smiled. "Not much gets past you does it. Hellfire and damnation, I can see Abby and my mother outside walking up to the front door with faces like thunder. They must have followed me. Perhaps something has happened."

Elizabeth rose from her seat. "Actually, I was also expecting them too ... have you all fallen out?"

"No, not really, but my mother can be so scientifically obstinate, wishing that all in the garden is well and thriving with this catastrophe, and Abby these days has been so jumpy and irritable. We've not been communicating properly like we always used to."

"What you mean is they don't believe you."

Maddie laughed. "Yes, in a nutshell, but I don't know how they know I'm here? Meeting you over the past month has been a secret." She looked again at her phone. "Oh gosh, I accidentally put Ada on my text to Abby, I'm so sorry ... wasn't thinking."

"No problem whatsoever for me, Madeleine. Hey, I'm the curate of this parish, I heal the sick and the troubled and they certainly look very troubled. Look, I'm going to let them both in then you continue from where you left off and we join intellectual forces and work this through together. I do have some experience of time travel too. Just like old times isn't it."

Maddie smiled. "Yes please, you're absolutely right."

Once the door was opened, Maddie could hear muted voices in the hallway. Some kind of discussion was in full swing led by Elizabeth then Abby was the first to dash through the door and give Maddie a swift hug. "Vikki and I came as soon as I read your text ... we think you're absolutely right but where on earth do we go from here?"

Maddie looked up at her mother stood alongside Elizabeth and looking quietly anxious, having been digesting everything she could think about on the way including the implications. Maddie knew very well how her mother analysed problems. "At long last it appears we're all on the same hymn sheet, so to speak. I really never thought you were going to come out of the garden of red roses, Mum."

Victoria wasn't going to reply to that. One day, when she's older and wiser, Maddie might understand that the first natural reaction of a mother is not to think the worst when her children are in danger. However, now she accepted Maddie's hypothesis it was time for action and as Elizabeth said at the door, a pooling of problem-solving minds was paramount. "Two things stand out to try and work out. First, where is Mauveine who may hold the key to this situation? Do you remember, Abby? Just before that incident on the Queen Lusitania, when we kept seeing Mauveine? She said something about needing to find Fenella. Second, what and where is the Warrior Queen?"

Abby nodded before dashing over to the plate of Chelsea buns and cutting one up for herself. "Mmm … I'm starving. I almost feel like I'm eating for two lately," she said blithely, then realised and quietly poured more tea for everyone. Victoria shot a glance across but said nothing. The expression had simply passed over Maddie's head as she was furiously searching on her phone for anything to do with 'Warrior Queen.' Elizabeth stared at Abby, stuffing herself with half a bun and looked at Victoria's implacable expression. They all had a separate discussion coming at another time and the unusual implications were immediately crystal clear in Elizabeth's mind, a situation far too common amongst her former aristocratic, married friends. Now, in this time period, there seemed to be something called the pill, a medication she urgently needed to explore, curate or no curate.

"I may now be able to help with the first question having also been vexed with that conundrum for the last four weeks," Elizabeth said, opening the brown envelope she was about to start on as Madeleine arrived. "The second question I am at a loss presently but from what Madeleine said a few minutes ago when she described where siblings and friends were, that is to say, the Black Anchor public house, then I suspect the Warrior Queen is a ship."

"A ship?" Victoria replied, "Why?"

Elizabeth smiled mischievously then continued. "Because that Liverpool public house in 1841 was a notorious hotel which served the needs of sailors, coming and going from the George's Dock, with drink, accommodation and loose women. At the time, Julian would regale me in my carriage on the way to the races with his vast local knowledge of maritime history, especially the more salacious kind. Quite the seductive storyteller, he was. That may also pinpoint the where. We are still in the locale, hopefully."

Victoria grimaced. She knew all about seductive storytelling. Modern Julian had played the same spiel to her in 2010. It still rankled that Ada, as was, had somehow managed to enjoy all the courtship tricks of bastard Julian in a very short space of time. She sighed inwardly but was resigned to reality. 1841 had been and gone and they had serious work to do. Her scientific mode was kicking in once more. "Maddie, find anything from your searches?"

"No, not a thing except the name of a girl band in Sweden. Shit … sorry, Mum."

"We'll come back to that in a second, I have an idea," Elizabeth said, reading the letter quickly before handing it to Maddie whilst Abby continued to noisily work her way through a second bun in-between slurps of tea.

Maddie gazed immediately at the address listed in bold at the top of the letter: Oddington Cottage, Canal Lane, Burscough. The information had been provided by a Miss Andrea Cullen, senior researcher at a family history society based in Ormskirk. What was this supposed to be? Then she realised, reading the explanation, that the address was taken from an 1861 census analysis for which the sole occupant and head of household was an Isaac Fazackerley, aged twenty-two. This must have been where Isi was living before he met and married Mauveine. Maddie handed the letter to Victoria and Abby, looking puzzled towards Elizabeth who grinned.

"This information may not be as abstruse as it may appear to you all," Elizabeth said. "I've been reflecting on my initial experience of landing into the year 2026 when I found myself walking around my old and much loved former abode, number twelve St James's Square. Admittedly, I had to quickly adjust from the shock of the change to business offices, but more importantly, it may be that an a priori rule of disruptive time transfer is to return to a place of comfort and safe familiarity. On the day, the Reverend Thomas Langton conducted Morag's funeral, which was held in London at St George's Church in Hanover Square, why there I still don't know, but I spoke to Thomas briefly at the end to express my condolences whilst his wife, Alice, with Michael Faraday, was busy organising other mourners to a private chapel down the road. I had no intention of heading there. Thomas said how much he once loved his tranquil cottage in Burscough by the side of the canal where he lived before marrying Alice. I thought no more of it until, thinking now about where Mauveine and Isi, as they really are, could be. There are, of course, two of them. Mauveine would naturally have landed back in Orsbrick Hall but as Maddie confirmed, there has been neither sight nor sound of either in any way."

"Not even any psychic feelings, a complete absence," Abby said, "which tends to give confidence that they haven't become ghosts again, or Maddie and I would know. So, either they are still in 1840's or 1850's time forever, or maybe some other time altogether which is my deepest dread."

"You don't think either of those possibilities is likely, Elizabeth, do you," Victoria said, having been quiet and intense in her own thoughts before suddenly emerging back into the discussion. "And neither do I. But a logical landing place could also be an Isi past residence rather than a Mauveine one. We never thought of that, I'm impressed."

"Exactly," Elizabeth cried, handing around the rest of the buns quickly before Abby devoured the lot. "So, on advice from the church grave researcher, I contacted this family history person for any historical data on the ten-yearly census records ongoing from 1841, knowing by their ease of dress and local mannerisms that Mauveine and Isi were originally from some other decade in the later Queen Victoria period. The question is does the address exist now?"

Maddie was already ahead and tapped furiously onto her phone, quickly identifying some old online 1890 maps of Burscough. Canal Lane was in evidence then and a number of cottages identifiable as well as linked streets with terraced housing. She'd never heard of Canal Lane but bringing up a modern Google map alongside saw, that the two-up two-down poor housing, like many old properties and lanes in the area and in fact the whole area, had long been flattened and was now the small Parkside industrial estate. "Canal Lane is now Parkside, Mum."

"Really? Then I suggest we go there straight away. Fuck, I need to go back for the car and I don't want Julian and Lynton asking awkward questions again." Victoria replied, irritated.

"I have theoretical access to an old horseless carriage of the vicar's in the former stables," Elizabeth cried, excitedly. "It's a Mit…Su…Bishi. What is it about this technology influence of

Asia? In my day, the only things China was good for were Ming vases and opium. But I have no idea how to ride one of these carriages yet. There's a starter object in the drawer here."

They laughed with the welcome release of tension, old Ada humour and a feeling they may for the first time be getting somewhere finding Mauveine. "Give it to me," Abby cried, picking up the ignition key. "I've only had one gin and tonic, unlike the downing of half a bottle by everyone else."

"I can drive too," Maddie suddenly announced. "Passed my test the day after my birthday. Sorry, Mum, I was keeping that a secret, not even Belle knows. And I've had no alcohol at all today."

Victoria shook her head. Maddie always had a surprise up her sleeve and grabbed the key off Abby and handed it with a smile to her daughter. "Let's go. You can tell me how you managed all that later, Maddie. My insurance will cover you."

The Mitsubishi turned out to be a rusted, forty-year-old Landrover lookalike with thick chunky tyres and a split-screen, but the big diesel started first time. Perfect for Maddie who had learned to drive in such a robust farm vehicle and so she decided, having thrust the old beast into four-wheel drive, they would go the quick, scenic way along the bridle track and drive through the deep river ford at the back of the industrial estate. Bumping along, Elizabeth felt quite at home, luxury even, and was quite mesmerised by the drive, but Maddie had to eventually slow down and keep away from the bumps, seeing Abby turning into her Queen Lusitania colour of seasick green, especially when they splashed their way through the axle deep muddy river.

Victoria felt proud sat alongside her capable daughter. Maddie had become a grown woman under her nose. From that day, onwards, she would offer no further critiques of

Maddie's choices, lifestyle or decisions, only whatever support she could provide. Maddie deserved the same independence of spirit, she acquired in Amsterdam many years before at the age of eighteen. Abby was absolutely correct, it really was time to let go.

Maddie drove slowly through the sprawling industrial park which, although not huge, had been expanding exponentially over the last year. An array of various sized high-tech units came into view. They had no idea what they were looking for until Victoria shouted to stop in the car park of the small, new unit on the next corner. Fittingly, she had spotted the name first, just visible on the fascia board in yellow … Xanthania Dyes Ltd.

Victoria turned to Elizabeth in the back seat. "I have to say, your scientific detective work may well have paid off—this has to be the place. Xanthene was the chemical basis from which we prepared the drug medication for James McKenzie's typhoid. Do you remember?"

"I certainly do, I witnessed the miracle cure in his room with you at the time and Alice, your sister as was, helped with the preparations in Morag's laboratory I recall."

"She more than helped," Maddie said, opening her door. "Mauveine invented Xanthene. Oh gosh, what will they look like? Abby, are you alright? You still look green, sorry for the bumpy ride. What's up? Have you not been well lately which is why we haven't seen much of you?"

Abby took some deep breaths and nodded, her smile returning again. They climbed out and looked around. Everywhere was quiet, a few cars were parked nearby. Many of the new units were awaiting tenants. A couple of old bicycles were propped up against the wall.

"Abigail, I'm afraid I must say it, I'm too familiar with all the signs and symptoms. Just like Medora. Are you with child?" Elizabeth suddenly asked, oblivious as ever to discretion. Her old and privileged habit of straight gossip amongst her married aristocratic social set, where illicit pregnancies occurred on a daily basis, remained. Victoria winced and Maddie looked startled and very surprised.

Abby answered immediately, what was the point keeping her predicament a secret. "Yes, I am. No good hiding it any longer. I'm really sorry, Maddie, I know I should have told you earlier but I've literally only just found out and there is a …"

"And I'm not at all surprised either. But Abigail, you'll have our full support to make sure everything goes well,"

A familiar posh sounding voice with a deep Lancashire accent rang out. They all turned to see a tall figure, dressed in blue skinny jeans and a tight green t-shirt. A long white lab-coat was loosely wrapped around her and she wore a pair of protective goggles and latex blue rubber gloves, her long brown hair neatly pinned in a tight bun.

"Mauveine? Oh, thank goodness, I feel so happy, we've found you at long last," Maddie shouted and ran immediately to give her a giant hug. Abby smiled with the relief of both coming out and now finding Mauveine. She felt markedly better instantly.

"Careful Madeleine, I've just finished a distillation. You don't want this red dye on your nice clothes. Isi is clearing up. I saw you drive in through the window. It's truly wonderful to see everyone. Enter please and I'll explain. I'm intrigued how you found us."

"That was completely down to Elizabeth and Maddie and their determined joint detective work," Victoria replied, grinning.

Mauveine smiled and quietly embraced first Victoria, then Abby and finally Elizabeth. "We owe the escape from the 1841 time-trap solely to you. Isi and I warmly thank you so much. I see you have changed identity, Ada. A good idea, although we've interestingly kept ours, official on the documentation we found in our new abode here. I'm Dr Mauveine McKenzie and the guy opening the door is unsurprisingly Dr Isaac Fazackerley. And I can't wait to understand why you're wearing a dog collar, Elizabeth."

They turned again to see a familiar and smiling Isi at the entrance, dressed similar to Mauveine but without the goggles, his hair cut shorter and still sporting a beard, but clipped in a fashionable, modern style. "Come on in," he shouted, friendly and casual as ever. "Kettle's boiling."

Very quickly they engaged in an update about one another, summarised to essentials; time was tight. Amongst the quiet of a very up to date and well-equipped laboratory, Mauveine and Isi had unexpectedly found themselves transported into a future period and environment they knew instantly would suit them well. Already, Isi's former acquiescence of the life of a man of cloth, albeit a profession for which he showed a gifted talent, was being quickly forgotten. They were and always had been scientists and had returned to what appeared natural. The trigger date of disruption was, as Elizabeth surmised, the date of Mauveine's birth. The space-time envelope could not contain Mauveine's existence and birth occurring simultaneously, an exclusion principle which they all realised was one of the fundamental laws of McKenzie family time-travel. Mauveine and Isi had been around for the past three days and decided initially to try and adjust to the new environment like Elizabeth had been attempting before then heading from London to Orsbrick Hall. Settling down had been easier for Mauveine and Isi as they had prior experience of the present period. Former ghost memories had been unexpectedly retained, but also, like Elizabeth, they quickly realised they had new knowledge implanting into their heads through the time forwarding process, relevant to the age they arrived at rather than left. Each day they awoke to find this information was dramatically increasing, which meant, alongside their years of ghostly observations, they were adjusting fast and with confidence. That was another reason they had decided, on day three, to start undertaking some familiar dye experiments and chose to recreate an old red azo compound that Mauveine had originally invented to become an effective mordant for dyeing silk. They had walked into a fully equipped, modern laboratory which made their hearts beat every time they entered. Everyone now understood that time flow, whether past, present or future, was observer relative, exactly like all other space-time, and was not the same for all participants. So, their three days' worth was as long as Elizabeth's one month. Why? That enigma would have to wait for a future explanation. Another dark energy mystery Maddie wished to explore in her new studies.

"So, do you miss being a former man of the cloth?" Elizabeth interrupted with a sly grin. "You were very good, Isaac, I loved Morag's funeral sermon."

"I believed that was going to be my vocation for the rest of my days," Isi said soulfully, "and I confess I did enjoy it very much although I know my dear wife hated being the wife of a vicar, but she played her dutiful role remarkably well. I shall always look back on those ten years with fond memories."

Mauveine glared at him. Dutiful roles always made her bristle. "I didn't exactly have a lot of choices, my dearest. It was the paternalistic 1840s after all, but now things will be different.

It's my turn," she implored, smiling at Victoria and then turned to Elizabeth. "It appears that you and Isi have swapped jobs," Mauveine continued. "So, are you are going to explain your intriguingly uncharacteristic role and attire?"

Elizabeth quickly summarised why and how she had become a curate and Mauveine gasped at the peculiar transition of the Reverend Thomas Langton and wife Alice into an unexpected, elderly version, so unlike her and Isi. They marvelled how Elizabeth had worked out how to find them.

Isi shrugged his shoulders. "Well, that's time travel for you. I'm pleased we're truly ourselves again and there's so much exciting work to do. There's even a contract on Mauveine's desk to research a new compound for Burscough Dyers Ltd, whoever they are."

Victoria burst out laughing. "That's my factory," she exclaimed. "We're certainly starting off well, but I'll be cracking the whip with you Isi, so being a scientist again won't be all smiles!" she added, eyes twinkling.

Mauveine nodded, that's what she liked to hear, lots of whip cracking and Isi under the thumb. "Good, indeed, excellent."

Isi went quiet once more and sat down with his tea and biscuit.

She turned and her eyes narrowed further, looking Abby all over. "Now Abigail. You're very subdued so unlike you but are amongst your very best of friends and can be unfearful to be candid. Being with child is a fabulous surprise. However, I can recognise by your demeanour that you are balancing an inner dilemma which many Victorian women once faced, is that not so Elizabeth? A specific 1841 dilemma, if my logic and timing are correct? Where is Madeleine?"

They looked around and saw her outside, on her phone, speaking earnestly to someone and scribbling on a pad.

Abby found her moment and took a deep breath. "Look, I give in, hands up. Yes, both you and Elizabeth have worked it out and Victoria knows. I don't want Maddie to hear this, at least not yet. A slight problem may exist with ... err ... paternity, either ... okay, truth time, straight to the point. It can only be the very same John Ruskin I had an unforgettable dalliance with or the peculiar, sex-crazed Dr Lynton Grey who I succumbed briefly to in Morag's study that first night we all met, thinking it would feel the same, and it didn't, absolutely dreadful. I'm beside myself with worry. What on earth can I do?"

Isi blushed, unused to direct female sexual conversation; he had never been as liberally broad-minded as his wife.

Mauveine noticed. "Ignore him, Abby. As a former vicar, you would think he'd heard it all, but clearly not. I think Elizabeth and I would concur with the recommendation I shall make from extensive experience of our time that you've come back from. Look after yourself, have the baby, enjoy the experience with Lynton as is, your husband. He'll accept it as his own, they always do. I would think very hard about attempting any explanation of what actually happened, which was very justifiable at the time."

Elizabeth and Victoria murmured in agreement and Isi nodded. Abby smiled. "Thank you all for the vote of confidence, it does make me feel much better. What you've said makes sense and I so much appreciate the candour. Anyway, that's an issue for another day. We have far more important problems to solve and Maddie is coming back. She seems to have discovered something important, by her expression."

Abby wanted and needed to talk on her own as soon as practicable with Maddie about becoming pregnant. Maddie was too astute not to be working out any implications. And she wasn't convinced in her own heart of that well-meaning advice of Mauveine, but this wasn't the time to question it further. The logic was sound but Abby's emotions rang out deep inside her mind differently. Crossing that road would be a topic between her and Lynton only, and she would choose the right time and place when she had thought about everything to tell him the way she wanted. And right then, a real crisis was encircling them all.

Maddie rushed inside waving Elizabeth's letter. "I've just spoken to the family history researcher, Andrea Cullen," she began excitedly. "Her father is a curator at the Maritime Museum and we've just had a three-way conversation, whilst he searched through their online archives, and he's found an obscure record in 1863, not publicly disseminated, which is why I couldn't find anything on Google. The Warrior Queen was indeed a large sailing ship operating from Liverpool and they traded in covert salvage for treasure, so you were correct, Elizabeth. But here's the really interesting thing. It was owned and captained, almost uniquely at the time, by a woman, a fearsome individual with the name of Fanny Kirkby. It doesn't take too much nous to extrapolate from Fanny to …"

Abby suddenly interrupted. "Whoa, Maddie, you're running ahead of yourself. We haven't explained the other reason we are here yet and now we must." She had seen Mauveine's contorted expression the moment Maddie blurted out Warrior Queen. Something extremely relevant was coming together and Mauveine needed space to absorb what had been happening.

Mauveine looked over sheepishly to Isi. "The Warrior Queen?" she said in a low, deep voice, her expression severe and her eyes flashing real alarm. "So, the rumours are true, that was where she ended up. No wonder I couldn't find her at the same time I couldn't find you either, planning and plotting with your crazy scheme at Orsbrick Hall ... but we've all long forgiven that transgression."

"You mean Fenella, don't you, Mauveine." Abby continued. "You were looking for Fenella on the Queen Lusitania, you told me on the deck. But who is Fenella?"

Victoria shot a glance over at Abby. Why such a stupid question, they all knew who Fenella was? It had been explained. She hadn't died at Morag's birth but had been rescued and brought up by her grandfather, Lord Kirkby.

Mauveine ignored Abby. She needed to first know what had happened to raise up the memory of the Warrior Queen and from Madeleine's lips only, and looked Maddie straight in the eye with that intense stare only her mother ever normally gave her. "Tell me exactly what you know, Madeleine, and what has gone on in the absence of Isi and me."

The room went quiet whilst Maddie expertly described the sudden doorstep appearance of Fenella on the same day they had returned in time. She continued with Fenella's story of who she was and why she was at Orsbrick Hall on April 20th, 1865, followed on by the unexplained disappearance of Belle, Ned and Zac, with Fenella and the others, from the Black Anchor Hotel in Liverpool, concluding with the odd message from Zac on the black holes app.

Mauveine continued to listen intently, never moving her gaze from Maddie and never asking a question until the explanation came to an end. Madeleine's sister and brothers had been taken ... back in time to 1865 by Fenella and held prisoner on her ship. But why?

There was another silence as Mauveine, very pained, looked at Isi who was shaking his head. Victoria, Abby, Maddie of course and even Elizabeth were hoping and expecting that she would have all the answers and knew what to do. But she didn't.

The only thing Mauveine was certain of was something evil and cunning had been perpetrated and there was only one sensible action to take. "We must head back, now, to Orsbrick Hall and confront what may be happening. I fear we have no time to lose given the date. Fenella, the captain of the Warrior Queen, was my sister, my true and real sister."

Victoria sat bolt upright. "Your sister? But surely Mauveine, don't you mean your aunt?" The stunned silence remained. Mauveine never reacted and remained impassive. Victoria pondered more, her brain running at warp speed when the puzzle instantly became crystal clear. "Oh my God, Mauveine. By real sister, you must mean you had not only the same father, James but also the same mother?" She turned to Abby recalling their fateful London visit with Morag that turned everything upside down. "Abby, remember. Morag eventually explained in the carriage going through Mayfair, why she was so upset on the way to the Royal Society meeting. She'd discovered, in the dead of night, that James had unknowingly fathered a child named Fenella, with a sixteen-year-old boatgirl, an unsavoury encounter at the back of the George, aided and abetted by the equally irresponsible 1841 manifests of Ned and Zac, roundly blamed by Morag for encouraging loose morals. The newly born baby had, after Morag's swift personal intervention, been supposedly bundled off to America with Puritans and everyone paid off handsomely by Morag to keep quiet."

Maddie hadn't taken part in that London visit. She had been kept back at Orsbrick Hall with Belle. But she did immediately recall the old letters to James McKenzie, written in the 1870s when he was severely disabled from a stroke that she and Belle had discovered in the library. They were from a Jake Gibbons, his former factory foreman who acknowledged that Mauveine, found by James on the canal bank, was James's biological daughter by Jakes's wife, who had died soon after giving birth. Jake was unable to cope and left the baby girl alongside the towpath deliberately. James must have had a further illicit encounter with the former young boatgirl, but who by then was legally married to Jake Gibbons. Maddie said nothing but Mauveine turned deliberately to her and began to speak, quietly and firmly.

"My mother's name was Robina, Robina Gibbons, and yes, she was a boatwoman. But you know that Madeleine don't you because it was Isi and me who facilitated your finding the evidence in the library."

"Yes," Maddie whispered back, her voice croaky. "So who is the Fenella who arrived at our door a month ago?"

"A very good question? I don't actually know," Mauveine replied. "But one thing is very clear. Isi, can you confirm the true facts, please."

Isi came forward, red and flushed from the same realisation as his wife that something very serious was now happening. "Morag's baby, Fenella, was definitely stillborn. I know because tragically I was present too at the time for both their deaths, having been urgently summoned by Dr Emmanuel Kirkby, the baby's father, when Morag took a serious turn for the worse during a very long labour. Having conducted a few simple prayers, I remained until the undertaker arrived when both bodies were sensitively removed. Dr Kirkby issued a certificate confirming their deaths but finally could no longer retain his professionalism and control his emotions. He broke down completely, comforted by Agnes the housekeeper and other staff. Morag's children had been fortuitously sent away a few days earlier, I don't know where to, so they were not present. Hence Fenella Kirkby was not spirited away by her grandfather, Lord Kirkby. His first presence at Orsbrick was when his son,

Manny, soon after, committed suicide in the surgery and he arranged immediately for the body to be returned to his estate in Liverpool for private burial.

Mauveine continued, her voice low and whispered. "When Morag was buried in London, the baby, enclosed in a tiny matching wooden coffin, was interred fittingly alongside her."

Victoria was feeling increasingly alarmed. "So the Fenella who turned up at our doorstep was lying for all the time she was with us. She perfected an amazing deception; she had a whole credible life story to relate and live through for our benefit to hear. More importantly, who is she if not your sister, Mauveine? The Fenella who was supposed to have been sent away to America on a ship? And why all the deceit?"

Elizabeth suddenly spoke up. "I've been doing my best to try and assimilate the complexities unfolding and put some logical context to the string of events but like Victoria, I'm struggling too with the complications. Mauveine, earlier you said we had to get to Orsbrick Hall, given the date. Today is the 20th May, exactly a calendar month after Fenella arrived. What is so special about today?"

Mauveine spoke again slowly. "There were rumours, originally emanated through the Orsbrick servants. I heard my father speak when I was a child that this person, Fenella, had not been sent to America but instead had been packaged off to an aristocratic household and formally adopted. Later, in April 1865, I was told one evening by my father that I had an older sister. I learned from my father that the family was indeed Lord Kirkby's. Somehow, Morag, my grandmother, had secretly engineered this change of plan through Dr Emmanuel Kirkby, her lover. Why she did this I never found out, nor did my father. That secret died with her because neither of us knew who the family was or even that my father had begotten a child until Lord Kirkby formally contacted him with legal documents the month before, outlining the whole revelation. My father was at first shocked, then astonished, and both of us became even more astounded to learn that my sister, his daughter, now Lady Fenella Kirkby, had run away from this privileged background as a young teenager and had apparently ended up on the high seas as a sailor, and now it appears, from Madeleine's research as the infamous Captain Fanny Kirkby, owner of her own ship, the Warrior Queen, who aggressively raised and sold sunken salvage from along the Lancashire coast. She was coming back to claim her share of the Orsbrick inheritance with the support of her now reconciled grandfather, Lord Kirkby. We were supposed to all meet on the 20th April 1865, but my sister didn't turn up ... and was never seen again. Lord Kirkby was devastated. He adored his adopted granddaughter; she was likely a form of proxy for the loss of his own son's daughter. He became a broken man and his legal claims never materialised. It was only years later that Isi and I picked up odd rumours, indeed from that very public house the Black Anchor no less, that my sister had vanished, presumed drowned, at the mouth of the River Mersey, on a packet passenger ship which sank heading for America. She must have decided, for reasons unknown, to amass all her accumulated wealth from treasure and quietly emigrate for a new life. She was clearly a very independent minded and enterprising woman, like all we McKenzies. Perhaps she had met someone or even got married, we will likely never know that either. Now, Abby, you can understand the connections and why, at the time, I was also searching for Fenella's spirit on your Queen Lusitania voyage. There were far too many psychic family coincidences, past and present, happening and not making sense. The interactions were making me feel very unhappy until

I finally found Isi and we triggered the return of all of us to the year 1841."

Abby, wide-eyed and Victoria, uncharacteristically silent, both nodded.

"And finally, to answer your question, Elizabeth," Mauveine added. "The date of the 20th May was, we were told, the date when the passenger ship, the Mountain Moon, sank and on which my sister was travelling."

Maddie was still tapping furiously on her phone and had found an old Liverpool Post reference from their online archives to the sinking of the Mountain Moon with the death of all three hundred passengers and crew. "Mauveine is absolutely right. We must leave now, the six of us for Orsbrick Hall. I don't know how we can handle it with Dad and Lynton present but I'm certain such a confluence of past, present and future may again force a potential psychic energy clash which disrupts the time-travel process and sends Belle, Ned, Zac, Nancy and Dottie back to the present, away from the clutches of this evil masquerading Fenella manifestation who has somehow materialised out of our original return from Morag. This may be our only hope to get them back. I know it's risky, but I can't think of an alternative now."

Victoria smiled, impressed with Maddie's foresight and clear thinking once more. "I agree with Maddie, there is none. In fact, Mauveine, from what you've said it may be that Zac, who Fenella had become very close to, is being lined up to escape with to America in some kind of warped parallel universe, by manipulating the space-time events and travel parameters back to 1865. That's the reason they've gone back in time."

"Oh fuck, gosh, sorry Mum, but it's not Zac … I bet it's actually Ned. Fenella had a secret crush on him, he was her manly ideal potential lover from the Victorian time and she hated Nancy."

"How do you know all that, Maddie?" Abby queried, shaking her head.

"Because she told me the day before they disappeared."

Elizabeth immediately waved everyone to order. "That's it. We've solved the conundrum for the time being but we have to get to work, now. That old carriage, Madeleine, you call a Jeep outside, has two spare folded seats at the very back I recall. Grab your starting key, please. I think we can all squeeze in. Let's commence travel right away!"

Chapter Eleven

After difficult manoeuvres during the night in an unexpectedly strong breeze, the Warrior Queen finally docked in the small berthing bay at Southport alongside the red stone quay. Helping with the loading of the salvage into the large carriage, Ned could only gasp at the value of the historic commodities which included masses of coins, a selection of rare jewels, two landscape paintings by Turner in a sealed trunk, various guns and pistols, swords, knives and even a heaped triangle of blackened cannon balls. Four hefty shire horses, steam pouring from their mouths and eager to go, were finally secured onto the thick shafts.

"They're big bastards, you never see them this size now in our time, except in exhibitions," Ade murmured to Ned, both watching Zac gently pat the front shire, mottled in brown and cream. "Give us a lift with these brass cannons, they look tiny but they pack quite a weight. Last thing I want is a hernia."

Loading them over the hefty rear wheel storage, the suspension sagged alarmingly and Zac began to peruse the state of the recent repairs to the carriage, which didn't exhibit the best of welding. "Hopefully, we haven't got far to the salvage broker. The weight of this lot and the bad roads are going to be a delicate balancing act."

"No, the place is somewhere in the centre, off Lord Street, so it can't be far. Shit, this area has changed, tell you what, I can't see the fairground," Ade remarked, laughing stupidly before stopping short. "Fuck me, look at the sight of who's coming, Ned."

Ned turned and took a deep breath seeing René, dressed in his Sunday best, striding off the gangplank but it was the sight of the person accompanying him which made the three stare extra hard. Fenella was coming too but instead of her familiar working sailor's uniform and Captain's regalia she'd exchanged them for a long, red and flowing frilly dress, set off with a lovely embroidered jacket, smart black boots and a matching hat, perfect now the wind had dissipated and the sun was already out. She was wearing extensive makeup and carried a dinky parasol which she waved to effect with a dazzling smile, motioning Ned to walk over to her.

"You're a lucky fucker, she does look fit," Ade growled, as Zac glared across. "Well go on, the lady is summoning. Move your arse."

Ned awoke from his stupor of surprise; by any criteria, Fenella looked decidedly gorgeous. "Yeah, right," he mumbled and strode over confidently. His tall and well-built physique stood out prominently from the other ill-fed sailors, still working hard to bring in fresh supplies and do necessary maintenance and repairs on the ship. He had also put on some decent and clean mid-Victorian clothes with a stylish corduroy cap, rummaged out of the cabin trunk and now looked the equivalent of smartly casual, wishing he could have grown a thick moustache like the other fashionable males walking up and down the front. He had even managed to shave with a dangerous cut-throat razor in Fenella's cabin.

"Mmm … you may kiss my cheek, Ned darling," she purred, commenting on his spicy aftershave which he'd found in a corked brown bottle alongside the razor. Hooking her arm into his, they strolled for a brief walk along the front, an opportunity for him to stare over at the sea and the sand dunes like a tourist visitor rather than a captive prisoner. Ade was right. Outside of the immediate docking area and further down, Southport was quite unspoilt.

"Now, whilst the crew finish loading the salvage, we can enjoy the sunshine for a bit." Fenella began, staring dreamily into his eyes "Look, over there, a little kiosk selling hot drinks and fish snacks for breakfast, so treat me please," she cried. "Once we've sold off this batch of treasure and replenished my coffers, I have a pleasant surprise for you. We will then set sail for somewhere exciting and new and embark on a real adventure, Ned, a new life, you and me together. I think you'll like that. But don't ask where as I refuse to say yet. Is that acceptable?"

He forced a smile, already feeling a sharp conflict of guilt and mixed feelings that the three musketeers had planned to escape. Fuck, should he just stay with Fenella and enjoy the good life unfolding? She was clearly crazy over him. He wasn't realistically going to see Nancy again and he wasn't ever going to return home in 2026 either, that was all Zac's nerd fantasy. It was almost like he had been destined for this lifestyle on the waves. He walked across to the tiny stall next to the familiar cast-iron pier, looking almost new, and bought hot coffee and a plate of mussels, crab and whelks with a hunk of brown bread, all doused with vinegar sauce. They sat down on a bench and began to pick at the food using quaint wooden forks, slurping the mugs of black coffee.

"So, what are you thinking about, Ned?" Fenella continued. "I surmise you've forgotten the old life already, haven't you? All those dreary rules, regulations, doing as you're told by your parents, day in day out. Now, together, we are free as birds, independent and can conquer the world."

She pecked his cheek again and he took her in his arms and gave her another passionate kiss. Damn it, he was losing the battle big time … Zac and Ade could leg it on their own, back to Orsbrick Hall and take their chances. His destiny was set up with Fenella. But he had one nagging question. "I just want to know one thing Fenella. What has really happened to Nancy, Belle and Dottie? Did they also come back in time? If so, where are they?"

Fenella went silent, her face reddened with anger. "You have no need to consider their dubious fate, Ned, they are irrelevant, nondescript, a speck of dirt in the passing sands of time. Only you and I matter in all of this."

"I just need to know that's all. I owe it to Belle, she's my sister and Nancy was my …"

"No longer," Fenella cried, interrupting sharply. "I could lie and tell you that they are still in your old time, waiting patiently for a lost cause, your return. Because I must tell you, Ned, you cannot retrace that step again, it is done, complete. That last part is true my dearest, but yes, I will not lie to you. They are here, already living new lives as befits their 1865 destiny, working class women toiling, in service, in Liverpool. You three are forgotten already as if you were never known, and completely replaced in mind and body. You understand my meaning Ned, don't you? When we are married, you will share my great wealth. We will build an empire together, beget lots of children and create a future dynasty. Nancy will die in destitution of the pox in a few years time, the others of poverty, overwork and disease. That pathway is already willed and set in stone. Nothing can change the irreversible wheels of time."

They stopped eating and Ned looked at her hard, struggling to take all that crazy situation in. "Marriage? What seriously? With me?"

"Of course, my darling. The ceremony is arranged tomorrow in the newly built Holy Trinity Church. That was part of my surprise. Your brother can be your best man," she replied with a smirk.

"And, they're actually here in Liverpool? Belle?"

"Yes, but you will never know them and they will never know you. Forget Nancy, Ned, history is rewritten. She was only ever a small perturbation along your true road to fame and riches. This is your real future, the first of my planned fleet," she said calmly, pointing back to the Warrior Queen, majestic amongst the other smaller vessels, sails unfurled and primed for sailing away once more. She now wished she had been her normal ruthless self and had the three put down permanently, especially Nancy, rather than leave them with the opportunity to live … a moment of rare beneficence but she was confident in what she said to Ned. No way would their miserable lives in servitude be worth living and smiled inwardly at the thought of harlot Nancy, readjusting to her daily rigorous routine being pimped in the Black Anchor. That was the way those bitch's futures would unfold, hard and unrelenting survival every day, hour and minute, which would take over their lives from the very beginning.

Clattering down Lord Street, the cobbled main road was traversed slowly, given the doubtful nature of the suspension, as the strong shire horses pulled their load steadily. From the outside rear step, Ade and Zac gazed in admiration at the magnificent architecture of the pristine Georgian buildings, everywhere busy with couples out shopping, stalls resplendent on the pavements and horse and carts clattering up and down. René was precariously perched, driving, outside at the front. Inside, amongst the secured crates, Ned and Fenella sat huddled together on the luxurious red leather seats, her body wrapped closely against his as she cuddled and whispered sweet nothings in his ear.

But Zac had already observed that his brother, on returning from the stroll around the pier, was decidedly quieter and taciturn. He turned to Ade and shuffled up the step closer, the racket of the wheels almost drowning out any ability to talk. "I think Ned's gone over to the dark side, he's acting odd all of a sudden," he said into Ade's ear.

"What the fuck are you talking about, Zac? You mean he's having doubts about the planned escape?"

"I hope not but something's up that's for sure," Zac replied, his forehead furrowed whilst they clung on hard. "Fenella is getting to him; she's a mistress of seduction."

"We'll see when we arrive, hey up," Ade shouted. They suddenly swayed from side to side when the carriage swerved sharply to the right. "We're turning off down some narrow alley, blimey only just wide enough for this cart, but should be there shortly."

Within half a minute they stopped. The narrow lane, dark and dingy, was strewn with dilapidated buildings rising up high on either side blocking out the sun, quite a contrast to the majestic main street. They jumped off and a large, mangy dog ran out of a house like crazy, barking ferociously at Ade who promptly kicked it hard in the face with his full eighteen stone and heavy boots. It ran off, frothing and bleeding, with a loud yelp.

"Bastard, the thing looked rabid. You have to be on your toes around here," he shouted back to Zac, watching René alight promptly and then open the door to hand out Fenella with Ned following closely behind. Ned looked sheepishly across to Zac and had finally made up his mind. He immediately took charge. "Right, first thing, let's get these crates unloaded onto the side. I assume that's the shop, Fenella?"

They turned to see a very dilapidated front, the peeling signage of Parbold Antiques just visible, with poky windows that could barely be looked through, the grime thick and longstanding. There were protective iron grilles over the windows and door, but the wooden sign said open.

"Yes, the place is actually far more interesting inside," Fenella replied. "The owner is quite a connoisseur but a little eccentric. I have to admit, he never leaves the place. I'll just alert him we're here." She pushed open the creaking front door and strode in. The six heavy crates, all meticulously packed, were soon unloaded by the four. Muffled voices could be heard inside.

Zac stood alongside Ned. "Bro, I can see that something's up. Are you still with us on René's plan?" he whispered heavily but before Ned could answer, the door opened again and Fenella strode out smiling.

"A good price has been agreed," she shouted over. "We can get on with the exchange but as usual he needs to see and confirm the salvage first before any parting of cash so let's get these crates inside." She drew a hefty pistol out of her bag and looked around carefully. "I never trust this shit neighbourhood, too many thieves around."

But dead on cue, Henri suddenly appeared, running like crazy around the corner of the adjacent alleyway. The plan was happening. "Captain, my Captain," he shouted, red in the face and catching his breath. "I'm glad I caught you, Madame, in time. There are real problems back at the ship, some of the crew have started fighting with the locals and they're threatening to torch everything."

Fenella grimaced. This was the last thing she wanted to hear, damned unreliable crew again. She needed to return quickly. René had come alongside her. "Captain Fanny, I think I'd better take you back in the carriage immediately. Henri can stay here and help Ned to take the crates in and conclude the deal. I know you trust him, so once we've sorted out the trouble I'll return and pick them all up."

Fenella gazed at Ned lovingly and laughed. "So, can I trust you then Ned, not to run off with all my money?" she said with a grin. "Mind you, where are you going to go?" She kissed his cheek lightly. "Don't let Lynton Grey cheat you out of a penny. I want my full seven hundred and fifty guineas."

Ned felt an immediate startled kick in the brain but stopped himself showing any reaction. He glanced over at Zac and Ade who were staring stupidly at the floor. They too probably had the same thoughts. It was not credible, in fact totally impossible but what a bizarre coincidence. Fenella and René set off in the carriage quickly back to the ship and Henri and Ade began to lug the crates to the front door of Parbold Antiques.

"We haven't got long," Ned began, wistfully watching her disappear into the distance. "I'll go into the shop and sort this Grey guy out and get the money sorted, we'll need to split it as agreed. Zac, you'd better help Ade. Some of those crates are very heavy."

"So, you're with us and not against us then?" Zac cried. "Ade was betting on you jumping in the carriage with her and doing a bunk. I would have been very disappointed with you, bro. So what swung the decision then?"

"Nancy, Belle and Dottie are here … marooned in Liverpool at the Black Anchor."

Ade and Zac stopped lifting. "You must be joking," Ade shouted, red in the face. "How did you find out?"

"Fenella let slip when I pressed her to tell the truth. They've been put in a dire situation deliberately by Fenella. I owe it to Nancy and my sister to get them and Dottie back in our own time with us. Once we check out Orsbrick Hall, we can muster a gang together to help us rescue them quickly. We'll have enough cash to grease palms and buy guns and together we can then all try and return from Orsbrick … we'll worry about how then. Anyone got a better idea?"

"Sounds like a plan, bro, I suspected all along they came back with us," Zac said. "I'll come in with you."

Ade nodded, a large grin spread over his face.

Ned pushed open the creaking shop door and a dull bell rang. A depressing gloom pervaded the filthy interior, damp and a bad smell filled the air but incongruously, splendid looking paintings adorned the walls. Another door opened and an old man with a dirty long mop of blonde hair shuffled out.

"You got the goods, young man? I see you admire my beautiful Turners, worth a few bob, I'll be damned. Don't I know you two from somewhere? Age is such a disintegrating state and my memory is not what it used to be, sharp and icily ironic." He laughed heartily then began to cough, hard and rasping and immediately lit the stub of a cigar sat amongst a pile in a huge brass ashtray on his desk. "Ahh, that's better, so much better."

Both Ned and Zac stared hard at the dishevelled, hunched figure in front of them, the features were unmistakable. Old, lined and croaky, the individual was a caricature of the man they knew and loved but there was no doubt whatsoever in both their minds. The impossible had somehow gotten possible.

"Lynton? Is it really you?" Ned stuttered, not knowing what to say.

The old man looked hard at the earnest young faces before him and smiled. "People forever say they know me, that's a fact. Comes with my worldly artistic fame, accumulated over the years, name constantly in the press, my boy, all of those worthy things. Dr Lynton Grey is indeed my name, art connoisseur and agent once to the rich and famous of London but that sadly was a very long time ago. I got tired and younger, fashionable, nimble men overtook me, just like you two. Now, I have to import and export to make a living in these harsh times."

"But what about Orsbrick Hall? And Abigail, your wife?" Zac interjected. He was ahead of his brother as ever and realised that this shabby individual was some sort of distorted creation from their minds, fashioned through the return in time with Fenella but living in this time. It was worth asking as Lynton Grey might be able to shed light on relevant happenings at home before they descended on the place later.

Lynton Grey stopped and grimaced, throwing his arms in the air. "That damned evil place! Ever since Lady Morag McKenzie died, the entire fun and laughter there vanished like a will-o-the-wisp and that horrible son, James, a man of rabid need for flagrant excitement and I thought I was extreme in my day. He bankrupted me did James McKenzie, cold, deliberate and clinical, but I came back in the end, I always bounce back. The bastard doesn't know I'm here and don't you boys be telling him either."

A voice rang out at the other end of the shop. "Where do you want all these crates?" Ade shouted, ducking under the low ceiling and pulling in the first two, opening the lids for immediate inspection. "Fuck me, it really is you, Lynton. My God, time travel has aged you badly. Sorry, didn't mean to offend."

Lynton, appearing deaf, ignored him and walked over to the goods. He looked approvingly inside the crates as Henri hauled in the others. After a quiet but thorough inspection, he finally spoke, waving his arms and glared at Ade. "None taken, young man. Unlike your friends here, I don't know you from Adam and don't especially want to. I must say, sir, you're an ugly great brute of a giant and talk nonsense riddles and I prefer sophistication, always have." He turned to Zac. "But yes, I do recall Abigail, Morag's cousin. How could I not, she was such a beautiful, sensual woman and could paint like an angel. She had a talent I have never seen before or since in a woman, but regretfully, sir, I did not marry the lady. She ran off with that unctuous flim-flam, John Ruskin, who calls himself an art critic; that's a hilarious joke if ever there was."

Zac winked at Ned who was mystified by this mutation of Lynton talking nonsense but quickly becoming bored with his effete affectations. Besides, they had to get a move on. The other crates were assiduously looked over and the box with the rare Turner seascape paintings carefully opened. Those two alone were probably worth double what Lynton was offering Fenella but Ned wasn't concerned with the deal niceties. He simply wanted the money quickly. "Seven hundred and fifty guineas then, Dr Gray, and we'll be on our way."

Lynton was about to start his normal barter but when Ade sidled up alongside Zac and began lovingly wiping one of the daggers on his sleeve he changed his mind. He went into the next room where they could see a large black iron safe bolted to the wall. Lynton closed the door, tumbled the locks and returned with a mixture of five and ten-pound notes which he placed carefully into a large leather bag. He went back in the room to salvage coins from a desk drawer.

Ned suddenly whispered to Ade. "What's a guinea, clever clogs?"

"Fucked if I know," Ade replied, his mouth twisted.

"You're both a pair of thick heads," Zac said with a wide smirk. "One pound and one shilling, old English money, twenty shillings to a pound so that's seven hundred and eighty-seven pounds ten shillings exactly."

Lynton returned and handed the bag of notes and coins over. Ned thrust it to Zac. "Check it, know-all," he growled.

Zac flipped through the notes and quickly added the coins. "There's five pounds too much, Dr Grey."

"Your commission from me. I know how tight-fisted that Fanny woman can be. Get yourselves some beers, lads. It's been good doing business with you." He shook Ned's hand when there was a loud rap on the door. Lynton looked apprehensive and picked up a loaded pistol from his desk.

"That'll be René, no problem Lynton. Thanks for the bung. We'll be on our way now."

Henri opened the door and warmly welcomed his friend, René, and they all strode into the lane, looking around for any sign of Fenella but everywhere was deathly quiet, not a soul to be seen. A series of bolts slid shut on the inside of the shop door, blinds were drawn and the closed sign hung in the window. Fenella's carriage was standing outside. René pointed further up and a man in a top hat could be seen loitering on the corner. "Your carriage is waiting there to take you to the wherry further up the coast. It has blackened windows but you must all lie in the back and cover yourselves with blankets. There is no time to waste. Captain Fanny will be wondering where I've gone and by now, being smart, will realise there has been no real disturbance. I fabricated a few fights to buy us some minutes but she will then come looking for all of us. My half of the money please, Ned."

Henri was shackling up the carriage again and watered the horses from a bucket outside the shop. Zac counted out René's cash. He smiled warmly, embraced the three in turn hard and jumped on top of the carriage with Henri.

"Go now, Fanny is ruthless and will turn on a sixpence. Take great care, she will offer no mercy to anyone who betrays her, not even you Ned. Au revoir, my friends. Allez Henri, vite, vite."

They were gone as quick as they came. The man in the top hat was now waving at them frantically. Ned stuffed the leather bag into his haversack and they ran up the lane. A large two-horse carriage was stood waiting, exactly as René promised.

"Can we trust this fucker?" Ade grunted, out of breath.

"We've no choice now, we'll have to," Zac replied, hastily.

In a moment they were inside, covered over in smelly blankets and the horses whipped to a fast pace. Escape was now reality. Ned pondered about what they must do next. If Maddie was right, Orsbrick Hall will hold the key to facilitate their return but they had to try and find Belle and Nancy, who he was desperate to see again despite severe guilt about his behaviour with Fenella. He presumed Zac was likely fretting over former girlfriend, Dottie, as would Ade who wanted his sister he had always been close to, back badly.

Chapter Twelve

Nancy carefully counted the money she had accumulated after searching around again where Henri had dropped the takings in a drunken stupor and found another wad of lost notes under the sofa. The total amount came to thirty-one pounds, seven shillings and sixpence, more than enough for them to escape. She hid her bag under the bed and ventured quietly downstairs to look for Rory in the stables and begin afternoon work cleaning the horses. It was hooves day. Rory was already shovelling hay and washing the piebald mare down. Nancy glanced at him as she strode in wearing her new jodhpurs and long black boots. Well … she had to spend some of her ill-gotten gains on a few treats including makeup from the old chemist shop, hopefully not containing arsenic. He looked back with a murmur and returned his gaze with a more protracted perusal which Nancy was very happy receiving. Her innate attention seeking behaviour from men she rather liked the look of had definitely not abated, travelling back in time. She reflected sadly on Ned for a moment but reassured herself such thoughts were a waste of time. No way would he be walking through the stable door, ever again.

Rory was tall, slim, hard-working and very good looking. He appeared far more intelligent than she would have expected from a guy shovelling horse shit all day, and although diffident and obviously shy with women, he occasionally tried to flirt clumsily but gave up when she cannily ignored him. He would have to try harder than that. But Nancy realised he could read, after spying him on his break, surreptitiously immersed in a tatty leather book which he kept closeted in his bag, whilst supping a half-pint of Henry's complimentary ale. He even scribbled a few notes in the margins with a stubby pencil, so he could write as well, unusual for a stableman of that period. On one break, when he dived to the bottom of the yard to use the outside latrine, she rooted around in his bag to see what he was reading. Amazingly, she pulled out a well-thumbed copy of 'Five Weeks in a Balloon' by Jules Verne and not long published and then she spotted, at the bottom, a couple of scented pink letters. A quick scan revealed he was receiving love notes from a Lady Eleanor Pilkington, living in a manorial hall outside St Helens. Rory was turning out to be a man with secrets and had been brought up in an educated environment. There were other sheets of paper too but she saw him tramping back up the yard and closed his bag immediately, returning to scrub Benji, the black foal.

Retrieving her bag of tools and implements, grateful that her former veterinary training had given her some useful survival skills, she began the process of cleaning out the hooves of Anthony, the black stud and father of little Benji. Normally, according to a short and concise expletive from Rory when she first started, Anthony would never allow anyone but him to tend to his needs. However, she had her ways and charm with temperamental male horses as well as men, having learned the hard way on too many Lancashire farms. He quickly became pliant and whinnied softly as she approached. Rory once again peeked over with a slightly jealous glare. Anthony had developed a slight limp on his left front leg. She suspected an infection and carefully raised the leg to see, sat firmly on a stool. Sure enough, a stone had been deeply embedded for some time and with a few swift snaps of the clench cutter and a light hammer tap she removed the poorly installed horseshoe and took the offending pebble out with a small pincer. There was some inflammation present and in anticipation of such problems had already persuaded Henry to allow her to buy bottles of carbolic acid and iodine from the local chemist, the best remedy she could find. She felt his leg tremble but Anthony remained calm, confident that his new friend would look after him. After a further clean out of dirt and pus, she dabbed the antiseptic around and already Anthony stopped trembling. The pain must be relieving. With a deft swing of her special hammer, she reinstated the shoe with new nails and he put his leg down with a quiet whinny. She thought he definitely looked like he was smiling a big horsey grin. She let him out to graze again in the adjacent small field belonging to the pub, amazed that in this part of the Liverpool city centre there were still fields. Although extensively built up, diverse patches of land for cultivating crops and animal rearing remained dotted about. The field had become an NCP car park long ago, after the old townhouses on it, built later in the nineteenth century, were subsequently demolished.

Rory had been watching this activity with a measure of curious interest and walked over, pitchfork solidly in hand. "May I ask, Nancy?" he said, quietly and slowly.

It was then she noticed for the first time that his accent was much purer Lancashire, akin to around Manchester but with no Irish lilt. He was probably from some area to the east of Liverpool given his aristocratic girlfriend lived in St Helens, a town halfway between. Accents had always fascinated her and she had already become intrigued by the difference between the mid-nineteenth century, Irish and Lancashire influenced soft

Liverpool accent, spoken by most of the pub customers and the distinctively harsh sounding 'scouse' guttural tones she had always been used to in modern time.

Rory continued. "You have an unusual capability with horses. Where did you learn those skills? I noticed too that you treated Henry's dog, Butch, earlier with an infected wound. Both seemed very pleased."

Nancy smiled. An opportunity for the first time to perhaps have a decent conversation rather than the cursory grunts and bland instructions she had received over the last few days. She fluffed her mane of red curls and decided to make it up, who would care? "My mother taught me everything and she learned from her mother. Tending to animals goes back generations, whether on the farm or with pets. I was born and brought up on a landowner's estate out towards Wigan where we did all the cures we could, I was an only child, you see. Sadly, my mother died suddenly a few years ago and I had to find work elsewhere, which is why I'm here. How about you Rory? Hey, it's time for our break. Shall I get you a beer, which is what you normally have? ... I wouldn't mind one myself."

Rory looked at her shyly. She was very forward and confident, unlike Eleanor. "Err ... yes ... you can join me if you like. I bought a couple of apple pastries too from the shop down Temple Street. Would you like one?"

"Cool," Nancy replied, not thinking.

"Pardon?" Rory remarked, baffled.

"Cooked? They don't want heating up in Henry's oven then?" she replied quickly, thinking she really must watch her language as Belle had warned. It was too easy to slip into modern slang, she nearly did the same with Henry's idiot son over breakfast.

"Err ... no, they're best eaten cold, I reckon."

"Yes, I agree," Nancy said, running off into the bar to retrieve two glasses of cool brown ale, so much nicer than the modern brews, real beer for a change. She returned with a bar tray, a couple of plates and forks, plus a small jug of fresh cream, nicked from Henry's cool larder, and a wet flannel. Rory had made a comfortable place in the thick pile of hay and was finally passing her sophistication test, looking surprisingly relaxed with the picnic style break. After Nancy wiped her hands, he did the same before retrieving the brown paper bag of pastries from his bag and placing one on each plate. She caught sight of his book again.

"I saw you reading that book yesterday on your break. What is it?" she asked.

He laughed and pulled the red leather copy out. "Don't suppose it's much good to you, not being able to read. I was lucky, the gamekeeper who adopted me as a baby taught me as a child, given me much pleasure since. It's a novel by Jules Verne, a new French author, called 'Five Weeks in a Balloon'. I've bought another one just published, 'Journey to the Centre of the Earth.' They've been translated into English fortunately. At the top of Dale Street, there's a very good bookshop."

"Actually I can read and write, very well. Appearances can be very deceptive in a woman, Rory," she replied with a giggle and took the book from his hand. "I once read this novel in the original French," and immediately quoted the first paragraph en français. English and French were her best subjects at school.

"Really?" he said, his face pleasingly stunned. "Only women I know who can read and speak languages are rich aristocrats. You are truly a lady of many surprises, Nancy," he said trying to evaluate her working class harlot image which he had assumed, at face value, was the person beneath. His attitude to her changed instantly. He moved closer, both now filling their faces with forked apple tart smothered in cream.

"I see you're enjoying this pleasure," she said. "This is how you eat apple pastries in Holland."

"You've been to Holland? I love to travel but now have little opportunity, this job occupies my whole life," he replied wistfully, clearly implying he did have another life once, perhaps better and more affluent than this one.

"That's evident from the books you like to read. Wait 'till you read 'Around the World in Eighty Days,'" she added cheerfully and then realised, it was yet to be published. Shit. "He's writing it," she continued, thinking on her feet again. "I was told a few weeks ago when I was in the library, someone there knows his publisher."

"Well, I look forward to that. Novels are a great way for me to relax, I hate this job ..."

She breathed an inner sigh of relief and interrupted.

"... And this lifestyle, I suspect, Rory. From your accent, I would guess you're not from Liverpool, perhaps more towards Manchester?"

He smiled, gazing at her luscious red lips which matched her hair, but he didn't have the nerve to try. Nancy was both astute and educated, a bit of an enigma rather like him. "More half-way, in fact, near a growing town called St Helens. Do you know it?"

"Vaguely. I know where it is but I've never been there. Is that where you were brought up, I mean by the gamekeeper?"

"Indeed, our cottage was on the estate of Lord Pilkington but ... well, there was a bad accident at one of the shoots my father regularly organised ... Lord Pilkington accidentally shot him. My father subsequently died three days later. That was a couple of years back. I had to leave the worker's cottage for his replacement. Lord Pilkington took it all badly, was beside himself with grief and guilt and couldn't bear to look at me again. I spent much of my childhood living amongst and being educated with his own children, almost as if I was adopted by his Lordship. He had seven, six boys and a girl, Eleanor, almost the same age as me. I miss Eleanor very much. I'm almost twenty-one now, getting old before my time. Haven't ever talked about this to anyone before. I'd be grateful if you don't mention this conversation to Henry, he has no idea of my background, and especially my urge to ditch this position and head back to the estate for Eleanor. The only relative I have now is my Uncle Jack. He works in the docks and got me the job so I'm grateful to him for that but I have to see Eleanor again, we're sort of engaged, informally like."

Nancy suddenly thought. "Has Uncle Jack ever mentioned the ship, the Warrior Queen to you, Rory?" she said softly, looking hard into his eyes.

He laughed hard. "Yes, quite recently, it came in for fresh supplies. That ship has quite a reputation, or should I be more specific, the owner and captain, Fanny Kirkby. She does things which are not fit to be spoken about to a woman of class like you, Nancy. Why do you ask such a strange question?"

Nancy breathed hard. "I need to trust you. Can I do that?"

He patted her hand affectionately, but then withdrew shyly. "Yes of course, totally. You've been a great help to me, got my thoughts back on track."

"My friends, Belle and Dottie, Henry calls her Peggy, who run the bar, their brothers are we think on board, sort of conscripted. And one brother, Ned, is my fiancé. We need to try and find them. Have you any idea where the ship is heading?"

"No, but I can find out. I'll see Uncle Jack tonight for a drink when my shift ends at seven. You mean you're engaged too?"

Nancy blushed. She felt uncomfortable telling lies using Ned given all the circumstances, although in many ways they were engaged and had been planning a life together as vets. "Sort of informal as well," she replied awkwardly. "You and I have a lot in common, don't we?" she continued, forcing herself back to her normal light-hearted self.

Rory grinned. "We do and that's a wonder, like our coming together is a sign. We'd better get back to work quickly. I can hear Henry marching down the path, those heavy nailed boots are very distinctive. I'll seek you after work once I find more information out."

Nancy returned to check on Anthony who was already walking normally, just as Henry clobbered around the corner, a wide grin of pleasure over his face seeing his favourite horse back to health so quickly.

Pitching and rolling in the growing swell of the coastal currents, the steam powered wherry slowly chugged along at a steady rate. Hiding under a small hanging lifeboat with a large, blue tarpaulin covering them was not exactly the height of comfort, nor was sitting upright on some old, smelly sacks which stunk of tobacco. They had embarked secretly, smuggled on board once dusk approached and given some bread, old cheese and an orange each, by the captain and told to stay out of sight of the rest of the crew or they'd end up overboard.

Ade, chewing at the stale bread, peered out through a tear in the material before the light finally died and could discern the coastline again at a distance. They were sailing roughly parallel to it with a large load of cotton and sugar. "I'm gagging for something to drink and could really do with a shit too."

Ned groaned. "For fuck's sake, Ade, not here. You'll have to hold it in until we land, it won't kill you."

"It will. I'm going to find somewhere, back in a minute."

He slithered out from the rear, out of sight of the rest of the crew and scampered under the lifeboat on the other side.

Zac watched apprehensively. "Typical of Ade always has to be doing something he shouldn't at a critical time. I calculate this will take all night," he whispered, peeling the orange. "Wouldn't it be good to have some decent food again?"

Ned nodded but felt guilty. Fenella had treated him to her luxury rations whilst he had stayed in her cabin so he'd done better than the other two by far, but he said nothing. She will be on the warpath now undoubtedly; the quicker they land the better. Fuck, why did Zac mention Orsbrick Hall to Lynton in the shop? If Fenella brings out her legendary pliers then Lynton would spill the beans immediately, not that he had any teeth left to pull.

Suddenly their tarpaulin moved again and Ade stumbled back in. A large smile had reappeared across his face. "Christ, I needed that," he muttered, "and look what I've found, guys, there was a crate of them left behind us." Three bottled beers were gently laid on the floor. The evening light was fading fast through the crack at the end and they could barely see each other. The thick green bottles, all different sizes, were strongly corked as Ade took the largest one for himself and shoved the top against a piece of dowelling sticking down from the lifeboat. "Have to push these inside," he said quietly. "Don't have the luxury of a corkscrew." He downed half the bottle in one gulp. "Ahh ... that is so much better. This ale is better than bottled Guinness."

Ned and Zac followed suit. They rearranged the sacks to form some crude bedding, listening to the thump-thump of the slow running steam engine below. Darkness had fallen. Ned lit a few matches so they could settle, relieving themselves one by one at the other end of the space before lying down. Sleep was all they could do. Dawn would break around five am.

Henry decided to close the hotel and empty the bars a few hours early, despite earnest protestations from the regulars, claiming he had 'urgent business' to attend to. This happened once a month apparently but the nature of his business remained shady and secretive, although he came back very late, long after midnight and usually the worse for wear. Down in Chinatown, existed a couple of notorious gambling dens and an ongoing scurrilous rumour circulated that Henry liked to regularly indulge in stud poker, playing for high stakes. They were places where much money changed hands, opium was smoked, fortunes won and lost and bodies were regularly found bound and gagged, floating in the dock. But Henry was that kind of man, fearless and loved life to the full on a day by day basis and despite his overweight, haggard appearance never seemed to be short of lady friends.

Rory had left Nancy a note to meet him and his Uncle Jack at the Horse's Head before closing but as Belle and Dottie now had the evening unexpectedly clear, they came along as well. Nancy updated them on all the intimate details of her discussions pursued in the afternoon, except the quick cuddle in the hayloft before he left.

"This place is a somewhat classier environment than our dump of a hotel. Gosh, someone even cleans it," Belle gasped, pushing open the ornately painted front door. The hotel, once of Regency origin, looked out over the waterfront, with lovely views of the berthed sailing ships and was evidently a stopping point of choice for rich couples and groups of men to eat and socialise. Numbers of them were sat around communal tables in a large and pleasant restaurant area, feasting on plates of very appetising food. A board hung over the bar with a special dish of the day chalked up in large letters: 'genuine Norwegian fish lobscouse - only sixpence for a plateful.'

Further along, they could see another smaller room, more traditional looking with a long standing-only bar for the regular drinkers and a few old tables at which men played cards and dominoes. But unlike the Black Anchor where any man or woman was welcome no matter what state they looked, smelt or staggered in like as long as they paid, there appeared in the Horse's Head to be a dress code enforced by nineteenth-century bouncers. And there were definitely no ladies of the night prowling around either. Nancy was glad she had washed her hair, which had been full of stable grime, no mean feat in their apology for a bathroom, and they were all pleased they had put on their best dresses.

"Any sign of lover boy then, Nance?" Dottie casually remarked, looking around for any eligible young males.

"Rory is not my lover boy," Nancy growled. "He's quite a gentlemen actually and sensitive."

Belle laughed. "I suppose that's more than can be said for Ned, sorry Nance, only a joke. I'm sure you miss him."

Nancy ignored Belle, nor was she sure whether that was even true … but conceded deep inside maybe she did really. "No, can't see him anywhere, in here or at the bar. We're probably early. Tell you what, I'm starving. I wouldn't mind a plate of scouse and a beer."

"Me too," Belle started to reply but they were interrupted by the sudden arrival of an apron-clad waiter, uneasy about three attractive women standing and staring aimlessly about the restaurant.

"Would you ladies wish to dine this evening?" he asked Belle politely.

"Yes, please. Is that place available over by the window?" Nancy replied, pointing to a large table which had just been vacated by three couples.

"Certainly madam, please follow me and I'll just fetch a clean tablecloth and some cutlery."

They sat down, staring quietly out of the window at the lovely view across the water and the tall sailing ships gently bobbing on the water. The sun still had an hour or more before setting and the evening displayed a clear blue sky and remained quite warm.

"Would you mind if we joined you, Nancy?"

The three turned to see a smiling Rory, unexpectedly dressed up in a smart pair of light brown cotton trousers and a white shirt, with matching waistcoat and blue necktie. He stood alongside a much older man with a thick head of grey hair and a droopy moustache, very alike in looks and also dressed similarly. Because it was a warm evening they had left their frock coats behind but were holding bowler hats.

"Rory, how lovely to see you," Nancy cried, shaking his hand gently. "I'm sure you've seen my friends Belle and Dottie in the bar but may I formally introduce them."

He shook each hand in turn with a smile and a greeting, staring hard into Belle's eyes. Where had he met her before? He would return to that conundrum later and quickly introduced Uncle Jack, who seemed very pleasant and friendly.

"Do please join us both of you," Nancy said, looking quickly at Belle and Dottie who nodded approvingly. They had a vested interest in finding out what they could about Captain Fanny Kirkby. "Have you eaten yet?"

The waiter returned with more cutlery and soon they were sharing out platefuls of the special Norwegian lobscouse fish stew spooned from a huge tureen, accompanied by a tray of glasses of ale. A great slab of brown bread was brought and a sharp knife, and Jack began methodically slicing it up to accompany the main course, explaining in detail how this meal had once been a mainstay for many sailors and still was, having himself once been on the sea for a long time, even fighting in the Crimea. Jack had a fascinating history. He enjoyed relating entertaining tales that made Nancy, Belle and Dottie gasp and laugh heartily. Rory insisted Nancy had to try the hotel pudding, a traditional treacle sponge made with Jamaican molasses and served with genuine and very popular Birds custard. Nancy protested that it would be bad for her waistline but was overruled by everyone, their raucous laughter attracting attention from some of the other tables, as they served out huge portions from one freshly made whole dessert looking like a giant yellow Christmas pudding, left steaming on the table alongside a massive jug of boiling hot custard.

Finally, it was time for coffees and the opportunity, at long last, for Nancy to ask Uncle Jack. "I understand from Rory that you know something about the Warrior Queen?"

Jack, sipping his coffee slowly, put his mug down and indicated for them to huddle up closer. "Yes, I do indeed. Loaded the very same ship up with my gang, three days ago in the George Dock. That woman, Captain Fanny Kirkby, is not a person to cross. She has, I am told on excellent authority, a deviant personality and her crew, many of them French, are well known for their overenthusiastic recruitment of suitable strong lads to help in their salvage operations up and down the coast. Notorious and ruthless she be and always needs divers you see, and they're not easy to come across in these parts. In the old days, we called it impressment, forcible enlistment into the Navy which was ended legally in England after Waterloo and the defeat of Napoleon. But of course, the French don't bother about that and Fanny definitely couldn't care less. She's very rich and buys off anyone who tries to interfere with her ways or else they disappear. One persistent policeman was found hanging from a warehouse crane a couple of years back. Never found the perpetrators but everyone knew it was her, especially because his private parts had been hacked off … she's said to do it herself, a speciality. So that's the background. Sorry if it be a little gory."

Belle drew breath, alarmed. She remembered how Ned loved diving after his previous summer school holiday in Croatia. She didn't like the sound whatsoever of retro-Fenella, positively evil. Had she been playing a game in 2026, specifically intended to lure them all back to her time? But why exactly? Orsbrick Hall was their only hope to find any answers.

"Do you know where the ship was heading?" Nancy asked tentatively.

Rory sensed the unease behind the question. "You can trust Uncle Jack, Nancy," he whispered. "I said you had close relatives who may have been press-ganged onboard."

Belle felt positive about that trust. They needed help. Rory and perhaps his uncle were their best hope. "My brothers have disappeared and we believe they may be on board against their will. One of them is a diver."

Jack nodded. "Understand," he said softly. "I won't ask what you want to do, that be your business, ladies, only I reiterate, take great care. A couple of the crew did say they were heading for Southport and had salvage to sell towards the end of the week, so likely they are there now if that's any use. Captain Fanny restricts treasure searches only to the Irish Sea and the

Mersey at present, plenty of rich pickings from sunken vessels so they won't be far. Anyways, must be off or the wife will have my hide. Ladies, I insist because it has been such an entertaining evening that the bill is on me so I'm just going to pay it then I'll creep away."

"No, no," Nancy said, instinctively always wanting to go Dutch, but before she could say anything Rory gently held her arm. "Uncle Jack insists," he said softly.

Belle, knowing the conventions of the time, instantly intervened before there was any misunderstanding. "Thank you, Jack, we've had a wonderful evening and very much appreciate your kindness and generosity. As he rose from his seat, she held out her hand which he kissed with a wink and a smile, followed by Dottie and Nancy.

"Now I know where I've seen you before," Jack suddenly said, staring at Belle's features. "You're that young lady with the strange name … used to come in here a lot with your fancy man one time. That lady who hails from Orsbrick Hall."

Belle felt a deep chill, the time frames were all wrong. There was a twenty-five-year difference with 1841. What was going on? Then she realised. Both she and Maddie had quite a resemblance. Of course. She had to think very fast. "You mean Mauveine … she's my cousin, yes we are alike."

"Good Lord in heaven above, yes, that was the name, you're like twin sisters, I do declare," Jack replied, taken aback. "Told me all about her work with dyes, I used to be active in the cotton trade before I went to sea. Real fascinating it were. I assume you're wanting to head to Orsbrick, don't worry, secret's safe with me. Give my regards to Rimmer, the head butler. Worked with him once, a most peculiar man but he saved my life when my hair, long in those days, got caught in a factory belt, sliced it in half with an axe there and then. I'm off to the wife, ladies. See you next week Rory."

In a trice, the bill was settled and Jack had vanished.

Rory ordered more beers and turned specifically to Nancy. "The restaurant only closes when the last person leaves," he said, "and some of them here will be around until two in the morning. But I reckon, Nancy, after this one we'd probably all better be getting back. Early shift in the morning, busy day tomorrow."

Belle, watching his expression as he spoke to Nancy, had a sixth sense that he wanted to converse with her alone and urgently. "I'm going to powder my nose. Are you coming Dottie?" she said, pointing to the sign which said cloakrooms. Dottie, equally attuned, got up promptly and they marched off to find the ladies toilets.

Rory knew he didn't have long. Henry had asked him in the morning to take the hotel waggon over to the canal terminus at Clarke's Basin on Old Hall Street to bring back a load of goods needed and also look at more horses in the Bootle auctions, so he'd be out all day and he needed to say it now to Nancy. "I've decided after what you said this afternoon, I'm leaving for good tomorrow and I want to help you three escape and find your brothers. You will need to go at the same time."

Nancy blinked hard … was she hearing him correctly? "I'm sorry Rory, I don't understand. You escape and we escape, all of us tomorrow? But how and when? This is all so sudden."

"I've worked out a plan," he whispered. "Your friends are coming back. I think we should tell them and I'll explain the details to all of you. Do you have enough money?"

"Plenty, I won't say where from. And you?"

"Yes, been saving a long time for this. Good."

Belle and Dottie slipped back quietly into their chairs.

He continued slowly. "Now, Nancy and I have something important to discuss with you, then we can all retire for a good night's sleep …"

Everything, for once had gone like clockwork. They followed Rory's instructions throughout the day, exactly. He had a fine mind for military-style planning, officer material Uncle Jack had once said proudly. No suspicions at the Black Anchor were aroused, but Belle's original proposal to depart by train as an aristocrat with her two maids was ditched. Instead, they were galloping hard across fields and country lanes in the light of a nearly full moon, peering closely at Rory's redrawn map and already were on the edge of Martin Mere. At this point they had to take great care; the water and the paths through the marshes needed careful navigation. They at least knew where they were, recognising various villages on the way, but were astounded at how rural and isolated this part of West Lancashire really was in the mid nineteenth century when little outside of Liverpool was built up. There had been a last minute change of plan. Uncle Jack had caught up with Rory mid-afternoon, just as he had purchased four prime horses at the auctions and was tying them up to the back of the waggon. Jack helped Rory bring the horses back and they were finally tethered in the yard of one of Jack's numerous lady friends, half a mile from the Black Anchor. But Jack also had new intelligence on the whereabouts of the Warrior Queen. The ship had prematurely left Southport and was proceeding inland to berth at the mouth of the River Douglas, from where Fanny was likely heading for Tarleton. So, Belle had taken a critical decision … they would head for Tarleton too as it was more than likely Ned, Zac and Ade were with her.

Rory had arranged for one of his friends to pack some food and then warned that their horses would tire halfway and should be rested and so should they. It was important that they got some decent sleep and be alert in the morning. On the map, he circled Scarisbrick Hall, where a cousin another gamekeeper, lived in a cottage with a barn about a hundred yards east of the main entrance. They were to knock and say Rory's name and Margaret, Charles's wife would put them up for the night and feed and water the horses. The couple were childless and had plenty of space. Rory handed a five-pound note to Nancy and insisted, despite her protests, that she uses it to pay Charles for his time and trouble. From Scarisbrick, they could follow the route taken by the railway, east over the fields and a shortcut onto the main road into Tarleton. Although only a small village, it was an important trading centre being the focal point where the Leeds and Liverpool Canal spur from Burscough joined the River Douglas. A complicated lock gate provided a vital gateway for transporting goods inland from the sea. Rory also suggested that the one excellent public house, the Cock and Bottle, would likely be where Fanny Kirkby would stay if she had arrived in Tarleton. Nancy felt disconsolate when they were about to leave Rory, all packed up with his own horse, Lightning, the black stallion in the field. Another time, era and place and she could have fallen for him in a big way. He was a perfect match but was heading immediately to St Helens to elope with the love of his life, Lady Eleanor Pilkington. She reached up impetuously before he galloped away, tears falling down her cheek, and wrapped her arms around him, topping off with a full-on kiss for a whole minute, much to his embarrassment. That was the least she could offer, a personal thank you for all he had done, ignoring the blatant amazement followed by sighs from Belle and Dottie who had never witnessed the hard-headed Nancy so emotional.

A couple of hours later and the magnificent Victorian Gothic outline of the great Scarisbrick Hall could be seen ahead, the full moon directly above the unique one hundred foot tower at the end of the building. This country house was one of the grandest abodes in Lancashire and a very fine architectural creation, in a league well above Orsbrick Hall in opulence, having belonged for many centuries to the aristocratic Scarisbrick family. Belle was aware of some of the history and had visited the Hall a few times, sadly in 2026 now an upmarket hotel and reliant for much of its income on television filming. But at least, unlike many stately homes in Lancashire, the Hall had not been demolished. The horses were visibly tiring especially Dottie's smaller mare and they began to quietly and slowly trot past the entrance and down the adjoining lane. A splendid three-storey white thatched building came into view, standing apart from the other run-down, ramshackle farm labourer tenements, often containing different poor families living in the same divided row of cottages.

They dismounted and began to walk the horses towards the entrance. They could see light flickering behind the curtains of two downstairs rooms. Agreeing beforehand that it seemed appropriate for Nancy to knock and explain, she walked up to the front door, surrounded by wisteria just coming into full leaf and the magnificent white flower buds emerging. The door opened almost immediately and a short, pretty woman, her hair in a tight bun, probably aged late twenties but it was always hard to tell, stood holding a candle and smiled warmly.

"You must be Nancy, I can tell by your hair," she said with a laugh. "Do come in all of you, you must be tired and hungry. I've got some vegetable soup warming."

Nancy blinked, not at all what she expected. Belle and Dottie stood silently, their mouths had dropped too. "You must be Margaret, I assume, but you're expecting us?" she said, her voice croaky with the wind and the riding.

"Don't look so surprised," a male voice shouted from inside and then Charles appeared alongside his wife. "We had a letter from Rory this afternoon. Very good post here being the Scarisbrick Hall and all that and he's explained everything and what you ladies be needing. A pleasure to welcome you on board. I do apologise, still think I'm in the Royal Navy some days. I'll just tether those horses in the barn and feed them, whilst Margaret sorts you all out."

Belle decided to take the opportunity … he likely was aware of Orsbrick Hall and may know something useful. There was always a close informal network amongst the gamekeepers. "I'll help you Charles, no problem, two horses each? My name's Annabelle."

He grinned. "Thank you, young lady, that'll make it easier for sure."

Nancy and Dottie walked inside. The cottage was unusually spacious and a log fire was blazing quietly in the hearth. The nights were definitely chilly and they were not adequately dressed for riding as they normally would have been. Indicating for them to sit at the table already laid out, Margaret returned with a warming tureen of thick soup accompanied by chunks of bread and ladled out a bowlful each. She took their thin coats to hang up and watched Nancy shiver. "Warm yourself up first by the fire, lass," Margaret said in a very broad Lancashire accent. "Neer cast a clout till May is out, Nancy, but given circumstances, you've all had to come in what you've got I suppose."

They heard the front door open again. Charles and Belle had returned already, the horses had been quickly settled. "Well I never, Margaret," Charles began. "This young lady is a cousin of Miss Mauveine of Orsbrick Hall, James McKenzie's daughter."

Margaret looked hard at Belle. "Aye, I can see the family resemblance, she must be about your age too, Annabelle. Mauveine McKenzie sometimes rides over here on a Sunday with her stable hand friend, Isaac, I believe. She has a beautiful white horse and has become very friendly with Lady Ann Scarisbrick who moved back to the estate four years ago. I understand Lady Ann acts like a grandmother and mother to Mauveine who sadly has neither so I understand and gives family advice and so on. Must be difficult for the girl living with only her father although she works for him in that dye factory they built there, she be very well educated too. Anyway, I've prepared three beds in the attic room at the top so you'll have a comfortable night after you've eaten. We've got an iron boiler behind the fire, a new fangled thing. They look after Charles and me at Scarisbrick, and we now have hot water, isn't that wonderful? There's a sink and tap up there and you can all have a wash too. I've left clean towels; water closet is through that end door."

By then, the three were sat around the table hungrily devouring the excellent soup. "Thank you so much," Nancy said in-between mouthfuls. "You are both extremely kind and generous and we are merely passing strangers. May I provide you with some recompense for all your troubles?" She pulled the five-pound note from her dress pocket.

317

Margaret grimaced and waved for Nancy to put the note away. "No, absolutely not, you keep your money, my girl. Likely you will be needing it along your journey. Charles and I are always happy to help out Rory when he requires it, we're a close family, always have been."

Nancy blushed and smiled. "Thank you."

Margaret turned again to Belle. "I understand you're heading, in morning, for Tarleton to find your brothers. There's a bridle short cut through the estate and across the fields, following a brook, which even Rory doesn't know. Charles will show you where you must go."

Charles was sat in his armchair reading the Ormskirk Gazette under the light of a dull candle and puffing slowly on a curly pipe, the sweet smell of the tobacco filling the air. "Aye, no problem at all, ladies, have to head that way and check some traps first thing," he said before putting on his wire glasses and continued reading.

Shortly afterwards, Belle, Dottie and Nancy retired upstairs, exhausted with the adrenaline rush and the ride and flopped into their comfortable beds for a very welcome sleep …

The difference between the night before and the morning after fully justified them taking Rory's advice and making a break at Charles and Margaret's cottage, helped further by generous lashings of bacon and eggs and mugfuls of hot tea for breakfast. Slowly following Charles on his well-cared for steed, they eventually found the narrow and well-hidden bridle path. He wished them well and with a final wave they trotted on at a brisk pace, Belle holding onto a new map and leading the way. Stopping by the brook to gather their bearings, a profusion of spring flowers and late blossom amongst the shrubs cascaded around them. Dottie needed to ask what was going on earlier.

"So are you going to tell me and Nance what Margaret whispered to you when we were leaving? You both looked very serious," Dottie said, sitting on a fallen log.

Nancy, wiping some earlier mud off her boots in the brook, looked up. "I never saw that exchange so come on then Belle, what big secrets were you two sharing? They were such a nice couple, Rory is lucky to have a great family."

Belle dismounted slowly and walked over. "Actually, it was a bit odd. Margaret gave me a warning. She'd been doing tarot after we went to bed. She's a bit of a practising spiritualist and claims to be psychic. She said to be very careful if we meet up with Fenella or Fanny as everyone knows her by. Margaret's take is that Fanny is pure evil, in league with Satan, and knows a lot more about her but was reluctant to say."

"Normally I'd say you don't believe in that claptrap surely Belle, a rational scientist like you," Dottie replied. "But let's be honest. Thinking laterally, what's happened to us as a likely consequence of something Fenella has activated means all bets are off on being a doubting Thomas. Everyone who's had contact with Fenella describes her as evil personified. They can't all be wrong, I suppose. We do need to take care whatever the rationale; she'll be vengeful seeing us."

"Yes, but we've got this far and we're almost there, we have to try and find the boys, they'd do the same for us," Nancy said, patting her horse.

"I agree," Belle said, "but ... look, I can't say anything more, we don't have time, although I suspect when we get to Orsbrick Hall the full explanation I owe you both may well come clear. The McKenzie family is ... err ..."

Nancy laughed and interrupted. "Listen, Belle, like we said earlier, Dottie and I are fully aware that your family have certain, let's say unusual characteristics having been around

319

Ned and Zac long enough. Ned has already said jokingly you and Maddie see spooks, like the ghost of Mauveine riding on horses but he doesn't see anything."

"And even Zac says he's seen Mauveine a few times in the grounds," Dottie added. "That strange happening of the burning barn last summer and the weirdo who walked out with the horses wearing strange clobber who then vanished into thin air. But now we're here in 1865, the clothing isn't so odd, it's normal for the time. Zac said it was Isi we saw … is that short for Isaac the same as Margaret mentioned? Was Isi Mauveine's boyfriend or husband, Belle? So, Nance and I saw a ghost too?"

Belle sighed. "Yes, on both counts, the explanation's complicated. And yes the McKenzie family, through the female line, have enhanced abilities to see into their own family past. That includes Mum and Abby, who as you already know is also part of the family ancestry going back to the sixteenth century. No explanation offered. Maddie and I only speculate the whole business is something to do with advanced physics, space-time, quantum theory and dark energy. Anyway, that won't help us here but I'd better explain now how I've been back in time before, then you'll understand better why we need to head to Orsbrick Hall and what we may encounter."

Nancy slithered back off her horse, almost falling to the ground. Momentarily, with all the action moving at a fast pace, she had forgotten what Belle had said when they encountered one another in the Black Anchor

Dottie seemed less surprised, she was expecting more at a suitable point in time. Belle had been too vague and reluctant to talk until now but they had truly escaped and were nearing their goal. "Having experienced this situation before certainly explains why you've been much more relaxed from the beginning and thankfully have been able to take the lead and steer me and Nancy out of various troubles. We're both really grateful."

Belle drew a deep breath. "Okay, but I'll be brief. It was the same time as you two witnessed the barn going up with Dad and Lynton, when Mum, Abby, Maddie and I we are on the Queen Lusitania, cruising across to America to Harvard. Mauveine and Isi somehow facilitated a return to 1841. We ended up at Orsbrick Hall with Lady Morag McKenzie, Mauveine's grandmother. There was a purpose and a problem … to change history so Mauveine, Isi, and all our family would be born. We did it and returned from Orsbrick Hall. The four of us haven't told anyone, not even Dad and the boys."

"But the Queen Lusitania never sailed, it had engine trouble," Nancy said, her eyes wide.

"That was part of the changed history, our McKenzie family history. For you two, outside of it, nothing happened. Time seems to be able to exist in different universes that in certain conditions you can pass through, like a wormhole in space. But now you're both part of this, effectively, as a result of something Fenella has done, we've passed through another wormhole to her time in 1865."

"So how did you get back?" Dottie said, frowning. "Sorry I know this is difficult for you but actually it's better that Nance and I understand so when we end up at Orsbrick Hall we have some idea what to expect and can go with the flow like I assume you will."

"That's fair enough, Dottie, and a good point and I should have thought of that before but to be honest I didn't know where I could start and had been leaving it till the last minute."

"No worries, we're all in deep shit here," Nancy said, "I understand fully, Belle. No detailed explanations needed, just give us a few pointers."

Belle smiled. "Okay, it seems that whenever the past, present and future collide unexpectedly or accidentally, like someone's future death being announced, it creates some kind of imbalance or discontinuity and everything is reset back to what it was. In other words, you find yourselves back in your own time, but in the McKenzie case, some history will have been altered. And that's how we returned. There was an argument between Mum, who was acting as a governess and Morag and in the heat of what was said it was realised by all in the room that we were from the future and being forced to make a death prediction for someone there ... an incompatible circumstance. Immediately there was a bright light and some kind of explosion like we experienced in the Black Anchor and next thing we were back to normal time."

"So you're hoping that the same could happen when we get to Orsbrick Hall, either naturally or we engineer it, but clearly we want Ned, Zac and Ade with us as well, which is why we need to find them, urgently," Nancy replied.

"Yes, now we're all at last on the same page, I feel much better," Belle said.

"Me too. What are we waiting for? You've got the map, Belle. Lead on," Dottie cried, as they hitched up the horses, mounted and rode off at a brisk pace.

Sunrise was just breaking through and Zac awoke with a jolt, alerted from his fitful sleep by the sudden change of the engine chugging. The wherry was slowing down. He rolled over carefully to the gap in the tarpaulin and peered out, the skies blue and cloudless. A beautiful calm morning was unfolding and he could see they were heading for a huge landing jetty somewhere. He didn't recognise the surroundings, a few cottages and buildings dotted about, but they were near the muddy bank of what looked like a wide river, definitely not on the coast. They must be in the estuary of the River Douglas. However, rousing Ned and Ade was like waking the dead.

"Jesus, Zac, what time is it?" Ade snarled, raising his fist. "Christ Almighty, you don't have to shake me so fucking hard, my head hurts real bad."

Ned also was groggily re-emerging into the real world looking equally bad. "Zac, I know you're not normally tee-total but refusing more of that bottled ale was a wise move, bro. That stuff is way, way strong, puts Carling to shame."

"Yeah, well neither of you had to down another six bottles each. Honestly, Ade, you see a crate of beer and you have to consume the lot. The crew will go apeshit when they find out."

"They won't, I tossed the crate overboard, nobody will be any the wiser," Ade replied, finally cracking his usual sneer and raising the sagging tarpaulin higher into the lifeboat so they could sit up properly. "Hey Zac, where's the bacon and eggs, my good friend?"

"You'll have to make do with this?" Zac replied, throwing one of three stale buns, which he'd saved from the previous night. "You'll likely need some energy. I filled those three bottles with water from the rain barrel after you two crashed out so you can get a drink. Anyway, the captain said he'd fetch us when the crew had alighted and they'd gone to a farmhouse nearby for breakfast."

They just finished their buns and swilled down the cold water when the tarpaulin was raised and the captain and his first mate beckoned them out. "Okay you three, time to scarper quick," he growled. "That'll be a tenner, Ned."

Ned fished into his pocket and gave him twenty. "Many thanks, Captain Birdseye, you deserve every penny for getting us away."

The captain snatched the note and his first mate, smirking, winked to Ade … it was him who had left the beer crate deliberately. "Name's Birdsley, young man, don't know where you get Birdseye from."

Ned kept a straight face but it took much effort by Ade and Zac not to crack up laughing. The seaman certainly looked a spitting image of the eponymous 1980s advert for fish fingers, recently re-run on the television. The captain continued, pointing south down the river bank. "If you walk that way to the start of the river channel, follow the river about two and a half miles and you'll end up at the lock where the canal and river meet, on the outskirts of Tarleton. There's a packet boat runs from there to Burscough and a cafe where you can have something to eat. River is still tidal there. Don't be drinking any of it, will give you the right shits."

Ned smiled. "That's great, we're very grateful."

"You should be," the captain replied. "Look yonder, across the deck towards that row of tall ships docked down estuary. Recognise the big one with the cream sails?"

They peered through the early mist and Ned's heart sank. "Fuck, the Warrior Queen, they must know we're here."

"Not necessarily. Ship does dock there, regular like, before usually heading up the coast towards Lancaster for more booty. But best going the way I say. If they're looking for you, they'll assume you're on the road with horses. Whatever, I'd keep well away from the village centre and the Cork and Bottle public house where Madam usually stays. If you've upset her lad be warned. She's been known to string a man naked across the deck and personally cut his bollocks off with a machete for less."

Ned paled. Ade grimaced and thumbed towards the wherry's boarding plank. "Let's get going, the quicker we get to Orsbrick the better …"

The horses were making good progress having been fed well with prime hay at the cottage. In the distance, about half a mile on as they rode up a small hill, they could see what looked like two rivers running alongside one another in the distance. To their left, at a similar distance, the beautiful church spire in Tarleton village rose up and various cottages and farm houses were clustered about what appeared to be some kind of centre.

"That was quick," Nancy shouted. "We've a choice to make. Either we look for them in the village or we head for the lock over there. The nearest waterway is the start of the canal and the other one is the River Douglas. They meet there and it's possible the boys could be heading for the canal."

Belle pondered and decided. "I think we should heed the advice Margaret gave and at least start with the canal first and if nobody has seen them we can head into the village, but we'll need to take real care then."

Dottie and Nancy both agreed and immediately they set off at a gallop down the final stretch of the bridle track and onto the main lane which branched off towards the canal lock.

It had been a struggle to walk along the river. Much of the path was waterlogged or full of deep mud with many diversions and unavoidable wet feet emerged as they slowly tramped through reeds and marshy clumps. What was around three mile felt like thirty but eventually, up ahead after turning the last corner, they could visualise the unmistakable canal lock and a few large wooden buildings. A landing stage of sorts had been built and the junction of the canal and river was in sight. As suggested by

Captain Birdseye, a passenger barge, which he had called a packet boat, was berthed on the canal. A number of passengers were already onboard and others were milling around, some sat on tables, eating and drinking. It was still early, none of them had watches but they reckoned, going by the distance travelled and sunrise time, it was about six-thirty in the morning. But it was Ade who suddenly, uncharacteristically excited for the time of day, turned to Zac, shoving him hard in the back.

"Both of you turn around and look. Fuck me, am I hallucinating still after that ale binge or are you seeing what I'm seeing?"

Ned turned around sharply, the three of them peering hard towards the lane leading to the berthing area. "Jesus Christ, it looks like Belle and Dottie on those horses and ... fuck, that must be Nancy but not how I recognise her ... she's got a weird mane of red hair and looks really wild ... actually very sexy ... mmm ...."

"Forgotten Captain Fanny already have we, Casanova?" Ade sneered, although Zac was suddenly quite fixated on Dottie. Perhaps they could get back together again.

Ned turned to Ade, in an unusually aggressive manner. "Not a mention about me and Fenella, dick-head. I'll tell her in my own good time, got it."

Ade shoved him away. "Hey, keep your hair on. I'm only joking, what do you take me for, Ned?"

Ned relented and smiled. "Okay, sorry, we're all on edge. They must be here looking for us I reckon. Come on hurry before they ride off."

Belle, Nancy and Dottie had stayed on their horses and were scouring the people around and the passengers on the packet boat but no sign of Ned, Zac and Ade.

"Doesn't look like they're here, we'd better set off towards Tarleton village, I never did like that Cock and Bottle pub, Fenella or not," Belle murmured.

But Nancy, looking the other way, was smirking. "Don't think we need to do that Belle. Look who we have here."

They turned the horses to see the three musketeers puffing and panting up the hill, not daring to shout in case it caught undesirable attention, but undoubtedly that was Ned in front waving at them, despite the growth of scruffy stubble over their worn-out faces.

The girls dismounted and tethered the horses. Belle was overjoyed and ran over to greet them first, hugging each one in turn. Dottie and Nancy walked up behind briskly and Dottie immediately hugged her brother but just as quickly grabbed hold of Zac and gave him a big hug and a kiss like old times again.

Ned finally loosened Belle's grip and stared at Nancy, standing there, aloof in her seductive harlot dress and black boots, her mane of curly red hair glistening in the morning light and her lips and cheeks matched in colour with some rouge she had brought with her.

"Hellfire and brimstone, Nance, I love the retro look. You look amazing. Jesus, am I glad to see you again," he burbled, his eyes on stalks. Any lascivious thoughts of Fenella had already vanished, especially after the machete warning.

"Come here idiot, you can tell me what you've been up to later."

Nancy ran up and gave Ned a huge hug then a long lingering kiss to groans all round. Wherever he'd got that fancy attire, he certainly stood apart from everyone else and looked a real country gentleman, apart from his soggy boots. A few claps and hurrahs from the passengers alerted all six that they were drawing attention to themselves and they stood apart.

A boatman walked forward briskly. "Barge is leaving in twenty-five minutes, once horses are fed again. If you want seats you'd better pay now. There's room on the butty boat behind for your horses if you want to take them, otherwise, I'll have 'em if you're going to sell them," he said with a wide toothless grin, his two grimy children with matching caps stood alongside.

Belle turned to Ned. "We'll take the horses. They're very strong and can take two riders each. I assume you're heading for Orsbrick too."

Ned looked puzzled. "Yes, how did you know?"

"Women's intuition," Nancy replied, eyeing up Dottie and Zac still holding and mooning over each other like long lost lovers. "We can catch up on our respective stories onboard, although we're pretty sure now what you've been up to."

Ned looked askance, feeling a stupid blush come on. At some stage, he'll have to tell Nancy the unsavoury truth. On the other hand, dressed like that, what's she been up to?

"I agree," Ade said. "Pay the captain, Gentleman Ned, you're the man with the money. Zac will put the horses onto the back barge."

Ned fished out a roll of notes from his pocket. "How much is it please?"

The boatman smirked, that was the first time anyone had said 'please' to him in a long time, especially his dumb wife and twelve kids. "Altogether, including them horses, that'll be ten shillings and sixpence. You've just got time to fetch a hot sausage bap from the stall over there if you hurry."

Ned gave him a pound note and indicated to keep the change. He felt generous, especially with Fenella's money.

Quickly they were seated inside and out of the cold in the top corner around two tables they had pulled together, enjoying surprising comfort for a canal barge. They began eating a plateful of sausage baps and homemade apple cake alongside mugs of hot tea, with milk provided, as the packet barge slowly pulled away to a steady speed of four miles an hour, towed by a couple of hefty black shire horses.

Each of them thought the same thing. There was a lot of selective catching up to do. But most importantly they needed to listen carefully to Belle as she outlined a plan of action once they arrived at Orsbrick Hall. The key to creating any kind of instability to try and get back to 2026, Belle explained, would be meeting up with the very young Mauveine. Hopefully, that would be the case and trigger a cataclysm for their return.

Chapter Thirteen

Careering along the busy main road, it wouldn't take long for Maddie to drive the old jeep home to Orsbrick Hall, now loaded up with six people. Mauveine and Isi were jammed into the children's small seats at the back, although both of them cheerfully stated that the ride was a hundred times more comfortable than a nineteenth-century horse-drawn carriage, even a luxury one. A certain sombreness filled the air. Each person quietly mulled over their personal concerns, everyone recognising it was impossible to formulate a plan of action because nobody could offer any clear idea of what to expect, except this day, was significant. The potential for breaking and entering the return in time which Fenella had orchestrated by mysterious means was becoming closer.

For Victoria, journeying back to Orsbrick Hall with Mauveine represented the best chance of accelerating the return of Belle, Ned and Zac although how and by what mechanism remained an elusive mystery. Fenella and the circumstances surrounding her from the beginning of her arrival had increasingly acquired a bizarre set of complications, extremely difficult to fathom, with too many unknowns and outliers. At least when they had been forced back in time to 1841, they quickly discerned from Mauveine and Isi a valid reason and a principle of a plan they could enact that eventually worked. But this time everyone was in a void of darkness, anxious and frightened except for a vague notion of the Fenella they knew being at total odds with her genuine past. But why had this happened? That key question still needed scientific evidence as well as clarity, with the dangerous possibility that everything might come together in one giant cataclysm, with no winners to emerge, past or present. But that was the risk they were going to have to take. What else was open to them?

Victoria remained especially jittery about Elizabeth meeting up with Julian again. It wasn't whether she could trust 2026 Elizabeth. She did in principle, as she had, in the end, trusted 1841 Ada. But it was evident that Ada's inherent naughty and mischievous character had unsurprisingly travelled across the time barrier. Elizabeth, despite her avowed wholesome curate airs and graces, had displayed a recurring need to occasionally shock and awe for the hell of it, just like the old times.

They agreed, before setting off, that on arrival Victoria would introduce Elizabeth as the new curate. That part should be easy as Julian was already aware of a curate expected in the parish. But Mauveine and Isi were a serious problem. Julian and Lynton were fully aware of their ghostly existences, and the beautiful picture of a very young Mauveine in her 1860s laboratory still hung in the hall. But neither saw Mauveine or Isi as ghosts on a daily basis. They didn't possess the psychic capabilities to recall and remember. What was not understood, however, regarding Lynton, was whether he had any latent memory of experiencing Mauveine and Isi on horseback from the prism of purpurine crisis in the priory, although McKenzie history had since been rewritten. Abby was sure he remembered nothing, but introducing Mauveine and Isi in the flesh and using their names could trigger a memory flashback to past happenings, as well as raising all manner of issues and questions, which for the moment were too difficult to explore and answer when the task was to focus solely on returning

Belle, Ned and Zac. Mauveine had already reasoned along the same lines and suggested that Victoria introduce them using other names as new suppliers to her dye business, which was true at least. Mauveine opted for her former nickname, once used daily by the servants and Isi volunteered his middle name which he never used and his mother's maiden name as their surname. Sighs of relief all round, one less problem hopefully.

Abby remained deeply uneasy about her pregnancy. The fact that she hadn't yet told Lynton or explain who was the father of the baby … the latter scenario would destroy her marriage in one fell swoop if the truth came out. Everybody agreed wholeheartedly that nothing whatsoever about her physical state would be mentioned, let alone hinted at. Abby, at some future time, could deal with it, solely on a personal level between her and Lynton. Abby felt reassured and confident, her perky self gradually emerging again as they continued, Burscough Bridge finally coming into view. She needed to be as alert and distraction free as she could. If a horrible situation happened she might have to use her old singing skills again, thinking hard about those archaic Latin chants she used to good effect at the Orsbrick Priory. But that was to dispel a seething vent of malice and evil surrounding the Rimmer ancestry. There was no evidence thus far that such bad and awful intent lay behind this new situation for Belle, Ned, Zac and their friends. Fenella may have been strange but she seemed genuinely kind in her own way. None of it properly added up.

Instinctively, Abby felt that Mauveine hadn't yet revealed everything about Fenella. Something, perhaps a past secret was still lurking, and more telling, her head was not pounding as they approached. The usual and definitive psychic sign of something life-changing and imminent was not happening. As

Maddie stopped at a set of temporary traffic lights, Abby suddenly had a realisation. Maddie, even more psychically attuned than her, was not affected either, that was patently clear. Perhaps this time around, with whatever had specifically evolved with Fenella, neither of them was involved, unlike the previous happenings. Was underlying this predicament solely something between Mauveine and Fenella in 1865? And were Belle, Ned and Zac to be used as family leverage for whatever objective Fenella was pursuing, which is why they had been dragged back into Fenella's time and situation? Shit. Abby said nothing but knew, at the earliest opportunity, she needed to confer alone with Victoria. Maddie was too emotionally close to Mauveine. All they could do would be to see what, if anything, transpired once they were at Orsbrick Hall and react as best as they could. But it seemed increasingly possible that the solution to this crisis lay solely in Mauveine's hand. They were all bystanders in an evolving saga from another time.

Besides concentrating on the driving, Maddie had her own cascading flow of thought. She was pleased she had finally told her mother about her driving test, albeit in a way not at all expected. But she felt confident that her mother would support buying her a car, in fact, she really fancied a large jeep like this one. It was such fun to drive and she loved being high up on the road if her father was prepared to dig deep into his pockets. Belle would be envious, but knowing her sister, envy in a nice way. Anyway, Belle could easily learn to drive as well. It was then Maddie felt an acute pang of loss, fear and longing. What if she never saw Belle again? With Ned and Zac, they were such close siblings, especially her and Belle. What if they remained locked forever in a time period of the mid-nineteenth century, as she could have been in 1841? Or even worse, they reappeared by replacing Mauveine and Isi as ghosts from the past, new disembodied spirits having suffered their own traumas in their new lives being lived in the Victorian past? The awful thought made her shiver and go cold inside. And back home there were other responsibilities with a sickly Janine to look after, although she should now be on the mend. How could all this be explained rationally to Janine? Her life had become terribly complicated.

They were now on the final back road to Orsbrick and would reach home shortly. Elizabeth, in her usual upbeat manner, was making everyone laugh on the grounds they had become far too serious inside her carriage, with her recently acquired curate knowledge of topical hymns, explaining that the number 127 had a mathematical significance nobody understood in the slightest, not even Maddie. So instead, Elizabeth and Abby decided to sing heartily in gusto harmony with a rendition of 'Come all Ye Faithful', joined in by Isi, his loud and sonorous baritone at the back well honed from his former stint as the local vicar.

Suddenly the familiar black iron gates came into view and Maddie swung the heavy jeep through the opening and up the gravel drive, to park next to Lynton's new Mercedes electric coupé. Elizabeth looked around curiously, wondering what had happened to the huge original oak gates but admiring instantly the magnificent conversion into a modern stately home with such beautiful gardens, her sharp eyes taking in all the nuances of shade, colour and design. Curate, she may be but she hadn't lost her former deep love of fashion and beautiful houses.

Victoria took a deep breath. The first hurdle would be Julian, inevitably the suspicious sceptic who she had got away with inventing stories and diversions all their years together. He gracefully chose to ignore them most of the time because he loved her and was never bothered about her idiosyncrasies. But equally, alighting from a car with Elizabeth, Mauveine and Isi was far weirder than she could sensibly express, although they seemed miraculously quite at home and relaxed. Of course, for Mauveine and Isi they had never left and been part of the entire house and history for all those years. So for them, physically stepping onto the front gravel must be like coming in through the tradesman's entrance. The last three months had been an almost never-ending succession of strange happenings so why, she logically reasoned, should she be fazed with this scenario? All she wanted was to see Belle, Ned and Zac back unharmed. On the upside, both Maddie and Abby were remarkably calm considering, as if this coming together was just another social occasion. Perhaps they were a step ahead in the psychic stakes and undaunted by scientific logic and rationality which constantly plagued Victoria's decision making at critical times.

Once out of the car, Elizabeth remained fascinated with the change in the surroundings since she was last there, in 1841, flaunting herself with her grandiose luxury carriage, opulent dresses, and boundless energy for intrigue. But, as she had remarked a number of times one month ago when they first re-collided, her brain had updated through the time warp with modern overlays of knowledge, so she understood why the ornate wooden windows had been replaced with modern triple glazed frames. But the overall fabric of the building, albeit somewhat more weathered, remained the same. She smiled as fond reminiscences of Morag, Victoria, and of course, the infamous Julian Fazackerley cascaded back into her Ada reserve of past memories. So where was the tantalizing new Julian?

Maddie pointed to the side of the house where the outline of the familiar woods and pond could be seen. A loud whining noise could be heard from Julian's workshop behind. "Dad must be inside working on something," she said promptly.

"Probably with Lynton. I'll fetch him in a minute. Shall we go in first? I'll just pull the bell, so you can meet Claire."

"Claire?" Elizabeth queried.

"We still have a housekeeper, Elizabeth, even in this so-called modern day and age and also a cook, called Danielle." Victoria intervened. "But they're not servants like in your day, more an integral part of the family. The house is too big for me to manage on my own, especially with running my business, although as you can see around, Julian enjoys doing and making things, rather like an estate manager. I'm sure you approve."

Elizabeth grinned thinking that new Julian may not be the village blacksmith but he certainly had the same practical capabilities, which she had always admired. She decided she was looking forward to seeing him after all. "Absolutely, and so you should, Victoria. Good servants are invaluable but I like this modern style of integration and equalised status. I always felt that way about my closest servant companions but my thinking then was far too radical for such a patriarchal and class-conscious society of idle rich aristocracy, especially my husband, William. Inside, I was always like Madeleine, what you now call a radical feminist."

"As too are Mum and Abby, and Annabelle don't forget," Maddie said, patting Elizabeth's arm gently. "And of course, Mauveine."

"Here, here," Mauveine answered, standing at the back and looking at Isi who grinned. "I endorse all of that sentiment, a McKenzie characteristic which has never wavered through the ages. Ahh ... the door is opening."

As it was pulled open, Maddie began chattily. "Hi Claire, we ..." then she stopped, mesmerised, so too were Victoria and Abby. Standing before them was decidedly not Claire or anyone else they knew for that matter. A tall, very blonde and attractive woman in her early twenties, with bright green piercing eyes, held the door. Wearing a short denim skirt and a tight t-shirt, she appeared like a model from a Paris fashion show with her long legs. The woman carefully took in everyone in the group for a few seconds then smiled back warmly.

"Good afternoon Maddie, and you too Victoria and Abby. Please accept my apologies for the confusion; I can see from your expressions you were not expecting me. I only arrived a few hours ago. My name is Erika and I'm from Latvia. Claire and Danielle have been inducting me with all your day-to-day household requirements."

Erika stared hard at Elizabeth, who was especially intrigued by this particular servant variation. Who was this Erika woman in a very provocative dress? Erika slowly repeated the visual interrogation with Mauveine and Isi. "I'm so sorry, but you three people don't compute, but as you do not pose an imminent threat then I'm comfortable," she continued blandly.

Victoria, never one to abide strangers in her house particularly opening the door to her, realised immediately, as did Maddie and Abby, although she had no idea beforehand, but was not surprised from the attire. "Hello, Erika. I think I understand now. So, are you a replacement for Sabrina?"

"Yes, Victoria, but hopefully much improved."

Before Erika could reply further, loud laughs and merriment of a familiar nature rang out from behind and Claire appeared at the door, smiling and affable as ever whilst Erika went quietly back inside. Everyone turned to see Julian and Lynton struggling to carry a heavy electrical insulator attached to a shiny metal box which they were lowering into a large wheelbarrow. Julian strode over with Lynton behind.

"Hello everyone, I'm Julian, Victoria's husband and my helping hand here goes by the name of Lynton," he began cheerily, wondering why everyone was so quiet and staring oddly.

Elizabeth needed no convincing. The likeness to her former lover, Julian Fazackerley, was remarkable. Tall, well-built and mature, with greying hair and rather sexy spectacles, he was just as adorable looking but then she always liked older men as long as they had some life left in them and new Julian seemed to fit that requirement in spades and more. But she had to be ever so careful in front of Victoria. Besides, there were enough complications around without adding more, at least for the moment she mused mischievously, holding in her strong desire to be flirtatious again.

Julian continued laughing whilst Lynton sidled up to Abby and kissed her gently on the cheek. "Sorry Victoria, I should have texted you but Erika only arrived an hour ago and I was just as surprised when the white van turned up again and she climbed out. Ash Kolinsky has been building her for some time. Following my feedback, Erica has acquired Sabrina's old memory chips so can build from that local knowledge but is much more intellectually capable, especially in mathematics for the benefit of Maddie and Belle and will be able to actively help with your dye and science business ... and your gallery artwork too, Abby. I thought that would be more useful."

"And is she musical too?" Abby interjected in a dry monotone, glaring at Lynton who immediately stopped grinning.

Victoria added her part to the observations. "I see the former North Korean attributes have been replaced with the latest line of Slavic ones. Professor Kolinsky certainly has an indisputable eye for the world's most attractive women, with matching dress style," she commented dryly.

"Err … yes …" Julian replied, uneasily. His good friend's too obvious predilections always brought the same reaction from Abby and Victoria and normally Maddie too but she was remarkably restrained for some reason. Why couldn't they simply accept that his friend Ash was an eccentric and a genius at the same time, forget her appearance and bask in the prestige and advantages of trialling one of the most advanced humanoid robots in the world? "Ash became … umm … disillusioned with Asian girls and now prefers the company of Eastern European females but he's become much more sensitive, as you can see, about his client requirements. Hence the improvements in intellectual working capacities and no, Erika has zero musical chips."

Maddie laughed out loudly followed by Abby, whilst Claire went to make tea and continue with Erika's domestic update.

Elizabeth couldn't remain quiet any longer but, as ever, was much more fascinated by the amazing 2026 technology than the ethics alluded to. Who was she to criticise a man's tastes? "Hello Julian, I'm Elizabeth Milbanke, your new parish curate. May I ask, is Erika a working manifestation, or should I say prototype of the so-called artificial intelligence revolution?"

Julian looked hard and removed his glasses to wipe them, seeming more nervous than a moment before. "I assumed as much, the dog collar was specifically noted," he replied forcing a grin again. "Yes, that's one way of putting it. Erica is one of the world's most advanced robots which we have the unique privilege of testing out. I thought at first you might be the new vicar. Sorry, I don't head over there very often, rather busy with the growing estate lately. But don't I know you from somewhere?"

Victoria's head jerked up from perusing the headlines of the local newspaper left in the porchway. Abby stared askance but Maddie remained her usual calm and resolute self. "Julian and you too Lynton," Victoria began. "Now you've met Elizabeth, how rude of me not to introduce you to Mo and Herbert Edmondson who are my latest factory suppliers of new dyes, having recently set up a research unit on the new industrial estate. Maddie and I have just paid them a visit. We almost forgot earlier and bumped into Elizabeth doing introductions around the factory units."

"I like to be proactive," Elizabeth said quickly.

Lynton immediately held out his hand to Mauveine and Isi in turn but his face displayed a further degree of puzzlement. "Sorry for also being a party pooper but today seems to be an uncanny déjà-vu time all round. Don't I also know you two?"

"Unlikely, Lynton," Isi replied gently. "Unless you've been to Göttingen in the last fifteen years where my wife and I have been living as technical researchers for the Bayer Company."

"Err ... mmm ... absolutely not, must be mistaken, my sincere apologies," he replied. "Anyway, it's a pleasure to meet you both. Family in this area?"

"Yes," Mauveine said without flinching, looking casually at Victoria. "We wanted to be nearer to them as well as continue our work with Dr McKenzie whose reputation in the dye industry is second to none of course."

Claire suddenly appeared at the door once more. "Afternoon tea is being served in the drawing room, courtesy of Erika who is learning the domestic ropes very quickly, so much better than Sabrina. She can also, I've just discovered, cook a lot more than bacon, egg, beans and pansanggi with noodles which will be useful when Danielle is off-shift. Anyway, would you all come in please?"

Victoria smiled and led the way, Maddie chatting with Abby and 'Mo' as Lynton followed, pointing out the numerous pictures on the wall to 'Herbert' which he had picked up at various art auctions over the years. Elizabeth deliberately walked in slowly with Julian, both keeping a distance from the rest. Julian began to draw her attention to a number of seventeenth-century religious paintings over towards the scullery which had been obtained from a nun's monastery clear-out. She stopped and admired the rare and unique pictures, recognising the style similar to some she had once hung in her beloved townhouse in Mayfair. But this was a good opportunity to have a quick and quiet prod, out of earshot of Victoria.

"Tell me, Julian, do you like the Aintree races?"

He put his glasses back on and pondered, quizzically. "Yes, I go every year. Love a little bit of a gamble, usually with Lynton and the boys. Why do you ask?"

"You look like a man who relishes the lure of beating the betting odds and the hot vibrancy of an exciting race, as my father once did," she replied jerking back her head coquettishly and a little un-curate like. "My old friend in London was also an avid horse lover, quite wild really, she often held wonderful parties in the summer. I do miss Caitriona." She smiled and carefully gauged his reaction. She would soon tell if her instinct was correct.

Julian stopped. There was a pause for a moment. "Caitriona? Such a nice name." He took a breath and continued. "Anyway, it's time we joined the others. I'm curious to see the conjunction of artificial intelligence and lemon drizzle cake, are you?"

They walked off briskly but Elizabeth was very satisfied with the slight reddening of the ears and a tiny drop of perspiration on the forehead. He was good at hiding it but Julian was decidedly a man with secrets … and she had a strong instinct that Victoria had no idea.

The old barge was slow, especially loaded up with passengers and towing a heavy butty boat, but it was a good opportunity to swap boy and girl stories which they had respectively endured during their separation, although care on all sides was taken not to overdo every detail, especially noticeable with Ned and Nancy who undoubtedly would have some private reconciliation to undergo as and when appropriate. Fortunately, that difficulty was realised straight away by Zac and Ade as much as by Belle and Dottie, staying focused on their own experiences. Two hours went by quickly and they found themselves slowly drawing up alongside the towpath in front of Burscough Bridge and the docking area near the old warehouses, busy working environments where all kinds of goods were being hauled up inside on cranes. Alighting, Ned and Zac manoeuvred their horses onto land and with Belle, they led the three up the bank onto the main road in order to ride onwards past the church for Orsbrick Hall, a few miles west. Nancy was the first one on her horse, followed by Dottie.

Nancy called down playfully to Ned. "I can see by your face you don't like the idea of riding horse pillion with a woman, just as you don't on your damned scooter but on this occasion, darling, I take the reins 'cos he's my horse. Okay?"

Ned grunted and grumbled but Zac was already behind Dottie and holding her tight, so Ned reluctantly jumped on. It had been transparently obvious that Belle and Ade were not in the business of renewing their relationship whether it was 1865 or not, but Ade's reluctance seemed to be concealing some other problem.

"Come on Ade, jump on behind Belle, we're all waiting for you," Ned shouted down impatiently.

Ade's face had turned even redder. "Actually, I know it's not a good time, but to be really honest I don't like horses much," he said, anxiety gripping him badly.

Ned laughed. "A big feller like you, you must be joking. Ade, are you telling us you've never been on a horse?"

Ade winced. "The donkeys on Southport Beach were enough for me. I did go on a camel once in Egypt on holiday after ten pints of lager."

"Sorry Ade, we're not heading for the Orsbrick oasis, so get on the bloody horse will you for fuck's sake," Ned answered, increasingly not amused.

Zac dismounted and took charge. They could do without another awkward Ned and Ade stand-off at that very moment. Belle also immediately dismounted and between them, they pulled Ade's foot the right way in the stirrup and he heaved himself up nervously, Zac holding him firmly. Given his size, it was just as well that Belle had the biggest horse, which was very calm considering, clearly a mare used to novices. Belle finally hoisted herself back up carefully and took the reins in front.

"Hold onto me tight will you Ade, around my waist, I don't want you falling off. But don't get any other ideas, understood?" she hissed, and everyone laughed. From Ade's petrified expression, ideas were the last thing on his mind.

"Just get me there in one piece, babe," he replied, his voice croaky again as he shut his eyes.

They set off at a brisk gallop, Belle in the lead, and decided to go the quieter back lane, past the numerous farms and come in over the steep humpback bridge alongside the boatmen's cottages, which Belle assumed would be there as they always seemed to have remained a permanent feature through many decades before.

Drawing to a slow trot, Belle finally led the entourage towards the Orsbrick Hall entrance. The huge old oak wooden gates, prominently dominating in 1841, still stood proudly. It remained a mystery when they disappeared. The horses clip-clopped steadily over the cobbled drive towards the front entrance. For Belle, everywhere appeared much as it was twenty-five years previously under Morag's well-kept stewardship except for one building conspicuously behind the house in front of the canal. The imposing factory with large smoking chimneys, where James McKenzie would be busy distilling tar for the dye experiments and manufacture, stood prominently.

Belle remembered that Mauveine's original makeshift laboratory had been constructed in the basement where Victoria still experimented. The cellar entrance, which should lead initially to the scullery, could be seen towards the far end of the house, almost exactly as it still was. Belle felt unsure how she would react if Mauveine came to the door or for that matter when she inevitably will meet her … the logic of the time sequencing would be a sixteen-year-old Mauveine, not a ghost nor the mature Mauveine they interacted with in 1841. And Mauveine would have no idea who she was or why she was there. Similarly, regarding James McKenzie, Mauveine's father and the present Orsbrick landowner, who in 1841 was the twelve-year old menace of a boy and only son of Morag they had to cure of typhoid. She decided that the best starting point would be to claim herself as Mauveine's distant cousin, a Miss Annabelle McKenzie, living in West Derby. The family likeness at least would be evident although how recognisable Ned and Zac fared alongside the male McKenzie ancestry was debatable

... in fact they were unlike anybody except each other. If anything, discernible attributes like noses and ears were assigned from their father, who in turn resembled Isi most closely. She then remembered. Isi was at that time head stableman and gardener and the much older, secret boyfriend of Mauveine. When or if Isi turned up she would need to be especially careful and discrete. Already, what seemed like a sensible idea coming home to Orsbrick, was peppered with all manner of complicated threads. She desperately wished Maddie was alongside. The two always complimented each other's strengths when facing daunting problems and challenges. Although to be fair, Dottie, and especially Nancy, had been unexpectedly brilliant along the difficult time-travelled road so far. Another unwelcome recollection went through her head. Nancy had already met James McKenzie in rather fraught circumstances at the Black Anchor. If that encounter resurfaced in front of Ned, heaven knows what unpredictable consequences would erupt. She stopped halfway on the drive and turned her horse to the others.

"I just want to confirm … this isn't going to be so easy, and I want to change what we said earlier. I'll do all the talking initially at the door as Mauveine's distant family cousin, I'll use my full name, and explain that I'm privately studying science and keen to meet Mauveine who I've heard all about. Ned and Zac, you're my younger brothers so you go by your true names too. Ade, you're Ned's best friend and Nancy and Dottie are your two sisters. Sorry Nance, but if you meet James McKenzie you must deny you ever knew him and plead mistaken identity if he thinks otherwise."

"Why should Nancy need to do that?" Ned asked, puzzled.

"Because James McKenzie came into the Black Anchor and made a pass at me and I told him to piss off. He's acquainted with the landlord, Henry, that's why, got it?" she barked. This was not the time for Ned to act short-tempered, jealous and reckless.

"Yeah, sure Nance, honestly," Ned replied, remarkably unmoved. "Good for you. Anyway, you're dressed differently now and you've tied your hair back so it should all be cool."

"As long as you are," she murmured and smiled at Belle, knowing completely what Belle was fretting about.

Once Dottie alighted, Zac suddenly pulled his horse around to face the other two. "Tell you what. This place is eerily quiet, don't you think? Not a soul anywhere, yet normally you'd expect to see gardeners or stable hands and definitely servants. The house and grounds are amazingly tidy and well maintained. It's weird seeing Orsbrick Hall as it was but that's not the point. Where are they all?"

Nancy pointed to a set of posts near the barn. "Let's tie up there and just walk to the door and knock. Someone will be in. The family could all be at the back. Maybe there's a garden party or something going on, it is a nice day and a Sunday."

"Or at church," Dottie added. "I agree with Nance and it's definitely time for trembling Ade behind you Belle to get off his nemesis."

They laughed whilst a somewhat paler Ade, still saying nothing, nodded vigorously.

Ned pulled the long cord at the door and a deep resounding noise inside rang out, even louder than the contraption his father had rigged up. This was a real servant's bell. But when the door slowly opened all they could do was stare silently with amazement and shock. Standing in front of them was a tall, beautiful woman her hair in a bun and wearing a long yellow flowery dress. A leering smile crept across her face … whilst holding a heavy machete dripping with blood. Fenella had arrived.

"Well now, this is excellent, just in time. Welcome, everyone to my humble abode, or what will be my humble abode very shortly. Ned, how wonderful to see you. Please don't run off like that again, it really won't be beneficial for your future health. Oh, and before you all think of making a quick escape, I'm afraid that has now become a little tricky."

A sound of movement and rustling could be heard and they turned to see lots of men, very definitely sailors and not servants, approach from every direction, out of the woods, from around the rear and side, even out of the chapel, some holding guns, others swords and knives. Walking slowly, they finally stopped in a semi-circle fifteen feet away around the porch. Zac had been correct. They should have trusted his instinct and bolted immediately. They had led themselves into a trap. Fenella had got there before them but where were Mauveine and her father, James McKenzie? Or indeed, Isi and the rest of the Orsbrick Hall staff, servants, maids, everyone? And even scarier, who had been at the receiving end of that machete? Any thought of running or fighting was hopeless; they were outnumbered ten to one. Ned recognised some of the men, part of the original Warrior Queen crew, but the majority he had never seen before.

"Ned, as always I can read your simple mind. I've been recruiting heavily again whilst we were docked in Southport looking for you. Poor old Dr Grey, he let the cat out of the bag, I'm afraid, after some gentle persuasion although I must say he only confirmed my suspicion. Although any dreams he had of painting again will be much more difficult minus both hands but I did bandage the stumps up well and sent him straight to the hospital. Hooks will have to do from now on, sadly."

"Lynton? You did that to him?" Ned murmured uneasily, staring at the machete, sweat running off his body at the thought of what might be next for him.

Belle grappled in her brain to pull her wits together. This situation looked as bad if not worse than the Orsbrick Priory confrontation last year, quite likely much worse as they had no idea what was going on and Abby and Maddie weren't here. Dottie began shivering with fear and sobbed, a deluge of tears running down her face whilst Ade grimly held his sister tight. Nancy, silent and churlish, felt huge anger her face bright red. She was weighing up whether she could wrest that machete off the bitch if she was quick and hit her with it, but what good would that do in the end? Zac wished he'd kept the pistol he'd stolen on the Warrior Queen but was thinking hard. He whipped something from his bag … his old iPhone. Nancy watched him and did the same … both would try to send a message and double up the chance. They tapped furiously. Nancy sent her text to her boss, to find Victoria with the words 'trapped at Orsbrick'. Zac, however, sent another message on his space-time black hole app again, direct to Maddie. Something deep in his guts was telling him it might be their only chance.

Fenella laughed uncontrollably. "Sorry guys but hasn't someone told you this is anno domini 1865? No internet yet, but nice try and full marks for initiative. Unfortunately, you are all well and truly on your own. How those mobile phones arrived though is an interesting phenomenon, but moving on as they say. Next, on the agenda, we will be …"

Belle suddenly intervened. "Listen, Fenella. We don't know what you're up to and why we're here but at the end of the day you are family and everyone here has always been your friend and never failed to be helpful and supportive."

Fenella stared hard at Belle momentarily. For a fleeting moment, Fenella displayed the look and expression they knew back in their own time, kind, inquisitive, friendly. But she instantly returned to her true self. "I'm afraid this world we are in doesn't work like that Annabelle, so enough distractions. I'm being very rude. Do come into your own house."

They followed Fenella quietly inside. There was nobody anywhere but then they turned the corner of the hallway towards the drawing room, to be met by the grisly sight of two hooked spikes driven into the wooden beams in the ceiling. A human head, dripping with fresh blood, was hanging from each one. Dottie looked up and immediately threw up in the corner, Zac and Belle holding her gently. Nancy was unmoved. She had a stomach of iron and had seen enough grisly animal sights in her time but Ned and Ade were visibly shaken by what they saw.

"Why both of them thought they would get very far, I simply don't understand," Fenella said, drolly. "I knew immediately they had to be the traitors behind this plot and I was so disappointed. Henri, I could expect. He was always untrustworthy but not my dearest René, poor René. All those years of loyal service. It was hard to dispatch him this way, but he understood the risks. Some you win and some you lose. Ahh … here's Mr Rimmer, the head butler; he'll take your coats. I'm sure you'd all like a drink. Usual Ned? Malt whisky I assume? I do miss our riveting nights in my cabin. Oops, sorry Nancy, I almost forgot. I'm afraid little old Ned does have rather a roving eye, isn't that so Ned? We have so much to catch up on. Harold, please do the honours for our guests."

Nancy glanced warily, unimpressed at Ned then glared back at Fenella. Explanations would be prised out of him later, if there was going to be a later.

Belle, however, was staring at Rimmer the butler, who appeared anything but normal looking for such a position. He was dishevelled, his hair unruly and his yellow and black teeth an alarming sight when he smiled. He shuffled closer and leered horribly. "And what would you like Annabelle? You are certainly a true McKenzie female, that's for sure."

He started to cough, hoarse and deeply rasping, his body riddled with some bad malady like tuberculosis. Then Belle suddenly remembered: Abbott Rimmer and the prism of purpurine. Unlike Maddie, she only ever had a patchy recall of that experience being less psychic, but seeing this disgusting individual brought memories back to the Orsbrick Priory and that terrifying ghostly scene set in the 1660s she had witnessed. Her mind ran at lightning speed through the rest of the known events involving her mother, Abby, and Maddie including the library letters she and Maddie had later found, researched and catalogued with reference to some horrible incident Abby, in confidence, had recently told them about, although Abby remained sparse with the detail as it was so traumatic. A strange psychic incident happened at Orsbrick Hall many years back before they were born, when her parents were dating, relating to Mauveine and Isi and their former evil butler in the 1860s whose name was also Harold Rimmer. And, just as with Morag, the relevant McKenzie history had changed, with Abby's intervention, to remove Harold Rimmer from the face of the earth but here he was back again. All of this enactment, horrible Fenella, the whole situation around them felt decidedly evil and creepy … was it all connected with what happened before? Was this the explanation all along for Fenella's appearance and actions? Rimmer, murmuring incoherently, shuffled off towards the direction of the kitchen.

They walked on silently into the drawing room and sat down. Belle began to speak again. "What do you mean, Fenella, your abode? Where are Mauveine and James, her father? And for that matter, the rest of the servants?"

Fenella grimaced impatiently. "Always exactly like your sister, Annabelle, constantly asking questions and never content with things as they are. Well, as it happens, James McKenzie is away all day at the Liverpool races, driven there by head groom Isaac Fazackerley and accompanied by Mauveine and sister Lydia. A rare family get-together, I do declare. However, the rest of the staff, I'm afraid, have been temporarily detained down in the basement. As you can see, Mr Rimmer is always partial to serving the master or mistress who pays him the most, and his new mistress will be very generous and reward his shifted loyalty. Unfortunately, Mauveine, Lydia and her father won't be returning later. An unfortunate accident in their carriage has occurred on the way back." Fenella stared at the grandfather clock ticking slowly in the corner. "Mmm ... about now, actually, so we may as well move on. As next of kin, I now take over. I have the legal documents, of course, all above board thanks to you Ned, an excellent piece of diving. I shall enjoy my rightful inheritance at long last."

Nancy stared at Fenella with disdain. "And what about us? Where do we fit into your grand plan?"

The corners of Fenella's mouth moved into a sneering grin. The carefully worked out finale for Nancy was coming to a head. Harold Rimmer, accompanied by ten armed accomplices, had returned with a large whisky and a glass of red wine plus five small tumblers of what looked like water.

Fenella continued. "My benevolent and generous nature has come unexpectedly to the fore, Nancy. You have your friend Annabelle to thank for that with what she proffered before.

Very true, Annabelle is right; yes, we are all family and friends. So rather than undertaking my first option of you being bound and tied and thrown straight into the cess pit, I've decided to give you all a second chance and have changed my plans. You're going on yet another adventure Nancy, with Annabelle, Zac, Ade and Dottie, one to take you far away for good and to make a fresh start. Very shortly you'll all be on your way to America … New York in fact, as my guests on the Warrior Queen. Doesn't that sound like fun … and I know you're a fun-loving girl."

Nancy squared up, still defiant. Dottie was staring wide-eyed and Belle became totally confused. Zac remained silent at first but then spoke out. "So, what about Ned? What's happening to my brother?"

Ned had already worked out what his fate would be. Fenella had decided that before they escaped but he had kept silent to Zac and Ade and certainly to Nancy. Once more he was at a crossroads and had to make choices and create the best of it. The thought of being on the receiving end of that machete was not one he savoured; he was first and foremost a survivor. He got up and sidled over to stand next to Nancy, exactly as Fenella hoped, and addressed the others.

"I'm afraid Fenella's original plan will be taking effect," he said stiffly, his voice wavering. "Are we doing it tomorrow, darling?"

Nancy stood up smartly, her eyes wild and her body stiff. "What the fuck are you talking about, Ned?"

Fenella clapped loudly, excited that Ned had smartly picked up the cue and gone with her expectation, unprompted even. Clever boy, he did have excellent promise just as she always knew he should. "Of course, all set my darling. Rearranged, but that wasn't a problem. I can see you are all mystified but it's very simple. Ned and I will be married in Southport at ten a.m. sharp then we'll see you off on the Warrior Queen, a farewell bon voyage. Ned and I will return to Orsbrick Hall to celebrate our honeymoon as the next Lord and Lady McKenzie, quietly at home with new servants in place and a feast prepared. We have a future dynasty to catch up on, don't we Ned, as we agreed in bed before you naughtily absconded."

"You bastard, Ned, I hope you rot in hell," Nancy shrieked and spat on the floor. Ade grabbed her before she could strike him hard across the face. The guards moved closer. Belle stood open-mouthed, she couldn't believe her ears. What had Ned been doing? No wonder he was unusually reticent on the packet boat from Tarleton. Zac remained motionless. He felt his phone vibrate in his pocket. Dottie gripped his arm tightly whilst Ade silently weighed up how many of the fuckers he could take out if he grabbed that machete still lying on the far table.

Fenella took her large glass of red wine and Ned's whisky from the tray. "Sorry but no toasts I'm afraid. I want you all now to drink these potions, merely a mild and harmless plant sedative to knock you out fully for twenty-four hours, by which time you'll be safely onboard my ship and on your way. Believe me, it's easier this way. We don't want any fighting, Ade, I know your inclinations and in the end, they have their orders … you don't really want to be cut to shreds, do you?"

Rimmer, wiping severe perspiration from his brow, handed Belle, Nancy, Dottie, Zac and Ade their glasses in turn. "Down the hatch, all of you," he croaked before coughing up more phlegm.

"Wait," Belle suddenly cried. "What's that sound?"

Midway down the wide hallway, the ballroom door was shut tight but loud squeals of laughter and shrieking could be heard from behind. Lynton's only daughter, Judy, and her tribe of seven young children had apparently been joined by a multitude of others from the estate whose parents Claire knew, and all were continuing to have a great party. Walking through into the drawing room, Victoria was immediately met by Claire with Erica stood behind, dressed up in magician's fancy dress and carrying trays of jellies, cakes and fruit juice. A wooden box behind was full with paraphernalia including a top hat, cards and various glove puppets.

"This was Erika's idea," Claire said, passing. "We're going to help Judy out as the numbers of children have trebled, my fault I'm afraid for inviting them. I found all this gear earlier in a trunk in the library, once used by someone for entertaining children here, centuries ago I guess."

"I know a lot of magic tricks," Erica added, putting on the top hat. "In fact, I would estimate the origin of these objects by the style and dress to be around the 1860s or 1870s. They are definitely mid-nineteenth century. So, I shall entertain all the children for the remaining hour and then it should be time for bed. Judy's will be staying over, of course, I've got their rooms ready."

Victoria was warming to Erika despite an earlier cynicism although Julian always invited it. She had a much more normal family sense than Sabrina ever did. Glancing at Mauveine's profuse smile, Victoria sensed Erika's conclusion was correct. Mauveine was having a pleasant flashback to her own early childhood when her father, James, would amuse her and Lydia alongside his wife Susannah before she died, with Saturday night magic evenings, using skills and tricks he had picked up at Cambridge University of all places.

"Thank you, both. That's so thoughtful, Erika," Victoria said, directing everyone to sit down. "I'm sure Judy will be very pleased and relieved."

Lynton, seeing a large plateful of strawberry mousse cake, made a dash for the food and began to pour the tea. Julian was sat next to Elizabeth and couldn't find the right opportunity to relieve his baffled and perplexed thoughts. He reflected quietly. What on earth was Victoria doing and why were these people here? Of all days, when they were increasingly concerned about the whereabouts of Belle, Ned, Zac and their friends, why had Victoria brought these disconnected strangers home? She had shot off mysteriously with Abby and Maddie earlier in the afternoon without a word of where she was going or for what reason. At least, he genuinely had something urgent to repair in the afternoon and then Erika turned up and took his mind off the unexplainable lack of communication and Belle, Ned and Zac's disappearance from the Black Anchor. He wasn't convinced of any of the so-called reasons put forward by Lynton the eternal optimist, and as time marched on something felt increasingly wrong. Perhaps they ought to go to the police now. But he had promised Ade's brother they would allow a full twenty-four hours and the long night was only beginning. They needed to discuss their thoughts further as a family, privately, but instead, they were entertaining unexpected guests, pleasant though they all seemed. However, the curate seemed a strange individual. Something about Elizabeth was as far removed from a priestly calling as one could possibly imagine. She had a compelling magnetism which he rarely experienced with women, not in fact since he had first met Victoria, and the explanation eluded him. Also, Elizabeth had made some offhand comments which disturbed him, almost as if she knew. The last thing he needed right then was to go down that particular pathway, in fact, he never wanted to go there; too much water had long passed under the bridge …

Victoria could see Julian was not his usual outgoing and sociable self and realised he was both annoyed with her and wondering why strangers were sat in their drawing room. She had to think very quickly of a rationale, especially as neither she nor the others had any idea what might or might not happen with their appearance inside Orsbrick Hall. Lynton, always affable, chatted freely to Mo and Herbert whilst Julian warily forced more small talk with Elizabeth. Abby too was acting out of character, definitely not her normal self either, despite a small window of reverie during the drive over. She had reverted to an uncharacteristic and quiet withdrawal, likely fretting still about when and if she would tell the truth about her pregnancy to Lynton.

Whilst everyone chatted, Maddie had taken the opportunity to run immediately upstairs to see how Janine was faring, expecting her to have awoken from her deep sleep and perhaps be feeling better. Almost as quickly, they heard Maddie bound back down the stairs to re-enter the room flushed and perturbed. She called out to Victoria.

"Mum, Janine isn't there. There's no sign of her whatsoever and her bed's made up like she's suddenly improved, got dressed, and then vanished into thin air!"

Mauveine glanced up. She saw Maddie was overly worried and appeared increasingly on edge with everything happening. "Most likely your friend has gone outside for some fresh air and a walk if she's feeling better," Mauveine suggested, carefully.

Maddie cheered up, the simplest explanation and the most logical allayed immediate concern. Her mind was too choked up with psychic conspiracies and dire historical plots against the family again, but she felt absolutely nothing untoward in her head, unlike anything that had happened before. Making out the true logic of what was going on around them seemed impossible. "I'll just go out and find her, thanks, Mauv ... err Mo."

Maddie stopped in time and could have cheerfully kicked herself. She had to think clearly, exactly as her mother had spelt out earlier. Now was definitely not the time for revealing the impossible explanation to her father and Lynton. Both had accepted the principle of Fenella appearing through a time-warp, which Zac enumerated in clear steps that night at the George; at least her father seemed to have done in the end. Or was he simply humouring her, along with Mum and Abby, perceived as the principal architects of psychic nonsense? Certainly, her father had never mentioned anything since and just accepted the way Fenella had rapidly adjusted to twenty-first-century living.

Maddie wandered off down the corridor and out through the back door, taking the two wolfhounds slumbering quietly in the scullery with her. If she found Janine they could both walk the dogs through the woods quickly if she felt up to it. In any case, they needed letting out back to their kennels. Usually, Ned did that nightly.

Julian, however, was in severe mental turmoil and felt he had come to the end of the road. The only normal individuals in the house seemed to be Erika and Judy and that was saying something. Maddie's faux-pas hadn't passed him by either and merely confirmed what he had been musing over ever since they all walked inside. Not only was Elizabeth strange, although she had an excuse, she was a curate, but the more he watched Mo and Herbert, such odd names, who on earth was called

Herbert in the twenty-twenties, the more he suddenly began to twig. They certainly appeared genuine, listening to Mo rattling off more dye research work as she and Herbert chatted avidly to Victoria. Herbert was obviously as scientifically clever as his wife but much more reserved in temperament. But how could he have missed it before? Looking around the room, Lynton's observational skills were, as ever, conspicuous by their absence, with drink inside him or minus drink. He was chatting avidly to Elizabeth about religious Latin text and medieval scripts, an interest they both oddly seemed to share.

Ever since he had met and married Victoria, he had over all those years together tolerated her semi-obsession with family ghosts, psychic happenings and increasingly bizarre historical facts, fuelled constantly by Abby. He had to admit, on that first day in 2010 when they broke into Orsbrick Hall, he fleetingly saw the inexplicable sight of Mauveine and Isi riding their horses through the grounds although it had never been repeated. And he understood and was comfortable with how he was related to Isi through that past and old Fazackerley lineage, an amazing piece of historical research by Abby, Maddie and Belle. It was strange though that he and Ned seemed impervious to the family ghostly sightings, whilst Zac and Belle admitted to a few of their own personal encounters around the woods. However, now he realised he was looking at something he had absolutely no rational explanation for, thanks to Maddie's slip of the tongue. Despite the modern hairstyles, clothes and conversation, Mo was so much like an older version of Belle, with the same nose as Victoria, and Herbert had features alarmingly similar to him. More than anything, he realised that the picture hanging in the hallway of the young girl in a laboratory, whose mystery was solved back when they were renovating the place for the first time and he discovered the lab in the cellar, told the story. Staring hard again at Mo, there was no longer any doubt in his mind. He was looking at the girl in the picture, older certainly, and he was going to bring this peculiar situation to a head, once and for all.

"Excuse me Victoria, sorry to interrupt but there's something very important I'm going to have to ask," Julian shouted across the room. Conversations stopped and everyone turned. Abby, who had popped out the same time as Maddie had just returned, her face grey. She sat down quietly, unnoticed except by Victoria who saw immediately Abby was distressed. Before she had time to walk across, Julian's voice boomed out.

"Are you two really Mauveine and Isi? I want the truth please."

Lynton was the first to react. "Julian, what on earth are you talking about? Mauveine and Isi are ghosts. They've been dead for over a hundred and fifty years."

But Mauveine pre-empted any further discussion. "Yes, Julian, you're right. We are," she replied in her soft-spoken voice.

Lynton turned pale. Suddenly, he had flashbacks of horrible memories like he was recalling an old forgotten dream of seeing Mauveine and Isi walk through the back door and then lead him and Abby to the barn to mount up on horses. That was where he had seen Mo and Herbert. "Jesus fucking Christ, sorry Elizabeth. Come on Abby, I'm off. Things in here have become so bizarre I can't take it any longer."

Abby, clearly in pain, grabbed his arm hard. "No, Lynton, you're not going anywhere. Yes, they are Mauveine and Isi, so what? Remember our pact … love me and love my psychic?"

Lynton stopped and sighed, taking a deep breath. "Yes, okay, understood. But what's the matter darling, you don't look at all well?"

Victoria and Mauveine had both got up to walk over but Abby waved them to stop. "Listen Lynton, I want you to call the emergency ambulance, right now. I need to be taken to hospital immediately. Don't ask please, I'll explain when we get there, but yes, I'm in terrible pain," Abby said calmly, sweat pouring from her forehead. She gripped her stomach, her face had become very flushed.

Lynton was already dialling 999.

Julian was now up from his seat. "Abby, shall we lie you down on the couch and make you more comfortable?"

"No, no, thank you, Julian, I'll be fine. Just let me sit here quietly. I don't want to move until the ambulance arrives, I'll be alright, promise. Perhaps I could have a glass of water please and some paracetamol. I'm so sorry about all this."

Elizabeth poured one out and handed it to her whilst Julian found some strong analgesics in a sideboard drawer. Elizabeth knew that expression and acutely sensed the pain. She had suffered enough in the past and when it had become so bad she would writhe about for hours like a wounded animal until someone found more opiates. But at least Abby didn't have to endure the gross inadequacies and follies of nineteenth-century medical care.

Meanwhile, Maddie had looked twice around the house, but still no sign of Janine. After letting the dogs lollop over to their kennels and finally feeding them, she decided to look next around the woods? Why had Janine disappeared and where would she walk off to now? Not only was Maddie increasingly agitated about the whereabouts of her siblings, heightened by the possible activity of Fenella and whether they would ever see each other again, but now Janine was missing of all times. She took deep breaths and resolved to calm down and rationalise, sitting at the edge of the pond on the oak seat her father had made last year. Peering randomly at her phone which she hadn't looked at for hours, she noticed a notification alert against the space-time app she had been experimenting with, having received that peculiar short message from Zac, although how or why remained a complete mystery. She opened the message box and read it quickly.

'Reunited with Belle, Dottie and Nancy, arrived home and was met by Fenella, circumstance very bad, need help!'

Startled by the impact, Maddie felt a sickening lurch in her stomach. She was right. Staring at the timeline sent a couple of hours before, her mind ran over the implications before she was disturbed by a loud screeching of tyres on the gravel. A white ambulance with vivid blue lights flashing had suddenly arrived at the front door. In a matter of moments, two paramedics rushed inside. Maddie stared, totally bewildered, what on earth was going on? But before she had time to react any further, a firm hand pressed gently onto her shoulder. Mauveine was standing there.

Smiling warmly, Mauveine sat down beside her quickly. "I'm sorry I startled you, Madeleine," she said quietly, her expression as always caring but her mannerism resolute. "There isn't much time. I followed you out."

"Time for what?" Maddie replied. "What's happening inside the house? Why is there an ambulance? And look, I've just had this special message; somehow it's crossed the time divide." She showed Mauveine the notification from Zac.

"Excellent, it's what I had surmised was likely. I'm afraid Abby is not well; she's in a lot of pain. Listen to me Madeleine, Abby desperately needs you now. I know you are very close.

She requires you both as her friend and for psychic support. When the medical team bring her out I want you to go with her in the ambulance to the hospital, both of you need to be away from here."

Maddie looked up, perplexed. "I don't understand anything. Are you saying Abby and I might be in danger if we're around? What's happening Mauveine?"

But something else immediately caught her senses, realising that the sky was gradually becoming darker. She looked into the distance way over the fields towards Parbold hill and saw the sudden collapse in the weather. From a cloudless blue sky, deepening dark clouds lay ahead; the changing situation in the distance was dramatic. But this was no ordinary transformation; she knew the tell-tale signs intimately. The wind had picked up and the black clouds were scudding violently across the sky towards Orsbrick, tinged at the edges with a peculiar yellow. But she still felt no psychic pains inside her head. Abby was right, all of this terrible situation must be created around Mauveine.

Mauveine patted her hand. "Now you know. A confluence of events with enormous implications is about to happen. A singularity of a grave space-time conflict has been created by Fenella or whoever she really is, but I too have been active behind the scene to try and counteract it. The next stage will be between me and them only, which I suspect you've now already realised. Because of your hypersensitivity, you and Abby must leave this to me. It will be dangerous, I can't say otherwise but you have to trust me. I must try and resolve a festering historic dilemma, now once and for all."

The front door abruptly opened with a loud bang. Maddie and Mauveine stood up and watched as the paramedics ran out again carrying a stretcher with someone covered over by a blanket, only their red hair visible. This was followed by Lynton, very distressed. Victoria was standing anxiously by the door. Maddie's heart sank again. Fuck, that was definitely Abby but what had happened to her? Lynton didn't follow the stretcher but instead jumped into his Mercedes, clearly going to follow on and likely fetch things for Abby once she was inside the hospital and being looked after.

"Now, Madeleine, run and jump in the back of the ambulance before they drive off, go, go go," Mauveine cried, watching Maddie sprint hurriedly towards the rear doors, the paramedics deftly placing Abby inside. Victoria, about to close the front door and go inside, saw Maddie racing over and began to walk out but Mauveine also marched across and waved, to distract Victoria and meet her before she could reach Maddie.

With an athletic jump, Maddie was inside and the doors slammed shut when the ambulance raced away, lights blazing and sirens wailing at full decibels. Lynton, wheels squealing, followed behind in hot pursuit. Victoria stared disconsolately at the disappearing vehicles as Mauveine reached her.

"My God that all happened in a flash but I'm glad Maddie is with her. If Abby needs anyone now that's who it should be. I think she's losing the baby, what a terrible, terrible tragedy," Victoria murmured, her eyes filled with tears

But Mauveine stopped her mid-flow. "That may or may not be true, Victoria, but it is important now neither of them is here. Look, over there in the distance."

Victoria's heart sank seeing those familiar coalescing clouds gathering pace. Her fast mind immediately understood the implications. "No, surely not now? But Belle, Ned and Zac? What will happen to them and to us? I can't believe this is happening all over again."

Before Mauveine could explain, Victoria gave out an involuntary cry. Her emotions were finally overwhelming her, and she ran wildly around to the back door. Someone had stupidly closed the front door on them. Flinging the scullery door open, she rushed inside and down the winding corridors towards the drawing room where numerous chattering voices could be heard. Mauveine followed. She understood Victoria's reaction but it didn't matter anyway and the family inside needed to know the truth. Events now had to take their course, whatever that may be.

Panting with exertion and her face contorted with fear, Victoria was met by a startled look, first by Isi followed by Julian who jumped out of his chair. "Jesus Christ, Victoria, what the hell is the matter? What's happened outside? Is Abby on her way to hospital, is she okay?"

Mauveine had by now walked in and joined Isi, quietly.

Everyone had become stone dead quiet. Mauveine's eye's narrowed. She instinctively realised that Julian, naming her and Isi for real, had triggered a time clash response amongst the McKenzie multiverses with unallowable knowledge. But what would be the final consequences?

"We have to do something, the thing's all happening again," Victoria screamed. "Something catastrophic and explosive is coming for us all, right now," she hollered, her voice cracked and contorted with emotion.

Julian, his patience and understanding finally exhausted, thrust himself aggressively at Victoria and grabbed her arm tightly, shouting even louder into her face. "Victoria, what the fuck is going on in this house? Has the whole place become completely and totally crazy? What are you going on about, something happening again? I don't for the life of me understand anything."

She stared silently back up at him towering over her, fearful of his uncharacteristic behaviour, his full six-foot-five bulky frame quivering with aggression. Never once had he ever been violent with her. Julian was cracking up with the strain. He knew so little and she knew too much. This was probably what Fenella had planned all along. Divide the McKenzie's, cause chaos and rule.

He felt a sharp tug on his arm, turning immediately to see Elizabeth confronting him face to face, but calm and rational. "Julian, I'd politely suggest letting go of Victoria and listen to me. You're frightening her."

He turned back to Victoria and released his grip, mouthing 'sorry so sorry' tears running down his cheek and desperately upset with his own irrationality. She rubbed her arm still saying nothing as Elizabeth directed him to sit down over in the other corner. Joining him, she began a whispered conversation which nobody could hear whilst a strange throbbing sound pervaded the whole room.

Victoria rushed to the window with Mauveine and Isi, all staring at the ominous black clouds that rushed along towards the house, faster and faster, driven by a whining gale. A deep yellow light had configured behind the woods, casting an eerie glow through the tree branches.

"Mauveine, what do we do?" Victoria muttered weakly, shaking still with the tension and watching the outside world change dramatically. "I don't understand. Neither Abby nor Maddie felt any warnings, like none of us, are involved."

Mauveine placed her arm around Victoria and hugged her tightly. "You're not involved. Belle, Ned, Zac and their friends have sadly been pawns, bargaining hostages in a long thought out and devious celestial game. Because I think now I finally understand the motivation. No, Victoria, this whole mess is solely concerning me and Fenella."

But Victoria was distracted, warily eyeing Elizabeth still in deep conversation with Julian. Elizabeth had grabbed hold of the decanter on the sideboard and poured herself and Julian a good half-balloon sized glass of best Scottish malt each before continuing a long and intense diatribe which any curate would have been proud of. Whatever Elizabeth was saying, she undoubtedly had Julian's full attention, appearing suitably mollified for that moment.

Victoria turned back to Mauveine. "Are my eyes deceiving me or is this room becoming hazier?" Victoria suddenly cried, watching the bold striped Regency wallpaper on the opposite wall attenuate into fuzzy strips of green, waving and flowing strangely like a fluid jelly.

Mauveine gripped her arm and Isi gathered the three into a tight circle. "Hold on tight," Mauveine shouted, ignoring Elizabeth and Julian. The time had come and it was simply too late. The room erupted into a great roaring whine and filled up with a dazzling light that immediately dimmed after a few seconds. Everything was swirling about dizzily, the rooms rotating in a blur of motion. Victoria, gripping Isi's hand tightly, peered through the haze and began to make out shapes and she could hear fresh sounds. More people were now in the room and voices were shouting and screaming, voices that were very familiar. Ned, bellowing out loudly and Belle screaming for the noise to stop, both materialised in front of her as renewed clarity and form condensed before all their eyes.

"Oh, my God Almighty," was all Victoria could utter, terrified and totally disorientated by the new sights around them. They were inside a weird, shimmering netherworld, partly thrown back into the nineteenth century and partly remaining in 2026. Victoria felt an arm pressed around her and realised Belle was now alongside, holding her hard, tears streaming down her face. Alongside, were Dottie and the bizarre spectacle of Nancy, all wild curly red hair and vibrant blue and orange dress, a long dress, similar to what Belle was wearing. They were still in their 1865 clothes, as were Ned and Zac, stood together with Ade and grinning madly. They were back but something had gone drastically wrong. They hadn't reformed as normal in the twenty-first century. But as Victoria ran forward holding Belle close, Ned and Zac, striding out of the fog, had pulled their father up out of his chair to give him an emotional hug each. Elizabeth, now smiling, had rejoined Mauveine who watched with intense interest but her face remained stern and unyielding. This wasn't all over yet, she knew that. Their return was only the start.

Once the haze and smoke cleared and the dizzying rotation stopped it was evident that they were still stood in their drawing room but in some strange hybrid world. Half the furniture was exactly of the moment but the environment had imploded, mixed alongside with artefacts which had once filled their drawing room in 1865. Even stranger were the walls, ghastly semi-transparent. There was a hush as everyone in their own way was trying to establish their time and place bearings, realising that they were caught in some strange McKenzie multiverse, neither a fish nor a fowl, or to be precise, Victoria immediately shouting in her loudest voice. "We're no longer in either 1865 or 2026, so where in heaven's name are we?"

Julian was desperately trying to adjust to where he was and what he had experienced but it was nigh on impossible. Only minutes before, Elizabeth had told him of the madness of travelling through time and that she herself was not of this world either. This situation was a million times crazier than any of his novels. Whilst Belle, Nancy and Dottie embraced hard, all gathered in one corner, Julian, with Ned and Zac behind, strode over to Victoria, Mauveine and Isi.

"Where on earth are we?" he muttered plaintively, scratching his head, his glasses furiously rubbed meticulously on the curtain and reinstated. Shaking his head, he gazed through the semi-transparent walls into the kitchen and scullery through one side and at the staircase from the other.

"Mauveine is right," Isi replied. "There is more to come. We're in the grip of something I desperately fear is totally unique, maybe as evil and unreal as one's imagination can ever create. … Oh Lord above, look."

The room instantly went silent as what appeared to be a crumpled up bunch of rags in the corner began to move and unfold, suggesting a butterfly emerging from its chrysalis, except this, was no butterfly. Fenella was being reborn. Smiling, she emerged rubbing her hands with glee, an evil Fanny Kirkby smirk which finally gave way to a loud announcement. Everyone watched horrified as she stood upright, dressed in her slick captain's uniform and holding that damned bloody machete once more.

Julian stared in disbelief. "Fenella? What the fuck?"

"Well, well, it looks like I won," Fanny screamed, her face contorted with the sight of her apparent nemesis who stood alone, calmly at the back, watching intently but saying nothing. "A very good attempt to create a disruption of our time," Fanny continued. "But with unforeseen consequences, Mauveine dearest. Because inadvertently, you've now entered my world that sits between heaven and hell and in which I have full and total control. Sadly, for you, the unintended consequences of your attempt to destroy me have assisted my planned programme of elimination. Now I can destroy the McKenzies together, in one combined space-time zone, each and all of you. But I promise we'll make it quick, I'm not a monster, despite everything they say."

She clapped her hands and a dozen armed sailors walked through the permeable walls, menacingly holding swords and knives. "All, of course, except one of you," Fanny continued. "And you know darling Ned, who that has to be. Once again your escape has been thwarted. I do wish you'd learn to behave. But I promise, you'll come to love this new abode of ours when everyone else in the room has shortly been eliminated, past and future and more perfectly than even I imagined. Thank you, Mauveine, and that miserable wretch of a husband beside you. Finally, you and I get even and I acquire what I have always deserved, the Orsbrick estate in perpetuity."

Harold Rimmer, prominent at the rear of the sailors in his incongruous butler dress, laughed hoarsely, his disfigured body convulsing with the effort and coughed up a great ball of yellow phlegm which he spat over the floor.

Nancy was whispering quietly to Belle. "Who on earth is that despicable individual?"

"Someone called Harold Rimmer, the former McKenzie butler," Belle whispered back. "If only Abby and Maddie were here, he could have been destroyed again. Where are they?"

Mauveine, with Victoria alongside, was stood behind them and caught the aside. "Rimmer was destroyed and every single atom eliminated, which leads me to believe all we see is not what it seems. Rimmer is an illusion, not real but a conjured-up manifestation, like a physical hologram."

Victoria had immediately noticed something else. Elizabeth was missing. What had happened to her? Was she absent because she never was part of the McKenzie history, sent back to her own time in this new convulsion of warped space-time?

But then she realised Ade too was gone, until everyone turned to see him reappear through the walls, pulling, using all of his great strength a heavy chest of Julian's outdoor tools. Ned and Zak ran and helped and in less than a blink of an eye, pickaxes, a large lump hammer, a heavy wrecking bar and a chainsaw were in the hands of each of them including Julian and Isi. The men grouped together in their own circle around the women to match Fanny and her band of maritime protectors.

Ned shouted out to Fanny, caught off guard for a moment not expecting this scenario. "I'm not coming and what's more we're going down fighting, all of us, this is the McKenzie way. Remember what happened in 1665? We may be outnumbered but we're bigger and stronger than all of your men. That sort of evens the odds up don't you think?"

Belle stared at her brother. How did Ned know or even remember the grisly scenes at the Orsbrick Priory, where he was nearly hung, drawn and quartered by Abbot Rimmer? He never had any idea or memory before? But of course, Belle realised. The letters and the history in the library, Ned must have read them all avidly, quietly on his own as Ned did.

Fanny scowled. "You disappoint me again Ned. Don't make me do this … and eliminate you too. I have more men outside. You will all die but you know how I feel. You and I have a future together that will go on forever."

An eerie silence fell across the entire room. Everyone looked at Ned and waited.

"No Fanny Kirkby, you don't have any future, because you underestimated every eventuality. I'm here, the real Fenella and I'm not incarcerated forever in time where you thought, back in Boston. I always knew this day would come. I have planned too."

A piercing and disembodied female voice had filled the room with a strange echo.

They turned to see Elizabeth walking down the stairs and then through the door, holding the arm of a striking and tall, dark-haired woman. She wore a flowing, long white dress and black boots, her dark hair falling down her back to her waist.

Victoria gasped, she couldn't believe what she was seeing. "Janine?"

But before she could rush over, Mauveine grabbed her arm strongly, aided by Belle. "No, whatever you do, don't," Mauveine cried, firmly.

"This is why Abby isn't here," Victoria replied, quietly and calmly to Belle and Mauveine. At long last, she finally realised and understood why this time calamity had engineered Abby and Maddie out of the situation. "Abby knew all along with her faultless sixth sense that Janine was not all she made out to be and I stupidly thought the whole concept was too far-fetched. Janine is the real Fenella McKenzie, illegitimate daughter of twelve-year-old James McKenzie and the newly born baby who was spirited away with a Puritan family on a steamer to America by Morag. Remember all of the fuss and trauma at the time? Janine is the long-lost sister, Mauveine, you've been searching for physically and spiritually all this time."

Visibly alarmed, Fanny Kirkby gasped making a peculiar gurgling sound and began to back away behind her guards who remained rigid, waiting for Ned, Zac and the others to attack. But everyone patiently stood their ground. Whatever was going on had taken a course and direction totally unexpected.

A radiant Janine turned to Mauveine and smiled. "Dearest sister, it's been such a very long time and I did escape from the sinking Mountain Moon as I'm sure you suspected, as this evil manifestation before us also tried to discover. Victoria, I'm so

371

very sorry for the cruel deception but it was the only way. I promise that Maddie will always be my friend and remain in my heart, believe me. But above all else, I had to find my sister, just as she had to find me."

Belle said nothing. She was stunned but Victoria could see immediately that she had taken in and understood what had happened and that Maddie would be seriously upset, her dreams and hopes for the future with her special friend vanishing into the netherworld of the contorted McKenzie past. Whatever the implications of this unbelievable appearance of the real Fenella, the effect was palpable on evil Fanny.

Mauveine held her arms out to Janine and they embraced warmly, watched quietly by everyone after one hundred and seventy years apart. A peculiar rasping wail finally broke the silence in the room. Fanny had become extremely agitated, muttering obscenities to herself. Everyone turned to watch the strange sight of Harold Rimmer, rigid and immobile, become increasingly transparent, his bones visible through his clothing like a peculiar x-ray image and then he was gone, vanished into thin air, a hologram whose light had gone out.

Mauveine looked up towards Fanny. "Time I think now to reveal yourself, demon. We know you're not Fenella my sister because she's here. You can't impersonate her. And Fenella Kirkby, Morag's daughter you were claiming to be, truly died at birth because Isi and I witnessed her death and burial. Your entire make-believe was a profound lie. So who are you? As my sister said, you are truly an evil manifestation."

"But I know the answer to that question," a loud voice from outside sounded out.

Mauveine and the rest turned to see another woman walk briskly and confidently out through the wall of the ballroom and in through the drawing room door. She was not dressed in

1865 clothing and looked her usual familiar self. Judy, of all people, had appeared from nowhere. In the dramatic unfolding, Victoria had forgotten the other people in the house including Lynton's daughter.

"You obviously had no idea I too was here did you, Fanny?" Judy continued. "But the time has arisen for you to finally be unmasked. You are Rosemary McKenzie, the long-lost depraved half-sister of Lord Robert McKenzie, secretly banished by ship to America in 1678. Witchcraft was your speciality too wasn't it, Rosemary, exactly like your mother, Zelda. But they never did find you after escaping from the trial courtroom in Salem, condemned to be burned at the stake. And exactly like Zelda, your end is approaching because a unique confluence of the McKenzie past, the present and the future has unexpectedly occurred together in this room at Orsbrick Hall. This enunciation, to follow, is for all the centuries of severe pain and distress you have caused by taking on various spectral forms and manifestations of the McKenzie family to do harm and evil. Unforgivably, your last and final attempt to become the spirit and adult form of that poor baby, Fenella Kirkby, who tragically died at birth and knew no life whatsoever, can bear no mercy or redemption. Especially, I deliver to you this denouncement for my poor father, Dr Lynton Grey, who today died of his excruciating wounds which you personally and violently delivered to a helpless old man. Isi, please undertake and complete the highest celestial sentence on behalf of the three Fenellas: Fenella McKenzie, Fenella Kirkby and Fenella Grey."

Fanny screamed out a high-pitched cry, her face wildly distorted and her body wrenching itself into unnatural contortions, whilst her voice cracked into a hoarse and deep gurgling sound. "You will all die first," she yelled, "everyone in this room, a horrible lingering and painful extinction especially you, Ned, for your betrayal. Hundreds of my men are coming from outside, the gibbets and fires are already prepared." Pointing at her remaining guards in the room, she screamed a deep bellowing and guttural moan. "Disarm and kill them all,"

Mauveine calmly stepped forward. "That is not going to happen, evil spirit. Look at your guards. They too, like Harold Rimmer, have become immobile holograms, bodiless apparitions, which in a few minutes will dissolve into their constituent photons and fly away into the ether." Mauveine grabbed hold of Ned's scythe and swiped effortlessly through the form of the nearest motionless sailor.

Fanny watched incredulously as did everyone. Elizabeth couldn't contain her glee and clapped mischievously, each guard turning gradually transparent in turn. Simultaneously, the walls began to solidify back to normal. The sky through the windows had darkened dramatically again, sending a huge roaring wind to batter against the rattling panes. Fanny bellowed and roared pitifully in strange tongues, trying to conjure up the most formidable evil forces she knew to overcome the catastrophic clash of past, present and future that Mauveine had engineered. The room shook and then shimmered, blurrily rotating in a dizzy circle back and forth like a kaleidoscope, with changes randomly mirroring various captured historical instances between 1865 and 2026.

Mauveine waved her arms for everyone to gather into a close circle. A sharp and circular yellow sun-like object could be seen through the window, hovering in the distance. She called out to Isi. "The time is opportune, my dearest husband. You know what to do. Expunge this evil demon forever from our lives."

Isi grinned and stepped forward, chanting variants of complicated exorcism rituals, loudly in old Latin one after the other, his sonorous booming baritone voice resounding everywhere, stabbing his finger at Fanny now alone and trapped inside the room unable to flee, all the walls solidified and the door locked shut. Her attempt at conjuring up countering forces was futile. Her body began to bloat up hideously and her fine facial beauty peeled away and dripped into bloody fat globules onto the floor, resembling the 1665 horror visual of Zelda which Abby and Maddie had called up in the Orsbrick Priory. Suddenly her long hair thickened and matted into a writhing mass of hissing snakes, exactly as Zelda, her mother had metamorphosed into.

The room shook violently again as Julian clung hard onto Victoria, Maddie and Belle, Ned and Zac doing likewise with Nancy, Dottie and Ade. Mauveine grabbed hold of Elizabeth as Isi stepped forward, shouting loudly with the final denunciation to exorcise the room, the house and the entire universe of the iniquitous demon, Rosemary McKenzie. A brilliant orange glow filled the room. Outside a giant burning ball was pressed against the window causing everyone to shield their eyes from the intense glare. Fanny Kirkby screamed a blood-curdling wail whilst the two Fenellas, silent, watching and waiting, rushed forward. Each took Fanny by the arm and hurled her across the room head-first through the window pane and into the orange ball. Immediately an immense, deafening explosion let rip across the entire room, the air filled up with a bright white light and a huge wind picked the circle of everyone up, like battered leaves in a roaring gale, hurling them one by one out into far-flung reaches of black space and a final oblivion ...

Chapter Fourteen

A rhythmic clattering of noisy wheels was sufficient to jolt an exhausted Maddie out of her quiet slumber, sprawled in the corner of a waiting room of the private maternity clinic at the rear of the general hospital. Watching a couple of nurses and a doctor push a large trolley full of equipment, she rubbed her eyes hard as they ran down the brightly lit corridor towards an emergency at the other end, where a noisy group of people were milling around. She had stupidly dozed off waiting for news about Abby's condition after they had wheeled her into the examination room. Staring at the clock, she was startled to see over four hours had passed since they arrived. It was late, she was hungry and desperate for a drink. Finding a lone one-pound coin in her pocket, she walked briskly to the machine near the main door and with a little rattling and persuasion managed to retrieve a small bottle of still water which she downed eagerly, reflecting on the traumatic journey from Orsbrick Hall. Abby, in desperate pain, had begun shouting and screaming in the ambulance that they had to hurry as she was losing the baby and in the end, became uncontrollable and hysterical, with Maddie desperately trying to calm her and then hold her down whilst various pieces of equipment and bags went flying. One of the paramedics panicked and finally managed to give Abby a sedative injection whilst Maddie held her tightly. Whether the dose was larger than it should have been or because Abby was so emotionally and mentally far gone, she quickly passed out into a quiet deep sleep so at least the rest of the journey proceeded safely. Alerted in advance, a team of medics were waiting and Abby was rushed into the clinic with Maddie stumbling along behind. Abby had forcibly demanded, before passing out, that the private Canal Clinic was where she must be taken.

Maddie pondered quickly, her mind running over with dread what may or may not have happened at Orsbrick Hall, but that would have to wait. Her priority was to locate Abby and check out whether she was alright. Where had Lynton ended up? Despite turning off half-way to take a short-cut down some back lane and arrive more quickly, he wasn't there when they arrived and only close relatives were allowed past a securitised door into the examining and ward area. When Maddie said she was Abby's younger sister, they looked hard, not wholly convinced, but allowed her through anyway. Abby was still out for the count, made comfortable in a bed inside a private room, but after a couple of specialists and two nurses arrived, Maddie was politely asked to take the lift down to the first floor and wait near reception. How on earth she had slept solidly for nearly four hours was beyond her and she couldn't remember what floor they had initially taken Abby to, everything blurring into a flying whirl.

For a hospital, all around her seemed extremely quiet, but then again it was a private wing which was likely why. Turning the next corner, she saw the reception desk. Nobody was there. She pressed a brass bell when an elderly but pleasant nurse-receptionist wearing a label saying Iris appeared immediately from the back and recognised Maddie straight away.

"Ahh ... you're the young lady who came in with your sister, Dr Abigail Warren. Madeleine, isn't it? She was asking for you earlier. Let me check on the ward whether you can now visit. She'll be glad you came back."

A lengthy phone discussion ensued but Nurse Iris returned smiling. "Yes, you can go up, take the lift to the third floor and look for the Boatman private ward; she has a room in there. Dr Warren is awake and eating dinner. I can arrange something for you too if you want? It's smoked salmon tonight with fruit salad."

Maddie grinned, food at long last. "Yes please, that would be great. But may I ask? When you said come back, I never actually left. I've been sat in the waiting area but fell asleep, unfortunately. Not sure how long exactly."

Nurse Iris laughed. "Sorry, we looked all around the waiting room, no sign of you anywhere and my colleague on the earlier shift definitely saw you going out the main door. Anyway, no problem, you're here now that's what counts. Your dinner will arrive in ten minutes."

Maddie frowned. That surely can't be true, how strange, but whatever. Avoiding the lift, she promptly raced up the stairs to the third floor, following the arrows and quickly arrived at the ward where a kindly matron took her straight to Abby's room.

As they walked towards the door, Maddie suddenly thought. "Is my sister's husband ... err ... Lynton with her?"

The senior nurse shook her head. "You obviously don't know."

Maddie stopped, alarmed. "Know what?"

"Unfortunately, it appears on his way he had a car accident, so Mr Grey is here but in the main hospital. They were short of beds so he's in the psychiatric ward. Don't worry, he was very lucky, some mild concussion and two broken ribs but we're keeping him in overnight under observation. I expect, assuming no complications, he'll be out in the morning."

"Does my sister know?"

"Yes, she's much better than when she came in and quite calm about her husband, happy to wait until the morning and he's awake. They gave him a sedative and painkillers."

"If you don't mind my asking, Matron?" Maddie continued in a whisper before opening the door. "Has Abby lost her baby?"

Matron was noncommittal. "I think your sister should explain it all herself. She said she wants to do that to you personally and nobody else. You are, I gather, both very close."

Maddie nodded. "Thank you, that's fine," she replied and proceeded with trepidation to open the door, immediately seeing Abby upright in her bed inside a lovely bright room with flowers at the end and Monet picture prints on the walls. Abby was smiling, tucking into her food as usual in her enthusiastic and nonchalant way, certainly not giving the appearance of a woman who had just lost her baby.

Maddie rushed forward to give Abby a hug.

"Hey, watch my dinner, this salmon is cooked to absolute perfection as are the vegetables, I might come here again," Abby cried, excited to see Maddie at last.

A knock on the door was followed by a shout from Abby to come in and a female porter brought in another steaming tray of food, pulling up the large trolley and spare chair alongside the bed for Maddie to eat. Dishes of fruit salad and a pot of tea were carefully put down too. Abby implored Maddie to start her meal before it went cold.

Maddie still couldn't reconcile at all what was going on. From screaming, uncontrolled hysteria, Abby had transformed back to her normal, calm and smiling self and into a state of well-being which had not been seen by anyone for some time. But Maddie was so hungry she had to start eating and after a

379

few satisfying mouthfuls, she began tentatively to speak. "So, Abby, you seem … err … very content … is the baby … is he or she alright? I'm assuming so by your transformation. And what about Lynton?"

Abby laughed. "I assume you know. Lynton is fine but very lucky. He skidded on a minor road just off Southport Road doing about seventy miles an hour on a pile of oil which had spilt out of drums off a pickup truck. The driver was trying to pick them up, couldn't wave him down quickly enough and the new Merc ended up upside down in a ditch. I saw him before, briefly." Abby pointed to a wheelchair in the corner of the room. "They're keeping him in overnight. He was very woozy and the doctors have bound up his chest, only one broken rib but pulled muscles and he hit his head on a branch, which came through the window as the car flipped and was concussed. The tree took most of the impact, saved his life as well. Good German engineering. I think it's all part of the plan."

Maddie sat up. She wasn't getting any of this. "What plan? So does Lynton know about the baby now? What does he think?"

Abby went quiet momentarily. "Maddie, look at that calendar on the wall."

Maddie looked around, baffled. "Eh? I've just realised, did you say Southport Road?"

"The ambulance brought you and me from the Red Lion. It's the day before. And there is no baby. Never has been. Countless tests have been done over the last three hours. They say I'm an unusual case, seen very rarely, exhibiting a type of phantom pregnancy which fools the medics as much as it fooled me. So I'm not pregnant, never have been and hopefully now, never will be, in fact, I'll make sure of it. So, there was nothing to tell Lynton, except my kidney stone, which has been lodged there for twenty years and never gave me a problem until now, suddenly deciding to become mobile. I've peed it out an hour ago, ping, straight into a bedpan. I've never felt better for years. That's why I'm smiling so much"

Maddie gasped, and finished off her last piece of salmon, also feeling a hundred times better. "Something's happened at Orsbrick Hall hasn't it? We're both in a history change again." She passed across a fresh fruit salad bowl and frantically began to search her phone again which she had switched off when she first arrived.

Abby nodded carefully. "Mauveine must have taken over. She desperately wanted both of us out of the situation."

"I know, she almost shoved me head first into the ambulance, it was all so surreal," Maddie replied. "But I read Belle's message as meaning she, Ned, Zac, as well as Nancy Ade and Dottie are fine. But there's no mention of Fenella. Why? Is she there?"

"Mmm … time to contact Victoria. I think you'd better phone your mother now. If some transformation has taken place, Belle will have some recollection as maybe Zac does. Ned, as always, will know nothing and nor will their friends. But Victoria, hopefully, is the one remaining crystal clear, and Mauveine and Isi of course as well as Elizabeth. How have they reverted?"

Maddie opened up her screen again frantically. "Oh my goodness …"

The silence around her was punctuated solely by the three local blackbirds outside singing in unison one after the other. Mating and nesting was still continuing unabated through the warm early summer. Victoria looked around and gently rubbed her heavy eyelids. She felt like she'd been fast asleep for centuries. She really thought that what she went through was the definitive ending of all possible endings. The last thing she remembered was spiralling around wildly, alone inside a hot ball of orange light and flying upward into the dark sky before everything went blank, like the inverse of emerging from a bad dream. But she was back in her drawing room, sitting in her comfortable armchair and gazing out towards the pond. The furniture looked normal, definitely not reflecting the nineteenth century. Had she emerged from that horrendous Fenella nightmare alone and in the same time period it had all started at? There was not a sound or soul anywhere but a pot of tea, milk and a porcelain cup were sat on the coffee table in front of her. She placed her hand over it, boiling hot and freshly made. That was encouraging. Just as she commenced pouring the tea, a knock on the door sounded. She looked over. Her heart pounded as the door opened and Erika walked in holding a tray with a black mobile phone and some kind of cake. Thank goodness, Victoria reflected. She had already met Erika, and despite the unexpected sight of a Sabrina replacement robot, it was a good sign that she had returned to some time-zone that had sensible meaning.

"I've brought your phone, Victoria, in case you wondered where it had got to. I found it in the scullery inside the bread-bin oddly. I made this treat earlier for the family and thought you might like to try it first, a Latvian speciality. Sour cream and walnut filling spread between layers of honey cake."

Victoria smiled, already feeling a welcoming glow of normality. "Thank you so much, Erika, that's very thoughtful and sounds delicious. I can see you've really taken to cooking and baking already. I wish you could share this wonderful creation with me."

Erika laughed. "Technically, I can also eat and drink, one of my modifications. I am bi-energy but the chemical conversion waste disposal doesn't work as efficiently as I would like presently so I prefer to plug in at the end of the day. But when I go next for a service, Professor Kolinsky hopes he can upgrade my hardware fully. Now, what was it you wanted to talk to me about?"

Victoria smiled, liking the concept and terminology. Flexible energy sourcing, a first step towards making robots superior to humans. She picked up her phone immediately, glad to see it … good thinking of Erika. She opened up the screen to check the date. This time she wasn't surprised. Twenty-four hours had been lost so the disappearance into thin air of Belle, Ned and Zac from the Black Anchor hadn't yet happened. Her mind began to race through something credible she could ask Erika without appearing to know absolutely nothing of what, where or how everyone else around might be existing. "I just thought it would be useful to know how you feel you're settling in with the rest of the family, Erika," she said tentatively.

Erika sat down on the couch opposite. She was dressed very similar to Maddie and Belle in skinny jeans and a top, the micro skirt seemed to have vanished. "Thank you for asking, Victoria. I must admit my first two weeks here have been hectic but I've been so grateful to Claire for showing me all the household requirements which I think I've mastered well and also Maddie and Abby for showing me different fashion styles which I much prefer, and Maddie's clothes fit me perfectly, we are so similar in size."

Victoria realised timelines had been altered beforehand. Erika has been here for some time. "Do you know when Maddie will be back?"

Erika was silent and thoughtful for a moment. "It depends on when Belle returns and when the children's party at the Red Lion, which Maddie, Abby and Judy were organising finishes but she said not too late."

Victoria inwardly sighed with relief. At least she knew where Maddie and Abby had surfaced as well as Judy. She took a chance with a follow-up. "Where has Belle actually gone? I missed her earlier."

"Into Liverpool with Ned and Zac and three friends, I think they were having a birthday celebration. Again, Belle expects to be back before midnight."

Victoria nodded approvingly, that scenario sounded positive. Her brain ached with non-tortuous ways of eliciting the last of the conundrums they had left behind in the half-world of the three Fenellas. "I'm certainly pleased we got rid of Maddie's friends before you started. You wouldn't have wanted guests to look after as well until you settled in," Victoria said, fingers crossed, another risky question but she had to know.

Erika grinned. "Perhaps not but my multitasking is highly refined and I did check the guest rooms. Nothing whatsoever to do in there apart from a quick vacuuming. Claire had tidied up well after your last visitor left."

Victoria pondered. The evil Rosemary McKenzie, masquerading as Fenella Kirkby, had indeed disappeared but what had happened to Janine, unexpectedly turning out to be Mauveine's sister, Fenella McKenzie? It sounded like Janine in this new history-time never arrived. In fact, did she exist at all? Something difficult was pending to iron out with Maddie as soon as possible. Victoria desperately needed some thinking time to put everything into perspective and where was Julian? "Thanks for your time, Erika, that all sounds good to me. I'll leave you to get on with what you were doing ..."

But as she was about to finish her sentence a loud bang made both of them jump, hearing the scullery door open wildly. A clattering of feet indicated someone was running in. Julian suddenly appeared, out of breath puffing and panting heavily. "Jesus Christ, Victoria, you'll never guess? I've just had a phone call from Judy, for some reason only my phone here is on her mobile. Lynton's in Ormskirk General with mild concussion and a broken rib after a car accident."

Victoria leapt out of her chair. "What? How did that happen? Is he alright?"

"Apparently, he skidded off the road in the Merc speeding to the hospital because Abby had been rushed in by ambulance suffering terrible stomach pains. Maddie has been with her all the time. She's just passed a long-lodged kidney stone which I never knew about and is feeling much better and they're keeping Lynton in overnight for observation. Judy is going in a pickup truck to pull the new Merc out of a ditch, a write-off, he was really lucky."

Victoria's mind was now going round and round. Julian obviously had no idea what had happened. As ever, his memory of psychic events was zero, thank goodness. But he made no mention of babies and miscarriages. What was happening? She needed to get over there quickly. "We'd better go to the hospital then," she said and jumped up ready to find her coat.

"No, no Victoria, Judy has made it very clear. They'll both be out tomorrow. Lynton is fast asleep, sedated and Abby is fine with Maddie, no problem whatsoever. I think Abby wants a bit of peace and quiet. So instead, if you want, you can come with me."

Victoria's eyes narrowed. "Come where?"

Julian beamed like a child who's just found a huge bag of sweets under his pillow. "I know this is not normally me but I'd gone over to see the churchwarden. They need some faulty electrics in the church vestry looking at and had heard I don't charge, church funds are a bit low. It's been some time since I've been in there I must admit, not since Judy's wedding. And I bumped into the new vicar who's just started and they've invited us for a sherry at the rectory, very friendly they seemed and already quite knowledgeable about the parish. I was just on my way over when I got Judy's call. Want to come?"

"Err … well … yes, okay, why not," Victoria mumbled, not sure whether that was a good or bad idea. "What's the vicar's name? I didn't know someone new was taking over already since Reverend Thomas Langton and his wife suddenly retired a few weeks ago?"

"Yes, a real shame, they'd hardly settled in. His arthritis became bad very quickly. Not like you to be in the dark, or me for that matter being ahead of the game on important ecclesiastical matters of the parish," Julian said, somewhat bumptiously, but he could tell by Victoria's scowl his witticism hadn't gone down well.

"I'll just find my jacket, I'll join you in a minute," she said suddenly looking at her phone again impatiently. No messages from anyone so she bashed out a quick text to Maddie to contact her urgently. Erika had discretely vanished to help Claire with the evening meal.

"I'll just put that inverter I've repaired back into the workshop for fitting tomorrow, had to use your lab bench and multimeters to test it out," Julian replied, marching out towards the scullery door.

"Hang on, Julian, you never said. Who is the new vicar?"

"Oh … err, the Reverend Herbert Edmondson and his wife Mo. Very trendy and casual, he's a polar opposite of what his title conjures up, quite young too, both of them. She's some

386

sort of scientist actually, I'm sure you'll be interested … see you outside in a minute."

Victoria felt a trickle of light-headedness permeate through the inside of her skull and took a deep breath. Events around them were taking unexpected and peculiar turns.

"Come on Belle wake up, please wake up."
Staring up at the bright afternoon sky, Belle was vaguely aware that she had been in some deep sleep. Someone was shaking her shoulder hard and then she gasped with incredulity at her surroundings. She was sitting with her knees up on dry sand at the bottom of a dune, oodles of razor-sharp grass stood upright around her acting as a barrier from the sea breeze. She opened her eyes to see Nancy, wide-eyed and just as disorientated, standing over her. Where were they?

"Thank God you're awake, Belle," Nancy cried. "I thought you'd croaked. Fuck, what has happened to us? One minute we're all about to be executed in your drawing room by the wicked witch of the sea and then, next second, there is one almighty explosion and here you and I are. I think we're in the sand hills at Formby beach."

Belle stood up, wobbly in the soft, dry sand, and hugged her friend hard. "Nancy, we're alive and I reckon we're back. As I described before, with a bit of luck, history has been rewritten to take account of the obliteration of evil Fenella or Fanny or whoever she really was. But where are we and why? Hey, hang on, you know. You remember everything, well do you?"

"I certainly do," Nancy replied, smirking.

Belle also realised they were dressed in tight jeans and summer windcheaters, exactly as they had been originally in the pub.

Nancy continued. "From the moment we found ourselves with Henry and that mutt of a son in the Black Anchor, right through to the escapades in the dock and the delicious Rory, then finding Ned and co. How can I forget Rory? I do rather miss my tarty look."

Belle was truly mystified. There was only one explanation possible. "Nance, this is truly amazing because for you to do that not only must you be a hidden psychic but there has to be some linkage of your family into the past McKenzie ancestry, but that will have to wait. First, let's check our phones and catch up."

They delved into their pockets and peered at the screens. Nothing seemed unusual except … they had lost a complete day. Belle smiled, an encouraging time-shift had occurred. The Fenella cataclysm was wiped out like it never happened, exhibiting the same time-shift effect as the fated trip on the Queen Lusitania with Maddie, Abby and her mother.

"Belle, do you hear that shouting behind this dune. I recognise that loud bellowing, it's Ned isn't it?"

Belle listened hard. Sure enough, the unmistakable Ned roar was very apparent and then they heard Ade and a cacophony of other voices, like some sort of game was going on behind them. "Let's creep up the top and see what's happening. But before we do, the fact you and I are here and they're all over there will mean, as usual, they likely won't have a clue what's gone on; no memory whatsoever. For Ned, Zac, Ade and likely Dottie, what you and I experienced, a brief foray of life in 1865, never happened. And Fenella has never existed either; time will have shunted her out altogether. Maddie and I learned to improvise on our feet before with this experience. Zac is the only one who sometimes has a weird flashback much later but right now we can discount him too because he never takes any serious notice.

The only ones we can share this with will be Maddie, my mother and Abby. Are you game?"

"Improvising is my big thing, Belle, as you know. I reckon you and I made a good team back there. Dottie, bless her was a bit out of it all in reality and probably that's because of what you said before. I've always had what I thought were strange dreams, but we can do the ancestry trail another time. Follow me."

They carefully stepped slowly up the side of the sand dune, peered over the top and gasped at what they observed. On the beach, about fifty yards ahead, they could see Ned, Zac, Dottie and Ade playing volleyball over a net with another half a dozen strangers. There were other groups of people gathered around a football game further along and a number of old Landrovers pulling large, gaily decorated trailers, were parked on the beach. Behind suitably erected canvas windbreakers and tents, more people were cooking food on a couple of barbeques, with tables laid out. As Belle and Nancy watched, a loud whistle blew and the volleyball game ended in large cheers from a myriad of people stood watching, with a television crew finishing off filming beside the pitch on the sand. Ned, playing his usual centre-stage attention-grabbing routine, shouted instructions then grabbed a chef's hat and began flipping burgers.

Nancy turned to Belle. "Now I remember. Something Ned said weeks ago. The Black Anchor was going to run some sports events to raise money for that poor child featured in the Liverpool Echo with a very rare eye cancer, to have a new immunotherapy treatment in America. Look at the logo on the banners, that new government 'fight cancer' advert. This must be the event."

"In that case, somehow in the time contraction, we've all ended up from the pub to here," Belle replied. "Okay, let's go for it. Ready?"

"You betcha, as Maddie's Janine, aka our 1865 Fenella McKenzie saviour would have said. I have a feeling that the story ending there is going to be painful."

"Yes, I agree. How come you know about Maddie and Janine?"

"Maddie's inclinations have been obvious for ages. Nobody's bothered whatsoever, who cares nowadays about gender fluidity but unlike you and me, she has an almost child-like, antiquated view of relationships. On that, you and your sister are very unlike peas in a pod. I think we're going to have to try and alleviate the emotional hurt somehow."

Belle reflected for a moment. "The fact that Janine may not even exist you mean? That's why Mauveine was keen for Maddie to be gone out of the way. She and Abby were there before the first explosion which brought us all together. When the ambulance came for Abby who had suddenly become ill, Mauveine almost shoved Maddie into the ambulance. Mum told me briefly whilst Fanny was grandstanding over Ned's affections on the podium. I think Mauveine knew something was coming to a head."

"I wondered why Maddie was not in the room. Right, okay, first things first. Let's go, I'll wave to Ned."

Walking briskly onto the beach, Belle and Nancy strode towards the activity. Lots of people were milling around the food, helping themselves to burgers, kebabs and sausages with chef Ned dishing out onto plates. He looked up, handing over to Ade and ran to meet them. "Hey you two, you've missed all the fun. You should have stayed and played volleyball with us, we won by miles. I hope your stomach feels better Nance. Too

390

many gin and tonics in the pub I reckon, you were going some at lunch time. Grab a plate, all expertly grilled by yours truly."

Nancy caught up with him and planted a kiss on his cheek. "Thank you, master chef; I never knew you had it in you. Yes, I'm feeling much better thank you. Belle and I walked as far as the River Alt. We needed some quiet sea air to chill out for an hour and had some catching up to do."

Belle laughed, that was some understatement, piling up salad and chilli dressing onto her chicken kebab. She nodded and turned to see Zac and Dottie, hand in hand, casually wandering towards them, Fenella clearly a non-existent memory. "Dottie and I won the mixed football," Zac chuntered. "Well, our team did. I'm glad Walter invited us to join this charity bash, aren't you Belle?" Happy with his day, he hugged Dottie harder whilst she gazed at him lovingly. Dottie, too, clearly had zero memory of her recent time travel in Victorian England.

"Yes, definitely. How much has been raised?" Belle proffered.

Ned finally finished with the cooking and hand in hand with Nancy, sauntered into the conversation, a double-decker cheeseburger dripping with tomato ketchup clutched in the other. "Brown Dog, the hippy guy over by the trailers who organised this lot, reckons with both the sponsorship of the matches and the monster quiz nights in the Black Anchor then we've managed to raise nearly seven thousand pounds. That's pretty good I reckon, every little helps Richie Barnes and his mother get over to the Wills Institute for that special eye treatment. Hey Ade, how's it going? I see the ale has started."

Ade, his chef's hat askew, trundled over effortlessly carrying a large crate of bottled lager and plonked it down in front of Ned. "Deffo, guys," he grunted, wiping his brow. "I just hope that half-wit brother of mine got our leckie scooters in the van like he promised and delivered them back to Orsbrick. I've persuaded Jimmy who lives in Newburgh, the ugly bearded one with the tatty Landrover, to give us all a lift back later, much later," he said mischievously. "Save us a load of hassle on the late night bus. But you'll have to feel hardy and get plenty of ale down your gullets, I'm afraid. Not a time to be nesh. His motor's the one with only half a canvas cover full of holes." He pulled three lagers out and opened them up.

"Oh yes, brother dearest? And what about the ladies, then?" Dottie demanded, giving him a sisterly shove. "Don't we get a look in too? I'm afraid Ade's always been a dick ever since birth!"

Ned guzzled down his first half bottle instantly. "Here, here to that," he shouted to roars of laughter. "Anyway, I think we've earned a few beers. Beach party starts in a minute generously supplied by the Black Anchor."

Soon they joined the rest of the party-goers. Landrover Jimmy had towed a generator onto the flat sand and disco lights and an accompanying giant sound system were rapidly rigged up. A few more pickup trucks arrived with additional crates of beer as well as plenty of soft drinks. The charity bash beach party had revved up immediately.

After half an hour, Nancy carrying two bottles of lemonade, sidled up in a quiet corner to join Belle, watching Ned and Ade centre stage on the dance floor, raucously gyrating in Gangnam style together and encouraging lots of screaming others to join in. "I've had enough of him for a bit," she said, out of breath. "I have to say, Ned can be the biggest idiot on the planet but he makes up for it with his unique social skills. He's one of the best motivators I've ever seen. It'll be a big asset to him if he ever grows up. Zac and Dottie have wandered off into the sandhills somewhere making up for lost time. I haven't quite worked it out but they appear to have just got back together again after a separation so at least that part happened like before. I've been very careful what I say to Ned but I reckon pretty well everything remains as it was previously until the last few days, minus any mention, sign of or appearance of bitch Fenella which makes our storytelling so much easier!"

Belle grinned, pulling out her phone. "I noticed that phenomenon last time when we returned from 1841. Good."

"You'd better message Maddie. We should make sure she knows we're safe and all is cool again."

"Just going to do it," Belle replied tapping furiously for half a minute. "Done and Mum as well. I just hope they're both okay. I'd rather talk to them tomorrow, still need to reflect on what's gone on."

"Actually, Belle, I want to tell you something important. Ned is going to go ape-shit. You know that application I made for the Veterinary School at Cambridge University? I only told you, Ned has no idea. He thinks I'm going to be hanging around in the vet's practice for him. I've been accepted after passing their entrance test. I had a great interview a week ago and I'm going. I'm sure my apprenticeship in the vet's practice helped enormously, I was streets ahead of the other interviewees."

"Wow, that's fabulous news, well done Nance," Belle replied, excitedly throwing her arms around Nancy's neck. "You're absolutely right, you have to make the most of yourself now and get that degree, and you've certainly got the ability. It's not your fault Ned's a year younger, he can apply next year. Let's face it, Dottie is going on to Oxford to do English so Zac will be in the same situation. They'll both have final Diploma exams to pass next year."

"I'm going to take everything as it comes, we'll see how it goes. I still feel very committed to Ned and a future together but I'm not going to be rigidly bound by it either. We're both too young."

"To be fair to Ned, I suspect he's gearing up for something like this anyway, just a few comments he made to Maddie a while back. He's more mature and reflective than he lets on. Anyway, now I've changed my application to medicine at Cambridge, fingers crossed I get in too. We can have a whale of a time then, I've applied to King's College in the city centre. This calls for a celebration, shall we have another lager?"

"Great idea, start as we mean to go on," Nancy replied, pulling over a full crate.

Walking with Julian along the canal bank to the rectory, Victoria heard her phone ping and quickly read Belle's message. She felt a welcome wave of immediate relief. Their safe return had been confirmed at long last. Julian had grabbed hold of her hand earlier, she looked up surprised, his face seemed relaxed and happy and evidently, he was feeling romantic again, the first time for a very long time.

"It's Belle, darling, they're all on the beach at Formby with some charity event organised by the Black Anchor and will be getting a ride back home later," she said, gripping his hand tighter as they walked gingerly over the slippery, unmade part of the towpath.

"I know. Ned told me earlier. Ade's brother arrived whilst I was outside, with all their electric scooters in his van. Had to look twice to recognise who it was, strange individual. He'd fetched them from the Black Anchor so they could go to this event in an old hired charabanc. I seem to be the only one who knows what's going on around here these days, like role reversal in old age," he said, grinning stupidly. Victoria ignored him.

It wasn't the surprise of seeing Mauveine and Isi again back in the rectory that forced Victoria to take a deep breath when she walked in. She was quite used to the idea of Isi as a vicar, but what startled her most was they had each lost about ten years of age and had the appearance of being in their mid-twenties, as if the trauma of the Fenella cataclysm in Orsbrick Hall had made even more of an impact on the historic time readjustment. Isi still retained his beard, neatly trimmed, but sported thick brushed-back black hair whilst Mauveine retained her long mousey locks. But one benefit of the reverse ageing combined with their very trendy dress sense was to throw Julian off any scent that they were surreptitiously related and Mauveine's glasses, which suited her well, also helped. After a quick sherry, Isi, now Herbert, wanted to show Julian inside the church and what needed fixing, so they happily went off to take a look.

Victoria was finally alone with Mauveine. They took the opportunity for generous celebratory hugs. Mauveine confirmed excitedly that like before in 1841 she could pursue her science dye research and had even walked back into her own room to the identical desk. But a contract was lying on top and signed up for a start-up industrial unit, Xanthene Enterprises Ltd. She would be independent again and Isi could pursue what remained long in his heart, ministering to the community, his true vocation. By some mysterious means, the time orientation after the explosion had brought their subconscious wishes back into reality. Victoria talked enthusiastically for a few minutes about dye collaboration, exactly as they had originally planned.

Mauveine interjected. "I'd better tell you first, Victoria, but you may have already suspected. During those final minutes, as you saw with your own eyes, Fenella, my real sister and I were finally reunited after a century and a half, which was wonderful for both of us. However, Fenella McKenzie has no place in this time. Her alter-ego spirit, Janine, that she created and adopted to effectively return and save us will not exist and will, therefore, have no footprint in time. Fenella McKenzie, in this history rewrite, will have returned to America in her own time and seen out her normal lifespan as was. This will be very hard on Madeleine and I owe it to her to tell her personally. So I've sent a taxi to pick her up from the hospital and bring her back here. She will know, of course, immediately she hears she is being taken to the home of the Reverend Herbert Edmondson and his wife Mo. I know about Abigail. I facilitated all of it to ensure both of them would be physically and psychically well away from everything about to erupt in Orsbrick Hall. What I hadn't reckoned on was that Abigail would emerge with no pregnancy, instead delivering a corrected kidney stone. To be honest, I don't know whether that will be good or bad for Abigail."

"Yes, Julian, who as you can see remembers absolutely nothing, said so earlier, I mean about Abby getting rid of the kidney stone, certainly no mention of babies. It appears everything kicked in for her, Lynton and Maddie from the Red Lion, not Orsbrick Hall."

"I know. Isi suggested that concept in order to facilitate even more distancing from the cataclysm. Madeleine will know anyway and so will Abigail that we've endured another McKenzie historic correction but not Lynton. His car accident was not pre-planned but a random event which unexpectedly threw itself into the mix. I was very nervous when I heard;

thank heavens he sustained only minor injuries. Anyway, they should both be out of hospital tomorrow and I will speak to Abigail by phone before she leaves. Is it acceptable to you if Isi and I tell Madeleine the truth first?"

Reflecting quickly, Victoria nodded and smiled. Mauveine had confirmed exactly what she had surmised. She felt a wave of deep and genuine relief. Without any doubt, Mauveine and Maddie could together work through all the reasons and implications of the vanishing of Janine far better than she could explain. And she was quietly convinced that deep down, Abby would be relieved too. After all, Abby never wanted children, despite justifying how it could all be wonderful from every angle, which was understandable at the time. However, the complications of conception and fatherhood were so out of this world, literally, that it would never have worked long term which is why, of course, she kept putting off ever telling Lynton. In some ways, the outcome for Abby was sad but not tragic. She hadn't miscarried because she had never carried, something Abby would probably find acceptable to come to terms with. But there remained one mystery which she and Mauveine needed to get to the bottom of.

Mauveine was perusing Victoria, still thinking quietly, and watched her stare at the empty wine decanter with more than a passing contemplation. "I'm afraid I don't know the answer to that conundrum, but she's definitely not here."

Jarred from her thoughts, Victoria looked up puzzled. "You mean Elizabeth has been written out of the recent history? What about her being appointed by your elderly predecessors?"

"I've already looked through their records," Mauveine replied. "Of course, they weren't here long, barely a month, but no sign of any curate and Isi, as subtly as he could, asked some of the long-time church volunteers whether they missed having a curate and they said they'd never had one in their lifetimes but extra help with the growing parish was a good thought if the Bishop found the necessary funds."

"But she must have resurfaced somewhere, surely?" Victoria said, wishing no harm had come to Elizabeth, despite her misgivings about her closeness with Julian, past and recent.

Mauveine frowned. "Logically speaking, one of three scenarios would have happened. Elizabeth has returned to another time, maybe back to her original era or she's returned but in another guise or she's gone the same way as Fenella McKenzie, my sister, and disappeared into a historic ether."

Victoria sighed, she felt suddenly deeply despondent. Elizabeth always pushed out contradictory emotions, just like in the 1841 days of Ada. Victoria genuinely missed her but was persistently wary, a mishmash of mixed feelings all at the same time. "We'll just have to see I suppose, but Elizabeth did play an important, indeed vital part in solving the Fenella dilemma."

Mauveine nodded. "I agree but first things first. Madeleine remains my biggest concern …"

They hadn't done one for a long time but Victoria decided, after checking the weather which was set to be a mini-heat wave, that having a small afternoon garden party to welcome Abby and Lynton back from hospital would be a nice and appropriate thought. Erika and Claire had volunteered to organise the party and manage a barbeque on the back lawn in front of the pond which, with the tree coverage, would provide a pleasant sun break area if anyone became too hot. The opportunity was taken discretely to invite the Reverend and Mrs Edmondson which delighted Julian who had happily hit it off from the word go with his new friend, Herbert the vicar.

As Mauveine predicted, when an intrigued Maddie arrived at the rectory during late afternoon the day before, the delight with their reunion turned emotionally fraught once Mauveine and Isi broached the subject of what had become of Janine. Maddie was already upset and suspicious because she had been completely unable to contact Janine by phone or email whilst in the hospital but had decided no news was good news, and believed there must have been a glitch with her phone which seemed to quickly run out of battery whilst she had been keeping Abby company. In any case, meeting up with Mauveine first was an excellent thought as she would find out the raw, unadulterated facts of what had happened at Orsbrick Hall.

Following copious tears, consoling hugs and a fortifying gin and tonic at the receiving end of Isi's excellent pastoral skills to heal troubled minds, Maddie began to slowly reconcile to an immediate future which would be very different from what she had planned. Not only would there be no Janine and no America but she would need to rethink how to pursue her graduate study. Taking a leaf from the book of Victoria, her mother, was already turning her mind to future options, very pleased that she had entered and passed her Cambridge scholarship exams with flying colours. Her excitement about artificial intelligence had become subdued. That area of study felt almost bare and lifeless without the thought of Janine alongside. Instead, she was reverting back to her original idea of taking lots of mathematics and theoretical physics or even astrophysics. Her childhood love of astronomy had been rekindled after endless discussions with Elizabeth. Talking this through with Mauveine was massively helpful. But what had happened to Elizabeth? They discussed the possibilities, likelihoods and realities but Maddie remained sceptical that

Elizabeth had reverted back to her original time. That outcome didn't seem fair, not that the laws of quantum space-time and dark energy whirling black holes really carried fairness and equity about them.

Isi eventually offered a helpful snippet ... he said that Janine never existing at all would be easier to come to terms with for making new decisions. The logical appeal of that simple truism had accelerated Maddie's reappraisal of her life and future and already, her potential depression was lifting. In any case, if Janine was there she would not want Maddie to be depressed either. The time had come for her to depart home and Mauveine waved a set of car keys in front of her nose.

"We've still got that old jeep you drove, parked around the back in the old barn. The Bishop told Isi that our previous incumbents insisted on donating it to the church for use by their successors. Both Isi and I will have to learn to drive eventually but to be honest both of us prefer to bicycle everywhere or use the omnibus, it's what we're used to. So, the jeep is yours on permanent loan. The church has taxed and insured it, whatever that means, until the end of the year, and then it's down to you."

Maddie beamed. She knew her father would likely buy her anything she wanted but the old jeep had a special meaning and resonance and she loved driving it. "Oh, yes please, that's fabulous Mauveine. I'm very grateful. That jeep has a real soul somehow."

Isi laughed. "I shall pray for both of you then!"

Mauveine smiled. "And don't forget. Outside of our small family coterie, remember to call us Herbert and Mo from now on, especially in front of the family males. Your father, Lynton, Ned and Zac will have no memory of what has just happened."

"Of course, understood, I won't," Maddie replied, fidgeting in her pocket. "I'd better be off home. I'm glad I know all that happened before seeing Mum. It makes everything so much easier and I'll talk to Abby on the phone later. Actually, I can feel my phone vibrating, I must have accidentally switched the ringer off again, bad habit." She pulled her iPhone from her jeans and stared disbelievingly at the screen. "This is the second phone surprise today. Hello?"

The weather the next day surpassed all expectations, perfect for their planned picnic. A warm and pleasant twenty-five degrees heat in the sun was accompanied by a very light breeze and heralded the likelihood of a hazy, crazy, balmy summer to come. Expectations of high summer temperatures were now the norm rather than the exception in the north west of England. One benefit in the last five years of the accepted climate change was the proliferation of fine English white and even red wines. Most vines grew presently in the south west and eastern regions of the country, with plentiful irrigation provided through a cheap and virtually energy free desalination discovery. Julian had been stocking up extensively in the Orsbrick Hall cellar being a strong supporter of everything British where possible in the way of food and drink, ever since the country had finally exited from the European Union three years back.

Following a last-minute appeal from Belle and endorsement from the family, Victoria decided to change the picnic venue to somewhere else untried: the newly opened and vastly extended Martin Mere parkland, an area of natural lake and bird marshes, where the regional government, a few years back, had offered one of a number of grants to persuade a return of the farmland to its former habitats and compensate farmers. Local young environmental volunteers had worked hard to develop the challenging conservation project on time, especially Belle, aided by Nancy, Ned and Zac at weekends. Added private donations, including from Victoria and Julian, in the end, surpassed even the generous government grant. The new Martin Mere, remodelled from the original huge and extensive inland lake drained in the seventeenth century, was already attracting much international attention and had provided a new lease of life to Scarisbrick Hall, whose grounds were one of the key focal points for visitors. It had been bought back into the family after nearly a century of absence and renovated extensively by an American female descendant who had made a billion dollars from computer software.

Belle and Nancy, mischievously creating an opportunity for some personal reminiscing, persuaded Ned and Zac to ride to Scarisbrick Hall with them on their horses, whilst Julian and Victoria, with Erica's help, would transport the food, drink, wolfhounds and picnic paraphernalia in the pickup truck. Ade and Dottie would arrive later on his scooter. They would be joined by Abby who offered to take the Reverend Herbert and wife Mo. Lynton, still slow, sore but growing cheerful, especially knowing Abby had made a full recovery and was back to her chipper self, would follow on with Judy, her husband and the children.

However, Victoria and Belle remained concerned about Maddie who had returned from Mauveine, resolute in her own mind about the future but subdued and remote, not a characteristic they had experienced before as a family. Ned, as usual, made some crass and ill-timed remark about moody females which garnered the severe ire of Nancy, so he had to make himself contrite and twice as cheerful and useful by cutting up sandwiches, humping drinks from the cellar and preparing the hampers.

In a secluded spot on the edge of the lake bounding the Scarisbrick estate, umbrellas were put up and Erika and Claire laid the food out on small trestles in the shade. Everyone, especially the children, seemed to be having a great time. Judy and Lynton organised them into teams to play a game of rounders on the well-mown lawn behind. Julian and Herbert had gone for a walk to the Hall to look at their new array of ground heat pumps which had recently been installed and Ned, Zac and Ade had decided to bring some binoculars and, with Nancy and Dottie, set off on a marked nature trail to the bird hide further up the bank and see what they could spot.

Victoria, Abby, Belle and Mauveine sat down around the picnic table and began munching at the delicious sandwiches and salads; they weren't going to wait for the others. Belle had been thinking long and hard about what happened over the last month, trying to reconcile what was impossible to have foreseen, and needed to comment. "I think what's been especially difficult for Maddie to accept," she began, "is not just that Janine was effectively an imposter she had fallen in love with but also how the Fenella we started with on the doorstep, who Maddie really liked and wanted to help, became such an evil and horrific individual, like they were two completely different people. I'm certain now the takeover by that horrible ghoul, Rosemary, Zelda's daughter wasn't linear or easy, somehow the Fenella initially may have been Janine in some form, I reckon, finally ending up, in the Black Anchor, as Fanny Kirkby. That makes it even harder for Maddie, if she's come to a similar conclusion."

Victoria looked up, suddenly deep in thought. "That's a very rational and sound observation Belle, I agree but how does it help us to help Maddie?"

Mauveine interjected. "Your conclusion is likely to be correct, Belle, given Rosemary's history over the centuries, but Maddie won't come to that deduction as you have because you were the only one to see, experience and remember all the shades of Fenella, from the shy doorstep mathematician to psychopathic sea-witch. And for you to come though that experience and remain as calm and collected as you have is wholly remarkable and something we all should be proud of."

Victoria beamed and nodded, rubbing her daughter's shoulder.

Abby, having hungrily devoured one pulled pork roll and ready for the next, picked up the bowl of mixed salad. "Maddie will be fine; the family sisterhood here will make sure of it. Now, let's change the subject, please. I have distinctly gone off the name Fenella."

They laughed and continued sharing around the plates of sandwiches and nibbles.

"Ned has finally done us proud," Belle remarked, laughing. "I reckon he should go into the hospitality sector rather than the veterinary business, he has an unexpected knack for food preparation."

"Yes, but only when under female pressure," Victoria said cynically, spreading a thick layer of her favourite chicken pâté onto her plate. "Now, where has Maddie got to? She should be here by now. She said she had something urgent to do first and would come shortly in her jeep. I'm still worried about her; she seems both manic and depressed at the same time. Belle, what have you said to Ned and Zac about Janine?"

404

"Maddie and I agreed a storyline that Janine has decided to continue her studies in California where her parents want to move to … to be honest they're so wrapped up in their own lives they're not bothered, although Ned did comment that he too was concerned that Maddie was taking this separation from Janine badly and that he was worried and promised not to tease her anymore, at least for one day."

Abby laughed. "That's fair enough I suppose coming from Ned. Hey talk of the devil, look over there. Isn't that Maddie walking across? Who's she with? Shit, I must get some new distance glasses."

They all peered at the far-off crowds towards the car park, not sure, and then Mauveine had the foresight to grab a spare pair of binoculars off the adjacent table. "Lord in Heaven above, have mercy on all our souls," she immediately muttered with a decided smirk.

"Steady on Mo, actually I rather like your new name, so much more informal. That expletive sounds very nineteenth-century. Here let me look," Victoria said as Mauveine handed them over.

"You may also find yourself replete with similar expletives," Mauveine replied, grinning.

Victoria readjusted the eyepiece and looked hard as the two people, walking briskly, were finally coming into proper view. "Fuck, hell and damnation, well I can't wait for the explanation. She even typically has her own fancy parasol. Give a warm welcome everyone in a minute or so to the irrepressible Miss Elizabeth Milbanke."

"What? Here give me those things," Abby cried, snatching them off Victoria, twiddling the knobs quickly. "My God, you're right, and she's carrying a bottle of red wine of course. Maddie looks very happy which is interesting. Well, that last mystery is solved and let's be honest we're all pleased, even you Victoria. But where on earth did Elizabeth land?"

"So, I hope you're all pleased to see me. You couldn't get rid of me into the furthest reaches of cyberspace that easily. I've got form on reappearing unexpectedly."

Belle grabbed another chair and hugs and kisses were generously exchanged, but intrigue filled the air seeing the new state and form of Elizabeth in her third reincarnation. In place of the black and uninspiring curate trouser suit, she was wearing a very trendy, yellow striped summer dress and expensive sandals. Her long brown hair had been replaced with a short blonde bob but the unmistakable features still held true as did the intellectual stare and mischievous expression.

Maddie stood apart, silently amused watching the reaction, especially of Victoria and Abby who were in abject disbelief. Without doubt, Elizabeth was a space-time chameleon with dedicated expertise. It was time for Maddie to reveal the truth.

"I think I'd better introduce the new Elizabeth to you all or should I say Professor Elizabeth Milbanke, Director of the new Cambridge University Astrobioengineering Centre. And if you look in those binoculars across the lake, to the left of the two sailing boats, you'll just see a low-domed roof glinting in the sunlight between the trees in the far distance. The building is situated between Hesketh Bank and the Ribble. That's the completed small observatory, replete with powerful infrared and X-ray telescopes. The rest of the building will be finished by the autumn."

Mauveine had taken the binoculars back and was avidly scouring the sky beyond, adjusting the focus until she found it and nodded.

Maddie continued. "That's the reason I was late because I agreed to pick Elizabeth up from her new office and bring her here. Good job I had the jeep as I could take a short cut over the fields to the main road because the constructors were busy with putting a bridge in place over the River Douglas to link to the A59."

Victoria, her mouth still open, finally spoke. "But why … and more importantly how?"

Elizabeth smiled, her eyes flashed with the satisfaction that once more, Victoria and Abby could be overwhelmingly surprised by her.

"So, I assume you don't want your old job back again," Mauveine said, somewhat sardonically. "Although if you did, Isi and I would have to create one as it never existed."

"No thank you, Mauveine," Elizabeth replied laughing. "I think I was more of a curate's egg than a real curate. That diversion, I'm sure, was my mother having a beyond the grave joke at my reincarnated expense. I'd better explain a little more. Basically, after the world imploded again, I found myself staring in front of a large desk in this wonderful building, all glass and light. A briefcase full of papers sat there with letters confirming my appointment following my detailed paper on the potentially important convergence of astronomy, artificial intelligence and cosmology through the exploration of life on other planets. Now, I had genuinely worked on sketching out that concept between curate activities and sent a paper to the Cambridge artificial intelligence faculty head who Maddie had been liaising with to change her course. Our regular discussions on all manner of interesting mathematical topics had inspired me hugely, as had the recently failed space missions to Enceladus and Titan, moons of Saturn. So, I thought I'd submit them a controversial paper, embellished with incontrovertible evidence that the survival of humankind would require colonising distant planets, sooner rather than later. Unknown to Maddie and me, this new discipline of astrobioengineering, which combines all those elements in my paper with computing, AI and philosophy, was already an advancing internal concept by Cambridge in partnership with the Universities of Liverpool and Preston and occupying a cabal of interested and internationally renowned specialists. Bizarrely, I had been recommended to pursue such theoretical research by a certain Professor Charlene Babbage from NASA who I had already been in correspondence with, old descendant habits die hard. It must be another space-time disruption joke. I appear to have some kind of astrophysics doctorate from Harvard and a certificate on the wall to prove it. So, the compact research centre is being built on prime West Lancashire farmland, at least my office and the high-tech observatory are so far, convenient for access by those other university partners. The land has been donated by an anonymous benefactor who has provided a generous trust to ensure the initiative is self-financing for the first five years. The centre will have a small staff of six, around a dozen postgraduates and a special class of ten top undergraduate students selected from around the world. Exciting isn't it? The stars, metaphysically and actually have quietly converged in my direction for a change."

"I can't believe I'm hearing all this. What an incredible transformation, I can see why you're so excited," Victoria replied, enthusiastically. But inside her methodical brain, she was trying to work out why this could have happened and stifle her intense academic jealousy.

"We should have a celebration, but we've no champagne," Abby chimed in. "However, we do have your rather exquisite looking bottle of red wine, Elizabeth."

"Actually, we do have champagne. Can't have a picnic without some chilled Bolly on hand. I sneaked in a bottle in the cooler box. Are you going to introduce me?"

Intensively engaged with Elizabeth's long tale, no one had heard Lynton silently hobble up behind, holding hard onto a cane walking stick as his ribs and ankle still hurt badly.

Abby turned and rubbed his arm. "Darling, are you okay? I hope you've been taking it easy with Judy and the children. This is ... Professor Milbanke, an acquaintance of Maddie's ... err ... at Cambridge University."

Elizabeth stared at him. What an interesting resemblance to the Dr Grey art critic bore who had tried to gatecrash her 1841 London house dinner party with Victoria and Abigail. Yet another confirmation of her secret hypothesis. "You must be Lynton. I've heard so much about you from Abigail here."

"Really?" he replied, totally mystified. "Nothing too bad I hope, I'll just find that champagne." He shuffled off to the vehicles, waving hard to Erika.

Maddie couldn't contain her own news any longer. "There's another finale to Elizabeth's new status. Amongst the student applications which Elizabeth has been approving today ... was mine ... which had been passed on for consideration by the University."

Elizabeth smiled and put her arm around her. "And I've approved it wholeheartedly. This degree programme will have everything Madeleine excels in and enjoys including biology. She will be one of only two UK students. The rest are highly gifted applicants from America, Europe and China and one from a place called Syria. Nine females and three males."

Victoria smiled weakly. "Well done, Maddie," was her only comment. Abby could sense instantly from Victoria's face there was all manner of complex concerns and emotions running through her mind. They would have to talk rationally later. Victoria was, as ever, over-demonising Elizabeth, who as a supremely gifted mathematician could be a hugely beneficial influence on Maddie's future potential and career. This was the most wonderful opportunity and Maddie could even remain living at home.

Belle, however, danced up and down with heartfelt, genuine excitement and immediately hugged her sister hard. "I hope my Cambridge medical application is also successful," she said, cheerfully. "I want to go with Nancy who will be doing veterinary medicine there in October. Oops … damn, sorry, I shouldn't have said that. It's still a secret."

"You mean Ned doesn't know?" Victoria queried, her eyes narrowing.

"No, not yet," Belle replied. "Nancy intends to tell him her own way and in her own time. Please, everyone, can you respect that including you, Mum. And he could apply anyway next year if he passes his exams."

"Yes, of course, Annabelle," Mauveine said quietly. "Every woman has secrets from her man. They need only be told when it's good for them. I should know!"

They all laughed, including Victoria this time. The diversion away from Maddie now complete, they watched Lynton approach with much more spring in his hobbled step, holding a large flagon of champagne. Erica followed behind carrying another table and a box of glasses. Further down the lakeside path, near the reeds, the Ned and Zac party of bird watchers were making their return and Julian and Herbert could be seen in animated conversation strolling back from the Hall. Judy and the children were already sat down on the grass, exhausted with playing games as Claire began preparing their jelly, cakes and ice cream. The rest of the afternoon continued in pleasant conviviality, Claire and Erika tirelessly ensuring everyone had plenty to eat and drink until Erika had to go and sit in Julian's pickup truck and plug into the power socket for fifteen minutes to boost her flagging energy.

Victoria and Abby, with Maddie and Belle, decided to go for a walk along the lakeside path leaving Elizabeth and Mauveine talking over a third glass of wine with Julian, Isi and Lynton. Judy and husband had taken the children back home to their Southport townhouse on the seafront, exhausted, with Erika's help, who had programmed her internal map scanner and database to be able to return to Orsbrick Hall unaided by public transport.

"Is this really what you want to do, Maddie? I mean study with Elizabeth for the next three years?" Victoria started as they all watched the bitterns nesting in the reeds further along.

"Of course, Mum. I can't think of anything more exciting. Elizabeth and I are really on the same academic wavelength and she has such a brilliant mind. Also, it's what Janine would have wanted."

Victoria took a deep breath. She had a comment to make but Abby interceded with a tap on the hand before Victoria said anything and began to add her own thoughts. "I agree with you Maddie, and about Elizabeth. This international programme seems to be a special flagship of one of the most prestigious universities in the world and attracting some of the most talented young people. Who would have guessed history could have rewritten itself that way. You were destined for it." She shot a glance across to Victoria who knew that signal of old. They would discuss this further between them privately.

Abby continued. "And, I'm so sorry about Janine. Nobody was to guess all that would transpire in a million years, not even Mauveine until it happened, but in the end, Janine, or as we

411

now know, Fenella McKenzie, appears to have been the necessary trigger to ensure Fanny Kirkby's evil plan would end and she brought everyone back. We should all be eternally grateful to Janine. I hope this is the last of these time-clash distortion episodes. In fact, something deep inside tells me it will be."

Belle nodded but Maddie deep in contemplation simply had to say it. "Actually, Janine was so sorry she had to deceive me and everyone including her own family."

A muted silence draped itself over them like an unexploded bomb on a damp blanket as the implications of that short sentence began to sink in.

Abby was the first to comment. "Hang on Maddie, how can that be? You weren't there. You sound like you've just been speaking to Janine."

"I did. She sat on the end of my bed and we chatted for a minute or two and then she vanished. She loved everything about Elizabeth's new course."

"When was this?" Victoria asked quietly, her insides turning queasy. "Maddie, are you trying to say that Janine has returned to Orsbrick Hall ... but as a ghost?"

"This afternoon before I left. Yes, Mum, I am saying that Mauveine has been replaced ... by her own sister."

Belle's face had gone pale. "This means Abby is wrong and we're back where we started. The story isn't finished ... living again in a house which is haunted. And we have the mystery of Nancy having a complete memory of what happened. Somehow she must also be part of the McKenzie family and we'll need to scrutinise the family tree again in minute detail."

"You won't find it," Maddie immediately replied. "Janine said so. Nancy is connected to Lydia, Mauveine's arty half-sister. She too had a secret."

"Does Mauveine know any of this?" Abby whispered. "Have you told her?"

"I don't know and I haven't mentioned it, not yet anyway," Maddie replied. "Where does one start? It's a complicated conversation to have by any stretch of the imagination."

Despairing again, Victoria couldn't hide her frustration. "I said this last time, just when you think it's all over it isn't. Look, there's Elizabeth walking off, she must be in a hurry to return to her research centre. I'm just going to catch her up, I need to ask something."

Before anyone, especially Abby could question, Victoria had sprinted off at a fast pace towards the car park where Elizabeth was heading. Soon, breathless, she caught up.

"Sorry I've got to fly so quickly, Victoria," Elizabeth began, somewhat surprised and stopped immediately. "Nearly forgot the time, I have a vital phone meeting shortly with the Vice Chancellor."

"I just wanted to say a sincere thank you, Elizabeth, for everything you did to help bring Ned and Zac back to their rightful time," Victoria began.

"Thank you, I do appreciate that. But let's be honest with each other and cut to the chase. You have a burning question don't you, Victoria. Well, go on, ask it. In fact, I'll ask it for you to save embarrassment," Elizabeth said softly. "You want to know how I managed it, return again like I did because I'm an outsider to the family, because I'm not a McKenzie."

Victoria blushed. Just as Ada always succeeded doing in 1841, Elizabeth in 2026 retained that sharp ability to anticipate her actions well in advance and take the moral high ground even when there wasn't one. "Yes, I admit, the observation has been playing on my mind."

"Your scientific mind I think, Victoria, to which I remain both highly attuned and admiring," Elizabeth responded, smiling. "Madeleine and Annabelle's impressive intellectual talents undoubtedly emanate from you ... I'm not quite so convinced of Julian's contribution in that area which brings me succinctly to the answer to your question. As I'm sure you suspect, Julian indeed holds the key. You remember, back in your drawing room, when he became full of despair and confusion as Fanny Kirkby's world and your world entangled together, a most peculiar experience but very interesting. It was then I realised in an instant that another pending time disjunction was about to happen. And unlike before, I needed to be an integral part of it, indeed to be one of the facilitators to ensure the energy release happened for my benefit as well as yours and your children, exactly as I managed when Mauveine and I traversed that icy, lone pathway of travel into the future and another chance to achieve things we never could in our original time. So, when I took Julian to one side, I told him who he really was and that I knew all his secrets, past, present and future ... that finally blew the doors off the wormhole tentatively connecting our two universes ... which with the unique and timely contribution of Mauveine's sister, sealed the deal as you guys say and here we all are, me included."

Victoria stood open-mouthed, suddenly wary and very uneasy. "Sorry, did you just say who he was? What secrets do you mean, Elizabeth? Are you alluding to your grubby affair in 1841 with that horrendous Julian manifestation who ignored and dismissed me as irrelevant ninety-nine percent of the time? I soon rationalised that behaviour as irrelevant to the task we had to fulfil but it still stupidly hurt as you well know."

"No, Victoria, I mean who Julian actually is. I had to think very hard for a long time about the one mystery that had eluded

Mauveine and you but the answer finally became crystal clear. Why did Julian and Lynton not traverse the century and a half back to 1841 with existing memories of 2026, as you, Abigail, Madeleine and Annabelle managed? The moment I met and quizzed the present Julian and now Lynton, the haze dispelled from my eyes. They are indisputably one and the same people, quantum adjusted to fit perfectly into the memory of time they happen to be in, as are your two sons, Ned and Zac. Their time travel signatures work differently from you, like a type of self-reincarnation, maybe because of differing dark energy interaction with female versus male which is why you four women exhibit what we have called through the centuries psychic abilities but they don't. Psychic capability and mesmerism, I suspect, are probably different variants of a mix of dark energy and gravitational properties travelling through Gödel wormholes at the quantum level. More work to do on that. A profound conclusion don't you think?"

Victoria fell silent, her fast brain racing ahead. Already, Elizabeth was so intellectually advanced at the frontiers of modern physics, which felt quite eerie exactly as Maddie alluded to. Was this why Julian had always been peculiarly uncommunicative on the details about his London life? She intended to find out more and fast.

Elizabeth unlocked her new Dutch bicycle from the stand. A large pot plant was sat in the front basket. "Victoria, let's face facts. You and I have always been on the same page and I can see from your face you've long harboured suspicions about unaccountable aspects of Julian's past life. I would suggest a starting point would be to confront him, subtly of course, about his sister Caitriona. Well, must be off, tally ho as we used to say in the bad old days, whip in hand. These two wheels, I have to admit, take some getting used to but what fun, as good as horses and so very Cambridge."

With a wave, Elizabeth sped off down the drive, weaving and laughing in the wobbly direction of her new observatory.

With heat rising fast through her body and her face glowing bright red with anger, Victoria watched Elizabeth disappear into the distance and pondered what other historical aspects of Julian's behaviour were destined to repeat themselves in the near future.

'*Aintree races anyone?*'

As for Elizabeth's final gem of a revelation?

"Caitriona? Fuck everyone," was all she could mutter, loud and clear.

But nobody was listening.

Have you read Mauveine?

MAUVEINE: Aged sixteen, wayward Victoria McKenzie flees desperate and confused from home in West Lancashire to a commune in Amsterdam and never speaks to her parents again. Now aged thirty five, single and fancy free, she is settled as a senior polymer chemist working in the ailing Ahrendolie refinery in Rotterdam. Following a serious and unsettling plant incident, she is forced into a long recovery break and plans to take off on holiday with Abby, her best friend and designer flatmate, always up for a new challenge. But Victoria is startled to suddenly learn of an unusual inheritance, Orsbrick Hall, taking her mind back to childhood events and places alongside the Leeds and Liverpool canal she never hoped to experience again. Intrigued by her news, she is summoned to a strange meeting with a Liverpool solicitor and bumps into the quaint Julian, an introverted steampunk writer, all grey hair and flying scarves. But what is it about the creepy Orsbrick Hall that nobody wants to talk about? Why does her past now unravel into an unexpected explosion of crazy scientific revelations and discoveries a hundred and fifty years before, which she would never have believed possible or credible? With Abby and Julian she must track down the source of past family secrecies and find out who the terrifying woman in the purple shawl really is. But will this unleash evil and powerful forces hell bent on her eternal destruction and damnation? And is Julian all he makes out to be?

An excerpt from Mauveine:

… She knocked on the pale green door and Victoria heard a firm but certainly elderly voice, in a very posh accent, reply. "Do please come in."

Mrs Grable held the door wide and Victoria walked into a large and very high ceilinged room, papered with a striped design she had never seen anywhere before and the walls finished off with a marbled Georgian coving. All around the walls were adorned with wonderful hanging pieces of fabrics, again like nothing she had seen, intricately designed and colourful, where she could make out themes of an outdoor nature, trees, water lilies, meadow flowers, orchids. She immediately thought of Abby, wondering why she was taking so long.

A high rear window from floor to ceiling, which could be opened out, and letting in lots of daylight, especially noticeable with the sun shining in brightly, took her gaze. Standing in front staring motionless at the view and holding onto two sticks stood a small elderly lady in a mauve cardigan and chocolate brown skirt, her hair white but thick. She turned around slowly, her soft complexion highlighted with a bright red lipstick and smiled. "Victoria, how wonderful to see you at last."

But Victoria, ready to move forward and kiss her cheek, stopped dead, frozen in her tracks as she looked into the beneficent face and her mouth dropped. The likeness was so uncanny, she couldn't believe it, like looking at herself in the mirror, admittedly a much older face, but Eveline had remarkably few lines, great skin and her thick white hair, cut in a fashionable bob, just a little shorter than her own blonde style. But the eyes and the intense look were identical.

Eveline looked quite amused and didn't seem in the least bit surprised. "Well, my dear, I must admit you have inherited the family likeness and are quite beautiful"

Victoria stared perplexed, who was this woman …?